# ALIEN CROSSINGS

# Laura F. Sanchez

Aakenbaaken & Kent

# ALIEN CROSSINGS

ISBN: 978-1-958022-04-7

Cover design by George Paloheimo
Cover art by Alex Sanchez and Laura Sanchez
Background photograph by Casey Homer on unsplash.com

Map of Washington State

# CHAPTER 1

### From *The Way of the Yunko*

*Deep into its Sixth Mass Extinction, Earth still chirps, growls, squeaks, and reeks with life. Screams with life. Screams with death, too, unheard by its dominant species.*

*This clamor of life overloads our Yunko senses–so much keener than those of Earth's native Sapiens–unless we constantly filter input. We must also conceal this greater sensory awareness from Sapiens; Sape curiosity is the second greatest threat to our hidden existence.*

Janelle Higgins sat next to me in third period physics class. Clarification: No way a Sape as spectacular as Janelle *wanted* to sit by me, but seating was alphabetical and my name, Goran Helin, came right before hers.

On the day things started to change, the teacher did a demonstration that ionized the air. The hairs stood up on my arms but not on Janelle's, so I experimented. I ran a pencil point up and down her arm, bare to the elbow. She made a face but the hairs did nothing. I blew on her arm. Nothing. Then I rubbed it with my fingers.

"Stop it, Goran," Janelle said and laughed, just as tiny hairs lifted from her skin.

I jerked away, afraid I'd offended some Sape idea of proper behavior. Or that somehow my Yunko biochemistry had triggered her reaction. "The hairs on your arm – did I shock you?"

"Course not. You just rubbed off all the body lotion."

And that was that. Her attention slid through me and back to her drawing of a girl wearing something frilly and puffy. I relaxed. Around Janelle I felt invisible, as comfortable as I ever felt around a Sape.

Walking home through the clammy dusk that evening, my mind wandered to the few times I'd touched a Sape female during the four years we'd been stationed in Seal Bay, Washington. But I wasn't *that* distracted–my senses still worked at full strength. In the wind off Puget Sound, I heard individual branches creak instead of a general rustling. The scuttling in the rhododendrons was a chipmunk, not a rat, and the buses hissing in the distance were the oldest in the fleet. I smelled the mildewed seat of an abandoned ATV, GrowMo fertilizer, and fish frying in old soybean oil. I noticed a raven flapping from tree to shrub to signpost as if pacing me.

A shout from behind startled the bird into flight and yanked my kaleidoscope attention into focus. Voices raw with menace grew louder, accompanied by the rapid whapping of shoes on pavement. I looked back. Four guys, visible in a streetlight's blurry glow, skidded around the corner I'd just turned. Looked like the Skull gang. I started running.

If someone follows us, we're supposed to lose the pursuer in a crowd or a stand of trees, but I'd been thinking about Janelle instead of checking my unfamiliar shortcut for adequate cover.

We'd just passed into the so-called "normal zone." Across the street, empty parking lots surrounded the huge GenAge Research building where Andrei, my older brother, works. On my side, a boarded up big-box store stood alone, not enough trash around it yet for concealment. Beyond it lay a garden center ringed by sharecroppers' withering vegetable plots – a possibility.

"You're dead, Goran, you filthy freak!" yelled a Skull.

Another voice panted, "Shut up. Save your breath."

That one sounded like Conroy, the only Skull with more brains than a clam. I glanced back. He was less than twenty meters behind me, dusty-blond scalp lock flapping as he ran, blue eyes blazing in the gloom from augmented infrared lenses. Didn't matter. If I speeded up enough to lose him and hide, I'd trigger his suspicions.

"You touch Janelle again," he wheezed, "I'll cut off your hand."

Janelle? They were angry about Janelle? I groaned out loud at the stupidity – theirs and mine. The Skulls routinely beat up guys just for looking at them disrespectfully. I should have realized that Conroy's girlfriend wore an invisible label reading "Do Not Touch."

Conroy's a six-three meatbot; I'm shorter than half the other guys in our senior class. I needed to take him down before he noticed a fight had started.

The garden center's sign sat atop a tall metal pole in the parking lot. I ran toward it, slowing down enough to let Conroy close in. When I reached the pole, I hooked it with my right arm, swung a 180, and rammed him with a full-on head butt. He's so tall I hit him in the gut instead of the solar plexus but down he went, mouth popping like a beached fish. I hoped I hadn't ruptured anything – we're not supposed to inflict injuries that require hospitalization – but I didn't have time to check. Jody, Wad, and Mongo galloped toward me.

A dried-up waterfall fountain stood against the garden center's fence. I raced toward it dodging potholes. Its fake rocks shook under my feet as I climbed high enough to vault over the fence's iron spear-pickets.

Inside, the aromas of fertilizers stung my nose, and paths twisted through piles of tools, pools of gloom, stepping stones, and trellises now used for drying fish. Behind me the Skulls cleared the fence with thuds and curses. I ran toward a jumble of yard statues and squeezed between concrete Virgins, gnomes, and Sasquatches.

Mongo yelled, "Hey, Freakface! I'm gonna rip your freaking face off!"

Our first Deflection Master had a favorite teaching: Anything you see can be a weapon. I scooped up two fist-sized stone frogs and hurled one. "How about a frog in the face, Frog Face?" I screamed, trying to sound like one of the guys. He yelped and clutched a shoulder. I threw the second frog and heard a bone crack. Collarbone, I think.

Conroy and Mongo down. Next up, Wad. He rounded a stack of wooden planters and stopped, head swiveling on his thick neck as he searched the dark maze. I caught a whiff of dull rage in his chemical signature. He spotted me. Judging by his uncertain stance, he couldn't guess whether I'd run or fight. So I deflected, dodging sideways along a row of sandstone slabs set up like dominoes. Wad charged. I shoved the last slab. It shifted slightly. Another shove and the rocks crashed forward, cracking into Wad's side as he tried to corner.

His yell brought Jody running. I bolted toward rows of young fruit trees, dived, rolled, and came up holding a sapling by its inch-thick trunk. When I spun, the heavy root ball hit Jody's torso like a giant war-hammer. He staggered sideways into a tree.

In the sudden silence, light steps galloped from the back of the garden center. Dogs! They weren't barking–probably trained to silently bite and hold. Three Dobermans rounded the building and hurtled down the path. Their panting breaths fizzed with alertness and purpose. I ran full speed for the center's back fence but the wind veered, soaking me in a cloud of stink so bad I gagged and stumbled. It came from an old construction dumpster filled with fertilizer made from fish guts, gull guano, and rotting kelp. I grabbed the dumpster's rim, pulled myself over it, and splashed into the ooze. Maybe it would burn out the Dobermans' sense of smell before it burnt out mine. The dogs flung themselves at the rim of the dumpster, claws scratching the metal sides, but it was too high. Finally, they pattered away.

I risked looking over the rim. A thrashing, yelling clot of dogs and Skulls rolled toward the front fence. Just as they reached it, a copcart skidded to a stop on the other side.

Two uniforms got out. They looked too skinny to be corporate dicks wearing body armor so they must have been Metro cops. One Tased the dogs instead of shooting them, which pretty much proved it; destroying corp property is the quickest way for Metros to lose their jobs. The other Metro took a shooting stance and aimed a hand weapon at the Skulls slumped against the fence. Then Taser Cop lifted a comm to his ear, probably calling the garden center owner.

Time to disappear – the owner would inspect the grounds for damage. I pulled over the side of the dumpster, dropped to the ground running, and then hauled my dripping, reeking body over the garden center's back fence and into the surrounding vegetable plots.

Sharecroppers sometimes booby-trap their plots with snares or zip guns loaded with birdshot, but harvest was over so I made it through undamaged. I headed toward home, bruises aching, scrapes stinging, choking on my own smell. But only two things really worried me: catching the Skulls' attention and Mongo calling me Freakface.

Had Mongo noticed a subtle Yunko difference, like my eyes set a little farther apart or one ear several millimeters higher than the other? I reassured myself that Mongo didn't do subtle; odds were, he just grabbed for some vaguely racist insult.

Most Sapes don't look very closely. They assume we're a mix of Asian and First Nation, with our straight black hair and high cheekbones. Close enough: Our human DNA originally came from the Evenki people who live in the Tunguska area of Siberia. But if someone asked, we claimed we were from a little-known First Nation band way up the coast in British Columbia.

Ten minutes later, I reached Ocean Vista Estates, a subdivision with zero view of salt water. These days, most of its peeling Craftsman houses have a dozen people crammed in and spilling out at all hours, but the October night was chilly enough that I only spotted three men in one side yard. They were too busy to notice me, intent on feeding their small fire and skinning some critter – maybe a raccoon, maybe a dog – stretched between the fence and a porch post.

Beyond Ocean Vista Estates lay open fields scarred by dusty graded roads meant for another subdivision back before 2028 when the Big Crumble halted most construction. Nine years later, in 2037, the fields were still empty except for weeds and blackberry bushes creeping slowly across the roads.

On the east side where the farmland gave way to foothills, the barn and the old log farmhouse still overlooked the empty cul-de-sac. We lived in the farmhouse and used the barn for a garage and shop. A derelict tangle of trees, fences, and blackberry thickets surrounded the two buildings, but I had rigged it into an effective perimeter. The place was too isolated to attract wasters and bangers, and it was a safe distance from the rising ocean, at least for as long as we would live there.

I slipped through the thorny dogleg and unlocked the barn's small side door. Inside, I gathered tarps to pull over me for warmth, along with a dust mask I hoped would block my awful stink. It didn't. I lay awake for a good hour, feeling cold, hungry, miserable, and stupid for fighting four Sape guys over a Sape girl who barely knew I was alive. My elders had been right: Avoid close contact with Sapes.

But at least I wouldn't have to face Andrei's wrath for a few more hours.

*

Sunlight shafting through the barn wall's cracks woke me. I slunk toward the house and eased through the kitchen door, but Andrei was already up and filling the coffee pot. When my smell hit him, he clanked the pot onto the counter.

"Go outside," he ordered. "Strip and wash off with the hose. Leave your clothes on the porch and then take a shower. Use my hot water allotment for a second shower if necessary."

The temperature was in the fifties but my older brother wouldn't care. I headed back out to clean up. When I finally sat at the table, he handed me a printout from a local newsfeed. "Read it," he ordered, his voice so harsh our two cats slunk from the room.

According to the story, Metro police had apprehended four male juveniles, names withheld, breaking into a garden center across the street from the GenAge Research building. They were treated for minor injuries, interviewed, and released. All four boys claimed their wounds came from fighting the guard dogs.

Normally, Andrei ignores everything except work, but he'd connected the story and my absence. "Where were you last night? And why didn't you comm me?"

"My comm was here, charging. And I didn't want to wake you so I spent the night in the barn."

Andrei never cooks, but he put a plate in front of me. It held half a kelp omelet. It looked suspicious. "Who are those boys?" he said.

"Call themselves the Skulls. Alpha gang at Seal Bay High."

"Skulls? What kind of name is that?"

"They have skulls tattooed on the back of their heads." I took a bite of omelet. It tasted like he'd stirred in a half cup of glue. "Keep their heads shaved so the skull tats show."

Andrei pondered a moment. "Is that not redundant?"

"They think it's scary."

"Did they initiate the attack?"

"Yes."

9

"Why?"

I shrugged. "When they're not hauling drugs or refugees around, they beat up other guys just for fun. I followed the rules: Inflict no serious injuries, demonstrate no unusual fighting skills. They'll think I just got lucky."

"Why were you at that garden center?"

Life would be easier if I could lie to Andrei, but our hyper hearing and sense of smell make lying to each other difficult. "On my way home the bus passed some guys playing pickup basketball." Already Andrei was frowning. "I got off at the next stop and joined the game. We played 'til nearly dark. I thought I'd get home quicker walking north past the GenAge building. I guess the Skulls spotted me and followed."

"Did they give any reason for attacking?"

I repeated the threats the Skulls had yelled.

"Who is Janelle? What did you do to her?"

At least we were off the subject of basketball. I described the incident in class and added, "Conroy's their leader. Janelle's his girlfriend. I was doing a science experiment, but they must have thought it was a sex thing."

"It is impossible for Yunko to understand Sapiens, particularly their mating practices. Any interaction risks our mission. Remember: Deflection before Confrontation. Always."

My defense was feeble. "But never speaking to anyone looks even more suspicious."

He took a bite of omelet. He probably thought it tasted normal. "We have survived   only because we follow the rules. You have to be strong, Goran. For our mission." He pried off another bite and added, "Will those boys mention your name to the authorities?"

I shook my head. "They avoid anybody official because of the drug stuff. Probably won't mention it to other kids either. Be too embarrassing. They'll just try to wipe me out the next time they catch me alone."

Andrei looked up, confused. "Do they not learn from their experiences?"

"Not so you'd notice." Sapes really should have named themselves *Homo sapiens idioticus* instead of *Homo sapiens sapiens*. I chased down my last bite of omelet.

"You're already late for school. Get your things."

"I'll need an excuse."

He rose, hobbled to a desk, scribbled on a GenAge note pad, and handed the sheet to me. It read, "Goran had to miss school this morning for medical tests. Dr. Andrei Helin."

At twenty-six, he was only nine years older than my seventeen, but it was getting harder for him to move around. Every time Andrei limped or groaned, I got scared he was going into the rapid aging phase. Rapid aging doesn't usually start until about thirty; in the space of two years, our people change from looking like someone in their fifties to someone so gray, shriveled, and decrepit they seem barely alive. Andrei's aging didn't show much on the outside yet except for his face, which looked as rigid as some old actor after too much plastic surgery. And his hair looked unnaturally black because he dyed it himself.

If we didn't find a way to fix ourselves soon, it would be too late for Andrei. But still, Andrei–my brother, my Researcher–was really annoying. I was his support staff and protector, doing all the repair work and scavenging and security and cooking – as well as going to that stupid school – so he could spend his dwindling energy looking for the cure that would allow us to all go home. But he kept wasting what little time we had by lecturing me.

# CHAPTER 2

## From *The Way of the Yunko*

*The training manuals for our field research teams include twice as many regulations for Seconds as for Researchers. This is not a criticism of our young people, who make it possible for Researchers to do their jobs. The imbalance simply acknowledges that Seconds are thrust into a more dangerous security situation. When they first go into the field, they are still too young to fully comprehend the need for secrecy. Their genome, more than 96 percent Homo sapiens sapiens, resonates with Sapiens of the same age, creating a desire for dangerously close connections with Sapiens teenagers.*

*Just as a Second must protect and serve a Researcher, a Researcher bears great responsibility to guide and counsel a Second.*

All the way to Seal Bay High School, Andrei lectured me about avoiding other students. Not easy in Seal Bay. It's a small town – fewer than four thousand people, not counting refugees. GenAge runs the town, so SBHS is basically a biotech boot camp. It has a good science track for future GenAge lab techs, decent business classes for future GenAge clerical workers, fabrication classes for GenAge maintenance, and that's about it.

Our senior class had barely enough students to form the standard cliques – the socials, the jocks, the geeks, the thugs, and the wasters. The oddball loner? That was me. We all knew each other, at least by name and stereotype. Most students showed up every day or had a solid excuse if they didn't. Our GenAge education bosses didn't much care who or what we were, but they cared very much *where* we were, and it had better be in school. Truancy lowered the productivity of their future workforce. Most of the kids showed up anyway just to hang with friends–there wasn't much else to do in Seal Bay. And for some, it was the closest thing to a safe haven.

Andrei let me off in front of Old Main. The U-shaped brick building enclosed a small plaza, now sprinkled with students on lunch break. But no Skulls.

At the entrance gate, I swiped the Immigration Control officer's pad.

She gave me a hard look but waved me through. SBHS was part of the "normal zone" boundary line running between the foothills and the rapidly shrinking coastal areas. The coastal part of town had given up any pretense of normal, mostly due to the endless waves of climate refugees from farther south. Our so-called government couldn't actually fix problems so they shoved the blame off on immigrants. Anyone who looked non-local drew suspicion. Schools, first responder departments, and medical facilities all hired Immigration Control officers.

First, I grabbed a jelly-fu burrito from a vending machine and then I searched the campus from Old Main to the playing fields that overlooked the bay. No Skulls.

That left the Rats' Nest, a maze of metal buildings crammed between Old Main and the steep hills to the east. I crept through overgrown brambles around the labs and training classrooms like a commando in some cheesy action video. Still no Skulls. They must have risked ditching for the day. At least it gave me time to figure out what to do about them.

At the next bell I headed back toward Old Main for biology class. Janelle Higgins strolled past before I could dodge the other way. She was talking with Kayla Midnight, who gave me a long, suspicious glare from deep brown eyes–I hoped the look was just Kayla's persona for the day instead of personal. Her hair was frizzed up in a wide band over the top of her head like a sideways Mohawk. The rest was retro-Goth – choke collar, tight top, and an outrigger thing of embossed leather around her hips like some punked-out Renaissance queen. Anybody but Janelle would be invisible walking beside Kayla.

Janelle gave me her standard goddess-in-training smile but kept talking. Sure enough, Conroy must have been too embarrassed to tell her about our battle. If their secret somehow leaked, the Skulls might go from being a worrisome threat to an all-out emergency.

After classes, I was waiting at the bus pickup when this girl in my math class, Lil Osborne, walked up to me. Lil's sort of tan and creamy, polished smooth like a piece of driftwood you want to run your hand over. I'm quiet and so is she; we've never talked.

"Hi," she said. "You weren't in class this morning."

"Uh, no."

"Want a copy of my notes?"

"Sure."

"Which bus do you take?"

I pointed out my regular bus in the pickup lane. I'm not great at conversation.

"Really? Where do you live?"

"Over where the foothills start." Since that described the whole eastern edge of town, it seemed vague enough.

She pivoted around me to look in my face. "I thought you lived near GenAge."

"Why'd you think that?" Why was she thinking about me at all?

"I intern there. Last night on my way home, I'm sure I saw you."

"Nuh uh. No. I wasn't anywhere near there."

Still peering at my face, she said, "I haven't seen the Skulls around today. You probably know what happened to them. Right?"

I shook my head and took off toward the bus. Did Lil somehow know about the fight? When she first started talking, I fantasized she might be coming on to me, but not one molecule of pheromone signaled any interest in mating. Her chemical signature seemed more like curiosity. I couldn't imagine how she found out about the fight when even Janelle didn't know. Her curiosity about me was sort of exciting but mostly dangerous. I needed to avoid her completely.

Riding the bus home, massaging my shoulder still sore from the previous night's tuck and roll, I realized Lil's own story was shaky. I think GenAge student interns go home about six o'clock, but the Skulls hadn't jumped me until after eight last night. So if Lil hadn't been leaving work, why was *she* hanging around GenAge?

*

Back at the house, I shot a few baskets before starting two jobs I should have finished the day before. First, I hosed off the solar panels. They were disguised as a a shed roof attached to the garage, hopefully concealed from corporate snoops bent on harassing people who generated their own power.

Then I started the long, miserable, scratchy task of cleaning dead branches out of the trees. But since Andrei wasn't home from work yet, I could use my magic landscaping tool – the Bubble Drive wand.

Lots of Yunko technology is based on the Bubble Drive. Scientists discovered its principles while trying to compress space-time in front of a moving object and expand it behind. It powers everything from prolonged acceleration for Yunko interstellar ships down to our personal Bubble Drive wands–four-inch long, hand-held gadgets with space displacement capabilities fine-tuned enough to knock a can off a fence post. Our wands compare to the devices powering the ships like a kitchen match compares to a ten-megaton nuke. Still, I must never, ever carry the wand outside a secure area or let a Sape see me use it.

I was displacing the dry, dead top of a Sitka spruce when I smelled a musky odor and heard the burp-yelp sound cats make with a mouth full of prey. I turned. Our cats picked their way down the steep slope behind our back fence. Zax had something brownish and smelly in his mouth.

Gwitchy bumped shoulders with him, trying to get in on the action.

Their ancestors were wild Pallas' cats from Central Asia. Their mountainous home had so few infectious diseases that the cats never developed strong immune systems. We've been modifying them for generations – larger size, shorter hair, and immune systems pumped until their leukocytes attack like killer bees. They're also easier to train. For cats.

They scrambled over the backyard fence and Zax brought the dead mole to show me. I praised him as a mighty hunter and Gwitchy for any assists she might have made. I was apologizing to the mole, its family, and any of its possible business partners when I heard distant barking.

The cats were instantly hostile to any perceived threat to Andrei or me. Zax dropped the mole and they dashed through the perimeter dogleg and down the slope toward the noisy invader. I chased, but they outdistanced me easily. Below us, a pickup with a barking German shepherd in back was turning around in a cul-de-sac. The cats were grayish-tan attack blurs locked onto the vehicle.

I aimed the Bubble Drive wand at a point a few feet below ground under Zax and Gwitchy and pressed. The dirt beneath the cats heaved and rolled backwards, while Zax and Gwitch, still running full speed, stayed in place. The driver motored away. Poor guy was probably lost – no one drives around aimlessly these days with gas so expensive. He'd never suspect that a limitless source of "alien" energy had just saved his dog from attack.

When I released the button. Gwitchy and Zax stopped, yowling with confusion before assuming the super-dignified stance cats take when they're seen doing something stupid. I scolded them, left them to play with the dead mole, and headed inside to start dinner.

Zax weighed nearly twenty pounds and Gwitchy wasn't much smaller, but from the kitchen window they just looked like fluffy kitty-cats playing toss-the-body-part. Anyone who was scared of those adorable kitties, much less lost a fight with them, would terminally lose face. As I put salmon jerky in the PlumpUp, I imagined the Skulls chasing me through some dark alley. Along come Zax and Gwitchy, purring and twining around the Skulls' legs. The Skulls stop to pet the pretty, friendly kitties, and suddenly Zax and Gwitchy are taking the four guys apart.

I wallowed in my revenge fantasy while I took leftover beans from the chiller and chopped seaweed to put on the potatoes. It would remain a fantasy. I was forbidden to do anything that might expose our true nature. Couldn't risk the cats. Couldn't use a gun because owning one would put us in too many data bases. Couldn't have a vehicle because Andrei thought two cars in the same family might draw attention. I obviously couldn't use the Bubble Drive wand. I couldn't reveal my full strength, which would seem exceptional to a Sape. I couldn't even use several of my favorite combat techniques.

But I'd caught the Skulls' attention anyway. For safety's sake, I had to back them off permanently. Even trickier, I had to do it without anyone noticing me do it. I didn't know where any of them lived, or where they hung out. They probably had illegal guns. They definitely had a car, although they rarely wasted gas driving their ancient Buick to school.

Andrei's hybrid crunched up the driveway. He came in, dropped his tablet on the table, muttered something, and went out back to sit on a large, flat rock. I hoped the meditation would cheer him up; he's been grumpier than usual the last couple of weeks.

During dinner he said, "I lied my way into the GenAge security center today. A dangerous move but I had to make sure their scanning equipment hadn't recorded your ill-advised adventure.

"Half their perimeter cameras are out of service, including the one across the street from the garden center." He gave me a stare. "You were very lucky that GenAge security didn't notice you. Even a random person walking by might have said something that could tip them off. Make sure nothing like that happens again."

Andrei's words about a random observer tickled my brain. I rose and stacked dishes in the sink. I needed to do some reconnaissance. When I said, "I'm going to my room," he nodded without looking up from his tablet.

Ten minutes later I emerged, cash stash in my pocket, smelling like a cedar tree from Andrei's hair dressing gel – have I mentioned that Andrei is vain? – and brushing my teeth to disguise stress in my voice from lying. "I forgot. There's a video and discussion tonight at the school library about the Mars mission. Our physics teacher said we had to attend. There'll be a test on it tomorrow. Can I take your car?"

"You should walk as much as possible. And be glad you still can."

The speedup of aging was beginning to obsess Andrei, but pointing it out had no upside. "Starts in fifteen minutes. I'll be late if I walk."

With a frown, Andrei handed over the car control. "Be careful. Don't ask any questions, don't volunteer information. And come home the minute it's over."

I took the control and left. The video and discussion actually were happening, but I had more pressing business. I grabbed Andrei's binoculars from our outdoor equipment stored in the barn, started the car, and set out on the hunt.

# CHAPTER 3

## Excerpt from the *Diary of Lil Osborne*

*After I fed and tucked Davy in last night, I headed for GenAge. About the time I reached the parking lot, I heard yelling and people running so I hid in the rhododendrons on the corner. This kid Goran Helin goes running by with the Skulls chasing him. They all climbed over the fence into that garden center across the street. Guess I should have called the Metros, but I was too busy trespassing, breaking, and entering.*

*Some noise must have triggered a GenAge alert. Erik Cheyne came out the entrance. God, I hate to even type his name! I guess Chief Cheyne called the city. A little later the Metros showed up and hauled the Skulls away. I stayed hidden until Cheyne's SUV left before I risked climbing up to the outflow grille.*

*Then today, no Skulls at school, but Goran showed up looking perfectly healthy. I barely know him – he keeps to himself. Kind of cute in a clueless way, but he acted like he didn't know where he was, much less the Skulls. He looks sort of First Nation and his name sounds maybe Russian. Thick, spiky black hair. About my height but twice as wide – all muscle. He could actually hang pants off his butt, but he belts them around his waist. Like I said, clueless.*

Andrei's brilliant when it comes to genetics, but I don't trust his observations on security matters. I wanted to check the GenAge security cameras myself before I went on to my main mission – nosing around the sketchy part of town until I found the Skulls' hangout.

Just past the garden center, an old three-story office building sits across the street from GenAge. I parked in the alley behind the building and got out. In games, alleys have spooky lighting and hot girls in catsuits. This alley had utility meters and garbage bins behind the two businesses that weren't boarded up. One unit also had a telescoping fire escape. The pull-down end of the steps rested below the second story windows, about the height of a basketball goal. I backed off and tucked the binoculars under my pullover and jacket to protect them. Then I ran full speed toward the ladder, jumped like I was slam-dunking a ball, and caught a rung. It clanked down and I climbed.

On the stairs' third floor landing, the railing was high enough that I could balance on it and grab a metal cornice around the top of the building. It held steady under a hard tug so I pulled myself up hand over hand, which set my shoulder aching again. I rolled over the parapet, dropped to the roof a couple of feet below, and crawled between reeking piles of trash left by people using the roof for a last-resort bunk and latrine–although the area's in the normal zone, those who're desperate enough get through.

When I reached the front parapet, the view of the GenAge property was great. The building's shaped like a boomerang, its arms angled to funnel people into the lobby. I pulled out the binoculars. Behind the lobby's glass front, a guard sat at the security station. He glanced up frequently, probably at video monitors above his desk for various cameras. Perimeter cameras were mounted on poles every eighty meters or so along the front property line. I aimed the binoculars at the one across from me. Another security guard appeared, walking the cracked, heaved sidewalk around the property. I decided to wait to see how long his route took.

His job looked as dull as my life's designated path. You'd think Seconds like me would spend our time on strategic planning and tactical drills. If only! Most of my time goes to scrounging and prepping food, and our overcharged metabolisms leave me constantly hungry.

Every month there's less to eat, and now there's some problem with farmers letting fertilizer runoff drain into the bay. Like I said, *Homo sapiens idioticus*. I guess it's not really my problem. Puget Sound's almost fished out anyway, but I won't live to see the last smelt pulled from the bay.

Waiting around on rooftops or waiting anywhere is hard for me. It reminds me of the minutes of my life ticking away. They taught us a little rhyme back in the Outpost's crèche: *Time has no duration./The Past is over and done./The Future can't touch us till it turns into Now,/and Now's the same length for everyone.* It's supposed to help us make the most of our short lives. Sometime it helps my Yunko side. Doesn't do much for my human one.

When I was five years old, I began training as a Second: deflections and defense drills, mechanics, basic cookery, and techniques for evading notice. Researchers start at five also, but their training in biology takes much longer. When we went into the field four years ago, Andrei was twenty-two in calendar years and I was thirteen. At best, we might have an additional four years here in Seal Bay before Andrei's body fails and I take him home to the Outpost to die. Unless we can find a cure for the evil stew of genetic bungling and interstellar radiation that drastically shortened Yunko lives.

Yunko's a slangy version of a Russian word for mayfly. We don't call ourselves mayflies because we're so delicate and beautiful, but because mayflies only live for one day.

I shifted the glasses back to the first security camera. It seemed to face in a slightly different direction, as if slowly panning through an arc. I could have verified it by watching longer, but I was antsy to get on with the main part of my mission.

Movement on the far right caught my eye. An old red Nissan crept into the parking lot of the next office complex and stopped at the far end. Someone got out and walked toward GenAge. When the figure entered the glow of a streetlight, I recognized Lil Osborne, wearing a backpack. She reached the GenAge property, glanced around like a spooked deer, and then darted toward the back of the building.

I lowered the binoculars and closed my mouth. Whatever she was doing, she apparently didn't want anyone to see her do it. I watched the building a few more minutes, but Lil never reappeared. Then I climbed down and walked around until I could enter the parking lot from the same direction. If she had been attacked or had an accident, maybe I could rescue her. I walked along the back of the building at a safe distance – just someone taking a short cut through the parking lot – but I didn't see her anywhere.

And she had a car. Gasoline in the United States was sitting at over ten dollars a gallon–if you had ration coupons to buy it. Prices had been about the same in Europe forever, but ten-dollar gas totally disjointed the U.S. People had wanted to lynch the President when he declared rationing. People crowded into substandard public transportation or walked or biked or ran private van-buses. In fact, the only people I knew personally that had cars were Andrei and the Skulls, and now Lil. Andrei got gasoline coupons because of his job at GenAge. Maybe they handed them out to interns too.

*

The closer you are to the water, the weirder Seal Bay gets, as if time ran downhill to splash into a collapsing future. In the normal zone–up by the foothills–the pre-Big Crumble world still hangs on, with places like our house, GenAge, and the high school as fortresses of failing calm. The zone line acts to funnel climate refugees fleeing from the heat and drought farther south along Seal Bay's waterfront and straight on towards Bellingham. Down by the flooded docks, life's a crazy carnival of desperate people twitching with a hundred needs. I figured it would be the likeliest place to pick up Conroy's trail.

I didn't want to risk Andrei's car along the waterfront, so I left it in the alley and walked downhill past the zone line. Immigration officers were off duty this time of night and all I had to do was step over the level-crossing bars. The whole zone line concept is about as effective as the old "gated communities."

I couldn't stop puzzling over Lil Osborne. It didn't add up. To me, Lil always looked like Ms. Perfect. No mistakes, no loose ends, no hint of rebellion. Something was either seriously off in my understanding of Sapes, or seriously off in Lil Osborne's life. There seemed nowhere else she could have gone except into the GenAge building, but how did she get in? And why? And had she also been sneaking around GenAge last night and seen the garden center fight?

When I reached downtown, I angled north towards the Moon Kitchen, an old city park one street up from the waterfront. There's a sculpture in the middle called the Moon Blender. It lined up with a wide street that ran all the way to the foothills. Five long metal rods strung with pearly orbs curved up from the base of the sculpture and back down in arcs that echoed the paths of the moon as it rose over the eastern foothills and set in the bay to the west – the solstices, the equinox, and in-between. I didn't understand the name until Andrei told me it looked like an old-fashioned tool used to blend pastry. I guess the "Kitchen" part came from all the deals cooked up in the park every night.

I couldn't use the Bubble Drive wand, guns, cats, or unusual combat skills. So my plan, if you could call it that, was to lure someone else into taking the Skulls out of action – and out of my business – by getting the Metros to lock them up. If I could find out where they stayed, I might find evidence of their criminality that was strong enough to set the Metros on them, while keeping my involvement secret. Yeah, basically I'd be a snitch.

The gang always seemed to have money from smuggling drugs and refugees across the Canadian border. And they possessed a four-hole Buick that was about eighty years old. But Conroy was only seventeen or eighteen. He probably hadn't acquired serious clout. He wouldn't be sitting in some mob-boss office letting people come to him – he'd have to go out and recruit potential customers. And if he met with customers, it was possible he did it at the Moon Kitchen.

Like some grotesque tourist town, the Moon Kitchen churned with local marketeers who served the refugees fleeing north from broiling heat, rising water, and new diseases. Yunko mostly avoid crowds, but the Moon Kitchen's level of weirdness rose so high that only the obviously peculiar stood out. I eased down a block of bars and gambling parlors and into the square. The noise was painful to my ears – generators thrumming, bicycle turbines swooshing, strained voices haggling. Honks and clucks and baa-a-as floated on a breeze of manure from the animal traders' pens.

"Looking for a ride north, buddy?" A short man wearing a purple skull cap with goggles on his forehead plucked at my sleeve.

Asking the smuggler if he knew Conroy seemed risky. "No," I said. He headed toward the food carts across the way.

A clutch of bicycle rickshaws rolled by. I followed them past drug dealers and infection stations for those who wanted to get their delirium on immediately. A young boy selling fake de-sal tokens pestered me until I told him I was with Desalinization Security. Lost-looking refugees slunk through the crowd. Just in front of me, a pitchman for a body mod shop stopped a couple with three children. Their weather-leathery skins hinted they were Texans. The pitchman demonstrated how you could see him chew his food through little transparent portholes surgically inserted in his cheeks. The youngest kid couldn't decide whether to whimper or giggle. I wondered if the body modifier paid the pitchman anything besides food to eat every night.

The refugees were clueless enough to be safe. I tapped Daddy Texas on the shoulder. "I'm looking for a guy named Conroy. Gives people rides. Maybe you've seen him lately?"

He shook his head, then looked down at himself as if wondering how I guessed he was a refugee. I pointed at his boots and walked on.

As I passed a straggle of contract workers, signs around their necks advertising services from standing in lines to assisted suicide, a melodious hooting pierced the general din. The odor of burning torches rose above the Kitchen's other smells. A path opened through the crowd. People tried to squeeze to the front.

Four dudes wearing blue and green robes appeared, blowing on conch shells. Following them was a robed woman wearing a headdress shaped like a nautilus shell. The robe was loose, but still, she looked like she got more to eat than most people. She carried a silver bowl at chest height. I knew what was in it–baking soda. The group called themselves the Gifts of Poseidon. I'd seen them hanging around the funky little aquarium a mile up the beach, praying to the jellyfish or something. They marched down to the docks every week or so to dump baking soda into the water, as if that would stop acidification from killing the oceans.

A ragged parade of priests followed. Some held torches. Others carried stout sticks and wore large bags slung over one shoulder. The fitful orange torchlight made their green and blue robes look gray. As they passed, they handed sandwiches from the bags to nearby outstretched hands.

Opposite me, a small figure wiggled to the front of the crowd and held out her hand. She looked vaguely familiar. Yeah. A kid two classes behind me, but I didn't remember seeing her this year. It wasn't hard to guess what she was doing now. Still skinny as ever, blue veins showing through fragile skin, but over the summer she'd grown impressive breasts. They were strapped up in a sort of double slingshot thing that matched the tiny, glittery skirt riding low on her hips. The passing priest ignored her and handed a sandwich to a woman two spaces down. The girl jiggled her hand and mouthed "Please" to the next priest. He wheeled and jabbed her in the stomach with his stick. She doubled over and sank back into the crowd.

It occurred to me that the ex-schoolgirl might know Conroy.

The priest offered the sandwich to a man beside me. I grabbed it and charged through the line of robed jerk-offs, intending to give the sandwich to the girl. A flash of glitter through the crowd marked my quarry's direction until a methane bagger pushed in front of me and his cluster of patched balloons blocked my view. I dodged around him.

# CHAPTER 4

## Excerpt from the diary of Lil Osborne

*Kayla found a new drugstore, so she came home with me this afternoon. She let Davy play with her personal defense gear awhile and then we set out on our Waster Chick & Wonderland Alice routine. Kayla walked in the drugstore and stood at the jewelry counter picking up things and putting them down so fast every clerk in the store watched her hands non-stop. While they were distracted, I drifted over to a wall of supplements, palmed a bottle, and walked out with a month's supply of Davy's Corfamdim! It seems to help him a little.*

*I wish to hell we could afford doctors to diagnose him accurately so I'd know better which drugs to steal. Tonight I'll search the GenAge databases for an espindolol drug that's just finished trials. It's designed to reduce muscle wasting in old people, but I think it's worth a try, even though Davy's only nine.*

Chesta? Cresta? No, Crescenda – that was her name. "Crescenda!" I yelled. No answer, but when I reached the stores that ring the Moon Kitchen, I found her, still doubled over and gagging, in front of a place that sold second-hand tools.

"Hi," I said.

She waved me away.

"Crescenda?"

She blinked and focused on my face. "I've seen you somewhere."

I held out the food I'd snatched from the priest. "I brought your sandwich."

She took it, lifted the top to check the contents. "Ugh. BioBounty tank meat."

BioBounty tank meat tastes like stringy foam infused with meat gelatin. Not even close to our Outpost product that comes from customized genomes with weeks of flexion to mimic muscle tone.

"I need to talk to you. I'll pay."

"How much?"

I guessed at a hooker's fee and upped it by half.

"Okay. C'mon." She touched her stomach again. "I don't want to work tonight anyway."

"Why'd that priest hit you?"

"Probably thought I was a hooker."

Uh, yeah, probably. I tried to phrase the next question politely. "What *do* you do?"

She peeled the slice of tank meat off and dropped it in the gutter. "Runner at a gambling place up in the foothills. I fetch chips and drinks and other stuff for the players."

Apparently she was doing well enough to avoid BioBounty tank meat. She nibbled half the bread and tossed the other half by the time we reached an apartment building a block away. I glanced around for any Metros, who mostly avoid the Moon Kitchen, and followed her in. A guy at the entry desk handed her a key. We climbed stairs to the second floor. Between the original hallway doors, makeshift entrances pierced the walls. Crescenda unlocked one into a room barely large enough to hold a single bed. Clothes hung from a row of hooks. Cosmetics, trinkets, decks of cards, and a comm unit cluttered the top of a nightstand.

She sat on the bed, pulled off high heeled boots, and patted the spot beside her. "Sit."

I sat and showed her the money. "You remember a guy from school named Conroy? Boss of the Skulls?"

She picked at her manicure a bit. "Yeah. Why?"

"Ever see him around the Moon Kitchen?"

"Few times."

"You know where he lives?"

"What's it to you?" She massaged her bare feet.

"I need to talk to him about a deal." I peeled a couple of the bills off the wad and made to stick them back in my pocket.

"A guy took me to a party at one of the waders coupla months ago. I think it was Conroy's place."

"Was he there?"

She nodded.

"Do you remember which house it was?"

"Nah. I wasn't thinking about addresses." She stretched her legs out and wiggled her ankles. "There was a fountain out front. Had a statue of a dolphin in the middle. Guy wanted me to ride it while he did some stuff."

"Can you remember anything else?"

"No."

"Okay. Thanks." I handed her the bills and rose. "Uh, Good food, dry bed."

"Same to you." She smoothed the money. "You want to mess around a little?"

I shook my head. "Messing around" was specifically forbidden. Besides, the darkening bruise on her stomach made me feel queasy. Getting information from her and then leaving seemed cruel, but I didn't know what else to do.

*

The three most desperate addresses in Seal Bay were the U-Squats where people live in their former storage units, the lawless Railyards, and the waders. For Conroy's illegal activities, the mostly deserted waders made the most sense. Stretching north from downtown, they used to be Seal Bay's Millionaire Row: huge beachfront houses bristling with glass, stone, and redwood.

Then sea levels rose. The owners tried to waterproof their basements and crawlspaces but the water kept wicking in. The warming temperatures also brought mosquito swarms that bred in pockets of standing water left after the breakdown of city maintenance.

I worked my way up Beach Avenue. The houses on the landward side were also abandoned. High tides were touching their front lawns, mired with sea grapes. Probably by 2040, they'd be wading too. The dwellings themselves smelled like mildew propped up their walls.

In the fourth house on the ocean side, light leaked past the edge of an upstairs window curtain. In the yard below, a head-high bulk in the middle of a circular driveway might have been a fountain. Everything was quiet. It seemed safe enough to study the place briefly. I moved into the shadow of a spirea bush across the street and took out the binoculars. Dull gleams of moonlight on the fountain hinted at the head and body of a dolphin. The tail and dorsal fin were missing, probably broken off by metal scavengers.

The huge house spilled down the slope toward the beach, its western rooms in the water. Bars guarded its windows, grates guarded the doors. Be hard to break in without leaving a trace. A shadow passed across the upstairs line of light. Another light came on lower in the house.

The scent of the ocean mixed with nearby smells of vegetation and mildew, along with occasional smells wafting from the Moon Kitchen–a thick soup of life brewed up in an oxygen-rich atmosphere. That atmosphere had led our ancestors to choose Earth as a laboratory to engineer our own species' survival. With mixed results.

The smell of diesel surged over other scents when a generator grumbled to life somewhere on the property. It didn't quite mask the sound of a door closing or of whispers and crunching feet that moved south on the beach side. Then, two lots farther down, shadows flicked across the street. I picked up the smell of more than one Sape. I didn't understand how the Skulls had spotted me, but it might be my best chance to learn more about their operation. When I caught their scent veering around behind me, I forced myself to remain motionless.

An arm circled my throat and jerked me back. Pain tore every nerve in my body. My limbs went rigid and I hit the ground like a plank. I would have screamed but for the paralysis.

When I could focus again, my wrists were bound behind my back with zip ties and Conroy hunkered over me, jiggling a Taser. "Well, looky here. Ninja boy's come a-calling."

"How . . . ?" I managed.

"Skinny lil' bird called me. Told me I might have a visitor."

At least I could stop worrying about poor little Crescenda at the mercy of the cold, cruel world. I really needed to start worrying about myself.

"Get him up," Conroy commanded. Wad and Mongo hauled me to my feet, Mongo favoring his possibly broken collarbone. They patted me down for weapons, took Andrei's binoculars, and shoved and kicked me across the street. Conroy pulled out a comm and said, "Bring 'em out. We're already late."

He pressed a control wand. Yard lights flooded the dolphin house. They didn't do it any favors – paint curled from the woodwork and trim swelled away from the walls. The left end of the place was taken up by two wide garage doors. A single-car garage facing the street joined the garage wing to the main house. Conroy strode to the single-car entrance, folded back metal security gates, and heaved up the overhead garage door. The interior was brightly lit, spotless, and empty. Meanwhile, Jody walked out the front door, waving someone to follow. A middle-aged man, a woman, and a teenage boy emerged. The man's face was bruised. They blinked in the glare.

The floor of the lighted garage jolted and then rose, revealing another space beneath. Slowly, majestically, its metallic blue paint gleaming under an anti-static nano-ceramic coating, Conroy's ancient Roadmaster Buick ascended into view on its very own car elevator. Conroy sighed with pride and drove the Buick from the garage. He got out, caressed the painted red and orange flames that gushed from the four vent ports on each front fender panel, and waved Jody over.

While Jody tugged the garage door back down and spread protective towels over the car's seats, Conroy handed his comm to Wad and pulled me over to the refugees. He posed me next to the woman and then threw an arm around my shoulders. "Smile, ninja boy, like we're one big, happy family enjoying our successful transport business." Wad took several photos.

Fear tapped my shoulder with an unwelcome message: I had badly underestimated the skill of Sapiens at deception. Conroy had neatly framed me, in the picture and as one of the gang.

Conroy said, "Okay, load 'em up." He walked to the rear of the vehicle and opened the trunk with an old-style key. "C'mon, kid. In you go."

Jody led the teenager over. The kid stared at the trunk in disbelief, then back at his mother. "I can't . . . you're not gonna make me ride in there."

"Stop whining and get in. If we don't get across the border by a certain time, you'll spend another twenty-four in the basement." With a few extra slaps, Conroy helped Jody stuff the kid in the trunk and close it. They put the woman in the front seat, with Mongo flanking her right, and Dad in the back between Jody and Wad. I braced for an attack.

Conroy walked back over. "Don't worry, ninja boy. We get back from our errand, we'll spend some quality time together." He gestured to Jody and Wad to get out of the car. "Lock him in the basement."

My plan to trap the Skulls needed major reworking.

*

Smears of moonlight leaked through three small wall vents into the dead black of Conroy's basement. Humidity: nearing 100 percent. Smell: something two weeks drowned. Sound: small, unseen things splashing under the half-rotted, five-inch thick wood pallets on the concrete floor.

I wasted a few minutes critiquing my plan in hindsight – going after the Skulls in the first place, trusting Crescenda, invading Conroy's territory on impulse. Next, I assessed the worst that could happen: The Skulls would kill me and leave my body lying around where officials would find it and autopsy it, exposing our secret presence on Earth. I tried to stop whimpering.

For another few minutes, I centered myself enough to think. The house felt empty, silent except for the slap of water against the wall facing the sea. All four Skulls must have gone north. Conroy's remarks hinted that they needed to get across the border while a certain border guard (or guards) was still on shift. Canada's once generous immigration policies had tightened brutally in the 2030s. Due to the floods of climate refugees, the only people allowed in now were people who didn't really need to immigrate.

If the Skulls planned to party in Vancouver, they might not be back until late tomorrow. If they just dumped the refugees north of the Canadian border, they might make it back in four or five hours, giving me a chance to get out of here.

So get started, Goran. I worked my zip-tied hands down over my butt and then pulled my feet through my arms, picking up splinters and scrapes from the rough boards. With my teeth, I centered the knot between my hands and jerked my arms back sharply to bust the tie loose.

Once my hands were free, I explored my prison, stepping across the uneven pallets like a minefield scout. My cell measured six paces one way, five the other. One cinder block retaining wall was blank, the next wall had the three vents at head height, the third was centered by three steps up to a steel door set flush with the other side. I'd heard them slam home the bolt as I tumbled through the door and down the steps. The light switch next to it was dead.

Halfway down the fourth wall, my foot hit a solid object. I pitched forward, smashing my knee against something hard. After a few moans, I felt the objects – a dozen bags of cement that the high humidity had reduced to big rocks in paper shrouds. Each one weighed about a hundred pounds, a possible weapon against anyone opening the door.

I was sitting on the bags rubbing my knee when a sound shrilled in the distance. I went still. It came again. Someone pressed the doorbell a third time, then banged on the door.

The visitor offered the possibility of a quick escape. I stood, lugged a bag of cement two steps and heaved it at the metal door. Massive clang. When the echoes died, I heard someone shout "Hello?"

"Come around the garages to the back," I yelled at top volume. Silence. The voice had sounded female. One of the Skulls' party girls? A waster looking for a fix? I stood next to a wall vent and listened for the splash of footsteps amid the waves. Time passed. And passed. At last I heard a bigger splash and a curse.

"Come to the first vent," I yelled.

More irregular splashes, then words floated through the vent. "Who's this?"

I knew that voice. But it didn't make sense. "Lil? Are you following me?"

"In your dreams, whoever you are." A pause. "It's almost high tide and I'm up to my calves in water, so who are you?"

"Goran. We talked today. I got caught in here accidentally."

"You are sooo lying."

"I need your help to get out."

A pause. "I can't afford to piss off Conroy," she said.

"He'll never know you were here. Actually, why *are* you here?"

"To buy something from him, okay?" Lil sounded peeved.

"I wouldn'a thought you were a waster."

"I'm not. It's medicine. And there's a security camera on the front."

I had noticed it mounted on one corner. "Get me out and I'll take care of it."

"I don't want any part of this."

Time oozed past me, oozed out the vent, and disappeared over the ocean. Regardless of when the Skulls returned, I wanted to get home before Andrei realized my "physics video" was nonsense. I didn't have the time or technique to develop a trusting relationship with Lil.

"If you help me get out, I won't tell anyone you're sneaking into GenAge at night."

A sharp breath, followed by a tense silence.

At last she said, "The door's locked and the downstairs windows have bars. How do I get inside the house?"

"You don't have to. You just have to get in the small garage." I told Lil about Conroy manually opening the door and my suspicion that the endless damp had either warped it past its tolerance or shorted out the electronic controls. The double metal grates were the real security for the car elevator. The Skulls had been in a hurry bringing me down in the elevator. Without the precious Buick inside, they might have left the grates open. "Once you get the door up, there's a control panel mounted on the side of the elevator. Bring it down a floor. Look for a bolted door on the side of the lower garage. You can unbolt it."

# CHAPTER 5

From an unpublished manuscript titled *Why We Came to Earth: The Yunko Voyages* by Yunko Chief Recorder Yevgeny Godunov

*Greetings, Dear Peoples of Earth. Please allow me to introduce myself. I am Yevgeny Godunov, current Chief Recorder of the Yunko expeditions to your esteemed planet. It is my hope that relating the story of our journeys will foster greater understanding between our peoples.*

*We had hoped to remain concealed and then depart Earth without ever disconcerting you in the smallest way. However, the recent arrival of another ship from our home world revealed our existence. Therefore, a decent respect to the opinions of humankind requires that we explain our presence. Our native world is the planet you call Gliese 667Cc. It is tidally locked around its star, with one side always in sunlight, the other always in night. We inhabited the twilight band.*

The bolt scraped back. The door cracked open. Lil cowered behind it as if I might charge out like a bull into the ring. I squinted against the glare and limped up the three steps from Conroy's foul basement into the spotless car elevator, protected from the damp by the spaces that surrounded it. Lil punched a button on the control panel and we rose to street level. First thing I did was pull the garage door down.

"Aren't you gonna disable the security camera?" Lil said.

"The feed's going somewhere inside. Probably Conroy's computer." I tried the knob on the door into the house. Locked. A solid core garage door, but set into a lightweight wood jamb. I stepped back and landed a kick beside the door knob. Something cracked.

"Stop it!" Lil grabbed my arm as I launched another kick.

I struggled to regain my balance. "What's the matter?"

"Conroy'll nuke out if you kick his door down."

"You have another plan for getting inside?" I didn't understand her objection, and I was running out of patience. "Either we leave now and the videotape nails you for releasing me, or we get inside and erase the tape."

"I don't want Conroy mad at me. I need a favor from him."

Took me a moment to catch her meaning. "You mean that medicine? Are you sick?"

"It's for my little brother."

"What's wrong with him?"

"Why do you care?"

"Just wondering why you're so tied up with Conroy."

"It's similar to Duchenne's muscular dystrophy, but it's complicated by other genetic damage."

"Conroy's sure no doctor. How's he get meds?"

"It's a sideline. He has a contact in Vancouver. Conroy sends him an order, picks up the medicine, then sells it to his customer for about a third what it would cost legally."

"So what do you want me to do?"

She lifted her hands, then dropped them in defeat. "Kick the door down, I guess."

I gave the door another hard blow and the jamb splintered. One more easy kick and the strike plate broke free.

We climbed a couple more steps to the entry and stood staring at the huge living room, kitchen, and dining room. The place looked and smelled like a two-month garbage party. Empty beer bulbs and cans littered the floor along with dirty dishes. A pile of sleeping bags lay against a wall. Not much furniture except for a long, curved, ripped up leather sofa, probably built in by the original owners. High on the wall, just under the roof peak, hung a Japanese scroll depicting a heron perched on a branch. Overlooking the mess, it probably felt as alien as I did.

Across the open space, more steps rose to a corridor. "That way," Lil said.

I followed her, kicking aside a pair of panties, sim goggles, and a knee brace. In the corridor, Lil opened the first door on the right. Clothing and a disassembled bicycle littered the floor. "Jody's room," she said. Across the hall, the smell of stinky cheese oozed under the closed door. We walked on. "Wad's room," Lil said. "He hoards cheeses."

"You know the Skulls real well."

She paused, her hand on the third door. "Just because I know them doesn't mean we're tight. I've been friends with Janelle my whole life. And with Kayla since middle school. They're close to Conroy. He moved in here back in the spring." She jerked the door open. Paint-stained overalls–an attempt at home-made camouflage – lay on the unmade bed. By process of elimination, the room was Mongo's. "And remind me again, please, why it's your business?"

No point in answering. Instead I pushed lightly on the door at the end of the hall. It swung open. "Hunh," I said. "Is Conroy a neatfreak?"

"Janelle stays here sometimes."

"Then she must have just left." Actually, the room looked like

Conroy might be attempting military order. Neatly made bed. Clean carpet. A long workbench holding tools, a computer, and a 3D printer. A display board on the wall pasted with stills from videos along with personal photos. Several were of Janelle. On showed a lanky kid leaning against a firetruck. I looked closer and realized that it was a younger Conroy. I sat in the office chair and woke up his machine. "Do you by any chance know Conroy's password?"

"Move. I'll try."

Lil ran through top defaults and commonly used passwords. None worked, so at least Conroy wasn't that dumb. She pushed the chair back in frustration and then typed in his friends' names. She searched the drawer beneath the workbench. She tried variations on Janelle's name and birthday.

She stopped in frustration. "So where'd they go anyway?"

"Looked like they were taking people over the border. A couple and their teenage son. Put the kid in the trunk of the Buick."

She stared at me, wheeled, and typed. Cursed. Erased. Typed again. Repeated several times. "Got it!" While I watched the screen change she said, "4HOLE1956. The car – the 1956 four-hole Buick." She sighed in satisfaction then added, "If I erase the security camera files, won't it send an alert to Conroy's comm?"

"They left maybe an hour ago. Be at least two more hours before they can cross the border and dump the clients. Then come back. We'll be long gone."

We left the way we arrived, through the splintered door back into the small garage and then under the overhead door. I left the grates the way Lil had found them – closed across the door, but not locked. Stupid of the Skulls to leave them unlocked, stupid to use a password tied to Conroy's precious car. But Conroy wasn't a stupid guy. Probably self-trained. Real bright, but he'd never had the formal training that obsessed over every little detail. I hadn't done brilliantly myself this evening, but Conroy's mistakes made me feel a little better.

*

Lil had parked her car up the hill on the other side of the zone line, near a high school hangout called the Last Resort. We headed for it, trudging up through mucky yards, keeping in the shadows of the jungly landscaping.

"Your turn to answer questions," Lil said. "How'd you end up in Conroy's basement?"

"A misunderstanding."

"About what?"

I related the silly incident with Janelle, hoping to divert her from more important secrets.

"Gawd, you're clueless." A block later, she said, "I'm hungry. The Last Resort stays open 'till eleven."

I was hungry, too, and I had bribe money left over. "Okay."

A few paces later, she said, "Your dad works at GenAge? I've seen a Helin listed somewhere."

"Dr. Andrei Helin's my brother."

"Wow! He already has his doctorate? Did he graduate when he was ten?"

"He's older than me." Needed to get her off that topic. "What do you do at GenAge?"

She rattled on about her work duties but I barely heard her. Wind off the bay kept whipping her long, gold-brown hair across my face, leaving tracks I could feel even after it slipped away. When the wind let up, her scent surged back – cosmetic smells, wild mushrooms and something like cumin, floating on top of a day's sweat and the smell of the tide.

Our mutual escape seemed like a bond. But was it close enough to provoke honesty? "Why do you break into GenAge?"

She stopped. I walked on. When I turned she said, "Things get really crappy around our house. Mom works night shifts at BioBounty Foods. That is, when she doesn't forget. That's how Mom handles stuff – she forgets it. But I don't. I'm never going to forget anything. I even write it all down."

Okay. "Your dad around?"

She drew even with me and we kept walking. "Yeah." A few more paces and she blurted, "But he drinks a lot. Hasn't had a job in years."

"Where'd he used to work?"

"Dock worker up at Bellingham. After the Big Crumble, the port silted up and nobody fixed it. Then that oil tanker ran aground on the wreckage of two offshore wind turbines the Oilheads blew up. SafeShip laid him off and he started drinking really bad."

There seemed no end to effects of the Big Crumble. The disasters of 2027–the Oklahoma Quake Storm, the Second Russian Revolution, the Saudi Depletion, and the Venezuelan Oil Tremors–sent the price of petroleum beyond reach of most people. Things have sagged along ever since. We had been insulated in the Outpost. I was only eight when it happened, and about all I remembered was the Change Lords and Bosses talking about how fracking triggered some earthquake in Oklahoma, which triggered some fault that triggered some other faults until the New Madrid fault let loose and killed a lot of people.

Lil finally got around to answering my question. "So yeah, I sneak into GenAge to search their databases for clinical trials that might help my brother. Or new meds. I found a promising one last night, wanted Conroy to get it. I'd do anything to find a cure for Davy. Anything."

"That's ragged." I tried to merge the Lil beside me with the Lil I saw around school, always looking so organized. And so obsessed with her little brother. Odd, how we were both involved in desperate searches for cures.

We rounded a corner and saw an island of light ahead – the Last Resort, about the only legal thing open past nine in podunk Seal Bay. The place was in an old dollar store, but its name came from murals of hellish vacation spots crowded with zombie-like visitors. The food was cheap, with red meat once a week. We stopped in a shadowed building entrance across the street and watched for suspicious activities, then ran to the restaurant's entrance. I flashed cash at the front guy to prove we could pay. He led us to a section near the back under the African Safari mural – starving refugees in big flowery sun hats lying on plastic lounge chairs around a scummy waterhole littered with animal skeletons. I guess they thought the murals made customers grateful for whatever the place served.

"You know my friend Kayla?" Lil waved at the wall. "She painted these."

"She's good."

A long history of food smells hung in the air, fueling my hunger. I felt strange sitting with a girl in public–a Sape girl at that. We ordered potatoes with cheese, the only dish they had left. Lil seemed uneasy, too, constantly looking around the half-full restaurant. I alternated bites with watching the occasional passing car through the large front windows. I couldn't think of anything safe to discuss. Lil rattled on about her little brother and various friends. They all seemed so connected, like a web that might capture any fly curious enough to approach.

We finished and headed for the door. We were at the desk and I was peeling off bills when the sound of an engine, more like a transport truck than a hybrid, swelled and faded. We walked out and I paused, looking in both directions. And listening. The low grumble sounded again, then sharpened to the rattling growl of a glass pack muffler. The four-hole Buick surged onto the street two blocks in front of us. I pushed Lil forward into a run and followed, hoping to dodge down a side street.

Mongo thrust his head out the Buick's passenger window, then half his upper body, aiming a pistol at me. "Hey, Bitch, we're gonna take you apart – "

I launched a tackle at Lil. She crashed onto the concrete with me on top, and we rolled into the gutter behind a parked car. A bullet hit the Resort's wall, pelting us with fragments of cinder block. I heard Wad yell, then the brakes screech, then two more shots. The car shielding us clanged and rocked under the impact. Beneath me, Lil heaved for air. Then the Buick pulled away, I think. I was too deaf from the shots to be sure.

I scrambled out of the filthy gutter and reached to help Lil. "You okay?"

She moaned, crawled over the curb, and collapsed on the sidewalk. Blood oozed from her abraded left palm. She grimaced, then used her other hand to pull bloody, torn fabric away from her right knee. "Why the hell did you smash me so hard?"

"Didn't have time to be careful." The few remaining customers pressed against the windows, staring at us. Lil fished a comm out of her jacket.

"What are you doing?"

"Calling the Metros."

"No!" I grabbed her hand and pried the comm from it.

She pulled away. "Those idiots shot at us. You gonna stand around till the Skulls kill you? And me too? Don't you get it? They saw us together! They'll know I helped you!"

"You can't call the Metros."

"Of course I can. They're pathetic but that's what they're for." She used the car to pull herself up and snatched at the comm again. I grasped her arm and tried to haul her around the corner before the Skulls came back.

"We have to stay at the scene of the crime!" she yelled.

I pulled harder and she stumbled forward. Behind us a manager and couple of servers rushed out of the Resort and started in pursuit. I couldn't let them question me, but escape was hopeless with Lil pulling in the opposite direction. I scooped her up, forced her over my shoulder, and ran.

She pounded my back, screaming and cursing. Got a fist far enough around to smash my nose. Warm liquid trickled down, but I didn't have a free hand to check whether it was snot or blood.

I made it around the corner, crossed the side street, and turned into the alley behind the next block of stores, Lil yelling and pounding all the way. Back yards lined the alley's other side. I kicked at each gate while gripping the struggling Lil. Near the far end, my kick broke a wooden gate free from its latch and we stumbled into someone's back yard. I deposited Lil on a patch of grass.

She glanced at the dark house fifty feet away from us and said in a furious whisper, "Would you please stop slamming me on the ground!"

It hadn't been a long drop. Why was she making it such a huge deal? Maybe she'd never had fight training, or played rough as a kid. I pressed the gate's latch holder back into the wood. Voices still murmured at the end of the alley but they drifted out of earshot. I braced my back against the gate and breathed deeply. I'd had it with the Skulls. Regardless of Yunko rules, I wanted to take them out. Unfortunately, there'd been so many witnesses to Mongo's attack, if anything happened to a Skull, I'd now be Suspect Number One.

The house stayed dark. The homeowners might be cowering inside, or the place might be abandoned. A few pears still clung to a twisted old tree by the back fence. I picked a couple.

Lil limped over. "You're one big walking target. You and anyone around you."

"Want a pear?"

"I guess." She put the pear in her jacket pocket. "Why didn't you let me call the Metros? It would have put Wad and Mongo on record at least, given us some protection."

I fell back on the official excuse for Seconds. "First thing they'd do is ask to see my driver's license. I don't have one – Andrei refuses to pay the bribe until I graduate."

"So just tell them that."

"Problem is, I drove Andrei's car to town. Left it over by GenAge."

She rolled her eyes. A good response since my story was pure nonsense. My driver's license was safe in my wallet, and my other IDs were perfectly adequate. Nothing like as tight as Andrei's, of course. One division at the Outpost does nothing but concoct identities for Researchers, who often work at high security labs. They keep track of places where records have been destroyed, of dead people whose identities could be stolen and transformed convincingly. They insert bogus information in databases all over the world. Andrei could have run for President, if he had wanted that ridiculous office.

But Lil kept focusing on my many mistakes. On and on she went: I was clueless; I was reckless; I was gripped by a death wish.

Finally I said, "Calm down. I'll take care of it."

"How? You and what army?"

"I have . . . other assets."

"Assets?" Lil blurted. "Who? All your friends? I never noticed you had any."

I should have walked away, should have let her angry aura fade, but the urge to hit back won. "No, guard animals."

"Guard – ? It's illegal for non-corporates to own attack dogs. If you use pits or Dobies – "

"They're cats."

Her mouth dropped open. She stomped around in a circle, shrieking with laughter. Maybe the gunshots had unhinged her. "You're insane. That's . . . okay, tell me why it's not the world's stupidest idea to go after a drug gang with a bunch of kitty-cats."

She made my fantasy sound as idiotic as it really was, but she was belittling Zax and Gwitchy. "Our cats have been selectively bred and genetically altered."

"For what?"

"A project that didn't work out. At a lab where my brother worked before. They were about to euthanize the test animals so we took a couple with us." She seemed to believe me. Much easier to lie to Sapes than to our own people.

"What kind of project?"

"Curing diseases caused by genetic defects." Sounded vague enough.

"Yeah, along with half the bio projects in the country."

She was good at sarcasm, but her expression changed in some way I couldn't read. She dug out the pear and took a big bite, ran one finger up the juice running down her chin and licked it. She never took her eyes off me.

Lil got me out of the basement and I got her in trouble. I didn't want to set her up for other dangers. At last, just to break the tension, I said, "Want to walk up to my car? Then I'll let you off at yours. Doesn't seem like a good idea to be walking around this neighborhood."

She nodded, and we set out. If I could just get her home safely tonight, maybe by tomorrow, I could come up with another plan. And all the while, a Yunko commandment pounded in my head: Yunko do not involve themselves in the problems of Sapes.

# CHAPTER 6

From an unpublished manuscript titled *Why We Came to Earth: The Yunko Voyages* by Yunko Chief Recorder Yevgeny Godunov

*During our centuries on Earth, we have reshaped ourselves so drastically in your image that our throats can no longer pronounce our ancestral language. When we first arrived in your year 1125 C.E., we learned your dominant language of that time and area, Latin. Thus we renamed our home world Orbis Noster. Since then, Latin has faded but Earth astronomy has made great strides. Now, we simply call our native world Gliese-C. We commonly refer to those of us on Earth as Yunko, yet still refer to those who remain on Gliese-C as Orbians. In our long quest to save our species, we have become, with great and sad irony, two species.*

I made it home from my adventures at eleven thirty-five. Andrei sat at the kitchen table. I wondered if he had sat there brooding the entire time I'd been gone.

"Took you long enough," he said. "I need to talk to you about what's happening."

Could he possibly know the truth about my evening? I braced for his anger, but he pushed a bag of apple chips toward me and said, "A month ago I mentioned that Beta Group's progress did not satisfy the stockholders. Beta Group was eliminated and I was transferred to Gamma Group.

"Yeah." I relaxed. Sounded like the problem on his mind was work-related.

He pulled his weary body straighter in the kitchen chair. "GenAge has collected millions of tissue cultures from cancer patients, along with patient histories. Those human tissue cultures are the only reason I'm embedded there. We can't match them for studying the dominant, human part of our genome. Gamma Group's main focus is searching the biobanks for natural mutations that inhibit tumor growth. Yesterday I ran across a tissue culture from a cancer patient that may hold the key to restoring our normal lifespans."

He paused, then continued in the sort of voice that religious people use to recite their creeds. "The tissue has a natural mutation that counteracts radiation damage by weakening atypical cells, allowing them to be more easily destroyed, yet restores normal telomere configuration."

"Great." I started to rise. I no longer pay much attention to miraculous discoveries.

"But there's a problem. They haven't yet decoded the entire genome. Therefore, I can't simply transmit the digital data for the culture to the Outpost. I will have to steal the culture itself. I don't dare wait until they've completed their research."

At that point, I didn't really understand the implications. "Great," I repeated. "Steal the thing and we'll run it across the border. Someone from the Outpost can meet us and take it home."

"Not so easy. The storage vault for culture and tissue samples is on the same floor as my new lab, but the door requires a key card with a higher security rating than mine. There's a significant risk I'll get caught trying to physically steal it."

Yeah, I thought, Andrei probably would. Then shame washed over me. My own performance that night had not been impressive. "What'll you do?"

"Enter the room with someone who has the right clearance so I can see the layout for myself. Then devise a way to break in, steal the culture from the vault, and smuggle it out of the building."

Then sprout wings and fly, I thought.

Andrei said something I didn't understand. "If I fail, your responsibility will become greater. I'll try to give you the information you'll need."

"What are you talking about?"

Andrei didn't answer. I tried again. "How can I do something if you don't tell me what it is?"

"In due time." He rose from the table, then stopped and scowled at me. "This morning was Remembrance Day. Did you do the ritual?"

I shook my head. If we kept track of Remembrance Day in Earth years, it would be simple–every year on June 30 we would commemorate the event that happened in 1908. But custom demands we observe the anniversary by the yearly calendar of Gliese-C, so in Seal Bay, Washington, Remembrance Day rolls around every 28.155 days.

Our older, conventional ships had successfully entered orbit around Earth for centuries. Then two of our new Bubble Drive ships arrived in 1908, slowing before they reached the solar system, The first ship – the almost empty one meant to carry us all back home – prepared to enter orbit over our base near the Tunguska River in South Central Siberia. A coronal mass ejection occurred simultaneously and the crew on board was killed when the increased atmospheric density interacted with the plasma of the Bubble Drive. The explosion released as much energy as 185 Hiroshima bombs.

It all seemed like ancient history when I desperately needed to concentrate on current problems, but late as it was, I followed him back out to the flat rock. We sat in silent darkness for a minute.

Then Andrei chanted the first call, "Frayka sent them from Light into Darkness."

I gave the response. "Sent the hundreds into Darkness stretching eternal."

"Until they once again encountered Light."

"Light from a star too bright to see."

"They fell down toward the light."

"Down to their destination."

"Down to the planet of their life and death."

"Into a Light too fierce to bear."

"We honor them, those of us who follow."

"Their quest is our quest."

"For it we live, for it we die," we finished in unison.

We sat a few minutes longer. The ritual revived my sense of mission and of unity with my people. It also turned my recent adventures – from climbing fire escapes to dodging bullets with a Sape girl – into embarrassing nonsense. Never again.

*

The next morning, neither Lil nor the Skulls were at school. Short on sleep and distracted, my mind rocketed all day from interstellar disasters to disappointing miracle cures to high school hassles and back. I had to cut these new entanglements with my Sape classmates, but I couldn't stop thinking about Lil. She was definitely an *asymtra*–something that presents an interesting aspect when viewed from any direction.

When I reached home that afternoon, Zax and Gwitchy were out hunting. I grabbed a jacket and set out for a walk. A trail furred with moss and tiny plants led up the rocky rise behind the house. At the top, a grassy meadow sloped toward the high country. As I crossed it, the cats' tails switched toward me through the tall, golden grass.

After the usual leg rubbing, we headed toward a weed-choked campground about a mile from the house. Rickety picnic tables sat among fire circles of blackened rock. The place was peaceful and fragrant with the vanilla smell of Ponderosa. I didn't think it had been visited in years.

Four years ago when we moved into the cabin, I found a small wooden nail keg among the junk in the barn. I carried it up to the campground, along with a 50-foot coil of rope, and rigged a pulley system so I could haul the keg up into a tree and out of sight. I used it to hide stuff I didn't want Andrei to see. I'd almost forgotten what it contained, but when I lowered the keg and opened it, there were still two ancient manga on the bottom, so mildewed I could barely make out the drawings of busty blondes and lusty octopi. I hoisted it back up. The cats and I noodled around the campground for a while, watching ospreys bring in fish to feed a nest of chicks, before starting back to the house.

On the way home, Zax and Gwitchy peeled off on their own business. I reached the barn, rounded the fence to the front, and looked up. And froze. A red Nissan sat in our driveway. Lil stood beside it, hands propped behind her on the hood, staring at me.

Quick terrain assessment: The alarms rigged around the perimeter were well hidden. So were the tripwire snares waiting for anyone who tried to penetrate the brush. The only security device visible was a glint off the wide-angle video cam mounted on the cliff face behind the house. Andrei wouldn't be home for hours. No problem keeping Lil away from the comm helmet, Bubble Drive wand, and other Yunko gear. Eagerness overcame caution and propelled me toward her.

"How'd you find our house?"

"Got Andrei Helin's address from the GenAge personnel files. Listen, Conroy called me last night about one o'clock. Soon as they got the security cam alert, they dumped their passengers and turned around. When they got home Conroy and Jody stayed at the house, trying to figure out what happened. Wad and Mongo drove around looking for you. Since they saw me with you, Conroy figured I'd let you out. Furious about it."

"What'd you tell him?"

She shrugged. "I said I just let you out because I thought you were injured. I didn't tell him you blackmailed me – he'd want to know how so he could use the leverage himself."

"Is he still mad at you?"

"I calmed him down some, promised him a whole sheet of gas ration coupons. Told him it was you that kicked in the door and broke into his computer." She shrugged. "He said he'd ask around about meds for Davy, but I'm not sure he'll do it. Actually, he acted sort of weird, like he was distracted, just going through the motions. But he's still major pissed at *you*."

"Uh, thanks."

She opened the car door but then gazed past me at something. "Oh, yeah. Your commando kitties. This I gotta see."

I turned and saw Zax staring at her from a safe distance. He ambled off, apparently convinced she was neither dangerous nor interesting. I disagreed.

44

Lil entered the dogleg path through the fence. I hurried after. Short of offing her and dumping the body, I couldn't think of a way to divert her. And I owed her big time. Might as well go through the motions of peeking in the house for the cats. But when we started up the porch steps, the living room curtains moved and a round head peered over the sill.

"There's Gwitchy," I said. "In the window."

"Gwitchy?"

"Um, native name." I didn't specify which natives.

"It's darling!" Lil said, a purr in her own voice. "Why are its ears like that?"

"They're descended from Pallas' cats. Her ears are set lower on her head so they don't stick up when she's stalking prey."

Lil knelt and tried to peer over the windowsill for a better look at Gwitch, who hunkered down. "Hey, you big, adorable thing, you're so beautiful and fuzzy," she crooned. "You're the fuzziest thing I ever saw."

I stared. She'd become a different person from the yelling, cursing she-devil outside the Last Resort. Even her expression was different. Maybe it was the look she gave her little brother.

She rose. "Can I pet her?"

"I don't think she'd let you. She's kinda feral."

"I won't scare her. Please?"

My better judgment took flight. I unlocked the door and stepped into the dim room. Lil pushed past me, eager as a kid hunting Easter eggs. Gwitchy started a low gurgling chitter.

Lil got a clear look at her face. "Her pupils are round!" She clutched my arm, way too suddenly.

Gwitchy sprang at my assumed assailant. I simultaneously gave the halt call, grabbed Lil, and fell backward, jerking her throat away from Gwitchy's teeth. I rolled over on Lil before the cat could do more than claw her arm. Convinced the strange Sape was attacking, Gwitch dug under me to get at Lil. I gave the second halt signal. The cat shrieked but froze.

Lil's harsh, shuddering breaths shook me as well. I tried to ignore her body pressed beneath mine, but I couldn't resist wiping the wild hair away from her face. Tears seeped from her eyes. She spotted Gwitchy and said, "Get her away from me."

I picked up Gwitch and carried her to my room. With words of praise for her vigilance, along with reassurance that I was okay, I locked her in.

Our home medkit can handle anything up to outpatient surgery, so I fetched it to the living room. Lil lay in a fetal position, clutching her arm. Blood seeped between her fingers. Seeing her there, I thought about an icon we studied as kids, learning about the Beautiful Twins of Light and Darkness. The picture showed them crumpled and bloody, as Frayka began punishing them for mating by melting them together into little droplets of blood that became their descendants, doomed forever by the battle between night and day.

I helped Lil up with the clunkiest words possible. "Have you had a tetanus shot?"

"About six months ago," she snapped.

"Come in the kitchen," I said. "I'll clean and bandage that."

Twice now I'd ended up on top of Lil, but not in a good way. As soon as she was bandaged, she stomped out the door and drove off before I could apologize again. Of course she did. When had a female not abandoned me?

# CHAPTER 7

## Excerpt from the diary of Lil Osborne

*So maybe Goran can take out the Skulls with his bloody, vicious, deeply evil cats, but I do not want any part of it! Freak! Even his house is weird. All brambled up outside. Inside the sofa's covered with this godawful blue hydrangea print fuzzed up with cat hair. First Nation weapons and masks hang on the scuzzy log walls like a frontier stage set. Then after his cat tried to kill me, he brought out this medical kit like I've never seen before, patched me up, and gave me antibiotic pills with no label. Black market? Clinical trial stuff? And final freakout – that cat had round pupils like a human!*

*I told Kayla about the Skulls shooting at us and about Goran's cats. She thinks Goran's scared of contact with the Metros because he's illegal. But Kayla thinks everyone's illegal and they all want to buy fake IDs from her. She wants to sneak Goran a big hit of tonic so he'll spout every thought in his head. It's an idea – Goran does bizarre stuff and he has access to weird meds. I keep wondering if he has info that would help Davy.*

*Later I searched "Andrei Helin" and I found a clinical trial he ran. I've read lots of trial abstracts because of Davy so I know how they're written–the language they use, what they include and what they leave out. Something seemed off in the language used for Andrei Helin's trial.*

Lil wasn't in math class the next morning, but I encountered Conroy when I took a shortcut through the Rats' Nest to shop class. I cut between two windowless metal training buildings that almost enclosed a dark, muddy rectangle reeking of motor oil and old cooking grease from the building vents. Jody leaned against the far corner.

Footsteps squelched behind me and I caught a smell that was becoming familiar. A hand gripped my shoulder and Conroy said, "We need to have a little chat."

I edged my feet farther apart and shifted, ready to pivot into Conroy hard enough to take him down. He felt the move and countered with a shift of his own. "Chill, man. This isn't what you think."

I turned. "What do you want?"

"The Metros picked up Wad and Mongo. Did you turn 'em in?"

"No. But the Buick's easy to recognize. Probably somebody in the Last Resort made the call."

Conroy nodded. "Sounds about right. I just wanted to see what you'd say."

Whatever Conroy had on his mind, I wanted no part of it. "You finished? I'm late to class."

Conroy adjusted the 16-penny nail stuck through his scalp lock. "Wad and Mongo are hitting a whole 'nother level of stupid these days. I didn't order them to shoot at you, much less at Lil. They're drawing attention I don't need. They're not Skulls any longer."

"Okay." I turned to leave.

He said, "I still don't get how you took all four of us down at the garden center."

"Lucky, I guess. I've had some training."

"You guys train with root balls? And dodging bullets–how'd you do that?"

I shrugged. "I heard the Buick coming. Mongo's a lousy shot."

Conroy said in a casual tone, "Wad and Mongo may be losers, but dumping them leaves me short-handed. I need somebody who can think on his feet, handle himself in a fight. Maybe somebody like you."

I didn't pass out from shock but it was a near thing. Conroy started a sales pitch about the perks of being a Skull but I hardly heard him, I was so busy looking for the trap. Did he need a fall guy? Cannon fodder? A mechanic for the Buick?

My comm vibrated. Andrei. "I'll think about it. Gotta take this call." I walked away. He didn't try to stop me. Out of earshot, I answered. "What's happening?"

"Emergency message from a Second, Maks Barsukov, in Corvallis, Oregon. They're in trouble and heading our way. Need our help."

"What happened?"

"I don't know exactly, but it got the Corvallis police after them. They holed up on the University campus in a bison barn where Vlad, the Researcher, works. Vlad's in bad shape. He's well into the rapid aging phase, and ten hours hidden in a storage locker has left him dehydrated and showing blood chemistry abnormalities."

"Why didn't they contact the Outpost?"

"The trouble started when they were away from home. Had to use the remote trigger to blow their house with everything still inside, including their comm helmet. They don't have alternate IDs, medkit, or extra cash. Maks hacked the ignition of a car in someone's driveway, switched the plates, and got out of town. I'm on my way to the high school to pick you up. We need to prep for their arrival."

*

We stripped the spare bedroom, rigged a bed with an IV for hydration and blood chemistry problems. Sterile sheets and disinfectants were the best we could do for a makeshift OR but the prep would serve for minor surgery. Andrei thought we might need to insert stents in Vlad's auxiliary breathing orifices under his shoulder blades to increase his oxygen intake.

Andrei answered his comm–the Immigration Control officer at the nearest normal zone gate checking whether we were expecting a Vlad and Maks Barsukov. Four minutes later, the surveillance cam showed an unknown car stop at the perimeter fence. Andrei pulled out his comm again, answered, and said, "It's them." I went out the dogleg first. I looked in the driver's window and thought I saw my own reflection, but when the driver got out I realized he was older, thinner, and taller. Otherwise he could have been my twin. Andrei quickly checked Vlad, who was lying in the back seat, and Maks and I helped him into the house. He couldn't stand straight and the wisps of white hair on his skull stuck out wildly.

I had shut the cats in my bedroom; I didn't want a replay of the Lil and Gwitchy incident. Their yowling made it hard to talk, so I tried letting Zax out on a leash. Maybe it was our refugees' Yunko physiology, but both cats were immediately friendly. The next two hours we worked on Vlad, hydrating and perfusing. Then I acted as surgeon's assistant while Andrei opened Vlad's "shoulder noses" to increase his oxygen saturation.

Our next priority was dumping the car Maks had stolen. Andrei instructed us to vacuum and wipe it down with sterilizers, drive it to the Railyards, and abandon it. He predicted the car would disappear within five minutes, never to be seen again. After an hour of cleaning the vehicle to Andrei's satisfaction, we took off, hands in disposable gloves, eyeing each other as suspiciously as dating service clients on our first outing.

I drove, cutting through a parking lot to bypass the zone line. We reached Main Street and turned south. Buildings grew grayer and shabbier, broken windows gaped, doors hung open. We passed the train station and lines of freight cars parked on sidings. The street dead-ended in a patch of dirt and broken debris bordered by a curb and chain-link fence with a vacant lot beyond. The rail companies had abandoned the derelict territory beyond the fence even before the Big Crumble. Now, the Railyards were home to people unwanted by everyone except the law.

A break in the fence looked big enough to admit a vehicle. I wanted to get away from the place as quickly as possible. "I'll drive through the hole in the fence and stop. Then we jump out and run."

Maks sneered at the running part, but he followed the directions. We bolted through the broken fence and jogged a couple of blocks before slowing down and shucking the gloves. I looked back and saw three figures crossing the vacant lot toward the car.

As we passed a long line at a soup kitchen, I tried conversation. "How was your trip?"

Maks shrugged. "We made it." He paused and sniffed his armpit. "Been wearing these clothes for three days. Anyplace in this town to buy new ones?"

"There's plenty of U-Squats."

"I said new."

"One store downtown, about four blocks from here."

"They have snap-wing sleeves?"

I tried to look too tough to worry about snap-wing sleeves and changed the subject. "Have any trouble getting from Oregon into Washington?"

"No. We used a half-ass old private ferry that still crosses the Columbia. Forget the I-5 bridge. They assume anyone heading north is a climate refugee, so it's strip-search, document check, and health survey. You run a fever, register any inflammation, state police guards in hazmat suits escort you to prison camp. I doubt you ever come out."

We detoured toward the clothing store. Inside, garments bright and dull were stretched on wire frames hanging from the ceiling like giant bats wearing party clothes. Maks batted his way through the overhead display to search the clothes racks beneath. I checked a price tag. Ouch. But Researchers like Andrei and Vlad who're embedded at Sape labs make good money. Maks found a shirt and pair of pants that met his style requirements. He threw another pair from the rack at me and said, "Your pants are embarrassing. Try those on."

I did. Somehow the pants made my thighs looked super ripped and my legs longer at the same time. But I didn't have credits on me so I stepped from behind the try-on screen and handed the new pants back to the clerk.

"Your friend paid for them." The clerk nodded toward the exit.

I grabbed the pants and caught up with him. Had I actually embarrassed Maks, or did he just regret being a jerk? Down the street, he turned into a liquor store. I followed. He put a pint of vodka on the check-out desk and the clerk didn't even card him.

Back outside, I said, "Thanks for the pants." He nodded. I tried, "How'd you end up in a bison barn anyway?"

Maks dropped the pint into a thigh pocket. "Took Blizzard out for her night walk. She's a . . . she *was* a Malamute-wolf cross. We happened to pass a bar. A girl was standing in the parking lot. I thought she was an underage student looking for someone to buy booze. Figured I'd help her

50

out."

I wasn't a complete idiot. I doubted Maks accidentally walked by that bar.

"We were talking," he continued, "when three guys came out – she'd been waiting for them. They started trash talking me. I tried to get Blizzard out of fighting range. Then one guy said something really gross. I let go the leash and punched him. Free for all. Blizzard had another guy down when the bouncer came out with a shotgun, stuck the muzzle against Blizzard's side, and fired. He held the gun on me while he called the Metro cops."

The loss of a guard animal made me feel hollow. I cringed at my notion of risking Zax and Gwitchy over a stupid high school face-off.

Maks continued. "Cops released me last night about midnight. I went down to a place by the river that stays open all night. When the early morning news came on, I saw the cops were after me again. I got out of there and commed Vlad. He'd already left the house, so we met up. He had keys to the big lockers in the bison barn; I hid him there. While I waited till the barn was deserted, I blew the house and stole a car parked on a residential street. Hacked the ignition system. Then I got into the barn, got Vlad out, and headed north."

We walked another block. "Why'd the cops release you, then go after you again?"

"How many years you been saving up questions?" he snapped. "They probably scanned Blizzard's chip. It has her breeding and DNA information, treatment protocols, stuff you wouldn't find on an ordinary chip. It alerted them there was something different about her." In a moment he said, with a shake in his voice, "You ever get in the same situation, cut your guard animal's chip out before you leave her body."

The thought flooded my mouth with saliva. We walked on in silence while I concentrated on not vomiting.

My curiosity got the better of me again about the time we reached Ocean Vista Estates. "Bison? They gonna shoot us up with bison DNA?"

"Back in the 1800s," Maks said, "Sapes nearly wiped out bison, then crossbred the ones left with cattle. But the University's bison are from a purebred herd up in Canada." He puffed out air. "Purebreds live longer and their meat's healthier. PanAgri wants to market purebred bison as health food and charge for it like it's caviar. Vlad was working on PanAgri's project, but he also isolated genes linked with the purebreds' longer life spans. Thought it might help with our problem."

I shut up. I still told myself we'd one day find a cure – either our scientists at the Outpost or one of our teams in the field – but studying geriatric bison seemed next door to hopeless.

# CHAPTER 8

From the unpublished Godunov manuscript
*Why We Came to Earth: The Yunko Voyages*

*In the Earth year of 1006 C.E., your people recorded a supernova in the constellation Lupus. While the supernova did no serious damage to Earth, twenty-two Earth years earlier, the outer edge of its gamma ray burst had hit Gliese-C.*

*At first we thought ourselves lucky. When the initial jet hit, the dark side of our tidally-locked planet was turned toward the blast and that uninhabited region absorbed the immediate damage. Casualties were limited to several hundred ice-cap miners working on the dark side. The single other habitable planet in our triple star system was destroyed.*

*But the "afterglow" energy emissions that followed, particularly the UV radiation, spread through our planet's protective atmosphere with devastating results. The dreadful event began the process of making our home world uninhabitable.*

Maks and I returned home at sunset. Vlad, still semi-conscious, mumbled something and plucked at the pillows that propped him on his side so his shoulder noses could function. Andrei was messing up the kitchen with something he called a stew. I took over and told him to go rest. Half an hour later I served up the pot of potatoes, onions, and beets, with a little goat sausage for flavor.

Andrei had contacted the Outpost again. The consensus was that Vlad needed a night's rest, and that Maks and I would take him to the border the next morning. Andrei had claimed a stomach bug as a reason for his absence, but he didn't want to miss a second day at work. He wrote me an excuse for missing nearly two days of school because of the same illness

After supper Maks said, "I feel like I've spent the last forty-eight hours stuffed in a box. Wanna go for a run?"

"Sure." We geared up and I led us out on my normal circuit. We loped down through the subdivision plots at a pace slow enough to talk.

"You think they'll send you two out again?"

"No," Maks said. "Vlad can barely work now."

He didn't seem chatty but he might be my only chance to find out things. "Then how will they reassign you when you get back to the Outpost?"

"Probably maintenance work. Or at one of our synthetics factories. Take your pick: making synthetic yew bark, tank meat, or blood from horseshoe crabs." He huffed out a cynical breath. "Assuming I just march along in lockstep with the program."

He was probably just talking tough. Maybe he had some dream of disappearing into the world of Sapes, but even if he did, he'd still die soon after thirty. "Maks, stop."

"What?" he said in an irritated voice.

"Do you ever think about it?"

"Think about what?" His voice turned sharper.

I was sure he understood my question, but I spelled it out. "You know. About dying of old age when we're thirty-one, thirty-two?"

"No. I don't think about it. What's the point? Eat, drink and be merry. That's what I think about. Shut up with the questions, okay?"

We reached an overgrown bike path that paralleled the highway along the coast. Maks increased his speed until I had no breath for talk. We were north of Seal Bay city limits now, running through a mostly deserted stretch of roadside businesses and abandoned houses.

Andrei and I never talked about our short futures, but it was always in my thoughts. As a little kid at the Outpost, sometimes I pretended I had been found in an orphanage for ordinary Sape kids–kids who'd live maybe eighty years if they were lucky. We age at about the same rate as Sapes through adolescence, but that galloping rate of change does not let up in adulthood. Then, when we hit the rapid ageing phase around thirty, we go downhill so fast you can almost see it. I'd worked out that Maks must be about twenty-one but he looked thirty, maybe thirty-five.

I wondered if it was the age difference when he stopped, bent over, and gasped for breath. "We should probably head back," he said. "Make sure Vlad's okay." He straightened and gazed toward the foothills where campfires glowed like fireflies. "What's that?"

"Climate refugees. The unlucky ones. Couldn't find a ride heading north so they're walking." The fires trembled in a wind off Puget Sound. "Or maybe they're the lucky ones. It'll be longer before they find out that while Canada's better–there's still a national government there to keep the corps in check–there's nowhere that's really safe."

"It's worse farther south." Maks pulled one leg into a stretch. "First time we went into the field was to Albuquerque, New Mexico. Vlad worked with tau proteins at the university. There wasn't much along the New Mexico-Texas border in the first place, but after the Ogallala Aquifer ran dry, the whole place fell apart. Poor sods."

Personal disasters, global disasters. We ran back to the house without further talk. Vlad was asleep and Andrei heading for bed . We ended up looking like geezers ourselves, sitting on the porch of the cabin, passing the vodka back and forth until it was gone. After spending four years in Seal Bay in isolation, for the past week–getting involved with the Skulls and Lil–I'd felt like I was living someone else's life. Then today, meeting Maks seemed like the first time I'd ever really talked to another person. All Andrei does is criticize, and I can't talk to Sapes without worrying constantly about revealing secrets.

Maks rambled on about some girl he liked and then some other girls. I couldn't believe he just roamed around hooking up with Sape girls in spite of all our rules. But I ended up telling him about Lil and the Skulls. He asked if Lil and I had gotten it on. I had to confess I'd never even kissed her, or any other girl. It would have been humiliating to tell anybody else, but Maks seemed like the first and last friend I'd ever have. And I liked my new pants.

*

The next morning we pulled out by seven. I drove, Maks rode shotgun, and Vlad reclined on the back seat. Since we were heading for friendly territory, we left the cats at home. Maks had little to say. I felt awful myself; booze affects us way more than it does Sapes.

We headed down to Sedro Woolly and took Highway 20 across the Cascades. Rain had set in, soaking the empty, weed-choked fields and draping the burn-scarred mountains in gray veils that thickened with distance. Lonesome little towns flashed by. Solitary gas stations stood abandoned, their signs bleeding orange rust. The countryside had emptied out once cheap gasoline was gone.

We reached Oroville just south of the Canadian border about noon. The dry, jagged hills around the town were still marked from old fires. The whole state looked like that: patches of green forest, then areas as black and blasted as Mercury or red and dead as Mars.

A few refugees cruised the town like dried-up grasshoppers hitting Lake Osoyoos for one last drink. We drove north along the skinny lake until I spotted the sign for the turnoff.

The golden orange billboard featured a Mongol warrior on horseback holding a short curved bow aloft and wearing a spiked helmet that trailed a plume. Great Khan Winery was painted underneath in exotic lettering. The road led into the steep terrain along the Canadian border. We topped a rise and spotted the winery, a green island surrounded by rocky slopes pocked with old mine entrances. A dozen other cars were parked in front of the main building. It was veneered with stone like an old castle. Some sheds off to the side had been rigged up to look like yurts. The air smelled like rock and snow and asphalt, with fruity undertones.

Maks and I walked in the main building and dodged around visitors to a reception desk. The guy behind it looked as if his features and thick black hair had migrated straight from Central Siberia. Possibly a distant cousin.

"Helin. Party of three," I said as instructed. "We have reservations for the one-fifteen tour."

"Very good, sir," the desk clerk said and returned the proper passwords. "I understand your party has special needs. Please pull around back."

We followed orders. Two other men helped Vlad into a wheelchair. Maks and I followed them back to the reception area. I bought a vac-pac sandwich from the snack bar while Maks oozed over to two teenage girls and started talking. As I studied how he walked, how he stood, how he leaned slightly over one girl, my own muscles shifted into the postures.

A tour guide directed visitors for the one o'clock tour to follow him toward a large, dungeon-like door. Everyone left but us. The girls looked back over their shoulders – Maks is a good-looking guy – but their parents hauled them toward the dungeon. A few minutes later another staff member came over. In a low voice he said, "You'll go as soon as this tour group leaves the cellars."

The two men we'd seen outside reappeared and led us through the dungeon door. They carried Vlad's wheelchair down a broad staircase between stone walls decorated with fake torches in brackets. Racks of huge wooden barrels filled the cellar, its far end lost in darkness. The wine smell alone was enough to give me a buzz.

Our guides rolled aside a rack of barrels to reveal a door marked Mechanical Room. In spite of the HVAC equipment and circuit boards inside, there was room for Vlad's wheelchair to pass through a sliding wall panel into a large elevator. We descended and exited into a corridor finished with sheetrock and linoleum and followed it for maybe 200 yards before reaching a keypad door that looked like something from a bank vault.

One guide opened a cabinet beside the door, took out a stretcher and handed us miners' helmets. "The floor is very rough beyond here," he said. "We'll need to carry your companion."

We all put on helmets and then settled Vlad on the stretcher. The guides opened the door onto a much darker passageway, an old mine tunnel. As we entered, the swing of our helmet lights threw writhing shadows on the gouged and blasted walls. I looked back at the door we had come through, but it was disguised to blend with the walls.

Our hike was both businesslike and creepy. I half-expected scary creatures to jump out at us like in a video. Maks trudged silently without making jokes. The floor was already rough, but soon the tracks for ore carts made another obstacle. The air felt hotter and heavier than normal, pressing down like the unimaginable weight of rock overhead. From the corner of my eye, shadows looked like moving creatures .

The tunnel began to rise steeply. Up ahead, light bounced dimly off facets of rock. One guide hurried ahead, then returned. "All clear." Soon we saw the sunlit arch of the mine's entrance, braced with timbers.

"Welcome to Canada," the guide said. "Wait inside." He walked into the glow of day. A huge RV sat in the flat area in front of the mine. Beside it, an elderly couple draped with binoculars and cameras looked like a hundred thousand other Asian tourists.

Our guide talked to the couple, checked the area with binoculars, and waved us forward. A younger man got out of the RV driver's seat. He opened a large door in the vehicle's side. A gorgeous girl in a white coat stepped to the ground and rushed to the stretcher to check Vlad.

Maks' jaw dropped. "Great Flaming Frayka!" he whispered. "Enough you make you jump in the nearest hospital bed!"

She waved at us to follow her and headed back to the RV. Maks almost dropped Vlad's stretcher hurrying after her. We transferred the stretcher to the two attendants, who lifted Vlad into the vehicle. Inside, it looked like a mobile operating room. Maks stepped in, still hypnotized by Dr. Love Goddess of the Mongol Horde. I don't think he even heard me say, "Bye, Maks." I wondered if I'd ever see him again.

*

Heading back through the tunnel to the winery and retrieving the car, my head buzzed with all the new input. The world was still falling apart. Our lives still ended at thirty-two. Andrei still had some crazy plan to steal a tissue culture from high-security GenAge. But the first operation I'd been in charge of had succeeded. A knot of anxiety loosened and it felt good.

The trip had also shoved Conroy's offer out of my mind. It returned as I drove alone toward home. I couldn't do it, of course, but thinking about it gave me a tingle–Goran, just one of the gang. Goran and his bros. Maybe I could join the gang but never mention Yunko stuff. The thought violated every inch of my conditioning, but I spent my life on guard anyway, like every other Yunko in the field.

Except maybe Maks. I mentally replayed our rescue mission. Maks had impressed me, appalled me, roused my curiosity, and pissed me off. The guy seemed to ignore the rules and restrictions imprinted on us from birth. And he seemed immune to the gloom that twisted its way through Yunko life. Most of all, he'd been my friend. I think.

# CHAPTER 9

From the unpublished Godunov manuscript
*Why We Came to Earth: The Yunko Voyages*

*Our Gliese-C atmosphere contained many of the same elements as Earth's air–nitrogen, oxygen, carbon dioxide, methane and other molecules–but combined in different proportions. When the supernova's UV radiation began breaking those molecules apart, some recombined to create growing amounts of free oxygen.*

*We evolved to breathe oxygen, but at a much lower percentage of the atmospheric mix than on Earth – we could have breathed easily at the top of your Mt. Everest. To get enough fuel to function, our bodies developed so that we could extract a higher percentage of oxygen from our atmosphere by using continuous intakes and outflows of air, like Earth's fish.*

After my last class the next day I was heading toward the buses, trying to walk like Maks, when someone grabbed my arm from behind.

"Where've you been?" Lil said. Kayla Midnight was with her.

"My uncle's wedding in Spokane." Our cover story.

She nodded at the girl slouched beside her. "You know Kayla Midnight?"

"Hi, Kayla." Everyone in school knew who she was. I think most Sape guys reacted to her like I did – half attracted, half scared. I remembered a single day when she'd come to school with her face mostly bare–dark eyes, full lips, a nose to reckon with. In one class we'd both taken, I remember her saying something that made me think her people were from New Mexico.

She had a new look today. A fuzz of hair covered her skull except for two four-inch hair horns. She'd shaved her eyebrows and painted dark blue Maori-style tattoos all over her face with little pieces of jet stuck along the swirls. Her torso was encased in a tucked, sequined, embroidered jacket from some duchess's closet. Metal skewers and handcuff bracelets fastened the front of the thick material.

Obviously she wanted to be noticed. "Great jacket. Where'd you get it?"

She slowly blinked to show the red cat eyes painted on her lids. "U-squat down by the hospital."

Lil tugged my arm. "C'mon. We're going to the Last Resort. Kayla said she'd treat."

Scary but intriguing. I imagined Maks laughing at my caution. "Okay." I hitched up my new pants – they rode a little low.

At the Last Resort we found a table in the Tropical Paradise section. I sat facing the wall. The mural showed ocean waves beating against crumbling high-rise hotels. Stick-thin people clustered on the balconies, along with cages of critters to cook for supper. Skeletal fishermen dangled lines into the waves so close below. Kayla was good. The painted figures were no bigger than my little finger, but each one looked like a real person.

All that remained above water of one building was curvy pink parapets and chubby turrets. "Where's that?" I said.

She twisted around and touched the pink turrets. "What's left of the Royal Hawaiian. Waikiki."

"You ever go there?" I said.

"Mom had photos."

"Mr. and Mrs. Midnight on their honeymoon?" I joked.

"I don't use their name."

The waiter arrived and wiped his hands on a grubby apron. "Ready to order?"

"Pickled kelp sushi," Kayla said. "Put everything on my tab."

Lil chose a veg stir-fry and I ordered fries with cheese and gravy. When the waiter left, Kayla said, "Conroy was arrested a week ago. Kept it quiet. He was arraigned yesterday." Her grimace made the tattoos jump. "He's out on bail."

"Huh." Lil glanced at me. "Where'd you hear that?"

"Janelle," Kayla said. She glanced up. "Speak of the devil."

Conroy jerked out a chair, greeted the girls, and whacked my painful shoulder. "Goran, my man."

"Heard you went to court yesterday," Kayla said.

He shrugged.

"Can they make anything stick?" she persisted.

"No. And no way I'm gonna be a slave working on the dams. Besides, it's getting downright dangerous. Some whacked out Oilheads tried to blow up Hoover Dam last week. Dam's okay. Dam security found a bloody foot still wearing a hiking boot."

None of us had a reply to that.

Conroy yelled at someone across the room, jumped up, leaned over me and spoke too softly for the girls to hear. "You been thinking about our conversation?" Then louder, "Catch up with you later." He walked over to join the other group.

Kayla said, "Janelle needs to get away from him. Before it all gets away from her."

Lil nodded.

As if to lighten the mood, Kayla dug a notebook and pen out of her bag and said through her nose, "Monsieur, I vill draw ze portrait of you. Oui?"

Odd, but I was curious about how she saw me. "Sure."

"Name ze artiste you prefer."

"Uh, guy that painted soup cans."

"Mais oui. Ze Warhol." She studied me a long time, then started blacking in the paper until my cartoon face looked back at me when she turned the page around.

She stared at me some more, then slapped the pen on the table and made a sound of disgust. "Can't quite get you," she said. "Something strange about your face. Eyes bigger and wider apart. Your ears are set kinda high. One looks higher than the other."

Not the Freakface thing! I'd read that Sapes are genetically programmed to notice tiny deviations in other people's faces. Was she setting me up somehow?

The waiter brought our food, saving me from a reply. Once we'd eaten past the first edge of hunger, Kayla started in again about Conroy and Janelle. "She comes over to my place, uses my equipment. The clothes she makes are amazing. One dress has a copper wire bodice. Probably Conroy stole the wire for her." She sighed. "I worry about her. I mean, Conroy's got a tiny shred of ethics – he doesn't use little kids like some of the other dealers. But the drug corps will take him down one way or another."

"I like her," Lil said, "but Conroy's bad news."

"Yeah," Kayla said, "And Janelle's folks are so gruesome, they make your family look jolly."

Lil glared at her.

"Well, it's true. Her folks make me glad I'm free of mine. Maybe she'll design herself into a big break." She waved at the waiter and then gave Lil a look and an elbow in the ribs. "Speaking of style, I just finished a piece – you two have to see it. Let's go over to my place." She looked at me. "It's not far, Goran."

Would Maks blow off an invitation to some girl's apartment to see her artwork? Ha! Feeling on the brink of adventure, I left with them. Our surroundings grew seedier the farther downtown we walked. I could see the Railyards in the distance when Kayla turned into an alley between old brick warehouses.

Halfway down the alley, she cracked a door into a small room. She peered around, then opened wide and waved us in. A board full of keys hung on the wall beside a grubby old chair upholstered with dirty pink teddy bear fur.

"Murphy's not here today. His nephew owns this place, pays Murphy about a dollar a day to sit there and keep an eye on things."

We walked down a hallway and climbed to the third floor, a large loft that Kayla used for a studio. She hustled us through a door from the loft into her apartment, a long room across the front of the building. A kitchen filled one end, two doors – probably closet and bathroom – were on the other, and all the jumble of Kayla's life jammed the space between. Three huge windows down the room's outside wall framed a million-dollar view of the bay.

"Have a seat." Kayla waved at a long couch, unzipped her boots, and padded barefoot to the kitchen. She opened the refrigerator and held up a can. "This new sports drink? It's not half bad." A curtain hung on a string hid half the kitchen. Kayla vanished behind it, then reappeared with three opened cans, sat on my other side, and propped her feet on a coffee table.

I gulped the drink and searched for something to say. Kayla seemed hospitable enough, but she had a spooky edge. I listened to her tell Lil about a toy she wanted to get for Lil's little brother, then ignored her words just to hear the hum of her voice, like bees in a hive. The low sun slanted under the clouds and through the windows. The girls glowed in the golden light. Flaming Frayka, but they were beautiful. It felt good to sit pressed between them, but part of me wished they'd move so I could lie down on the couch and sleep. They sipped and smiled at me. I wanted them both more than I've ever wanted anything.

I was feeling stranger and stranger. I tried to make a joke but couldn't remember its point. Suddenly I blurted, "You're so beautiful. You're the Beautiful Twins of Light and Darkness. Come to life. Here on Earth."

They stared at each other. Lil said, "Who are the beautiful twins of white and . . . uh?"

"Light and Darkness," I said, patient because they probably didn't know a thing about it. "The first cords Frayka wove – the light cord and the dark cord. You know."

"I'm afraid I've forgotten," Lil said. "Tell me about Frayka."

They were so beautiful. So desirable. I spoke slowly so they'd understand. "Frayka weaves our cords of light and dark. First they're almost all light, then more and more dark. The dark threads are matter, nothing but our flesh. The light cords are the energy." I tried to demonstrate with my hands, twisting them around each other in a rising double helix. It looked stupid. I giggled.

I caught my breath and resumed the story we all learned as children. "They all blend together, but Frayka weaves in more and more dark until our cord is . . . has no light anymore. Nothing but dead flesh. And then we die." I fought back tears.

"Then Frayka puts our cords away–either in the chest she keeps on the forever night side, or she lays them out in the everlasting sun of day so they can bleach back to white again. And then she weaves those light threads into new cords." I felt proud of reciting the complicated story after so many years.

Kayla frowned. Even with a scowl on her face, she glowed with dark radiance. "Some kind of religious thing?" she whispered to Lil.

Lil shook her head, her tan-gold hair waving in slow motion. "Maybe Indian. I think some of his people were First Nation."

"Or maybe he's stark raving," Kayla whispered back.

They had acquired a glowing edge that almost blinded. They thought I couldn't hear them, but I could hear a mouse's heart hammering from where it cowered between the wall studs.

I realized they didn't believe me. "I mean, you have to understand. That's why we chose Earth. The first time the Change Lords saw a Sapiens baby born, its cord pulsing with all that light and dark, this genetic highway, they knew this was the designated place."

Kayla rolled her eyes, picked up my hand and caressed the ridge of callus along its edge. She gave it a quick lick that I could feel all the way to my toes. Then she started touching my face as if to see me with her fingers. It was the most wonderful thing I've ever felt. I moved closer but a wave of dizziness hit me. Lil finally pushed Kayla's hand away.

Her turn to take my head in her hands and into her lap. Somehow Kayla was now sitting on the coffee table. "So Andrei's trying to repair defects in genes. What are the numbers of the genes he's working on?" Lil said.

I couldn't form an answer. She kept asking questions but I couldn't process them, and her words were beginning to mush together.

"I'm not a scientist," I said repeatedly. "I don't know." Finally I lapsed into silence.

She stared at me, a faint scent of red fury leaking through the golden swirls of her energy. "Oh, you don't know anything about anything."

It stung. I forced the words out. "We have the greatest getenisists . . ge . . geneticists in the world, in the . . universe. They're light years ahead of GenAge." I snorted at my joke – light years! – and tried to wiggle my face out of its numbness.

"What are you talking about? Who's 'we'? And who the hell are the Change Lords?"

That phrase – coming from Lil's mouth – hit me like a bucket of ice water. I went silent. The sparkly look of everything began to fade as the molecules slowed and dropped one by one from their ecstatic dance. The horror hit me like someone pumping acid into my stomach. I'd said way too much.

I rubbed my face until it felt more normal. Then I grabbed the sports drink can and sniffed it. Under the vegetable and seaweed juices, I detected something like mushrooms. It left an aftersmell, like an aftertaste, of melting plastic. It finally sank into my head that they'd drugged me. They weren't the Beautiful Twins of Light and Darkness. They were two high school girls who'd tricked me into betraying my people.

I struggled to my feet, desperate to redeem the situation. "You drugged me. Why?"

# CHAPTER 10

From the unpublished Godunov manuscript
*Why We Came to Earth: The Yunko Voyages*

*As Gliese-C's atmosphere acquired more and more oxygen, at first it seemed like a good thing. With more "fuel," our activity increased. An increase in nitrogen compounds stimulated plant growth. But then the extra plants started producing even more oxygen. And the nitrogen created less benign molecules.*

*Respiratory problems appeared, and our heavy gravity made the problems worse. We suffered illnesses similar to Earth's pulmonary inflammation, edema, and fibrosis. Our people grew sicker and sicker until we realized that we must change our atmosphere or change ourselves to survive.*

Kayla surged up from the ratty old couch. Silhouetted against the blazing sunset, she looked scary as a sea monster breaking the waves. Her voice whooshed. "What's your problem? Everybody lofts on tonic!"

I clawed my way back to sanity until she once again looked like your average Maori warrior instead of Godzilla. Data still flooded my senses. Paint smells from the studio dominated other odors – cosmetics, bread going moldy, coffee. "You have coffee," I said. "Make me some." Like alcohol, real coffee affects us drastically. Might clear the lingering effects of the tonic.

Kayla stalked into the kitchen. Lil followed. They whispered about whether I'd turn violent.

Movement seemed to reduce my dizziness. I walked back and forth in the long room. Between the two doors at the far end hung a large, unframed painting lush with color and detail – a party crowded with glamorous people standing around holding plates and glasses. The central male figure picked at his food with a stiletto. A woman faced him. The red splotch at her neckline was either a rose or a bloody wound. Between the adults, a small child scurried away. I wondered what the painting symbolized. Or recorded.

Two file cabinets supported a plywood desk top. A laptop sat on it–a high-end graphics screamer; Kayla must be making good money. The only other furniture was another small table below a lighted mirror. On it sat a fishing tackle box. Its lid squeaked when I opened it.

"Don't mess with my stuff," Kayla yelled from behind the curtain.

"You messed with my head," I yelled back. Tubes, little pots of color, sparkly stick-ons, and tiny bottles filled the box – Kayla's identity kit.

They emerged from the kitchen carrying mugs of coffee and sat on the sofa. I took the coffee table. I sniffed the brew. It smelled okay. When it cooled enough to drink I took a cautious sip, then gulped half the cup. I could feel my head clear a little. "Why'd you do it?"

They looked at each other. "My little brother's terminally ill," Lil said. "I came across a clinical trial your brother ran. I thought it might be something that would help Davy. But something about the report seemed off, like it had been faked to hide what they were actually investigating."

I had no idea what she was talking about. "Why are you looking at stuff that's still in trials? Why not something that already works?"

"Nothing works. And I couldn't afford it anyway." She took a deep breath. "I think you and your brother have some kind of big secret. Probably connected to genetic research. And whatever it is, someone's been using it on you. Not to be insulting, but there's something really strange about you." She sniffed. "We dosed you with tonic hoping you might say something useful, but all you did was babble nutty stuff about cords and twins."

I drank my coffee while she rambled on about Davy.

"I even went on a reality show," she said. "'Win Your Cure.' We made it into the top ten before they eliminated us. I guess we weren't cute enough. Or Davy looked too cheerful. Or I didn't grovel enough."

The image of Lil groveling for reality show judges just wouldn't form in my brain.

"Don't you understand?" she almost yelled. "The doctors don't think he'll live past sixteen or seventeen." She pulled out a comm, opened it and danced her fingers across it. "Here's his picture. He's nine years old."

Davy had the face of a cheerful ghost – thin and white but with a happy smile. He'd die before I would – a new thought I couldn't quite absorb.

"I could ask Andrei if he knows about any new meds for muscular dystrophy." I felt sorry for the poor little kid, but I also felt used. And confused. The last few days I've spent more time around Sapes than ever before. I used to regard them like strange dogs: maybe friendly, maybe ready to attack, always difficult to predict. But lately I'd come to feel almost on the same wavelength as Lil and Kayla, even Conroy. I should have listened to the higher-ups – we Yunko can never grasp the sly cunning of ordinary Sapes.

*

After dinner that night Andrei said, "Goran, will you check the comm helmet and calibrate it? I need to finish some calculations before I consult with the Outpost about securing the tissue culture."

"Sure." Andrei usually calibrates the helmet himself. The last real calibration I had done had been under mild sedation during my training at the Outpost.

We headed to the small room Andrei uses as an office. He gave me the coordinates and I got to work. The process took my memory back to the Outpost, to visiting the nearby Tsimshian and Nisga'a villages, to the smell of smoked salmon mixed with the smell of the sea.

I set the final values in the series and opened the channel. It felt like stepping through a door into space and disintegrating into a swirl of molecules. They asked me to identify myself. I told them I was putting the call through for Andrei Helin in Seal Bay, but I'm not sure I used words.

Andrei gestured for the helmet. I collected myself enough to carefully follow the Remove sequence, then handed it over. Some of the conversation spillover made sense. Andrei had noticed some very odd side effects in a particular line of cancer cells. His terminology soon lost me but I caught something about the age of the cancer patient, something about clock genes. Both Andrei and the person at the other end gave off a sense of excitement.

He snapped out of his absorption to say, "You can go. I don't need you any longer."

Fine by me. I was developing a headache from the day's mental acrobatics. I slipped out, wondering if the helmet's effect on me had been intensified by the tonic.

After school the next day, I bus-hopped around Seal Bay looking for beans, eggs, and cheese. With meat and fish getting so scarce, it was hard to maintain a high-protein, high-calcium diet. I was sick of fried, boiled and scrambled eggs so I decided to try a soufflé. Andrei came home just as I stuck it in the oven. He went briefly to his room and then out to meditate on the flat rock in one corner of the back yard.

While the meal was cooking I shot a few baskets at the goal attached to the barn and fantasized about actually playing on a team. I could steal blank medical report forms, look up normal values for the test results, fill them out and forge Andrei's name. In the locker room, there wasn't anything about me that looked much different. The extra ring of muscle around my lower torso, a relic left over from tripodal lower limbs, would just look like I'd bulked up a little. My "shoulder noses," the auxiliary respiratory outlets under my shoulder blades, had not been opened. The

67

only thing that showed were small, ridged lumps. And extreme bone density was invisible.

I took the soufflé out of the oven. You're supposed to eat them right away. "Andrei," I yelled out the door, "dinner's ready." He didn't move. I called again, then went out to see what his problem was.

"Sit down, Goran. We need to talk."

"We can talk while we eat."

"No, this is too important."

I sat on one edge of the flat, moss-covered slab. "Make it quick."

Ha! Andrei went into lecture mode. "Our ancestors' long interstellar voyages exposed them to large amounts of cosmic radiation. Dozens of new mutations hit those who made the first voyage. Then dozens more afflicted the members of the Second and Third Voyages. Mutations on top of mutations. But as we hybridized ourselves with Sapiens, we apparently solved those problems without damaging our natural life spans of several hundred years. Apparently."

"The tissue culture?" I prodded. If given the chance, Andrei would start every explanation back at the Big Bang.

He heaved a sigh like a last breath. "Our people transformed themselves enough to venture into Earth's open air and sunlight. But Earth's solar radiation was so much stronger they developed cancers, particularly skin cancers, at a terrible rate.

"So our scientists reduced our amounts of telomerase enzyme, hoping to control the proliferation of cancer cells. But that action also destroyed the protection that Sapiens genes had given us, and we were not able to simply reverse the action. We would have done better to change our skin structures, but we wanted to keep our ancestral chromatophores so we could still adjust our skin color when we return to Gliese-C."

I dropped my head in my hands. *When we return to Gliese-C.* Yeah, right. I didn't want to hear any more about how we'd solve the problem that was killing us. I rose, said, "Come on inside," and practically hauled Andrei to his feet.

As I served the collapsed souffle, he said, "I'm not finished. This particular tissue culture came from a twenty-one year-old woman named Zora Tislenko."

I looked up but kept eating.

"She has an unusual history. She also has metastasized melanoma. Her parents were children in Ukraine when the nuclear plant at Chernobyl burned. Their families were evacuated, but they refused to stay away from their homes in the Exclusion Zone. They returned and moved from place to place to evade the authorities; there is no way now to determine how much radiation they absorbed."

I took another serving.

"After Zora's grandparents died, her parents immigrated to Australia. When Zora was born, the doctor learned of her family history and convinced the parents to give DNA samples for themselves as well as the baby. Then at nineteen, Zora was diagnosed with melanoma, quite common in Australia. It had already spread to her lymph nodes and liver.

"But she began to experience spontaneous remission, a so-called 'miracle cure.' Because of her youth, her telomeres are much longer than in most cancer patients. Gamma Group obtained her neo-natal gene map. It doesn't quite match her current genome. Something changed her very genes. And I noticed something odd about the sequence in which her antibodies destroyed cells at the margins of her tumors."

Andrei seemed to fall into a bottomless well of thought. I risked saying, "All our research – has it come up with anything for regular genetic diseases? Stuff like that sickle cell thing? Or like muscular dystrophy?" I was making progress with disguising my lies.

He was too distracted to notice my deceit. "Easy in comparison. Just set up the replication of healthy genes to replace the damaged ones." He pushed his chair back and headed to his room.

That night I tried to catch up on schoolwork, but real-life questions flooded my head. I didn't know what mysterious role I might play in Andrei's plans. I didn't know what to tell Conroy. And I didn't know how to tell Lil that Yunko medicine could probably cure Davy, but he would never get access to it. It was almost a relief to think about Davy instead of my own problems. Was it harder for him, alone with his unknown disease, or for us, in the same doomed boat with all our people?

# CHAPTER 11

## Excerpt from the diary of Lil Osborne

*My dad's driving me crazy. He was home sick all day yesterday, completely unbearable. I stayed home from school today to take him to the doctor. The office was a mob scene, and it took all my latest paycheck. The doctor listened to his chest and said it was probably bacterial pneumonia. I'm so scared Dad will give it to Davy. We can't afford the antibiotic the doctor prescribed, so Dad's drinking and taking way too many painkillers.*

Saturday morning I worked out at an almost deserted gym downtown. I hoped it would keep me from freezing up with worry about Andrei. He had gone in to GenAge, determined to tag along with someone who worked weekends in the lab where the tissue culture was stored. He thought that once he'd seen inside of the room, he could figure out how to steal the sample. I wasn't so sure.

A few minutes after I left the gym, my comm buzzed. Lil Osborne asked if I wanted to go to the aquarium with her and her little brother. It took me several moments to process her words and to wonder who was entitled to the bigger grudge at this point. At last I said, "When?"

"We're at the aquarium now. How soon can you get here?"

Stranger and stranger. "I'm downtown already. Maybe ten minutes."

"Good. See you."

I couldn't believe Lil was suddenly hot for my company. I walked toward the harbor, suspicious but itching with curiosity as I pushed through the street market crowds that overflowed the Moon Kitchen on Saturdays. At the aquarium, Lil's red Nissan glowed against the parking lot's asphalt, cracked like sooty alligator skin, the gray bay, and the dark clouds roosting on the islands.

She got out and met me a dozen feet from the car. "Thank goodness you're here. We have a problem." She glanced back at the Nissan. "The city used to have wheelchairs, but the company that just bought the aquarium got rid of them. I can't carry Davy very far. Could you . . . carry him around to see the exhibits?"

So. She wanted a pack mule for her brother. I felt like such a total zero I said, "What's the matter? Can't you get your drug buddy Kayla to haul him around?"

It sounded spiteful even to me. I braced for her counterattack but she said, "Sorry about the drug thing. It was stupid and pointless. Anyway, I needed to get Davy out of the house. Something's wrong with our wheelchair, so I didn't bring it."

The car horn beeped. She went over and spoke through the open window, then returned. "Just for your information, Davy adores Kayla. I tried to call but her comm's off." She continued, completely merciless. "Visiting the fish and sea lions is a big deal for Davy. He imagines he's a fish, swimming around in some magical world with no pain and no braces."

As annoyed as I was, I couldn't quite take it out on a sick kid. "Yeah, okay. Whatever." I followed her to the car. She opened the door and fussed with the little boy inside, zipping his jacket higher.

Davy stared at me over her bent back. In his thin face, his nose was as sharp and suspicious as his eyes. "Who are you?"

"Name's Goran."

"Why are you here?"

There had to be a better answer than 'Because you're helpless and your sister suckered me into carrying you around.' "Hey," I said, "I won the Seal Bay High School carrying championship last year. You need someone carried, call an expert."

"That's silly. There's no carrying championships."

"Oh, now you've hurt my feelings! I thought I was famous. They just don't show carrying contests on TV 'cause they make less money than football games." I got a fleeting grin in response. When I bent to lift him from the seat, he felt like a large bird, skin over delicate bone. Too fragile to lug around piggyback. I slid my arms under him and lifted. "Lot of technique involved in championship carrying," I said. "Bet you could learn, though. I'll show you the basics."

Once I held him securely, I said, "That's good. You're exactly the right size. Now, drape that arm around my neck and grab my thumb with your other hand to steer me. Just pull my thumb right or left, like the reins of a horse. Give it a try." He timidly pulled my thumb to the right. "Whoa! You're a natural."

"Giddyup!" he cried, and we set out.

Inside the aquarium, a ramp wound down around a big fish tank. Davy yanked my thumb to stop me every few steps. He seemed familiar with most of the creatures in the tank. When he'd had his fill of fish identification, he pushed my thumb forward. We entered a small dark room lit by a tank of ghostly, phosphorescent jellyfish, endlessly rising, falling, pulsating.

After a while, Davy said, "If they got out? Like they were flopping around on the sidewalk? They'd just squish if you stepped on them, right?"

"Guess so." I remembered something from biology class. "But if nothing eats or squishes them, they live forever."

Davy caressed the tank with a frail hand, hypnotized by the otherworldly creatures. A couple of minutes later, Lil poked me and nodded toward the exit. The aquarium only has three real exhibits: the fish tank, the jellyfish, and a few half-tame sea lions. They hang out behind the aquarium on a wooden dock that extends past the seawall. It's right at the waterline these days. It runs around a small pool, with viewing seats a little higher and vending machines stocked with overpriced seal chow.

"Let's sit and watch the sea lions," Lil said brightly and then whispered to me, "Your arms must be about to break off." We settled Davy on a seat and the sea lions clustered below him. Lil bought a baggie of feed and he tossed them bits, nagging the beasts to be nice and take turns. When the sun came out and warmed the benches, he dozed off.

We sat on the seawall upwind from the smelly sea lions. I nodded toward him. "Is this too much for him?"

Lil shrugged. "It beats the alternative." The words seemed to escape without her permission. "Which is my father. He's home sick, driving everyone crazy." She checked the time. "I'm afraid Davy'll catch whatever Dad has. I needed to get him out of the house. I wish I could get him out of there permanently." Before I could think of anything to say, she added, "Don't tell anyone, okay? Nobody but Kayla knows how it really is at home."

"Okay." I had no one to tell. I wondered what other secrets Lil had beside a rotten home life and a secret way into the GenAge building. "What's the matter with your dad?"

"Doctor said it was bacterial pneumonia. He prescribed an antibiotic that works on most everything. But none of us has insurance. I can't afford it."

"That sucks." I didn't have money to help her – Andrei hands me the week's grocery money on Sundays, and I'd used up this week's cash.

I listened to the waves slapping the seawall for a while. I had access to another kind of help, even more powerful than cash. But I was honor-bound not to use it, wasn't I?

Davy yelped in his sleep. Lil tiptoed over to check him.

While we're forbidden to do anything that might reveal our off-planet origins, we're also ordered to act fully human if observed. Human decency demanded I share the remedy. The kid looked like a hard sneeze would carry him off, much less bacterial pneumonia.

Lil came back. "I guess we should head home." She squared her shoulders as if picking up a load again.

Human responses kicked the rules aside. "Can you give me a ride to my house? If you know how to do injections, we have an antibiotic that should cure your father."

She gave me a long dose of the squint eye. "Where'd it come from?"

"A doctor prescribed it for my brother last year. Gave him some extra sample packs." I was getting better and better at lying to Sapes.

After another long stare, she woke Davy and we headed for the car. On the way to our house, he turned his ferocious curiosity on me. Did I play any sports besides carrying? Did I have brothers or sisters? What was my favorite food? Did I have pets? He stretched my rapidly developing lying skills to the limit.

At the house, I said, "You two stay in the car. I'll get the stuff." Inside I opened the medkit and selected a packet that was definitely not available on the open market. Lil was more than smart enough to follow the directions. I hoped she wasn't smart enough to realize that the medicine we nicknamed Spitwad analyzes a patient's human lymphocyte antigens, then modifies the compound to optimize the patient's individual immune system.

Back at the car, I leaned in the open window and handed her the clear plastic pack with four components inside. "Okay, first have your dad spit in this thing that looks like a little petri dish. Then pour in the contents of the first vial and let it sit for an hour. Then pour in the second vial, shake it well, wait thirty more minutes. Then fill the syringe and inject it in his arm muscle. Then completely destroy the containers. We'd both be in trouble if they're ever found."

She opened her mouth to ask a million questions, paused, and said, "Just this one dose?"

"Yeah. For twenty-four hours he'll wish he *was* dead. Chills, nausea, aches, general misery. But it'll knock out the pneumonia."

"Thanks," she said. "For the day. And for this."

*

Saturday evening Andrei came in shuffling his feet and heaving sighs, his way of inviting a conversation. I cooperated. "Did it go okay?"

"Would I be here if it hadn't?" He rooted in his briefbag. "We need to discuss my plan. You prepare supper while I log everything before I forget."

I added enough seaweed to a pot of navy beans and onions to turn the mixture purplish. Then to make it bearable, I toasted some bread and cheese to go on top – French onion soup for nutrient freaks.

Andrei's specialty is designing transport cases for cell and tissue cultures. After dinner he took out the prototype transport case he'd brought home, a metal container about the size of two one-pound coffee cans stacked end-to-end, with keypad, latches, vents and ports, one for filling with liquid nitrogen.

"I told the lab guy I needed to check how their cryo-storage compartments were calibrated individually for air pressure and temperature," Andrei said. He punched numbers on the case's keypad. "That should suffice. The case is small, but the liquid nitrogen has a static hold time of eight days, which should be more than enough time to get it from GenAge to the Outpost. Did you watch? Can you set the controls yourself now?"

"Me? Why? You just set it."

"If I fail, it will be your responsibility to get the culture and bring it to the Outpost."

I did a double take. "What? That is so not gonna work. I can't even get in the GenAge building by myself, much less find the culture – "

"That's why I drew a map." He laid it on the table. The map was drawn Yunko style, which meant it looked like a stack of transparent boxes nested inside each other – probably the way a mole visualized its tunnels – instead of an overhead view like a Sapient map. A thickened edge meant turn right, left, up or down. Empty circles showed the number of things, such as doors, in a sequence, with a filled circle marking the one to take.

"We go in the front entrance to the elevators," I said, "and up to the eighth floor."

"There is no we. I am going in alone."

"No way! I have to be along to protect you if anything goes wrong – that's my job."

"As I said, you must complete the task if I fail. We cannot risk both of us being caught."

My mouth opened to argue again, but I realized he was right. I looked at the map. I slowly traced the corridors and doors leading to the correct lab. "What's that?" I pointed to a thing that looked like a peace symbol with an extra crossbar.

"Key card lock."

"How do you plan to get by that?"

He looked so proud of himself. "I'll go in early Monday morning. Step through the door with the workers who come in at six."

At least he'd thought through a plan. "That takes a lot of nerve."

He made a brushing off motion. "So continue with the directions."

"Okay. You enter the lab . . . what's the dotted line?"

"A negative pressure airlock. But it has no security check."

"So you get through the airlock and into the work area." I puzzled out three dots along the top of the square. "And you go through the middle door in the far wall."

"Into the cryo-storage room for human tissue samples." He pointed to six circles in a row. The filled dot was the last one. "The containment vats."

I nodded. "And that?" At the top was a figure that looked like a daisy with lines of circles radiating from a center point. One circle was filled.

"Each vat is divided into pie-shaped segments. The culture we want is in segment C, fourth shelf down from the top. I've printed the inventory number of the culture beside it. Memorize the number."

Okay. Andrei studied science. I studied tactics and strategy. And I was very familiar with the saying that no battle plan survives first contact with the enemy. Andrei's plan depended on a long chain of circumstances working out perfectly. I wanted to knock sense into his head, but I couldn't think of a workable alternative.

At last he said, "We'll continue tomorrow."

We spent most of Sunday going over the plan. Once Andrei had stolen the culture, he'd say he forgot something in his car, sneak the culture out of the GenAge building and head for the house. We'd pack it in the transport case, complete the protocol for leaving an assignment and head for the winery at the border, never to be seen in Seal Bay again. I refused to think about that part. Instead I spouted a stream of "Yes, buts," trying to patch the weak spots in the scheme. Andrei's only contingency plan was that if he failed, I'd steal the culture. Somehow.

Sunday evening before the last workers left GenAge, Andrei took the transport case over and topped it up with liquid nitrogen. Later, after I went to bed I heard his footsteps passing back and forth repeatedly. The outside door slammed, but sleep took me before I heard him return.

Monday morning he shook me awake before dawn. We dressed and ate without much conversation. I walked out to the car with him. He rolled down the window before starting the engine. "When people come on shift at six, there's more confusion. So I'll try to steal it within the first few minutes. I'll comm you when I get back to the car so you can be ready. We need to be out of Seal Bay before anyone starts looking for us."

All I could think to say was "Good luck." I watched him back out and turn, and I watched the car disappear into darkness. Then I called the cats into the house and shut their door – we wouldn't have time to chase them down. I started collecting whatever I wanted to take with us, but I couldn't focus. I wandered aimlessly. I stopped and tried to center myself. *Time has no duration –*

Suddenly Zax and Gwitchy yowled. Dogs howled in the distance. My skull seemed to vibrate. I ran outside and stared toward Seal Bay. The skyline showed black against the early morning sky. The weird feeling in my skull came again, along with a high shriek at the very edge of my hearing. The security sirens at GenAge. I checked the time. It was six twenty-five.

My head vibrated, my skin crawled, my hands went numb, my brain iced up in indecision. If GenAge security had captured Andrei, they'd search our house next. Protocol demanded torching the place to destroy all evidence, from DNA traces on everything to communication equipment. But if I burned the house and Andrei escaped, we'd have no home.

But we wouldn't need a home any longer because we'd have to disappear.

My feet switched to automatic. I stuffed the medkit in a backpack with other necessities. Then I dug out the cats' carrier; it's like a baby backpack for twins, made with layers of steel fabric sandwiched between heavy rip-stop nylon. I added the comm helmet and the tissue transport case. My tablet? No. Any more stuff to carry, I'd need a shopping cart.

My comm vibrated. "Goran," Andrei choked out, "I was in the lab. I had put on cryo gloves to remove the culture when another scientist walked in and asked what I was doing. I said I wanted the take a culture and check how it fit in my transport case. She said I couldn't take it out of that particular lab. She seemed suspicious. I said Okay, I'll go get the case. I left the room and got out of the building before they blocked the exits and sounded the alarms. They'll verify my absence any moment. Demolish the house and leave immediately."

"Where are you now?"

"Outside Seal Bay. I have the Bubble wand with me. Get the comm helmet, the case and the cats. Go to . . . the place where you hid your comic books. I left a package there last night with things you'll need. Hurry."

"Wait! Where are you going?"

"I'm heading for the place you took the others. Then on to the Outpost."

"So I'll head there too?"

"No. I failed to take the culture. Now it's your responsibility to steal it."

"But – "

"Your honor, your duty, and our survival demand it. No arguing, no more talk. You must start the demolition, Goran. Now." He cleared his throat. "You have been an exemplary Second. Thank you."

And then he was gone.

# CHAPTER 12

## From *The Way of the Yunko*

*We are so close to Earth's human population biologically that we must regularly remind ourselves of our differences. The following are common Sapiens medical tests we must avoid:*

*All DNA analyses*
*Blood tests other than lipid panels and liver enzyme tests*
*Most imaging tests of the torso and all DXA-type bone scans*
*Pulmonary function tests*
*Examinations relating to the central nervous system*
*External examinations of the lower torso and upper back*
*Tests of smell or hearing based on involuntary responses*
*Dermatology biopsies*

I grabbed a long roll and hunk of cheese from the chiller and stuffed them in a pocket. Then I moved the cats and other gear to the rear gate in the fence. I ran back to the house, turned on the vent fan to suck oxygen through the building and tipped over the fuel canisters already in place.

No point locking the door. I stood on the porch, still protected by the house's sturdy, solid presence. But it knew. With grief and guilt I ran my hands along the log walls and whispered, "I'm sorry. Thank you for your shelter." I shot three flares through the open doorway, then threw in the flare gun and my comm, and ran. After a quick detour to torch the barn, I snatched up the gear, whistled for the cats, and raced for the trail up the cliff.

Halfway up the narrow path, heat from the fire hit my back and legs. When I glanced behind me, smoke and flame were leaping for freedom through broken windows. I turned back to the trail. Its rough, rocky footing demanded full attention.

When we reached the sloping meadow that led to the high country, Zax and Gwitchy sat down and whined, annoyed at the different routine. I paused to catch my breath. Flames now pierced the roofs in several places. Twin columns of black smoke rose in the still morning air and merged. I nudged the cats and started across the meadow. In the distance, vehicle sirens wailed. For what it was worth, Seal Bay's all-volunteer Fire Department was on its way.

At the campground. I heaved my burdens on to a rickety picnic table and rubbed my knee where the comm helmet had banged it. The cats jumped onto the bench beside me. We watched the column of smoke through a gap in the trees. I munched the bread and cheese, giving the cats a portion.

Still chewing, I rose, untied the rope to the wooden keg and lowered it from the tree. A leather briefcase lay inside on the mildewed manga. I took it out and dumped its contents on the table. Out fell bundles of cash, new fake IDs, a copy of the lab map and a note with contact codes, instructions and advice. He had signed it "Sincerely, your brother Andrei."

Without warning, I wailed like a stupid baby, went into a coughing fit, cried some more, and tried not to throw up. I'd lost my brother. I remembered playing in the games yard with the other nursery rats when one of the crèche mothers led over a solemn twelve-year-old and said, "Goran, meet your brother, Andrei." He'd visited with me occasionally. We sat together at assemblies. Then, when we began training intensively to go into the field together, we moved into the same quarters.

We shared a fondness for scones. And cats. And martial arts movies, for different reasons – I studied the techniques, Andrei loved how the characters gladly faced death for honor and duty with no whining about their feelings. Our ears were shaped exactly the same. We had identical dents in our little fingers. Of course he was my brother.

I hadn't thought I even liked Andrei. Sometimes he seems like another species, though we're only two iterations apart – once at a checkup, I sneaked a look at my file and found out Andrei's a 6.5 and I'm a 6.7. But he's always so stiff, so focused, so disapproving, so . . . dependable. He'd carried the satchel up here last night. Climbing the rough, steep trail would have tortured his joints. And he'd known about the comics all these years without blasting me. His last words had been thanks for being an "exemplary Second."

Through my stinging, watering eyes, I looked up at the osprey nest and shuddered. I felt as lonely and vulnerable as one of the chicks, naked, unable to walk, hardly able to see, dumped on a highway somewhere at the mercy of any passing car or crow. And no help available, none at all.

The cats butted my legs with increasing urgency, aware something was wrong. They were right; I didn't have time to blubber. First, I needed a place to hole up. Second, I had to steal a tissue culture guarded by an extremely effective security force now on high alert.

I tried to think of potential allies, only to hit an even deeper realization that Andrei was the only person I had. I'd deliberately avoided making friends at school and the gyms around town. Maks could have been a friend, but I didn't even know where Maks was. Conroy? Possibly safe since he was neck deep in illegal stuff himself, and he wanted something from me. The wants of others made me think of Lil. Maybe more, maybe less than a friend.

And Great Flaming Frayka, the obvious fell on my head like an anchor. Lil knew how to sneak into GenAge. She might be my only hope, a thought both pleasantly tingly and frighteningly grim. The next thought had no redeeming qualities at all. If Lil tried to sneak into GenAge tonight, she might get caught in the heightened security. I had to warn her but I couldn't comm her. I didn't know where she lived, or her parents' names, and I'd thrown my comm with her number into the fire.

But I knew where Kayla lived. If I could reach her place, she could comm Lil. GenAge had no reason to monitor conversations between two high school girls. Kayla's loft was about three miles away, an easy walk except for my baggage.

As I tried to think where to stash my stuff, a convoy of three vehicles sped around the curve leading to our house. They looked like the black SUVs used by GenAge security. They'd made the connection between a fleeing scientist and a house fire just outside of town. And by now Andrei's dossier would have reminded GenAge of my existence. Time to run.

I'd have to leave most of my gear in the woods. If I made it back, no problem. If I didn't make it back, the cats had at least a chance of survival here. The comm helmet self-destructed if anyone tried to open it without the access code.

I transferred the contents of Andrei's satchel to my backpack, dug the cats' anchor beacon out of it, and headed into the trees. Well into the forest, I set the beacon to keep them within a quarter-mile radius until the battery ran down and stuffed it under a fallen tree. Comm helmet, transport case and satchel joined it. I piled leaves and duff over the opening. Then I slung on the backpack and set off along the edge of the heavily wooded escarpment. Behind me, the cats yowled demands to go along on my upcoming adventure.

*

I reached the alley beside Kayla's warehouse about two, and put one ear to the street door. Random sounds came through – a toilet flushing, boards creaking, faint snores from the amateur watchman. What was his name? Murphy? Yeah. I unslung my backpack and took out a small spray bottle. When I turned the door handle and walked in, an overweight, elderly man jerked, snorted, and peered at me.

"Afternoon, Mr. Murphy."

"Do I know you?"

"I came by once before. Hey, I was walking past the alley and saw smoke coming out an upstairs windows."

He heaved himself up. "Smoke? I don't smell smoke."

"It's mostly going outside. Come look."

I stood aside as he lumbered past, snapped my arm around him to immobilize, and pressed his carotid arteries. His poor old neck was so flabby I could barely feel the pulse. He smelled younger than he looked, but he only struggled for a couple of seconds before slumping. I hauled him back to his chair, settled him in it and aimed the spray into his gaping mouth. Engineered from red-tide plankton, the spray induces short-term memory loss, like a traumatic blow to the head but without the risk. At most, Murphy might think he'd had an odd dream.

Kayla's third-floor studio was deserted and her apartment door locked. I prowled her workspace to keep my mind off Andrei and my empty stomach. Kayla's art seemed to be about human-type shapes bound into bundles. The smallest one was half-sucked lollipops tied together with wire. The largest, old-style parking meters tied around a stake with what looked like human arms. And those girls thought *I* was weird.

Footsteps rattled on the stairs. Kayla's head rose into view, adorned with the hair horns and Maori warrior face paint, topping a Buddhist nun's brownish-red robe. She drew out a key.

I stepped forward. "Kayla?"

She spun around. "What do you want?"

I touched a finger to my lips. "Lil's in serious trouble but she doesn't know it yet. I need you to get her over here without mentioning my name. I have to warn her before tonight."

The patterns on her face writhed from her mix of expressions. "What's going on?"

"She might run into a security alert if she tries to sneak into GenAge tonight."

"You know about that?"

"She told me the other day."

Kayla fingered her key. "Why'd they call an alert?"

"Uh, guy I know – "

"Not good enough. Who?"

"My brother. He wanted to take something out of the lab."

"Did they grab him?"

"No. He escaped. But they might pick up Lil if she goes over there. I don't have a way to contact her."

"Not good. GenAge security – well, Erik Cheyne, to be precise – rattles her completely."

"Who's Erik Cheyne?"

"One of their top security guys. I think he's in charge of all the physical stuff – building security, personnel, espionage. Lil hardly ever mentions him, but once she said he liked to do interrogations himself. The way she said it gave me the chills."

"And I need a ride to pick up some stuff," I got in. "Soon as possible. Do you have anything to eat? I'll pay you."

She unlocked the apartment door. "Come on."

She shucked her boots. "There's leftover stew. I'll heat it."

"Can you call Lil while it's heating? Time's really short." I put a dollar on the table.

"Forget the cash. The stew sucks, anyway." She held her phone in one hand while taking a pot from the fridge and putting it on the stove. "Lil? It's me. Can you come over right now? It's really important." She listened, then said. "Well, take the groceries home, kiss Davy, and tell him your mom will be there soon. No, I can't tell you more. Trust me, okay? Bye."

She handed me a spoon and the pot of half-warmed stew. "Why didn't you want me to mention your name? Are you in trouble too?"

I had to tell her something but first I gobbled a couple of bites. "Since GenAge is after my brother, if they find me, they'll grab me for questioning. Don't know the details." I plowed through the rest of the stew – there was just enough to make me hungrier.

"Whatever." She sauntered to her computer and turned it on.

I slouched on the sofa, worrying, wondering what else was in Kayla's refrigerator. Before I had time to completely fray from impatience, the door opened and Lil walked in. When she saw me, she stopped so fast she stumbled.

"What's going on?" she asked Kayla, who shrugged.

"There's a real dangerous situation that's developed at GenAge." I stood. "I wanted to warn you. And ask your help . . . about something else. It's all connected."

Her eyebrows dive-bombed together. "Think you can manage some details?"

"C'mon." I took Lil's arm, glanced at Kayla, who pretended to be engrossed in her computer, and headed for the studio. I walked Lil all the way to the far end, wondering what to say. We're so conditioned to secrecy, I didn't know if my mouth could even shape the words. But I had to take the chance. I didn't think Lil would voluntarily rat me out – she'd sound like a crazy person, and besides, she had secrets of her own. I figured she'd believe our fallback story.

I looked over the rooftops to the bay for a moment, took a deep breath and turned her to face me. "What I'm about to tell you is a deep secret. Do you swear to keep it that way?"

She stared at me long enough for shadows to creep a millimeter across her face. "This has to do with GenAge?"

"That's a small part of it."

"Does it affect me? Or Davy?"

"Maybe."

"Okay. I'll keep it secret. If I can."

The best deal I was likely to get. I did not mention aliens or the Outpost, but I told her about Andrei's attempt to steal the culture and that GenAge security was after me too. The heightened security would be a risk for her if she followed her usual routine. "And that's not all. Now, I'll have to steal the culture. I don't know how to get in the building, so I need you to tell me how you sneak into the place." She stared at me. "And can you give me a ride right now to pick up my stuff out by the house?"

At last she managed to say, "Are you guys espionage agents? For one of the Asian or European corps?"

"No."

"Then why do you care about some tissue culture anyway?"

Put up or shut up time. "I'm from a people who have very short lifespans. It's a genetic thing. That's why my brother looks so much older. He's getting close to the rapid phase when we start aging so fast you can almost watch it. He thinks one of the cultures in a Gamma Group lab is the key to reversing the process."

I didn't know whether her expression was distaste or sympathy.

"You keep talking about your people. What people? First Nation? I never heard anything about bands up the coast dying young. Well, I mean, from anything other than the usual crap they have to put up with."

"Actually, we're not First Nation."

"Then what are you?"

"Right now we need to pick up my stuff. I'll tell you later."

# CHAPTER 13

From the unpublished Godunov manuscript
*Why We Came to Earth: The Yunko Voyages*

*Faced with the probability of extinction, our scientists on Gliese-C sought remedies. We designed breathing masks. We built underground habitats. We destroyed photosynthesizing plants until we had to ration food. We vacuumed various compounds out of the atmosphere. We pumped oxygen into caves beneath the Ring Sea. Nothing worked very well.*

"Get your car," Kayla told Lil, "and pull in the alley by the fire escape. I'll unlock the window so Goran can climb down without Murphy seeing him."

Very business-like, except for the tremor beneath her crisp words. Then Kayla hugged Lil and whispered, "This is too dangerous for you. Be careful – " Her voice broke, but her face was still unreadable beneath the fake Maori tattoos.

So I waited under the fire escape. Lil pulled around and parked, and I ran through light rain to her car. Just as I got in, a GenAge SUV crept past the end of the alley.

Lil's face seemed to shrink back on her skull. "What are *they* doing here?"

"Looking for my brother. Or for me."

"Why here? Are they everywhere?"

"Probably just a few patrols searching randomly. And a perimeter around town. Stopping every vehicle that tries to leave."

"Are we going to your house?"

"Near there."

"So won't Cheyne's goons be watching the road to your place?"

"Yeah, so we'll have to take another way out of town. You're not gonna like it. Head for the Railyards."

"You're not serious. Even the Metros don't go in there."

"Don't see any other solution. The Railyard gangs might hassle us but they aren't after me personally like GenAge is."

She drove south on Main Street, muttering to herself as the

surroundings grew more dismal. I'd first visited the Railyards long ago with Andrei when he needed to buy human blood plasma that couldn't be traced. Then my quick drop-off with Maks. I felt even more uneasy now. Railyards citizens were not disorganized or idle; they worked hard to provide everything that was illegal elsewhere. And the place had its own security force and its own laws, even if those laws were baffling and brutal to outsiders. It was the only route out of Seal Bay that wouldn't be infested with GenAge dicks.

Lil slowed to a crawl. She locked the Nissan's doors, as if that would do any good. I nodded toward the break in the fence, and she bumped over the curb and through the hole.

"Head between the sidings," I said, "and drive as fast as you can."

The rain came down harder, slicking the bare ground. Through the drizzle, I spotted a light that began flashing high above the rail cars. Lookouts had noticed our invasion. The Nissan splashed into a gauntlet of railroad cars. Doors rumbled open in their sides, and shadowy figures peered out to see who was trespassing on their turf. A few men jumped to the ground and slogged after us. Lil gripped the wheel and sped up, skidding in the mud. At one puddle the car almost hydroplaned. I watched for a route that would take us out the south end of the rail yard

Ahead of us, I could now see that the flashing light sat on the boom of a giant crane. It looked ancient rearing above the rail cars, but it creaked into motion. Its cable ended in a hook larger than the Nissan. A man clung to the boom, almost at the top. He waved, apparently signaling the operator. The boom lifted the cable over the sidings and lowered the hook into our path between the railroad cars. I glanced around. A dozen people were closing in on us. When I looked again at the hook, it was swinging away from us.

"Turn!" I yelled.

"Where?" Lil screamed back.

Good question. "Pull over next to the boxcars."

She nudged the Nissan to the right until it scraped a boxcar. The giant hook reversed direction, swung down, and toward us along the middle of the path. With a shriek Lil dived across the seat into my lap. Metal screamed as the hook swung past and took a swipe of paint off the side.

"Go now!" I yelled.

She sat up and floored the accelerator. We wallowed down the muddy trail, the hook chasing us on its return swing. We both screamed when it crashed into the car and hooked the rear. For a freakish instant the car slid along on front wheels only, banging us forward. Then the whole bumper assembly ripped loose and we thudded back onto four wheels. Lil was sobbing but still driving. The engine made a grinding noise that sounded like serious damage. I checked the man on the boom. He was gesturing to the operator to move the boom down the alleyway. Speed up? Slow down? Stop? I couldn't calculate the arc of the next swing.

Ahead of us, two men dashed across the path and disappeared between rail cars. "Turn where those guys ran," I said. Lil wrenched the car through a sloppy skid into a gap between cars just as the hook swung back and bashed our left rear fender. It catapulted us over the rails and into the derelicts' town square. A few vehicles sat between hole-in-the-wall shops thrown together from scrap and abandoned in the rain.

Across the open space, the two men struggled to push a wooden contraption – it looked like a huge truss–across an opening. "That's it!" I yelled. "The way out!"

The truss thing was mounted on a central pivot anchored in the ground. It could swing around like a giant turnstile until it blocked vehicles from driving through the opening in the wall of rail cars. The guys pushing one end of the truss around the pivot almost had it closed.

Lil bumped across the cinders and mud holes. "Slow down enough for me to jump out," I said. "Then shoot through the gap the instant you can." She moved her foot from the accelerator to the brake. I jumped out and raced toward the far end of the barrier. I braced my shoulder against it and pushed back. The motion stopped. My feet tried to slip out from under me, but I worked them into the mud with each slow step forward, forcing the truss back step by step. The two guys pushing the other end yelled for reinforcements.

I pushed until I thought my arms would crack out of their sockets. "Go!" I screamed when the opening was slightly wider than the Nissan. Once the car wiggled past and broke free, I flung myself to the side. At the sudden lack of resistance, the other end jerked my two opponents forward into the mud. I scrambled under the truss and raced after Lil.

She slowed and I jumped in. "You're getting my car filthy." She was trembling.

South of the Railyards we drove through a gigantic timber depot. The reddish trunks looked colorful against the gray world, and their spicy, sour smell penetrated the car's closed windows. I panted a bit, content to sniff logs instead of solve problems.

Lil regained enough breath to choke out, "You said you wanted to pick up your stuff. Not that you were gonna wreck my car and get me killed!"

"Didn't do it on purpose."

"What are you going to do about my car?"

I didn't know. "Did the medicine I gave you heal your dad?"

She paused a moment. "Yeah."

"So just trust me a little longer, okay?"

She blew several breaths through her pursed lips in odd little puffs. "Are we going to your house?"

I slumped and closed my eyes. "Drive south till you reach Bluffside Shopping Center. Take the road up the bluff to avoid the zone line and head back north." Before, I hadn't had time to be scared, and now I was too tired to waste the energy. I had no plan other than picking up my stuff and getting Lil to show me how to sneak into GenAge. Anything else, I could sort out later.

The rain poured harder. Maybe the change in air pressure triggered some state between migraine and hallucination. Flashing, squirming geometry danced on my closed eyelids. Then the colors shifted into the angular patterns woven into a shaman's coat, sewn with glittering, dangling objects. The patterns bobbed and circled in the drifting smoke that filled the shaman's hut until they faded out. Except I'd never been in a shaman's hut – it was ancestral memories creeping in again. All garbled together – memories of our Evenki ancestors, memories of our Yunko and Orbian ancestors. They seep through occasionally in times of stress, a side effect of all the brain re-engineering we've undergone.

"Goran? Goran!" Lil was shaking my shoulder. "Which way? The road's run out."

I shook my head to clear it. The rain had stopped. We weren't far from where I'd left my gear. "From here we walk." I amended my words. "I walk." GenAge might be watching my cache, and the cats would be wet, uncomfortable, and pissed. I needed to calm them down before they encountered Lil again.

Eyes slitted, she leaned back in the seat, oozing waves of frustration.

I couldn't think of anything to say so I got out and walked into the dripping woods. Barely a hundred yards in, I picked up faint sounds and smells behind me. Lil was following. Arguing would waste more time. If she stayed well back, maybe she'd avoid any trouble up ahead. I reached the campground and made a show of looking carefully behind me. With a flick of movement she dodged behind a tree. I headed on to the cache.

The comm helmet, satchel, and transport case were still under the fallen tree. The damp, annoyed cats had squeezed into the same cranny. I loaded up, petted the cats, retrieved the anchor beacon, and yelled, "Lil! You can come out now. The coast is clear."

No answer but the small splash of a leaf dumping its water. Then Lil stepped around a stand of underbrush and stalked toward me, mouth clamped, face red. She'd stoked up a good rage by now. "You tore up my car!"

"Didn't mean to."

"'Didn't mean to' won't get me a new one. I can't get to work on time taking the busses. Can't get Davy to the doctor. Mom doesn't have a car, Dad got his license yanked. You've screwed up our whole family."

I needed her help. I hadn't counted the money Andrei left, but it looked like a lot, enough to get her something better than the scuzzy old Nissan that smelled like burnt oil, stale popcorn, and ancient vomit. "I'll give you money to get it fixed. Or to get another car. But I don't have time right now."

"Got too many criminal activities scheduled? What are you mixed up in anyway? Something that'll get me killed?"

Having no answer, I turned away.

"I need the money now, before I get any deeper in this."

"How much?"

"Four hundred dollars."

Sounded about right. Abandoned, beat up cars were everywhere. I dug the roll of bills out of the backpack, turned my back to hide it from her view and counted out four hundred.

She took it, recounted, and stuffed it in her jeans. "So back at Kayla's you claimed you weren't really First Nation and I said "What are you?" and you said you'd tell me later. It's later. So tell me."

I started back toward the car. "Actually, we're part First Nation, at least culturally. We spent a lot of time with them when we were children."

"So *actually* you were lying, right? What are you?"

"Our . . . ancestors came from Central Asia. Siberia. Mostly from the Evenki people."

"Never heard of them. Why's that such a deep, dark secret? Why the BS about being First Nation?"

I looped around the truth to gain acceleration. "Mostly because everyone's so paranoid about immigration. Even if it's just from other states. You know how it is – Hey! Got a problem? Lynch an illegal. That'll fix it. So we want to sound as local as possible. Besides, we don't want to draw attention to ourselves."

"Why not?"

"Well, think about it. Say we fix our particular aging problem. People would jump to the conclusion – the wrong conclusion – that we could extend their lives too, and they'd kill us trying to get the secret. We just want to fix our problem and go home . . . to Siberia."

We emerged at the campground. Might as well dive in. "I'm desperate. You're the only hope I have. I'd be lost in there." I dumped my burdens on a picnic table and sat down.

Lil eyed the cats, sat on the table, and pulled her legs up out of clawing range. "You want *me* to help you? Look how helping you today turned out." She huffed in exasperation. "Can you guess what scares me more than anything else except losing Davy? It's Erik Cheyne getting me alone in a room. Again. Whatever he left of me, they'd lock up forever. And Davy would die too. That's what you're asking me to risk."

I stood. "Come over here." From the campground's edge, we could see down through the trees to the valley. "See that big black smear down there? That was our house. I torched it this morning to keep GenAge from getting it." Frustration made me angry. "Yeah," I snarled at her, "I understand the risk involved. I'd steal the stuff by myself if I could, but I can't." The smoke smell almost choked me but Lil seemed not to notice.

She backed up a step, looking blankly at the charred ruin. "I . . . I can't make that decision in two minutes. I need time."

"I don't have time. They'll search this area again soon. I have to get the culture and take it across the border."

"I can't think with you bugging me. I'm taking a walk. Tell you when I get back."

# CHAPTER 14

From the unpublished Godunov manuscript
*Why We Came to Earth: The Yunko Voyages*

*Eventually, our scientists proposed that, instead of trying to change our world, we change ourselves. We would genetically engineer our species to thrive in a high oxygen atmosphere. For political reasons, it was advisable to conduct the genetic experiments off-planet. And we expected the work to go faster with access to DNA from species already adapted to high oxygen atmospheres. We knew of three inhabited high-oxygen planets within twenty-five light years of home. After the first probes returned, the Change Lords selected your Earth, the planet richest with life, for our laboratory.*

Lil stalked into the forest. She'd probably get lost, I'd have to find her, and it would get dark, blowing the whole day I was supposed to spend stealing the culture and escaping. I quivered with impatience.

Then there was her car. It wasn't like I'd torn it up on purpose. She'd been the one driving. But I didn't know anyone else who might take me across the border.

Bored with sitting on the picnic table, Gwitchy butted my shoulder. I turned to pet her and saw a halo of diamonds beading her fur. The fog had crept in. I could barely make out the dark patch down in the valley that marked my former home. The hills beyond were invisible.

If the fog thickened, Lil might walk in circles. As I stood to go after her, the cats went tense. I followed their stare. From the mist-clogged forest, Lil marched toward me as if reporting for duty.

She swiped an arm across her damp face. "First I have to ask you a question. And you have to trust me enough to answer it honestly. That's the only way this is going to happen."

"Okay." I didn't have much choice.

"Can your people, whoever they actually are, do the surgery or genetic engineering or whatever to heal Davy?"

Her question didn't really surprise me. Maybe some corner of my brain already saw the connection. "After you drugged me, I asked Andrei about fixing gene-related illnesses like muscular dystrophy. He talked like it would be easy. So I guess they could fix anything similar to it." Her face lit up. I had to add, "But it would require getting Davy out of the country."

"To Canada?"

"At least. I don't know exactly which medical facility could do it." But that wasn't the big problem. "And my people would have to agree to treat him."

"Will they?"

I shook my head. "Way above my rank. My guess is, it'd be somewhere between difficult and impossible."

Lil took a deep breath. Then another. For a moment, she laid her hand on my cheek – I didn't understand the gesture. At last she said, "Any tiny chance beats the zero chance he has now. Here's my offer. I'll do my best to help you steal the cell culture. If. If you swear you'll take me and Davy across the border to wherever we have to go to get him fixed. And try your best to get their agreement."

The warmth of her fingers lingered. The deal seemed impossible. There were two escape routes over the border, the easy one and the hard one. With Davy, we'd need to go the easy way through the Yunko winery. Problem was, the winery escape route was definitely off-limits to outsiders. But we'd have to get him through somehow; Davy couldn't endure the hike over the border, even if I carried him all the way. "Can he stand a fairly long car trip?"

She hesitated, then nodded.

The car trip to the winery was sure to end in disappointment. The Change Lords had no reason to risk security for an unknown local kid. I glanced at the comm helmet case. The helmet relayed our real-time location to the Outpost, but not what was happening. A thought intruded: could I possibly lie to them through the helmet, keep them in ignorance about what was really going on? I shoved the thought away so violently I must have jerked.

"What?" Lil said. "What's your answer?"

"Okay. What you said. About Davy. I'll get him across or die trying." I sounded like an idiot.

Zax, who'd been threading my legs, started yowling, and Gwitchy joined in. I felt like yowling too. "They're hungry," I said above the racket.

"What about you? Have you eaten anything?"

"Not really."

"No wonder you sound weird. You need a place to eat and hide. Hang on." She pulled out her phone and tapped a number. "Hey, it's me. Yeah. Can we come back over there? Goran needs a place to hole up." She laughed. "You're awful. Bye."

Lil stuck the phone back in her pocket. "We can stay at Kayla's if we can get there. The car can't stand another trip through the stupid Railyards."

"Should be okay sneaking *into* town."

"What about them?" Lil jerked her head at the still circling cats.

"They can stay in the back seat."

"No way. Not in the same car."

"They'll be okay. I'll keep 'em calmed down."

"Goran, no! I still have scabs!"

"I'll put them in their pack. They'll be immobilized. Okay?"

She grimaced.

"You head back to the car while I get them ready." She didn't need to see me chasing and wrestling the cats, trying to stuff them in their pack, and generally looking like a fool.

*

Fog thickened, then thickened again. With visibility scarcely forty feet, it took forever to make it back to Kayla's warehouse. I had a brain fog problem too. The more I tried to work out how to steal the culture from GenAge, the more obstacles I saw. Then, moving right along, sneaking across the U.S-Canadian border with stolen goods and an invalid child. I needed to work on the car, now knocking slightly. Then figure how to cram three people and two large cats into it. Find fake papers for Lil and Davy. Get the Sapes through the winery tunnels. Face the Outpost leaders with an impossible request.

My head hurt. I hefted the cats' pack and we started up the stairs. I hoped Kayla would allow them in her apartment.

That became a non-problem as soon as we walked in. I swung the pack to the floor. Gwitchy and Zax started whining the way they do when I'm too slow putting treats in their bowls. Kayla turned in surprise, her eyes locking onto the cats.

In response to their complaints, she crooned deep in her throat, then ordered, "Let them out." I put the pack on the couch and unzipped their mummy bags. They tumbled toward her legs without pausing to check out their surroundings. She melted to the floor, as boneless and fluid as the cats. Maybe her hair-horns looked like cat ears. Maybe her Maori face paint confused them. Soon the three of them were in a pile on the floor, grooming and kneading each other. It felt like watching a new species evolve. But annoying. The cats needed to concentrate on their jobs, not their wonderful new friend.

I looked at Lil. She made a "Too twisted for me" face and started toward the kitchen. We found a bag of pasta and a few shriveled tomatoes and onions. Kayla tore herself away from the cats long enough to dig out bacon. She ordered us to fix half of it for Zax and Gwitchy, but there was

93

still enough for a pot of halfway edible spaghetti.

After we gulped the food, Lil got her laptop from the trunk of the Nissan. We had hours of planning ahead but we could hardly ask Kayla to leave. She was hard to read. I suspected she was very curious about what we were up to but didn't want to show it. The cat thing I couldn't figure out at all. Maybe we could go in the studio without her following.

Kayla stared at me, eyelids half lowered, Zax kneading her belly and Gwitchy draped around her neck. She lifted Zax to the floor, removed Gwitchy, rose, and fetched three beers from the fridge, then resumed staring at me. "An oyster could figure out you're planning to break into GenAge, then run for the border. Since I'm letting you stay here, I'm already an accessory, maybe a co-conspirator. So get on with your plotting and don't worry about me." She jerked her head at her monster laptop in the other end of the room. "I'll be over there out of earshot. Working on your new IDs. I hope you realize the first thing you'll need is really good fakes."

We gaped at her.

Lil went for the frontal approach. "Can you make one for Davy too? I have a photo that might work."

Kayla did a double take. "You're taking Davy? Don't you realize the risk?"

"With my situation, it's not as much risk as staying here."

"You mean . . . are you leaving for good?" Kayla's face twisted under the makeup. She tried to hide a quaver in her voice. "Thanks for telling me."

"Kayla, no. I wasn't trying to hide it – I didn't know till this afternoon." The two friends stared at each other out of their separate pain. "Let me help you." Lil hauled another chair to Kayla's laptop and they bent over the keyboard, heads together, murmuring.

I stretched out on the couch and stared at a painting of totem-pole creatures performing in a circus. Seemed like a hundred years since I'd heard the security alarm at dawn and realized Andrei had failed. I snapped awake when Lil poked my shoulder.

"C'mon. Your turn before the camera." She pointed across the room. Kayla had pulled down a window shade to make a plain, cream colored background, and placed a camera on a tripod before it. I stood in place. I already possessed falsified Yunko documents, all the way down to a tattered pass for the Seattle monorail, but I'd keep that to myself.

My brief nap had sifted out the biggest problem. "We need a key card to get the lab door open," I said. "Pretty high clearance. Even my brother didn't have one. He had to go in with someone else."

"Do you know who?"

I shook my head. "Someone working in Lab 8C."

She idly pressed the laptop's space bar a few times, then logged on. "They send us interns all over the building delivering stuff. I'm pretty sure the lab doors on the eighth floor have backup keypads as well as swipe slots. I can hack the personnel files, find someone working in Lab 8C, get the keypad access code from their file." She sighed. "We'll also need to steal a transport case for the culture."

"I have one with me. My brother brought it home, so it's probably the right type."

"Good."

"Okay. Our route. Do you know how to get around in the building?"

She gave me a superior look. "Remember you told Davy you were a carrying champion? Well, if Seal Bay had a tunnel rat team, I'd be the star rat." She described her breaking and entering route – a complicated procedure of climbing on a shed roof, crawling through ventilation ducts, getting into the central service shaft to go up, then more ducts. It sounded claustrophobic and hard to remember.

"I've been on the eighth floor lots of times," she said. "But I have no idea how to find the culture once you get inside the lab."

"My brother drew a map." I fetched the Yunko map from my backpack and smoothed it out on the table.

"That looks crazy," Lil said.

Kayla checked it out. "Cubism on acid."

I tried to explain. Lil still seemed confused, but Kayla said, "Come over here."

We followed her to the laptop. With a concentration so fierce that it felt like an attack, she closed one window and opened another marked with a 3D grid, grabbed the shape of the building footprint from an aerial view of GenAge and then said, "Okay, Lil, describe your route into the building."

While Lil talked, Kayla moused, typed, toggled back and forth from wireframes to surfaces, and pushed things around on the touch-pad screen. All in 3D, volumes grew, replicated, and piled on each other. Then tunnels burrowed through them. Soon a model of the GenAge building glowed from the screen, pierced with wormholes for Lil's duct runs.

"Give me the map," Kayla said. She asked what a few symbols meant. Then she began filling in the eighth floor until we all but walked through the halls and into the lab. "Try to visualize yourself walking through and memorize the route." She rose abruptly, popped a flash drive out of the machine and went out to the studio. The cats hurried after her.

My tired brain plodded back and forth along the route until I thought I could follow it in my sleep. We chanted the number of the culture vial until it was carved into our brains. I was hungry again but didn't see much chance of eating. "What about the central service shaft? Any cameras? Infrared? Will they have a guard in there?"

"Never seen a guard before," Lil said. "Don't know what they'll do after a security alert. No cameras in the service core. Rumor is the security contractor skimped on the cameras inside and outside, then threw change orders at GenAge 'till they renegotiated and reduced the number inside. And so many ducts run through the service core, the heat signature's pretty confused."

I hoped she was right. "How many guards total?"

"Two on each floor," she said. "One in the lobby and one walking around. Eight floors, so that's sixteen guards. At least two more outside."

We studied the building model until Kayla and the cats returned from the studio. She waved papers and laminated cards. "Your new identities."

When I reached for them, she jerked them back. "We need to talk about the price."

"What?" I rose.

"I'm your safe house, your forger, and your navigator. By now, I'm implicated up to my ears. I'm going with you across the border."

"That's impossible!" I stepped forward to seize the documents by force.

Lil darted between us and and grabbed each of us by an arm. "Kayla, you've never talked about leaving Seal Bay. Your . . . business and everything."

"You're not the only one who doesn't tell her friends everything that's going on." Kayla stared around her one-room home. "Dagmar down at The Paint Store told me someone came in a couple days ago looking for a girl who did art and used the name Regina Midnight. Dag said the guy dressed and talked like he was from the east coast. I figure it's time to disappear."

Lil caught her in a hug then released. "You think your father sent him?"

"I'd be a fool not to. Somebody knows I'm here, knows I hang out at art supply stores, knows at least one of my real names. Besides, I hate this pit." She waved her free arm, either at the studio or all of Seal Bay. "It's going down the tubes."

Sounded like a whole new mountain of complications. "There's no room in the car," I said. "Not for four people, the cats and our stuff."

"I'll hold Davy in my lap. Lil needs me to help with him anyway. And to keep her safe when she's doing something stupid. Or I'll just follow on my bike."

I needed a bucket of cold water over my head because I couldn't come up with a way of losing Kayla without also losing Lil's cooperation. I shrugged. Once I had the culture I could dump her.

Kayla smirked. She handed Lil a sheet of paper. "Before you use the IDs, hack your new names into these sites."

It reminded me. "I need a comm unit. To warn Lil if something goes wrong while I'm inside the building. Any place close I can buy one?"

"Not this late." Kayla frowned. "You mean you don't *have* one?"

"I got rid of it." I nodded at Lil. "With the house."

Kayla opened a file drawer and pulled out a tangle of electronics. She sorted through it and selected a cheap comm and ear buds. "Here's a burner."

"Thanks." I turned it on and checked it out.

Kayla returned the mess to the drawer. "What time will you hit GenAge?"

"With shift changes and janitors and everything," I asked Lil, "what's best?"

"Around three o'clock this morning. In five more hours."

# CHAPTER 15

From the unpublished Godunov manuscript
*Why We Came to Earth: The Yunko Voyages*

*The first ship we launched toward Earth was comparatively slow. It completed its 22.7 light-year journey in 1125 C.E. The crew spent most of the long voyage in suspended animation. The ship's shuttles landed in the middle of Earth's largest landmass, near the Podkamennaya Tunguska River in the present-day Russian region of Krasnoyarsk Krai.*

*Our personnel who survived the intense radiation of the voyage lived in the shuttles until they could deploy habitats and laboratories underground. Wearing protective suits, they explored the surface and took samples from local plants and animals.*

Lil and I could have been the last people left alive, floating through the fog in our Nissan space capsule. I heard every contact of her sneaker with the gas pedal, every breath and almost every heartbeat. I smelled her lemony shampoo over the faint aroma of spaghetti, at least until Gwitchy pawed my hair and blasted me with her meaty breath.

The downtown streets were cottony gray tunnels. Sound, more than sight, told me when we reached open ground near GenAge. Lil turned off a couple of blocks before reaching our destination and parked where she normally left her car when sneaking into the building. I hoped the motor's knocking hadn't carried through the fog.

I pocketed the anchor beacon, opened the door, and stepped out, the cats tangling in my feet. Tonight I had more trust in ears and nose than vision. The fog carried the smell of the bay from our left. I hoped it would keep us from walking in circles. I touched Lil's arm and pointed in the presumed direction of GenAge. We sniffed, listened, and guessed our way across the parking lots. At one point a hazy pair of lights crept by, maybe eighty feet away.

At last we found the GenAge building by stumbling over a curb and felt our way to an attached one-story shed. Lil climbed the metal ladder and I followed, boosting the cats in front of me, until we flopped on the flat roof just under the fresh air intake ducts.

"How long you think it'll take me?" I whispered.

"Maybe thirty minutes. Maybe till forever." She pulled at a grille. It fell out, exposing the points of loosened screws. Lil collected them.

"How'd you do that?"

"Got to it from the inside, removed the screws and replaced them with smaller ones. Told you I knew this building." She poked her head in to look, her hair wafting in the air current. "Sure you remember the route?"

"Yeah," I said, not feeling at all certain. I fed the cats into the opening. Then I pushed into the duct – as far as my shoulders. I pulled back and collapsed my chest and hunched my arms into my torso, trying to squeeze my upper body into a rectangle that could slide through the opening. Didn't work. I stripped off my jacket and shirt and squeezed forward as hard as I could but I just got stuck, scraping off a little skin when I wrenched loose. The cats emerged from the duct, sniffing at the blood and tissue.

"You're too big," Lil said. "And some of the other ducts are even smaller." Her voice rose in a strained, nervous pitch. "I'll have to go by myself. You're too clumsy and noisy anyway." She sounded crazy with nerves.

Bad. Way bad. I couldn't let her go in alone. But I didn't see any other choice. "The cats have to go with you."

"No. I don't want them near me."

"You have to take them. They're your only protection now." I handed her the anchor beacon. "Stick that in your pocket."

"I don't want them," she said in a near scream.

"The cats are going. They'll follow the beacon." I couldn't believe things had already gone so wrong. "Make sure you have your penlight and keep the comm bud in your ear."

"Tell them not to touch me." Her hand shook so hard she had to make a fist to hand me the screws. And then she crawled into the darkness. I lifted the cats in behind her.

Some hero I was, sending the princess into battle while I stayed behind. I wanted to hit something, to scream, to smash the hulking building until it crashed to the ground. Instead, I pulled my clothes back on. When I could stand it no longer, I whispered into the comm, "Where are you? What's happening?"

"Nothing," she whispered in return. "I'm still in the first duct run." I tried to stay with her mentally, visualizing her crawling over the duct joints, the cats butting her and trying to squeeze past.

After an age, Lil murmured in my ear, "Just turned the last corner. There's light through the grille ahead."

I could hear the soft bump of her arms and knees as she crawled, her breath coming faster. Then I definitely heard a gasp. "What?" I whisper-screamed.

"I'm at the grille to the big central stairwell. A guard just walked in an access door from an upper floor. They must have beefed up security." She gave a squeak, almost a sob. I heard a faint growling through the comm. "Dog with him," she said. "They're coming down the stairs."

"Back up. Crawl back as fast as you can. Around a corner so he can't see you if he shines a light in the duct."

Scrambling noises. A bark that sounded closer. Her sobbing breath. "The dog's right at the duct. It smells me. It's barking."

"Where's the guard?"

She rustled as she peeped back around the corner. "I can't see him through the grille. He must still be on the stairs."

Think. Think! "Okay," I said, "Did you loosen that grille too?"

"Yes."

"Do you have enough room to get the cats around in front of you?"

I heard a low snarl, then "Dammit," then "Ouch!"

"Okay, they're in front," Lil panted.

They must have been around the corner. Rumbling snarls came through as Zax and Gwitchy spotted the dog at the grille. "Hold the phone close to their heads." I gave the attack whistle as loud as I could. Claws screeched on metal. I heard the loosened grille clang to the floor when Zax exploded out the duct with a piercing shriek, Gwitchy yowling behind him. I mentally apologized to the poor dog, who was just doing its job.

Through the phone came a growling, howling riot at the zoo. "Oh. My. God." Lil breathed.

"Get to the opening. Be ready to go!"

"One's going after the guard," Lil gasped. "They're flying! It's like they're running up the walls and dive-bombing the guard. And the dog"

I'd seen them do it. Running so fast their momentum let them swarm briefly up a vertical wall. The cats would use the central shaft like a jungle gym. I heard a human scream and feet banging on metal stair treads. Then another scream and a thud.

Lil moaned. "The guard. He was fighting a cat and fell backward over the rail. I don't know if he's dead or just knocked out."

She mustn't freeze. "Is the dog still fighting?" I yelled.

"Yes," she squeaked. "He's going down."

"Go go go! The cats will break loose and follow the beacon."

She seemed to gag. "There's blood everywhere."

I took a deep breath. "Lil, climb out of the duct. Now. Put the grille back in place." I could hear a retching noise in the back of her throat. "Okay, Lil. Got the grille back in?"

She muttered broken whispers.

"Lil, don't look at the guard. Or the dog. Get to the stairs and climb to the eighth floor."

"The doors don't open from this side. I'll have to use my third floor duct."

"That's good," I said. "Get in the third floor duct with the cats, and then we'll talk about what to do next."

She choked back a sob. "The dog's trying to crawl back to this grille. What if they find it and guess somebody's at the outside end? They'll come after you."

"I'll keep watch. Now get up the stairs and into the other duct." I scanned the gray-white mist around me. Saw nothing. Heard nothing. I doubted anyone could see me lying on the flat roof, but it wouldn't be long before someone found the guard. No hope now of escaping undetected.

"Goran," Lil said at last, "I'm in the third floor duct with the cats. They're pretty bloody. Do you think that guard's . . . still alive?"

"Probably. Maybe the fall actually saved him from more damage from the cats." I was doubtful, but we couldn't afford for Lil to freeze up with horror and guilt. "We'll take care of the cats later. Are there any elevators or stairwells near you?"

"Stairs at the end of each hall, but a camera's pointed at them. And the guards in each lobby can see the elevators."

"There has to be a service elevator somewhere. They wouldn't haul heavy equipment or hazardous materials through the main lobbies. Where is it?"

"At the back," she said. "I think it opens into a storeroom."

"Bingo. Can you get to the service elevator on this floor without being seen by the camera?"

Silence. "I can get close using the ducts. I guess my knees can stand one more crawl."

"Great." I added, too softly for her to hear, "I'd do it for you if I could."

She started out. Every once in a while I'd hear a thump, an "ouch," or a whimper. It seemed she'd been in the building for hours. My comm said forty-three minutes had passed. And I thought we'd planned this so well.

"I'm at the ceiling grille in the storeroom."

"Can you drop into the room and get to the elevator?"

"Yeah, but I won't be able to get back in the duct."

"Any ladders or tables you can drag over?"

Before she could answer, the GenAge alarms went off, blasting all across my range of hearing, overwhelming at close quarters. I clapped my hands over my ears and rolled into a ball. At last the shriek subsided and I could hear a voice through the ear bud yelling orders on the building's PA system.

"What are they saying?" I shouted.

"Hang on," Lil yelled back above the clamor. At last the voice went quiet. "They're re-deploying security personnel. Sending Level A, the real badasses, to the exits. Level B, the investigator types, to the ground floor of the central shaft. Then – this is odd – they want the Cs, the barely-fog-a-mirror guys, to report to the animal facilities."

We paused, then spoke almost simultaneously. "They think lab animals escaped and attacked the guard and dog."

"Where do they keep the animals?"

"That's our first break." Lil gave a shaky laugh. "All the animal facilities are in the other wing. They're probably sending the Level C guys over there to see what's missing."

"Do they use cats? Or anything else that could leave similar wounds?"

"Cats, chimps, dogs, you name it."

"You have to get out of the ducts before they find the loose grilles," I said. "That leaves the service elevator. Take it to the ground floor. I'll meet you at the loading dock."

"What about the culture?"

"It just got too dangerous for you to try."

"Dammit, Goran, it's Davy's only chance. I won't stop when we're this close. If the elevator doesn't work, I'm zombie chow anyway. If it does work, it won't take much longer to reach the eighth floor, get the stuff, then ride down to the loading dock. How's the fog?"

Took me a moment to switch gears. "Still thick."

"Good. Work your way down to the loading dock and wait for me. It's about halfway down this wing, in the back. Okay, I'm dropping."

I heard two soft thuds as she tossed the cats to the floor, then a louder crash and a groan.

# CHAPTER 16

From the unpublished Godunov manuscript
*Why We Came to Earth: The Yunko Voyages*

*After their initial explorations on Earth, our researchers organized into two teams. The teams would research two possibilities for a new bodily form that could survive on both Earth and Gliese-C. One team proposed adding DNA for human organs to various organs and systems of our own genome to change our respiratory design. The other team hoped to modify a human genome with our DNA so it could survive on the surface of Gliese-C. To obtain human DNA, researchers stole samples from secretly anesthetized Evenki, the indigenous people of the area.*

I sat and stared at fog like a sailor drifting out to sea – for about ten useless seconds. If Lil and the cats were captured, the consequences would be too awful to think about. I had to get inside the building. The wall that disappeared into the fog above me was stone veneer and metal, too smooth to climb. I pulled my knife from its ankle scabbard and slashed at the membrane roofing of the lean-to, only to hit concrete.

Lil had said to wait near the loading dock. Maybe I could get in that way. I climbed down and crept along the building close enough to touch it in the fog. Eventually the chest-high dock materialized in front of me, its damp, gritty concrete smelling faintly of garbage and motor oil. I turned its corner and soon encountered a wide ramp. The blurred glow of a light mounted on the building wall illuminated a regular door beside a large, roll-up garage door. A vehicle could drive straight up the ramp, across the dock, and into the building to unload its cargo unseen. I hopped up and checked the doors – smooth steel set in steel frames.

A distant siren howled through the heavy air, drawing closer. Across the parking lot a faint blob of light widened and separated into the headlights of a vehicle heading toward the loading dock much too fast for safety in the fog. I raced for the edge, rolled over, and flattened myself against the ramp.

The SUV was big, black for maximum intimidation, and its grille seemed to snarl. It charged up the ramp and stopped halfway. Through the tinted glass, the driver's face was a pale blur behind the darker blur of a comm, maybe ordering someone to meet him inside.

The vehicle was my only chance. I rolled onto the ramp and under the SUV. It was fitted with the steel-bar grid of an under-carriage protection extender. Of course it was. This guy's fantasy life probably featured commuting to work every day across minefields. I grabbed the metal bars and hooked my feet into them just as the door rumbled up and the driver screeched forward. Even though I pulled myself flat against the bottom of the grid, my head banged against the concrete floor when he slammed on the brakes inside the building.

Two legs, camo pants stuffed into combat boots, jogged across the floor to meet the SUV. I pulled myself a couple more inches toward the other side.

"Chief Cheyne! Sir!" Camo Pants snapped. So. The big bratwurst himself had arrived to take charge of the manhunt – more accurately, the girlhunt.

As if I'd sent a mental message, my comm vibrated. Lil. Not now! I released the   protector grid with one hand and turned off the comm.

"Where's the guard?" Cheyne said in a flat monotone

"We were afraid to move him, sir. He's still in the core shaft."

"Did he say anything?"

"He's still out, sir."

"Did you call an ambulance?"

"No, sir. We called Dr. Roeffles, sir. He's on his way."

"Good man. Keep it in house. The dog?"

"Sir, we had to put the dog down, sir."

I mentally sent a formal apology to the dog, along with the acknowledgement that its life cord would now darken mine. What a bloody, botched up mess! At least the guard was still alive; technically we weren't yet murderers.

Cheyne got out. "Show me everything."

The garage door closed. Then his car door slammed. The two men walked across the floor. Cheyne moved well – loose, silent, balance shifting smoothly with each step. Their legs stopped in front of a door on the back wall, then passed through when it opened.

My arms screamed when I lowered myself to the floor. I flexed various parts, slid over behind a tire and peered around it scanning for cameras. Then I checked the other side but I didn't see any surveillance equipment in the large room, so I rolled from under the SUV.

The room – a maintenance and shipping area – was roughly a hundred feet long, filled with the stuff that nobody wanted to put elsewhere. Chain-link fencing closed off one end, with tools and equipment locked behind it and a forklift and golf cart parked in front.

Bags of landscaping chips and fertilizer filled the corners. Along the back wall, I could see the service elevator door and another door marked Stairwell. I turned on the comm and contacted Lil.

"Why didn't you answer?" she whispered.

"I'm inside the building." I didn't want to terrify her with the news that Cheyne had arrived. "GenAge personnel were too close for me to talk. Where are you?"

"Eighth floor. The cats and I are in a restroom. There's a guard walking in the hall."

"So the service elevator's working?"

"Yeah." She paused. "At least it was five minutes ago. But on this floor it opens straight onto the hall."

"Okay, I'm coming up. Right now. Leave the cats in the restroom and be ready to go out and distract the guard so he's not watching the elevator."

"Hunh? How?"

"I don't know. Do some girl thing. I'll comm you when the elevator gets to seven."

Our window of opportunity was closing. If Cheyne was smart, he'd shut down all circulation routes inside the building and clear it room by room. For sure he'd send someone to check the lab that Andrei tried to breach. I started toward the elevator but paused. A board hung with keys was mounted beside the doors. I read the labels, put one in my pocket, pressed the Up button, and got in. Floor numbers glowed one after another.

At Floor 7, I called Lil. She nailed the timing. The elevator doors hummed apart. Twenty feet away, Lil, wearing a white lab coat, slouched against the wall and smiled. The guard hurried toward her. She'd positioned herself so his back was toward the elevator.

I ghosted up behind him and used the carotid choke, then a double shot of the memory spray since he looked in better shape than poor old Murphy.

Lil opened the restroom door. Zax and Gwitchy tumbled out and headed for my legs. I knelt and felt them for injuries. Zax had a cut on one hind leg, probably from the dog, but his coat's so thick and protective, he barely limped. Gwitchy groomed blood from her fur but it wasn't hers. She seemed quite proud of herself.

"C'mon," Lil called softly from down the hall. She'd punched in the security code and opened the door to Lab 8C. "I accessed the work roster while I was waiting. Shouldn't be anyone inside tonight."

We stepped quietly into the lab, a shadowy sanctuary of long work tables lit only by tiny equipment lights, passed sequencers, mass spectrometers, and microscopes as complex as space stations. Across the large room, Lil opened a door labeled Tissue Storage. The cats and I followed her into a small room lined with more doors.

She flipped on the light, grabbed a leather apron and insulated gloves from a rack, and put them on. "Human tissue cultures in there, away from the other species." She jerked her head at the middle door and opened it. I glimpsed a row of squat metal cylinders. Eternity's freezers. A mist rolled across the floor. The cats backed away and whined. Lil shut the door behind her. Two minutes later she emerged carrying a capsule-shaped flask.

"What's in that?"

"The culture. In liquid nitrogen," she said, putting it on the floor. She shucked the gloves, then took off the apron and wrapped it around the flask. I grabbed the bundle and we hurried back through the outer labs, the corridor, and into the service elevator. I punched the Floor 1 button.

"And you're sure this is the right culture?" I was saying when the elevator jolted to a halt. Yowling cats skidded, Lil and I stumbled. The wrapped flask hit the floor. Over the door, the 4 lit up, then the 3, then back to the 4.

I slammed a fist against the Doors Open symbol. The doors quivered, slid apart an inch than closed again. It was enough to see that we were stuck halfway between floors. I cursed under my breath. "Cheyne must have seen the down arrow light. Must have some sort of emergency override."

"Cheyne's here?" Hearing the panic in Lil's voice, the cats stalked toward her.

I grabbed Zax and Gwitchy. "Don't think about him."

A waist-high grab bar stretched across one side of the compartment. I wrenched it with all my strength. One end came loose and I twisted the bar all the way off.

"Okay, hit the Doors Open button on the count of three." I stationed myself at the front of the elevator and dropped the bar at my feet. "One. Two. Three." When the slight opening appeared, I grabbed the two doors, forced them open, got my shoulder against one, and jammed the grab bar between them. "Put the flask out, step on my shoulder, and crawl out yourself."

Miraculously, she did it with no arguing. I threw the cats out after her, crawled out myself, and grabbed the flask. "Where's the stairwell?" I panted.

Lil pointed down the corridor and we took off. We had to make it to the bottom before anyone started up the stairs.

They'd obviously cut costs on this stairwell too: bare cinderblock walls, a thin layer of concrete poured in metal pans for steps, and railings made of pipe. Doors blank except for painted floor numbers. Echoes so loud we sounded like an army.

A door slammed below with a sonic boom. The treads shook with running feet. I handed the flask to Lil. "Go up a turn and hide. I'll tell you when to run for the first floor." I crouched low against the clammy wall and motioned the cats to my side. Steps pounded up the flight directly beneath me and hit the turn. The guard glanced up and saw me just as I vaulted over the railing. I hit him hard, smashing his head against the cinderblock. As he fell he got an arm under my shoulder and wrenched it with all the force of his fall. I screamed. He still struggled as I got my feet under me.

A shot in the stairwell from the second attacker half deafened me. Ricochets whined as I wrestled the guard around and launched him down the stairs at the man charging up. I whistled Zax and Gwitchy to attack and they flew over the railing, as eager as otters hitting the water.

"Run!" I yelled. Down Lil came, flashing past me and stopping at the whirling mess of snarling cats and screaming guards. I wrestled her past them and hauled her down the last flight.

"That's Cheyne the cats are ripping up." She sounded both terrified and excited. I pushed her through the door into the maintenance room.

"Hide behind the golf cart." I whistled for the cats. They came running and we slammed out after Lil.

Nothing to block the stairwell door. No, the stack of 50-pound fertilizer bags. I half-tugged, half-kicked a couple over and dashed back for more. My shoulder was beginning to seriously hurt. Gwitchy stalked back and forth in full Bitchy Diva mode while Zax hunkered down. They weren't seriously injured, but they seemed frustrated at breaking off their encounter. They followed me for a moment, then chased each other up a rack of shelves beside the door and bickered.

I dumped two more bags in front of the door before getting in the forklift and turning it on with the key I'd taken earlier. The thing was slow. Just as I got it to the overhead door, a bullet pierced the stairwell door. I'd never driven a lift before. I found the control to raise and lower the fork, but I couldn't get it low enough to slide under the garage door. Lil watched from behind the golf cart. Three more shots. The stairwell door pushed open, shoving the bags across the floor. I backed the forklift and turned just as Cheyne, badly bloodied, squeezed through.

With an indignant scream, Gwitchy plopped from her perch onto Cheyne's back. Zax hit the floor, then ran up him like a tree. The security chief screamed, tried to smash Zax with the pistol and then dropped it to protect his eyes. Zax, clinging to his head with all twenty claws, gnawed on his ear. Gwitchy switched sides and went to work on his crotch.

Like our Deflection Master said, everything is a weapon. I drove toward them, pressing the control to raise the fork, herding the three of them toward the metal mesh cage. I caught Cheyne between the rising prongs and advanced until the prongs pierced the metal links and squeezed him against the mesh, dangling a foot above the floor. The cats leapt free.

Now what? I tried to set the machine to keep up the pressure long enough for me to grab the door opener, but I couldn't get the thing to lock into position.

"Lil," I screamed, "get the door opener out of his pocket."

She slipped out of hiding, walked toward the bloody, dangling figure, and stopped.

"Search his pockets," I yelled again. She edged close enough to touch his leg.

Eyes opened in the bloody face. "I remember you," Cheyne said in a voice cold enough to freeze a furnace. "Our little bucking pony." Then he whispered something I couldn't hear. He grasped the forks that pinned him and tried to scissor his legs around her but she jumped back.

I pulled something that looked like a hand brake, jumped out and grabbed Cheyne's legs with my good arm. The cats closed in. Lil looked ready to pass out, but she raised her hand and dug into a pants pocket soaked wet enough with blood to show the outline of the opener. I took it from her, swiped off blood against my pants, and raised the door.

"Lil," I said, "get the flask and let's go." She backed away, still hypnotized by Cheyne's eyes glaring out of a sheet of blood. I physically turned her and gave a slight shove. She grabbed the flask and we all raced for the opening, jumping off the loading dock just as three more guards pushed through the stairwell door.

# CHAPTER 17

## Excerpt from the diary of Lil Osborne

*Can't sleep. No point. Dawn's almost here. Every time I close my eyes, I hear Erik Cheyne whisper, "Next time, Craig and I'll take turns with the Taser." Cheyne will kill me. I think he's always planned to kill me, he just hadn't picked a time and a method. Now, he'll do it as soon as he can find me. I still don't understand what's going on with Goran Helin, but Cheyne's the one who's an inhuman monster.*

*In a few hours we'll pick up Davy and head for the border. Crazy, but I've run out of other choices, if I ever had any.*

If you're addicted to suspense, try racing full tilt through fog. When we were far enough from the security guards, I said, "Stop, Lil." I handed her the flask and whispered, "Take the culture and head back to the Nissan. I'll decoy them in the opposite direction." If I didn't escape, maybe she would, with the culture. Somehow, someday, the Yunko might eventually track it down.

"Then what?"

"I'll meet you back at the car."

She touched my arm and then walked into the fog. I could hear the guards' low voices behind me. I raced away from the building with slamming feet, whistling for the cats to follow. We veered north, angling 180 degrees away from Lil's route. Commands echoed back and forth in the fog. Boots pounded after us. They were following nicely when I banged against a parking sign and fell. Zax and Gwitchy closed around me, snarling at the noise behind us.

I signaled them to attack and they silently bounded away. At a burst of yells and yowls, I took off again, whistling them to break off and follow. When I figured we were past the far end of the building, we veered left and quietly reached the street, crossed and cut behind the row of office buildings where I'd spied on GenAge a hundred years ago.

The murk was turning lighter. Headlights passed more frequently. Two blocks south, I ran across the street again to reach the lot where we had parked. The red blur of the Nissan materialized in front of me. It was empty. I called "Lil" in a low voice.

"Over here." She sat on the curb thirty feet away, invisible in the remaining fog.

Her hands were over her face and she was shaking. At last she said, "Seemed safer not to be in the car." She pulled the bundled flask from the shrubs behind her. "You okay?"

"Coupla bruises." I laughed and coaxed the cats into the car. Except for my shoulder, I felt terrific. We'd done the impossible! Lil and me! Stolen the culture that might save my people! And I was probably in love!

Or maybe twenty-four hours with lots of stress and little sleep had turned me psychotic. I was still chuckling when Lil started the car. It feebly knocked to life, which sobered me up.

"The car sounds bad," Lil said. "What if it dies?"

"Then we need to be as far away from GenAge as possible. Head for the back street without turning on your lights."

We noisily reached the street, but a mile away on the edge of downtown, the engine gave up. Lil steered the vehicle's dying glide to a curbside No Parking zone.

"Now what?" She sounded panicky.

"Got the penlight?" She pulled it out of her pocket and released the hood. When I raised it, a blast of burnt oil hit my nose. The feeble beam lit an engine block crusted with black. I closed the hood. "We have to leave the car here for now. Looks like an oil leak froze up the engine." I couldn't quite tell her the Nissan was now extinct.

"We can't. How will we reach the border? Do something, Goran!"

"We need to get out of sight. The fog's lifting and people are about." I looked around. A block away, a still-closed carryout place sat between an abandoned gas station and a block of apartments. Its outside tables were partially encircled by a weathered wood fence that shielded them from the wind. "Over there."

I let the cats out and we hurried down the sidewalk, Lil fretting about Davy. We cut around the fence and took a table hidden from the street. "We need to disappear. Call Kayla. She can pick you up on her motorcycle. And tell her to bring the cat's pack. We need to get them out of sight too."

"What about you?"

"I'll make it over there as fast as possible. Tell her to hurry."

While Lil made the call, I drifted off – the noise of Kayla's Kawasaki woke me. The girls hugged and talked. I stuffed the bloody cats into their pack. Lil climbed on the cycle's back seat and I handed her the pack to hold. She grimaced. They roared off through the growing light.

I tucked the culture flask under my arm like a football and jogged through the early morning streets imagining I could hear pancake batter hitting skillets, bacon sizzling, orange juice gurgling, coffee perking, forks clinking. But every cent I had was in the backpack at Kayla's.

Thoughts of food paled beside our other problems. Cheyne had identified Lil. If Cheyne was functioning, he'd check her personnel file and set up some kind of ambush around her house. But Lil wouldn't leave without Davy. I again considered ditching them all and heading for the border with just the cats. But how? Besides, I didn't want to leave her. We needed to get our of Seal Bay immediately–in another vehicle. By now GenAge might be searching all over the Northwest. Why did Sape stuff always get so complicated?

*

I scrounged a crust of toast off Lil's plate, sat back wishing for three times the amount of food. The cats, Zax with a shaved and bandaged leg, voiced dissatisfaction with their single sausage each. I'd given Kayla cash to go out and buy breakfast. I hoped the food would fuel our brains enough to come up with a new plan. While she was gone, I installed the culture in Andrei's transport case and tossed the flask. I also took the medkit into her small bathroom and pulled off my jacket and shirt. A careless tug made me suck air through my teeth. I ripped open a gel-pack from the medkit and molded the goo around my injured shoulder. It looked like a giant jellyfish. The gel infuses anti-inflammatories and painkillers through the skin, along with a compound to leach calcium out of the damaged muscles.

Kayla turned on a morning news webcast just as I stepped back out. "Come here!' she called, staring at the computer screen. Above a chyron "Schoolgirl and bobcats raid GenAge," a video showed the pixelated, back-lit image of a man sitting in a chair.

His disguised voice said, "The guard was unconscious. When he came to, Security asked him what he'd seen. He said the animals looked like two giant bobcats. And he thought he saw a schoolgirl with them. Said they chewed up his dog and attacked him." The video stopped, the newsreader beamed and chirped, "So how's that for a weird one? KBAY contacted GenAge but they had no comment. Tune in at six tonight for developments on an apparent break-in at Seal Bay's largest employer."

"So who's that?" Kayla jerked her head at the screen.

"Probably another GenAge guard," I said. "Maybe picking up some cash on the side. Maybe losing his job instead."

Kayla flopped on the couch. "We need a car. Big enough for my stuff, Lil's stuff, all that gear you hauled over here, two cats, the three of us, and Davy."

"Yeah, don't forget Davy," Lil said sharply.

"Or . . . what about the train that runs up the coast? It's really cheap," Kayla said.

"You'd still have to go through customs in Vancouver," I said. "It's too big a risk, particularly with a kid along."

"I'll call 'em and ask today's odds." Kayla tapped a number. In a moment she said, "Never mind. Odds are seventy-six percent that a storm surge in the next twenty-four hours will put the tracks under water at Blaine or Dakota Creek."

I couldn't resist. "Yeah, that's why it's so cheap."

"Hand me your burner phone," Lil said. "I need to call Davy, tell him I'm coming."

"They identified you," I said. "Your land line'll be tapped by now."

"I'm calling Davy's comm. Why would anyone be interested in that?"

I shrugged and handed her the comm. She tapped a number, waited a moment and said, "Good morning, sleepyhead." Then, "No, I had to work at GenAge and now I'm at school. Are Mom and Dad there?" Her lips tightened. "Listen, sweetie, can you scoot yourself across the bed and reach the curtain?" She squeezed her eyes shut and waited. "Great. Now peep outside. Any cars you don't recognize?" She held up two fingers to us. "Can you see how many people are in each car? . . . No, that's okay."

She stood up and paced. "Oh, I'm planning an adventure. Just for you and me. It's a secret." She pinched her nose with her free hand. "Yeah, it'll be a blast. But for right now you just snuggle up and sleep some more. Okay? Love you."

She put the comm on the coffee table and walked into the studio. I stood to follow but Kayla stopped me with a hand. "This thing with Davy is killing her. And I'd like to kill their parents."

I was forming the same opinion.

Kayla glanced at my pile of stuff in the corner. "Do you have any money?"

"Yeah."

"Like, a lot of money?"

Even minus Lil's four hundred, the wad of big bills was almost two inches thick. "Probably enough. Why?"

"I know someone who might help us, but he'd squeeze you big time."

"Who?"

"Conroy. He has his own reasons for wanting to leave town."

I started to object, since I trusted Conroy like I trusted quicksand. But he wanted something from me. He had something I needed. That had the outline of a deal, even if I had to be on guard every second. "Call him."

She grabbed the burner from the coffee table and tapped in a number, which implied she was pretty close to Conroy.

"It's Kayla," she growled. "Oh, stop bitching. You'd be up already if you were going to school today. Interested in a nice little deal?" She leaned over to scratch Gwitchy's head. "Giving some people a ride up north." A moment later she said, "Some friends. They're going all the way . . . let's say the equivalent of five people."

A moment later she said, "You're out of your mind. They can pay twelve hundred tops." She looked at me, eyebrows raised in question. I gave her a thumbs up. "C'mon, it's just a day trip up and back. You can do better than that. Particularly since I get the feeling you really need a change of scenery." Then, "Okay. Twelve fifty and I throw in gas ration coupons. How soon can you be here?" Pause. "Can't you make it sooner than that?" She turned to me and mouthed "Noon." I nodded, not having much choice. "Okay, untangle whatever it is and get here as soon as possible," she said. "Pull into the alley and comm me. We'll come down."

# CHAPTER 18

From the unpublished Godunov manuscript
*Why We Came to Earth: The Yunko Voyages*

*Our initial attempts at creating hybridized life were lengthy and brutal. Decades passed before our research teams created "interstellar cells" that lived long enough to divide.*

*Once that milestone was achieved, in 1167 C.E., the last survivors of the teams loaded their shuttles with samples and data, returned to their ship, and programmed it for Gliese-C; they would die long before completing the return trip.*

Lil sat on the floor, bent over the coffee table making a list. It seemed to calm her shaking. Kayla rambled around sorting through her stuff and readying her big graphics laptop for a trip. I was too impatient to sleep and too tired for anything else, so I thought about Conroy's car. The beetle-blue, four-hole Buick dated from the middle of the last century. Conroy had rebuilt its innards, and its body had to be mostly Bondo and fiberglass by now. It ran like a bat out of hell and looked amazingly roomy. Even better, it was too old to have any sort of GPS tracking system.

On the bad side, it was incredibly noticeable, it sucked gas like a bilge pump, and it was owned by Conroy. He regularly ran people – or product – to Canada in the car, but I wanted to stay far away from that operation.

"Crap!" Lil muttered. "Flaming, screaming, crappy crap!"

"What?" I leaned over to see what triggered her outburst.

She waved the list. "Clothes and meds Davy needs. I forgot to pick up Albuterol yesterday. He's almost out."

"Can't it wait till we get across the border?"

"No. It helps his breathing. I don't dare take him anywhere without it."

"Write it down," I said. "I'll hike to a drugstore, pick it up while we wait for Conroy."

She shook her head. "It's prescription. Have to get it myself. But with GenAge looking for me, I don't dare tell anyone my name."

Kayla touched Lil's shoulder. "We can get it like we get

over-the-counter stuff."

"But I'd have to get behind the druggist's counter." Lil stood.

"No problem. I went in a place at Fourth and Cascadia Boulevard one morning three weeks ago." Kayla snagged a pair of motorcycle boots from under the couch and started pulling them on. "Their druggist comes in at ten and rolls back the security grate around the drug counter. Then he drinks a cup of coffee and flirts with the two salesgirls for ten, fifteen minutes before he goes back to the counter. If we get there in time it might work."

Lil pulled on her jacket and laced her sneakers.

"Hey, wait a minute," I said, but they headed through the door and down the stairs

It finally sank through my fatigue that these two crazies were on their way to rob a drugstore. I grabbed my own jacket and chased after them, just in time to hear the motorcycle roar to life and see them flash past the end of the alley.

Running at full speed, I reached Cascadia Boulevard seven minutes later, gasping and sweating. A block away, the two girls sauntered past a few derelicts toward the drugstore. I bent over, hands on knees, for a few deep breaths before jogging after them.

The store looked pretty bare. Shelves lined each wall and formed two rows down the middle between wide aisles, as if they were trying to spread out their shrunken stock.

Kayla stood at a cosmetics counter near the front, fingering the makeup and applying smears to her already grotesque face paint. One salesgirl watched her with clenched jaw. The other flirted with the druggist. On a chair by the door, an aging security guard yawned non-stop. Lil was nowhere to be seen. I drifted down the center aisle until I could see the druggist's enclosure at the rear of the store. A ceiling-mounted fisheye mirror reflected her arm and shoulder as she squatted on the floor behind the counter, searching the lower shelves.

I pretended to study ankle braces and glanced at the guard again. He watched me for any sign of bandage theft. Suddenly his eyes shifted. He rose and yelled, "Hey, you! Freeze!"

Lil froze, holding the enclosure gate half open. The guard lumbered down the side aisle. Kayla shot past the clerks and out the door. Fat lot of help she was!

As I rounded the front end of the center aisle I grabbed a couple of shrink-wrapped toilet seats from a stack. I sailed the first one like a giant Frisbee. It banged into the guard's ample buttocks. He faltered but kept going. I threw the second seat like a cross-court pass and cracked him on the head, knocking off his uniform hat. He staggered against the druggist enclosure, veered to the right and out of sight. Lil screamed.

When I reached the back of the store the guard was gripping Lil's arm. She beat at him with her other hand, which held a pill bottle, frustrating his attempt to aim the pistol or to cuff her. I dived at the guard, tackling him below the knees. All three of us crashed against the far wall, with my injured shoulder hitting first. Lil pulled loose and butt-scooted backward. I scrambled up, pulled her to her feet, and ran toward the door.

At the guard's first shot I tackled her to the floor again and rolled us around an ATM machine sitting against the far end of the aisle. The guard fired two more shots. The clerks and druggist ducked behind the checkout counter. I looked for a safe path to the door. Or something else heavy to throw.

Outside, an engine shrieked up to max RPM. Kayla jumped the big 750cc Kawasaki over the curb, across the sidewalk, and through the drugstore's automatic doors. She screamed down the center aisle, swerving into the far rack of shelves. They crashed to the floor in a hail of toiletries. After a sliding stop, she revved again and crashed into our aisle, raining health products down on the hapless guard. "Get out!" she screamed at us. "Run!"

We ran, hitting the sidewalk and dodging left around the corner just as a cop car braked outside the drugstore. Kayla thundered out the door and skidded through a right turn. The cop screeched after her. I pushed Lil into the recessed doorway of an abandoned store and tried to hide her with my body.

"Stop jumping on top of me," she yelped.

A few people passing by stared. I was just trying to keep her safe, I promise. I'd seen plenty of couples get all over each other at school until you couldn't tell who they were. Obviously the safest way to keep anyone from spotting Lil was to kiss her. So I raised my arms to block anyone's view of her face and tried to do what I'd seen other guys do.

In spite of all my fantasies, this was unexplored territory. I pressed my lips against hers and made gobbling motions with my cheeks. Pretty soon she started working her lips around, so I did the same thing. Our mouths came open and then she was biting on my lips and it seemed like our lips got bigger and all the blood started rushing to odd places. It was the weirdest thing I've ever felt. I wanted to keep doing it.

At last she pushed me away. She stared a moment, then said, "That your first time?"

I wanted to sink through the sidewalk in embarrassment. How could she tell?

Then she grinned. "Well, you've got potential, but you need lots of practice." She took my hand and walked down the sidewalk as if nothing had happened. She was amazing, the way she'd start losing it and then pull it all back together. I think that's probably odd, even for Sapes. The street people ignored us.

A block later, businesses petered out. We passed a few houses, barely stitched to respectability by their scabby picket fences, and reached an overgrown park with rows of tables under shed roofs where they used to have farmers markets. Thoughts of produce – piles of berry pies, mountains of mashed potatoes – stoked my hunger.

Lil plopped on a table to re-tie her sneaker. I ran my finger over her hand and along her leg. "Will Kayla ditch the cops?"

"Probably," Lil said. "She'll head down to the old fish market. They can't follow her in or watch all the exits."

Fish market. I added steamed crabs to my fantasy. Bowls of cioppino. Halibut steaks glistening with butter and lemon, which somehow morphed into Lil wearing no clothes.

*

At Kayla's warehouse, her bike sat in the downstairs lobby. We whooped with relief and clattered up the stairs to thank her. Then I flopped on the sofa, dazed with fatigue, hunger, and horniness. Kayla was sorting through cases of makeup. "Goran, go out in the studio and stay there an hour. And take the cats."

She didn't offer an explanation and I was too tired to ask how many illegal habits these girls had. I whistled up Zax and Gwitchy and followed orders. In the barn-like studio I wandered around looking at her work, massaging my shoulder, trying some *kata* in hopes the calming, recharging movements would take the place of sleep. The cats vaulted to the heavy old trusses and played gymnastics on the beams. At last I leaned against the wall, looking out a window at the harbor and the islands to the west. I must have dozed off standing up. The next time I checked the time, it was fifteen minutes until noon. My hour of exile was up.

I stepped through the apartment door and stumbled to a stop. Two strange girls sat on the sofa. One turned and I recognized the line of Lil's face and neck. Kayla must have hacked off her long, shiny hair, leaving bangs that almost hid her eyes, and dyed her new 'do a deep throbbing red. She'd also worked on Lil's lips, which now looked huge, pouty, and superhot.

By clever analysis, along with the cats' delighted pounces, I deduced that the other girl was Kayla. Her hair, not quite straight, not quite curly, stopped somewhere between her chin and shoulders. Had to be a wig. Its color seemed to be every hair color on earth slopped together and then watered down. Her eyebrows were barely visible, her eyes naked and extinguished. She wore a dirt colored sweatshirt, pants and heavy boots.

She was the drabbest girl I'd ever seen. I wondered if this was the real Kayla, if there *was* a real Kayla.

She laughed. "Fooled you, didn't I?" She turned to Lil. "See? Even Goran didn't recognize us." She got up and demonstrated her new beaten down posture and walk. Then she reached in a pocket for her comm, flipped it open and listened. "Conroy's on his way. We need to get downstairs."

We hefted our stuff and filed out. Downstairs, we cracked the door to watch as the Buick pulled up to the curb, Conroy driving. Someone else sat in the passenger seat.

# CHAPTER 19

From the unpublished Godunov manuscript
*Why We Came to Earth: The Yunko Voyages*

*In the approximately 140 years of ship time between the day our voyagers left Gliese-C and the day their ship returned, our home world changed for the worse to survive the thickening atmosphere. Our population dwindled. Many took refuge underground. Others managed to live on the shade side of the High Peaks, a circle of mountains on our sun side pushed up by the weight of glaciers on our dark side; the arid range rose high enough to reach thinner air. But the thicker atmosphere below caused more heat to circulate to the dark side; higher temperatures melted glaciers, raising the level of lakes, rivers, and seas in the habitable zone. At the same time, more oxygen increased the action of rust and fire, ravaging the drier areas.*

Kayla recognized the passenger first. "It's Janelle."

Conroy assisted Janelle from the car as if she were made of crystal. It's hard to explain Janelle. She was the most beautiful creature I had ever seen. I mean, I was eaten up with lust for Lil – her amber looks, her burglary skills. But Janelle was worthy of endless contemplation. She had eyes as big as that Bambi deer's and was nearly the same color. All I really knew about her was that she was Conroy's girlfriend. And while I took notes in physics class, she drew pictures of pretty girls wearing bizarre clothes. Girls are always drawing pretty girls, like guys draw cars, but according to Kayla, Janelle's a really talented designer.

She didn't look talented today. She looked scared. "Hi, Lil," she managed. "Like your hair."

"What's she doing here?" Lil snarled.

"Riding up to Canada with us," Conroy said.

"No!" Lil said in a near-shout. "If she goes, there won't be room in the car for Davy."

Conroy frowned and moved in front of Janelle.

Lil's anger confused me. I thought she and Janelle were friends.

Janelle seemed bewildered also. "You're taking Davy?"

Obviously, Conroy didn't understand exactly what kind of trip we faced. I stepped closer to him. "Taking Janelle's not a good idea," I whispered. "This trip could be dangerous."

"Huh? Why?"

"We took something from GenAge. They'll be after us. And we can't head straight north to Canada because they'll be watching those routes. We need to head south first, then cut east before we turn north to the border."

He scowled at Kayla. "Dammit! You talked like this was a regular run. Straight north, straight back. Eight hours." Then he moved into my space, towering over me. "How long *will* this trip take?"

"Maybe a night or two on the road. I really think Janelle would be safer staying home."

Conroy pulled Janelle a few feet away and whispered. She shook her head. He whispered again, then escorted her back to the car. He returned to the rest of us, out of Janelle's earshot. "She has to leave. She's pregnant. Her mom already suspects, and her folks will kill her if they find out for sure. She's their meal ticket. They've . . . raised her under glass like a prize pumpkin so they can marry her off to some rich, powerful guy. Which is not me. They think she's at school this morning."

"She can stay at my apartment till you get back," Kayla said.

"I'm not coming back. If I risk waiting until my case goes to trial, I'll end up slaving on the New Skagit Dam."

"They can't sentence minors to forced labor," Kayla said.

Conroy tried to grin. "I turn eighteen in three days. So I'm across the border for good."

Lil jerked my arm. "But there's no room for Davy if Janelle comes along. And he can't stand a long trip. We need to take him straight north."

Kayla put her arm around Lil. "We can't leave Janelle. Particularly if Conroy's not here to protect her. I'll follow you on my bike so Davy can ride in the car."

Wall-to-wall disaster. Unthinkably messy from the Yunko viewpoint. I had no Plan B except somehow dumping the whole crew once we were on the road, so I leapfrogged to the next problem. "Okay, the car's here. We need to go by Lil's immediately and get Davy, then get out of town." I doubted we could get Davy out of Seal Bay, much less all the way to Canada.

Kayla and Janelle went upstairs while Conroy, Lil, and I headed toward Lil's neighborhood in the car. Even with three of us on the sofa-like bench seat in front, the Buick felt as roomy as a small apartment.

"Take the next right," Lil said. Around the corner, houses turned shabbier and yards trashier. Lil's was the last, most dismal house in the line-up.

Obviously a no-go. GenAge's signature black SUVs sat at each end of the block. A third one was parked to watch the rear of the house.

"Go around again," Lil ordered.

"Too dangerous," Conroy said. "They'll remember my car."

"Then stop. I'll sneak through the back yards to our house."

She reached across me for the door handle. I grabbed her hand. "No! They'll be all over you before your foot hits the pavement. No way can we smuggle Davy out right now."

She jerked loose, scrambled halfway over me and grabbed the handle again. "Let go of me!" She had the door partly open before I could pull her hand away, slam the door, cram her on to the floorboard, and flop on top to keep her there.

"You lying bastard!" she screamed, jerking, struggling, and elbowing me anywhere she could reach.

"Stop it, Lil. We'll rescue Davy later. It's too dangerous right now."

"I don't care. I have to save him."

"You can't. Not now. If you try, you'll fail. It'll be a trip straight to Erik Cheyne's office or dungeon or whatever. I promise: we'll get Davy."

She moaned and muttered and slowly returned to sanity. A miserable sanity. At last she said, "God, can't you do anything besides jump on top of me?"

*

Our journey was hardly the streamlined, low profile operation I'd visualized. Conroy drove and I rode shotgun, the cats at my feet. The three girls sat in back. Kayla had decided to abandon her bike and go in the car. I guess even her iron nerves craved company.

Lil had yelled about going back for Davy until we regrouped at Kayla's and loaded the car, even though every one of us told her it was impossible. Now she sat with a baseball cap pulled over her face, pretending to sleep, emitting waves of anguish and fury. Janelle sat in the middle. Kayla, projecting drabness with all her might, sat on the other side.

Conroy took the same escape route through the gap in the Railyards fence. Once on outlaw turf, he stopped, honked twice, then three times. A man emerged from the maze of rail cars and sauntered over. He didn't look First Nation even though he wore a traditional Makah hat, cone-shaped and woven of spruceroot, now tattered and filthy.

Conroy rolled down the window. "Need to pass through to the timber depot."

The sentry nodded.

"Might be somebody coming through on our tail." Conroy pulled out a small plastic bag, his hand hiding the contents, and handed it to the man. "Be good if you could change their minds."

"No problem," the sentry said. He turned and waved to someone hidden in the distance, then walked back in the direction he'd come. No one challenged us as we followed the same route between the rail cars. At least Lil was too upset to make a snarky comment comparing Conroy's ability to get through the Railyards to mine.

Once clear of Seal Bay, Conroy said, "I'll go down to the Anacortes turnoff, cut east to Sedro Woolley, and then turn north. We can cross the border at Sumas.

He still didn't understand. "Can't go that way," I said. "We can't risk crossing the border west of the Cascades. Head to Sedro Woolley, then turn south on the back roads."

"Well, that's stupid," Conroy said. "Why not just drive all the way around the world and come down from the North Pole?"

"Because I want to escape. And I'm the one paying for the trip."

"Then you better get ready to pay for lots more gas."

We rode in silence for several miles. Lil suddenly said, "Pancakes."

"What?" I turned to stare at her tear-swollen face.

"Pancakes. A big stack. Dripping with butter and syrup. With sausage and hash browns. I'm starving and I want to scream."

She sounded unhinged. Maybe she'd regressed to some imaginary childhood where Mom fixed loving breakfasts and Davy was still okay.

Conroy chimed in. "Sounds good to me." He jabbed at me with his elbow. "Treat us to a late breakfast, Moneyman?"

Janelle said, "I waitressed at an IHOP last summer. Near Sedro Woolley. But we probably can't afford anything that fancy."

People say IHOP used to be just an average diner, but these days it was rumored to still serve foods you couldn't find anywhere else. Just the thought made me drool. "Okay," I said. "We can celebrate getting out of Seal Bay."

"You could celebrate by paying me now," Conroy said.

"After we cross the border."

*

A few miles later the IHOP's steep, faded blue roof came into view. The waitress, several notches less dazzling than Janelle, seated us in a large booth. Even with half the items crossed out, the menu was amazing. When the food came we ate until we almost bulged out of the booth. It was an effort to chew by the time Conroy said, "So what's your super route to the border? The one that's so much better than heading toward where we actually want to go?"

I couldn't let Conroy take over this operation, and I didn't want to reveal the Highline route before I had to. GenAge was after Lil and me. The local law was after Conroy, and the drugstore's security tape now documented Kayla's mayhem. That left Janelle. "The crossing's east of here. They don't get many refugees, that far from the coast. When we get there, Janelle can probably drive the car through using her regular ID since the only ones looking for her are family. The rest of us will hike across. We'll rendezvous on the other side."

"What if the guards stop her?" Conroy said.

"Place is tiny. Just one guard. The local timber company that owns the crossing won't pay to link with large databanks. They wouldn't have any reason to suspect Janelle. Might not know that any of us are wanted, but we can't take that risk."

"Won't the motion sensors along the border pick you up?" Kayla asked.

I shook my head. "I know how to get us past the sensors."

"Oh, sure," Conroy came back. "How many days does this take?"

"Look," I said, "just two roads cross the Cascades north of Seattle and they'll both be watched. We need to go farther south before we head east over the mountains."

Frowning, he leaned forward. "South as far as Interstate 90?"

"At least."

"And you think this trip will get dangerous?"

I nodded.

He clinked his fork on his plate a few times. "So what if we go south, cross the Cascades on I-90, then head north by way of Wenatchee? My Uncle Wilbur lives near there. We could leave Janelle with him. I'll get the rest of you across, then come back for her."

Losing one complication seemed like the first positive development since Andrei's panicky call. "Sounds good."

Janelle looked horrified. "No, it doesn't." She tugged on Conroy's arm and whispered. In a moment they rose and headed outside.

I wanted to give him time to convince her so I asked Lil to bring her laptop from the car. When she slouched back in, I gestured to another table. We took our seats wordlessly, like some old couple unhappily married for decades. She didn't boot up the big machine, just glared at me.

"It'd be good," I said, "if we could find out what's happening at GenAge. Can you access their their security communications, or is that too difficult for you?"

Patronizing Sapes usually works. She powered up and viciously poked at the screen. Then she frowned. "They're on some kind of drill or lock down. Says, 'Currently on enhanced operational status. To report concerns, observations, or questions, direct your comments to Otis Lardner.'"

"Who's Lardner?"

"Head of Security," she said slowly. "Their suit-and-tie face man. Goes to board meetings and conferences, talks to clients and stuff. Cheyne's under him as top physical security officer, and some woman whose name I can't remember heads information security."

"So where's Cheyne? Why aren't they reporting to him?"

"Exactly. Maybe he bled to death. Or he's in the hospital."

I hated to say it. "Or in the field, directing operations. Or using a medical leave to come after us personally."

She gave me a look of pure hate and rejoined Kayla in our original booth. I paid the cashier and bought two more orders of sausage for the cats.

*

As Mt. Rainier, a hundred miles away, rose higher above the treetops; the gasoline needle sank lower. We pulled into a gas station unlikely to be connected to any high-tech network. Kayla forked over counterfeit gas coupons and I supplied wads of cash.

The Outpost could track the comm helmet, so they'd know I was out of Seal Bay and heading south. I hoped they didn't know I had a good chunk of the Seal Bay senior class with me. In any case, I couldn't wait any longer to contact them.

Once we'd fueled up and driven a few miles, I told Conroy to pull onto the shoulder at a rest stop where trees marched thickly down the slope. The cats needed to be loose for a while but I didn't want their distraction. I put them on their long leashes and looped the ends over a fence post. The group gave the comm helmet case curious looks when I took it out of the trunk but didn't come out of their food stupor long enough to ask questions. Lil faked busyness with her laptop so she wouldn't have to acknowledge my existence. I squeezed between the strands of a barbed wire fence and headed into the woods.

I'm used to being a loner. I was growing more comfortable with my companions, but after the longest twenty-four hours of my life, I needed a break. And I didn't know if using the comm helmet was safe around pregnant women.

# CHAPTER 20

## Excerpt from the diary of Lil Osborne

*For some stupid reason, I thought I could trust Goran. Ha! Now my little brother's left behind without me to take care of him. Goran's people probably couldn't cure him anyway. I think he just told me that so I'd steal the culture.*

*We're supposed to be on our big, desperate, top-speed escape, but we're just sitting around doing nothing while Goran's off fooling around in the woods. He took this weird thing with him. What the hell is he doing? Contacting foreign powers? Jacking off? Sleeping?*

*Jeez! He's been gone over an hour. I'm going after him.*

I found a flat spot and dropped to the forest's spongy mat of needles and moss, spread my legs for a wider base, and leaned back against a fallen tree with the helmet case in my lap. My position had to be stable enough to prevent injury.

In a complicated pattern, I touched the "decorative" bumps on the case to disarm the self-destruct function and then drew out the helmet. It looks something like a motorcycle helmet – even the amplifier/transmitter crest over the top looks a bit like the biker "Mohawk" in style years ago.

The helmet made me nervous. I did a couple of breathing exercises, pulled it on, adjusted the settings, and initiated the sequence. The familiar sensation of falling through space flowed over me as the helmet set about re-calibrating my brain.

First order of business: I reported getting the culture safely out of Seal Bay. A warm feeling of approval beamed back. I told them I was heading in a roundabout way to the Highline crossing since more direct routes to the border seemed riskier. They transmitted a picture of someone coming to meet me if I needed help, but I declined. Then I almost lost it as the reality of my actions crashed home. I was breaking every Yunko code, every commandment of our long survival, closing every path back to an honorable status.

I was lying to my people. My shame turned to gut-loosening fear. I didn't know if it was actually possible to lie to a comm helmet. I forced down panic long enough to change the subject, inquiring about Andrei.

They gave a nebulous answer and started quizzing me about how I was protecting the culture. I described Andrei's transport case. It was exhausting, trying to hide my thoughts from the force patrolling my brain.

Inspiration hit. I formed the words clearly and thought them at the same time. "If I'm in a public place where I can't use the helmet, can I comm you at a phone number?" Another presence seemed to join the conversation, launching a number to float in my head. I committed it to memory. I'd use it for any future contact.

I sensed more presences arriving. Then I could feel them physically, like needles pushing into my flesh. Just as the Yunko operator asked for more details about my route, the world flew apart. Pain lanced down from my head and out my extremities like Taser hits. I convulsed. My skull and shoulders hammered against the fallen tree until I managed to roll away from the log and bang against the softer ground. In front of me stood a bizarre creature holding the helmet it had jerked off my head. Rational thought fled again and the creature, a grotesque mashup of Lil and a red-headed woodpecker, faded.

A smell stung my sinuses, making me itch insanely until I was clawing at my clothes in the effort to scratch. I controlled myself enough to struggle to my hands and knees, but the earth tilted to the vertical and I crashed to the ground again. The groaning, creaking smell of forest rot deafened me.

I tried to tell the Lil creature to put the helmet back on my head but chewed my tongue instead. Warm blood ran down my chin. When I gestured to my head, I socked myself in the eye. The creature crept closer, clutching the helmet. I went into convulsions again. While I banged around on the ground, it jumped on my bucking body and forced the helmet back on my thrashing head. Darkness. The convulsions eased and then stopped. I seemed to float in space. Bright bursts erupted like a night battlefield as I bobbled through my own synapses.

I tried to sit up. My head reeled. When I touched it, I touched metal. Thank Frayka the helmet had begun re-wiring my brain map to normal functionality. My rapidly swelling eye pressed painfully against the helmet's contact surface. I wept for a minute, or an hour, while Zax and Gwitchy kneaded my belly.

A face peered through the vision plate. A strange girl with killer lips and hair the color of mahogany and sunset. Lil, after Kayla's makeover. I could hear her voice from a great distance. "Goran! Are you okay? Say something!"

"Sh . . .sh . . . shit!" I sputtered, pulling off the helmet. Wrung limp, I collapsed against my log. Lil stared at me, mouth open, irises circled by a ring of white. I tried to take deep breaths and spat blood repeatedly. Just when I needed to think like never before, my brain had turned to oatmeal.

At last I struggled to my feet, shoulder screaming, as feeble as thirty-one-year old Vlad, and shambled toward the trees. "C'mon," I said to Lil and the cats.

She must have been too shocked to speak. We trudged in silence until I asked how she had found me.

"The cats tracked you. I called to you, then yelled. It was like you didn't hear me. I thought you'd passed out or something, so I jerked that thing off your head." She paused, pulled a few needles off a fir tree and sniffed them. "Was that a bad move?"

"Don't worry about it." I wasn't sure we were going the right way until I spotted a deserted cabin I had passed. I hobbled over and sat on a weathered step to rest.

Lil looped the cat's leashes over a post and stood in front of me. "But you have to stop bullshitting me. You didn't come out of some yurt in Siberia. Tell me the truth. Or I'll tell everyone about you. And you'll never get the culture over the border."

Couldn't go back, had to go forward. "A little part of me is from somewhere . . . off planet."

"You mean, like, a space station?"

I shook my head. Bad move.

She actually sneered. "Then I suppose you're an alien?"

"Depends on how you define alien."

"Don't give me that. Will you turn into a slimy, drooling octopus if I piss you off?"

I sighed. "No. I'm pissed off right now, so what you see is what you get."

"Goran, stop lying. Space aliens who just happen to look like people from Siberia? Gimme a break!"

"Our people have been visiting Earth for centuries. We've slowly bred ourselves to look like, to mostly be, human."

She looked both disgusted and ready to run. "How? Raping Siberian women?"

I pressed my fingers into my aching head. What a mess. A vast, all-encompassing mess. "No. Hundreds of years ago, Researchers with the early expeditions collected local specimens, sometimes from people. But they just took DNA swabs. Then they wiped the people's memories so they wouldn't be traumatized when they woke. We never hurt anyone."

Lil couldn't seem to close her mouth. I wished I could permanently wipe *her* memory but the spray was in my backpack in the car. "Look, we've got big problems. We need to figure out what to do next instead of yakking about ancient history. Besides, I'm forbidden to talk about it."

She'd wrapped her arms around her body. Her face seemed distorted with fear. Or maybe transformed with disgust. "Bu . ..bu . . .but what do you *really* look like?"

Great Flaming Frayka! Sapes and their one-track minds! If I'm not just like you, then I'm automatically a monster. The truth would be better than her nightmarish fantasies. I thought back to holograms I'd seen of the First Explorers, their bodies preserved in the Hall of Heroes. "If you're thinking in terms of Earth creatures, I guess our ancestors most resembled, well, kangaroos. With skin like dolphins."

She gaped, then broke into hysterical laughter. Screams of laughter. Sobbing laughter.

Dammit! She was freaking out when she needed to act logical. "Shut up," I shouted over her racket. She slowly calmed down to giggles, but her eyes looked glazed. "What do you expect? We come from a heavy-gravity planet. We evolved with a tripod body configuration for stability. Big eyes, long ears to live in a twilight band – our planet doesn't rotate, so one side's always blinding sunlight, while the other side stays night. And our skin could lighten or darken according to the light level."

"Bouncy bouncy, hippity hop," she giggled.

I grabbed her by the shoulders. "Look, I'm almost ninety-seven percent human, and the other part doesn't show. A few genes from other Earth species. And the alien part mostly has to do with blood chemistry, bone density, breathing, and uh, my central nervous system a little bit."

"Like being a little bit pregnant?"

That snapped it. "Your comedy routine isn't helping Davy."

She jerked as if I'd slapped her. "You're either lying or crazy, and I don't think you can do anything for Davy. You can't even fix yourself. You made me wreck my life just to get your precious culture."

"Doesn't sound like you had much of a life, anyway. Come on. Before the others come after us." We started walking. "You think we can't help? You just saw a demonstration with the comm helmet."

"Well, don't help Davy like that. It'd kill him."

'Just listen, okay? Seventy, eighty years ago, Sape . . . Earth scientists finally discovered reverse transcription-polymerase chain reaction technology. For centuries, our people have used similar techniques to, uh, fix a gene and then get it to replicate throughout the body."

"Can't scientists do that here?"

"Yeah, but their methods are crude as a stone ax. Our techniques are far more advanced."

She stopped and gave me a long look, focusing on my swollen eye. "So you're saying you can repair the defect in Davy's genes all over his body?"

132

I nodded.

"What does that have to do with the helmet whatchamacallit?"

"Davy surely has muscle atrophy in his legs and other places. Human scientists used to think the brain was . . . static. That it basically couldn't change. Brain cells died and were never replaced."

Andrei had been very interested in Sapiens brain research, which seemed as quaint as Earth traditions about the four humours. I tried to remember details from his lectures. "Then humans started discovering more and more about the brain's ability to rewire itself, to repair damage or re-route around it. I mean, even full humans can learn to hear with their skin. Or write with their feet. Or see with a computer program. But your techniques are still like the worst, longest, most barbaric therapy that was ever invented. Only a few people are able to succeed."

"The helmet?"

"The helmet works by rewiring the user's brain into a mode that enables long distance communication. Then, when you're through using it, the helmet rewires the brain very quickly back to normal functionality. When you yanked my helmet off, it hadn't rewired me to a normal state."

"But Davy's really very smart, so how does that help him?"

"Body parts that humans would consider permanently destroyed, like atrophied limbs or damaged retinas? If we can't repair the problem, we can rewire his brain to use another area of his body to compensate for the loss."

We'd almost reached the edge of the clearing. On the grassy swath beyond the last trees, the Buick gleamed in the sunlight. The rest of our crew lolled around.

Lil stopped suddenly. "One more question. If you're so advanced and superior and everything, what the hell were you doing in a dump like Seal Bay?"

"Some of our people go out in pairs, as Researchers and Seconds like Andrei and me. We're scattered around the world, mostly where somebody's doing helpful research."

"A seventeen-year-old, uh, Second? Not hardly."

She still didn't get it. "Our lives are so short, by the time someone's learned enough science to be a Researcher, he or she is too old to do the physical stuff a Second has to do. Besides, I'm older than seventeen in several ways."

She shook herself. "If you're really aliens, why are you on earth anyway?"

The real answer was None of your business, but I didn't think the truth would help. "We aren't here to hurt anyone. We're . . . just working on ourselves."

"Working on yourselves? Like some twelve-step program for freaks?"

How could someone so desirable be so annoying? "Being on Earth has nothing to do with humans. But you absolutely must not say anything, ever, about what you saw and heard."

"Why not?"

"Because we'd end up in some lab being vivisected. If you get people after me, they'll take you too. We'd never get over the border and Davy would never see you again."

"Far as I can tell, we're not getting Davy over the border anyway. He can't make it without me. I'm going back if I have to hitchhike."

"Cheyne identified you. We'll get Davy. I swear it."

"Then what? Why would your secret space people blow their cover to help Davy?"

"I think I see a way. But you can't tell the others."

"They're not stupid. Kayla and Conroy know there's something sketchy about you."

"Just don't tell them, okay?"

"Tell them what?" Her voice broke. "You're mentally ill?" Deep breath. "Your eye looks really awful." She headed down the hill. I followed.

At the car Kayla ran a finger around my swollen eye and smirked. "Lovers' quarrel?"

"Ran into a tree."

In the confusion of leaving, I had forgotten something. "Wait. Give me your comms." I set down the helmet case.

Conroy pulled his comm out and held it at arm's length above his head. "Why?"

"So they won't locate us by pinging the units."

Janelle pulled out her own comm uncertainly. Conroy took it from her and held it up with the other one, expressionless, forcing the confrontation I'd hoped to avoid. "No way. Mine's got important info on it. What're you gonna do with them?"

"Put them where no one can trace them."

"How?"

I nudged the case with my toe. "Put them inside this. It'll block any attempts to locate them." Andrei had once said the helmet case acted like a Faraday cage. Except the Yunko could track the helmet even in the case, so I had to get it away from us too.

Conroy sneered. "You're one big bag of tricks, aren't you? Then what?"

"We mail it to where we're going in Canada."

"And where's that exactly?" Kayla said.

"We need to decide. I'll buy you burners in the meantime. C'mon." I held out my hand to Conroy and he tossed the two units, making sure I had to jump to catch them.

# CHAPTER 21

From the unpublished Godunov manuscript
*Why We Came to Earth: The Yunko Voyages*

*In response to the long emergency, our people on Gliese-C were changing too. Psychologically, we forgot we had ever engaged in wars or adventures or romance or art and music – we thought only of the all-consuming, all-out mission to survive as a species.*

Tree shadows darkened the narrow road from Granite Falls to Monroe, giving the Buick good cover from aerial surveillance. I was thinking about where we'd go in Canada when Conroy said, "Okay. Where do we cross the border and where do we head after that?"

Might as well tell him. "We cross between Danville and Laurier."

"Hell!" Conroy yelped, "That's almost to Idaho. And there's nothing there."

"Which makes it the safest place to cross," I said. "We just need to decide where to go after that."

"Nothing to decide, dude. Janelle and I are going to Vancouver. I've got contacts there and Janelle wants to start work on a clothing line. If not Vancouver, Toronto's her next decent market."

That seemed pretty definite. "Kayla?"

"Vancouver works for me. Lots of graphics work there." She added so softly I didn't think the others heard, "And it's still a continent away from my father."

Lil kept her head down, hiding her expression. "Like I have a choice? Davy can't stand any trip longer than directly across the border from Seal Bay to Vancouver."

"Okay," I said. "Next stop, we mail everything to Vancouver." For once the Sapes had agreed immediately instead of arguing.

Pastures and fields began to break up the forest. I tried to mentally push the car faster across the exposed stretches. The Buick escapes notice about as well as a circus wagon, and we could all be easily connected to Conroy's car. Anyone who bothered talking to Seal Bay students would find out that we knew each other, and that all five of us were missing.

If an alert went out for a 1956 beetle-blue Buick, halfway decent aerial surveillance would spot it easily. I hadn't heard any helicopters, but drones were often silent. Back when the government pretty much sold everything off to corporations, several big corps bought armed military drones. I wanted to ask Lil if she'd ever heard of GenAge drones, but she was already standing on the cliff edge of crazy. The idea of Erik Cheyne watching her silently from above might push her over.

Coming into Monroe, Washington, the highway passed a large shopping center. Several stores were still open. Conroy pulled in and we headed toward the apps store to buy burner comms.

Before we left the store, I asked a clerk where we could physically mail a package. She pointed to a storefront across the stretch of asphalt. "Mel's Mail. Truck picks up packages once a day, takes 'em to Seattle. They send them on from there."

It sounded insecure but it also sounded like the only game in town. U.S. post offices were mostly boarded up or converted to Rent-a-Lockbox places. At Mel's Mail, the clerk sold me packing filler and a large box. I put the comms inside the helmet, packed it up in the case, then in the box, as carefully as I could, and addressed it to the name on the ID Kayla had made, at a UPS Store on Cambie Street in Vancouver.

Before we got in the car, I pulled Conroy away from the others. "I'm worried about surveillance – air and ground. Probably not another car like yours in the whole state."

"You're right. I checked. It's the only one." He looked pleased.

"Yeah, well, we need to figure out how to get across the mountains without being spotted. The major highways are real bottlenecks."

Conroy looked around as if he could magically see all possible routes, then pointed with his chin. "Head south on Highway 203. It turns into Highway 202 and runs along the Snoqualmie River. Go down to North Bend, take a break until after dark, say, eleven o'clock. Then head east on some back roads I know. They'll take us more than halfway across the mountains. By the time we have to get on I-90, shouldn't be anybody watching."

"Why North Bend?"

"They're having fire trials. Today and tomorrow."

"Fire trials?"

"Yeah. Sort of a cross between a job fair, track meet, and death in the arena. With inland fires so bad, they need lots more firefighters. Around here, TopPick Fire Services does the recruitment and training. TopPick doesn't spend much on good equipment or training so they go through personnel pretty quick."

"How come you know so much about it?"

"Tried it once. Only jobs around were firefighter or being a pollinator

138

along with the refugees, slogging around fields and orchards all day long with those stupid little artist brushes."

"So did TopPick hire you?"

"Nah. They were still being total hard asses about age limits back then, and I was barely sixteen. But they keep sending notices to anyone who's ever applied. They hold the trials at North Bend's middle school. First day's mostly physical tests and checking whether you'll panic on a fire line. Then on the second day, whoever survived the first day takes written exams. They don't want to waste money training someone that won't make it. Probably be a crowd at the trials. Good camouflage. Lot of them'll want something that gives a little edge in the tryouts. I can sell some product and we can hang around till after dark. Then hit the back roads."

Just what we needed – Conroy selling drugs. Problem was, I didn't have a better plan. And since Conroy had specialized knowledge of sneaking around, I might as well use it.

*

We drove through sleepy North Bend to the eastern outskirts. Then we headed north until it looked like we'd run smack into towering Mount Si. Its rounded, wrinkly crest loomed over the middle school where the fire trials were underway. Conroy drove around the buildings to the playing fields in back. The parking lot was almost full, and a sizable crowd surrounded the near end of the practice field. He found an empty spot, turned, and backed into it. A thick band of trees edged the asphalt.

We piled out of the car. Even here, still west of the Cascades, smoke flavored the scent of pine needles. Conroy whacked my sore shoulder. "I'll go check out the crowd, see if it looks promising. It'll take a while. You wanna go along? Stay here? What?"

"I need to let the cats out for a while. I'll take 'em into the trees for a break. Maybe catch some sleep myself."

He shrugged, lifted the back seat, and took out baggies. I picked up the cat pack and walked into the strip of woods. A hundred feet into the trees, I found a fifteen-meter wide concrete circle, speckled with .moss and an occasional weed . Way too big for a tetherball court. Some kind of assembly area? Maypole, maybe? I set the cats' anchor beacon for a slightly wider radius and let Zax and Gwitchy out. Soon they were darting in short bursts, like kittens practicing sprints. I moved around the circle until I could see the car through the trees and settled down for a nap. Janelle had already found a nice patch of grass just outside the concrete and dozed off.

Across the circle, Kayla and Lil settled into a patch of sunlight. The tone and cadence of their voices sounded like an argument. I could almost see the balance of dominance flowing back and forth between them. Was that a Sape thing? A friendship thing? A female thing? I drifted toward sleep myself.

An hour later Lil shook me awake. She looked different, kneeling on the patchy moss. Her face was blotchy and her eyes were red, but she wasn't glaring or screaming at me.

When I sat up, she said, "Goran, can we talk?"

"Sure."

She told me Kayla had given her a rough time about distracting everyone, particularly me, putting us all in danger. "But ever since we left . . ." Tears started. She inhaled sharply, trying to stop them. "Whenever I close my eyes, I see some security goon throwing Davy on a cold concrete floor in some GenAge basement. With no meds to ease his pain." She broke down again. "And him thinking I abandoned him."

I scooted over and put my good arm around her shoulders. It seemed the proper Sape thing to do.

When she could continue, she said, "Kayla asked if I could call anyone who could check on Davy. I . . . couldn't get up the nerve so Kayla called Mary Lee Griffin – that's Mrs. Griffin's daughter. Mrs. Griffin lives next door and babysits Davy sometimes"

"What did she say?"

"Her mom went over to our house about noon and reamed out the GenAge stooges so bad, they helped her bundle Davy up and carry him next door to her house so she could feed him and take care of him."

Then the tears again. At last she said, all in a rush, "I'm sorry I blamed you for leaving Davy behind. It wasn't really your fault." Then she hurried back to Kayla and they went into another huddle.

So, no rants and curses today. I exhaled. I wouldn't fail her again. I sat and watched the two of them, wondering how Sapes always found so much to talk about. Then I moved my shoulder through a series of positions, most of which hurt. I tried to retrieve the faint traces of a dream that had evaporated when Lil shook me – some mashup of fables told to children. Something about an army invading a kingdom, and a hunter begging the king to let him spirit the princess away to a safe hiding place.

I couldn't remember how the story ended, or whether the tale came from Evenki legends or ancient Orbian lore. We were taught to listen to our dreams, but I had no idea what this one was trying to tell me other than the obvious: We were on the run. Was Lil the princess I had to rescue?

A large, black SUV with darkened windows circled through the parking lot. I slid farther down the tree I was leaning against. The vehicle paused as it passed the Buick. According to Andrei, black SUVs used to be as common as cockroaches, but few people drive the gas hogs nowadays.

The driver could have been a Fire Trial applicant intrigued by the antique vehicle. Or GenAge security.

We needed to disappear, and for that we needed a less noticeable ride. Maybe my dream had actually been about the car. Suppose I was the hunter, Conroy was the king, and the four-hole Buick was the princess. Maybe I needed to convince Conroy that the best way to keep his princess safe was to hide her away. I headed to the practice field to talk to him.

Much of the crowd looked about our age. Physically, they ranged from semi-skeletal to workout maniacs. Plenty of older ones too. Local farmers. Survivalist relics. Would-be midnight cowboys and Indian wannabes.

One group was on the football field, wearing numbers like track competitors and attempting events that looked much too difficult for them – running and climbing ladders while carrying rescue mannequins or wearing large backpacks, dragging heavy hoses, cutting down thick posts with chainsaws. On a podium marked with the TopPick logo stood three men wearing expensive outdoor gear. They held stopwatches and marked clipboards steadily.

Conroy was deep in negotiations with a couple of guys. I waited until they walked away before going over. "I need to talk to you."

He rooted in his backpack. "About what?"

I told him about the black SUV snooping around and added, "Anyone who sees the Buick remembers it." I frowned. "Might be an alert out for it. A drone could take it out easy."

"No way some puke's gonna damage my car."

"Where'd you find it anyway?"

"Where we're headed. My Uncle Wilbur's place near Wenatchee. I lived with him growing up. Worked all one summer for the Buick. Back then it was nothing but a hunk of rusted-out metal."

"What's your uncle do?"

"Auto repair shop. Collects old cars on the side. Still has a barn full of them. He thinks they'll be worth a fortune someday when the gasoline comes back."

It sounded promising. "When we get to his place and drop off Janelle, you think he'd hide the Buick in his barn, then lend us or sell us a different vehicle?"

"Yeah, 'cept he'd try to keep the Buick for himself, now I've got it all mint. So no, I don't want to leave it there."

We turned as the PA system squealed. One clipboard jockey read off a string of numbers and told those people to sit down on the bleachers. Then he read off another, longer, string and told them to go home. A fresh group of desperados took the field.

141

I tried one more time. "Leaving the car with your uncle beats a GenAge drone blasting it off the road with us in it, including Janelle."

"What's your scam, Goran? How'd you get GenAge after you and Lil anyway?"

I hesitated. "I can't talk about it. I took something because I thought it could save my brother's life."

"Is he sick?"

"Degenerative condition. What about the car?"

"I'll think about it."

We headed back to the girls. In the parking lot, security guards hustled a food vendor and his cart toward the exit. It was almost five o'clock. Might be our last opportunity to eat for the next few hours. Conroy loped after the eviction team and I followed. The security dicks lectured the guy about not paying the fee, gave him a couple of kicks, and left. We bought his remaining stock, which consisted of herring and cheese hoagies and breaded ratfish sandwiches, and headed for our patch of woods.

We handed out sandwiches and settled down. Conroy said, "I've been thinking. The Buick's too noticeable. We can leave it at my uncle's in Wenatchee and take another vehicle."

I didn't mind giving him credit for the plan if he'd just go along with it.

He added, "But first we have to get it over the mountains without somebody spotting it. I think we should wait till dark and then take some back roads I know."

I was itching to leave immediately, but I waited to see what the others would say. Lil started talking about returning to Seal Bay and cooking up a plan with Mrs. Griffin to rescue Davy. It was painful to listen.

Kayla interrupted her. "Camouflage it."

"How? Put a wig on it?" Conroy said. "You can't cover the Buick with clown paint like you cover yourself."

"Sure you can," Kayla said. "Way back during that war with the Nazis, my great-grandfather worked with the U.S. army painting these dummy tanks and trucks to fool the enemy. That's how he got the idea to start his company after the war."

"You're not putting paint on my car."

"What company's that?" I asked, curious about Kayla's history.

She ignored my question. "Why are you trying to eat with your left hand?"

I reached across and touched my right arm. "Bad shoulder."

They started laughing and joking about other things I couldn't do with my right hand. I focused on trying to eat and tearing off bites for the cats.

I'd heard of being alone in the middle of a crowd. But was this my crowd? Sitting around playing and joking like children? I wanted to join in, and I wanted to yell at them to stop dawdling and get out of here.

The PA system whined again. One of the TopPick weenies instructed the applicants to gather up their belongings and find a place on one of the firetrucks or in their private vehicles. The group would convoy to the wildfire test site just past Cle Elum.

Cle Elum. "Get up!" I almost shouted. "Get your stuff in the car. We have to hurry."

They gaped at me.

"Cle Elum's almost across the mountains. We'll join the convoy. Even if they spot us, what can GenAge do?"

The others grabbed their belongings while I caught the cats. We piled into the car and pulled through the middle school parking lot toward the exit road. As the convoy vehicles passed, Conroy nosed the heavy old Buick forward like a bulldozer, forcing his way into the line.

# CHAPTER 22

## Excerpt from the diary of Lil Osborne

*Worst argument ever with Kayla! She thinks I'm the problem for being mad at Goran for breaking promises. For distracting him. Like I should just forget about Davy? Act like Goran's normal? Pretend we're in some video game?*

*Just to make her shut up, I woke Goran and apologized for blaming the situation on him. Then I went back and told Kayla she didn't know the half of it. Told her Goran was mentally ill. Described what happened when I pulled that helmet thing off his head, which made him think he was a space alien. But he does seem to have contact with some sort of high tech operation he claims is in Canada. Or else he really is a space alien – at this point I wouldn't be surprised. Kayla didn't say much until Goran and Conroy came back with these awful sandwiches.*

When we reached the wildfire test site, a firetruck blocked the road ahead. Firefighters and TopPick personnel were waving the convoy vehicles off the two-lane road, through a gate, and into a pasture. More flunkies directed the vehicles to park in long lines.

Conroy parked the Buick. "That's a public highway. They'll have to move that firetruck pretty soon. Probably when the convoy's all inside."

I looked around. Cars were now parking in lines in front of us, and a large clump of scrubby junipers rose five feet behind. "You want to get out and wander around? Lend me the keys. I'll let the cats out for a few minutes, then lock them inside and catch up with you."

Conroy handed me the keys. They all got out and ambled toward a crowd of potential recruits that was sorting itself out. I took Zax and Gwitchy over behind the junipers so they could pee and sniff around.

By the time we returned to the car, a crew was heading toward the firetruck to move it. The car keys, cats, and culture were all in my possession. I could leave the others here and complete my mission properly. I tried to revive my Yunko sense of duty. I told myself I'd actually keep my friends safer by decoying any pursuers away with the Buick.

But as I watched the others, Janelle leaned against Conroy for support. She bent over slightly, maybe suffering nausea. With quiet gentleness, badass Conroy put an arm around her and brushed a lock of hair from her face.

No. I couldn't steal their only means of escape.

*

"Please stop."

Conroy swerved the Buick onto the shoulder and hit the brakes. Janelle pushed the passenger door open and leaned over, Conroy's hand on her back. Pregnancy – combined with car sickness, stress, and a dubious diet – was battering Janelle with nausea. At least she didn't actually heave this time. She just shuddered a couple of times and then got out and stood in the misty, chilly night taking deep breaths.

She got back in and slumped. "Sorry. False alarm." A moment later she added, "Goran, can I have another bonbon?"

"Sure." I dug a bonbon out of the medkit and handed the walnut-sized lump of highly concentrated nutrients over the front seat to her. My supply was getting low, but the bonbons seemed the only food Janelle could keep down. Her nausea had started soon after we escaped the fire site. After the first vomit stop, I'd switched places with her, hoping she'd find the front seat more comfortable. Didn't work. By the time we'd driven thirty miles up Highway 97, Janelle was suffering from a miserable combo of dehydration, hunger, and nausea. She needed nourishment she could keep down.

I didn't know what effect the Yunko bonbons would have on a seventeen-year-old pregnant Sapiens. An analysis of the nuggets would show a long, familiar list of vitamins, minerals and proteins, although in odd proportions, plus a residue that defied identification. But the situation seemed serious. I had pinched off a tiny piece. "See if this agrees with you."

"What is it?"

"A food supplement."

She put it in her mouth, savored it, and swallowed. "Can I have some more?"

"Wait fifteen minutes, see how you feel."

After that she gobbled bonbons as often as I'd let her have them. I still worried about their eventual effect, but her nausea calmed down. My shoulder felt better too, even though I was squeezed between Lil and Kayla.

I wanted out of the car. I could almost feel the Buick's memories seeping out of the leather and metal. I was pretty sure the car was trying to make me feel guilty about wanting to dump it. Even more, I wanted out of Washington State and over the Canadian border, particularly if snow was expected. Then there was the tissue culture. It had been in the transport case for nearly forty-eight hours. Supposedly, the case would keep samples viable for eight days, but I didn't really trust that claim. We needed to reach Canada ASAP for all sorts of reasons.

Several miles after we turned onto Highway 2, Conroy said, "Almost there." He slowed and turned right onto a gravel road. It ran uphill from the farmland through scrubby trees and rounded a couple of bends into a clearing. A shabby double-wide trailer sat on the right and a huge barn straight ahead. A light came on in the trailer, outlining a tall, bulky form standing in the door.

"That's Uncle Wilbur," Conroy said. "I'll talk to him." He got out and loped across the yard yelling, "Hey, Wilbur! Don't shoot! It's me. Conroy."

They stood on the stoop talking for several minutes. Then Wilbur disappeared inside. He returned with a flashlight and walked down the steps. Conroy got back in the Buick. "So far, he's listening. Don't know how much he'll charge us though."

Wilbur slouched across the yard toward the barn, his head sunk between his shoulders. When he reached the barn he stuck the flashlight in his pocket so that its beam played up the warped wood of the huge building. He threw his weight into rolling aside the double doors, stepped into the barn, and flipped on the lights. Conroy eased the Buick under the steep, three-story roof. It reminded me of video scenes where the space shuttle glides into the vast, shadowy sanctuary of the mother ship.

Wilbur walked backward, waving us farther into the dusty interior. He looked like Conroy after another thirty hard years, blue eyes faded to old denim, dusty blond hair just a fringe around his skull instead of a scalp lock on top. When the car stopped, we untangled our stiff bodies, staggered out and stared at the collection of metal relics backed into the former horse stalls.

Janelle opened the passenger door.

"Well, well, well!" Uncle Wilbur hurried over and helped her out of the car. "A fine looking lady in a fine looking car. Three beautiful girls you two guys brought with you!" He kept his hands on Janelle longer than necessary. Conroy's face tightened.

"Five o'clock's coming up," Uncle Wilbur chortled. "Time to start breakfast." He herded the girls out of the barn with excessive pats.

Once in the trailer, Wilbur urged us to the dining table.

"I need to just lie down on the sofa, " Janelle said.

"Me, too." Kayla started toward the trailer's main room. Lil followed.

"Whoa, you little fillies," Wilbur boomed. "You're not lazy bones are you? The kind that rolls around in the bed all day? You all come back to the table. Get some food in you, it'll perk you up."

They trudged back.

Whatever his story, Wilbur had plenty of food and he cooked it quickly. Before we could doze off, he set scrambled eggs, kippers and home fries before us. After a few bites, he jabbed his fork toward me. "Where you from, boy?"

"Seal Bay."

"Nah. I mean, where your people from? You don't look American."

"First Nation, way up the coast."

"Tsimshian?"

Close enough. I nodded.

Wilbur leaned back in his chair, stared at me, and then to my horror, unleashed a torrent of Sm'algyax, the Tsimshian tongue. He finished up with, "Well, boy, whacha say about that?"

I tried to dredge up vocabulary, hoping I had the correct tribe. "Uh, *smhawks,*" I said. I think it meant "I believe you," but it might have meant "southeast wind."

Wilbur roared with laughter, then asked Conroy, "Where'd you find this guy?"

Conroy, in an edgy mood anyway, eyed me. "He found me. And don't ask me where he comes from. Matter 'a fact, he's just stuffed with secrets." He jabbed Kayla in the ribs. "You know his story?"

"Oh, weirder than we could possibly guess, I'd say." She stared at me oddly. "Supposed to be an ordinary high school student. Fat chance."

"Yeah? What do you know about it?" I snapped. Breakfast was turning bad really fast.

"Why, it's the hereditary family business–making things look like something they're not."

"Then why're you hanging around with us?" I told myself to stop pushing, but stress, pain, and fatigue won the battle. "Why don't you go home and work at the family store?"

Kayla's face, the face she worked so hard to make forgettable, distorted into a near-snarl. "Family members who go home have a way of ending up dead."

Lil stood up and yelled, "Stop it! All of you."

Amazingly, we all did, staring around the table like guilty children. Wilbur chuckled.

When things get tricky, retreat is the recommended action. I rose. No one spoke. Outside, I whistled up the cats and headed down the gravel road. The drizzle had stopped but the air felt saturated. The cats nosed their way through the weeds alongside the road. Maybe I'd just keep walking until all my problems fell away like drips from the leaves. I had thought the others were becoming my friends. Wrong again.

I'd walked half a mile when I spotted a glow through the trees more distinct than the light pollution from Wenatchee. I scrambled up the muddy slope and through the brush to a small ridge. The light came from a decrepit all-night convenience store on the highway below me. The store might still have an old landline that wouldn't be monitored. I should probably contact the Outpost again.

We descended toward the store's predawn glare, Zax and Gwitchy high-stepping across the damp ground. Lights swept across the parking lot when a large SUV turned in. I ducked behind a pine and called the cats in close. I couldn't tell if it was the same vehicle that had been snooping around the Buick in North Bend, but I had to assume any black SUV meant trouble.

The vehicle parked. The store's lights silhouetted two men in the front seat, the driver with a cap, the passenger with something white around his head. The driver got out and headed into the store. I melted back a few feet and faded through the trees toward the rear, looking for an angle that would give me a better view of the passenger's face. He rolled down his window and tossed a drink can.

The heavy air carried his scent. The cats went tense. Zax started a low whine that rose to a scream almost shrill enough to rattle the glass storefront. Just as I grabbed the combative cat and dove into the weeds, the passenger looked toward the noise in the woods. I recognized Erik Cheyne, his head and ear – or possibly missing ear – circled by a bandage.

# CHAPTER 23

From the unpublished Godunov manuscript
*Why We Came to Earth: The Yunko Voyages*

*Our 1325 expedition began work on designing a respiratory system that could handle the atmospheres of both Laboratory Earth and Gliese-C. The most promising approach combined human lungs with the "gill tracheae" common to life forms on Gliese-C. The gill tissues could be activated as needed by either exposing them to air or covering them with skin grafts.*

I grabbed Gwitchy and lay on the struggling Zax. Trained they were, but they lusted for another sweet taste of Erik Cheyne's blood. I hoped he took the feline scream for an angry mountain lion.

The driver returned to the SUV, and headlight beams jerked across the hillside as they turned and pulled onto the highway. From my prone position, I couldn't see whether the vehicle turned east toward Wenatchee or west toward Uncle Wilbur's place. We lay on the soggy ground for thirty more seconds before I rose and ran back toward Uncle Wilbur's. At the last curve, I veered into the trees in case the trailer was under attack, but the clearing looked peaceful in the dawn light.

Conroy was asleep on the living room couch. The girls and Uncle Wilbur were nowhere in sight. I searched kitchen cabinets and set coffee to brewing before I shook Conroy awake and told him about spotting Cheyne.

"How the hell did he follow us?" Conroy mumbled.

"Beats me."

"That SUV, the one you saw in North Bend?" He sat up and scratched his scalp lock to stimulate thought. "Maybe they planted a tracker on the car. You said you were watching but you musta missed it."

"No."

"We need to check it again when it gets light." Conroy rose and filled a cup. "Goran, I trust you like I'd trust a fourteen-year-old tonic junkie. You got us into this mess and it keeps getting worse. How much danger are we in?"

"I don't know."

"Too lame. Try again."

"Okay. When they left the store, I don't know whether they took off or holed up nearby. Or whether they know we're here at Wilbur's or just in the general area. Much less how many personnel and their plan of attack."

"Think I'll still leave Janelle here. I don't want her scared and worried right now." Conroy put his cup down. "I'm gonna tell her we're taking off soon as we check the car." He rose and headed down the hall, silently opened a door, and slipped in.

Janelle and Conroy emerged from the bedroom arguing in whispers. They sat on the sofa, Janelle hunched in the corner. "Goran," she said, "did you tell Conroy to leave me here?"

I shook my head.

"Well, whoever's idea it was, you not leaving me behind. Do you guys even begin to grasp how creepy Uncle Wilbur is?" The two resumed their fierce whispering.

I didn't have enough information to come up with a decent escape plan. At last I said, "Janelle, we need to talk to Lil about GenAge. Can you get her and her laptop? Try not to wake Uncle Wilbur. "

She rolled her eyes at the idea and rose. Five minutes later she returned with Lil and Kayla. Both looked half asleep. I recounted my trip to the store and watched fear paralyze Lil's face. She put the laptop on the coffee table, then ducked into the kitchen and out of sight.

Kayla stared after her with a worried expression, leaned close to me, and whispered, "You shouldn't have told her about Cheyne. He's poison. I mean really. Rumor is, some mercenary force kicked him out during the Middle East wars. Too sadistic even for them. Lil won't talk about exactly what went down with him, but ever since, she's kept to herself even more."

"Hate to ask her but we don't have much choice."

Lil emerged, face stiff, holding two cups of coffee. She handed one to Kayla and settled herself.

"Can you hack GenAge security again?" I said. "Find out where they think we are now?"

She set her cup on the coffee table, opened the laptop, and booted up. Conroy stared into space. Kayla and Janelle started scrounging a snack. They probably figured we'd better eat whenever food was available. I sneaked down the hall to the bathroom to wash up.

When I returned, Kayla and Janelle brought over a jar of jam that had never seen a fruit tree and a plate of toast. Lil ate with one hand while working the keyboard with the other, her eyes glued to the screen so intently she kept missing her mouth with the toast.

At last she leaned back and sighed. "Found the expense log. Looks like about a third of the force are on field duty; they're filing expenses from the northern stretch of Interstate 5. And the copter's flying out of their Bellingham satellite office. Makes me think they're searching between Seal Bay and the border."

She grimaced, jammed her hands in her armpits as if they were freezing and stared at the ceiling. "The orders are still under the name of Otis Lardner, Head of Security." She heaved a sigh that was almost a sob. "So my guess is, the official hunt's still focused on the direct route to the border. And Cheyne's still officially on sick leave, but he's running his own private hunt."

"Why?"

"Revenge. On you and me. And the cats."

I wasn't convinced, but I said, "You think he'd go after Conroy and Kayla and Janelle too?"

She swallowed. "Cheyne's completely psychotic toward anyone who crosses him in any way. He'd probably hurt them just for helping you and me."

\*

With full daylight, Conroy drove the Buick out of the barn. While he searched the body and the interior for a tracking chip, I took Uncle Wilbur's flashlight from a tool pile and slid under the car to check its ancient metal underpinnings.

Footsteps approached. Someone kicked my foot. "Find anything?" Lil's voice said.

"No." I slithered out and stood. "Car's clean."

"Did the guy driving Cheyne look Asian?"

"I didn't get a good look. Why?"

"I've been poking around the GenAge public website. They have a 'Coming Soon' page that advertises half a dozen products still in development. One of them looks like Andrei's transport case. Another one is an implantable infusion pump for anti-rejection drugs."

I didn't see the connection but waited for her to continue.

"A couple months ago, this weird thing happened. The lab that's working on the infusion pump – Lab 4B – paged me. The lab boss met me at the entrance, handed me the case that holds the infusion pump, and said to take it to a fabricating lab on the second floor." Lil hugged herself and paced back and forth in the frosty clearing. "Each lab keeps its log book by the door, on the secretary's desk. But the secretary was gone and I didn't see the book. The boss said she'd already logged out the pump case."

Conroy had come over to listen. "What's that have to do – "

Lil held up a hand. "Hang on. The pump was directed to Craig Yamamoto. I took it down to the fab lab and left it with the secretary."

"Who's Craig Yamamoto?" I said.

"One of the machinists. Word is, he can make almost anything." She stopped again, grimaced as if her lips were numb. "And he's Erik Cheyne's flunky. Runs errands for Cheyne, helps him with . . . illegal stuff. Anyway, a few days later, I went back to Lab 4B with a hard copy doc the lab boss needed to sign immediately. I asked the secretary to carry it back to her boss's office. While she was gone, I flipped through the log book on her desk. No one ever signed out the pump case."

"Kinda odd," Conroy said, "you going back to the same office so soon."

Lil shook her head. "That's mostly what interns do – tote stuff back and forth that has to be physically delivered. We're cheaper than a pneumatic tube system."

"I still don't get it," Conroy said.

"The carrying case for a research prototype was secretly transferred to Yamamoto, the fabricating genius," Lil said slowly. "But why? What did Yamamoto do to it? It's a prototype. Andrei's transport case is also a prototype."

I was starting to see a fuzzy outline. "You think Cheyne's buddy Yamamoto is doing something to all the GenAge prototypes? Or their cases?"

She nodded. "Like maybe hiding a tracking chip on them. And they don't want anyone else knowing about it, so the chip probably transmits just to Cheyne's comm – "

"You're way out on a limb," Conroy said, "just 'cause you didn't see something in a log book."

"Okay, then you tell me why Cheyne and a guy who could be Yamamoto are hot on our trail while the rest of GenAge security is wandering around Bellingham."

Conroy stared at the sky a few moments. "I'm sure you can also explain why Cheyne and the machinist are bothering to mess with this."

"Money?" Lil squeezed her eyes shut and pressed both fists against her skull to force thought. "They track the prototypes . . . so they can divert them. Like, long enough for a rival corp to steal any breakthrough technology before the GenAge product hits the open market." She opened her eyes. "Does that make any sense?"

"Not a whole hell of a lot," Conroy said.

I tried to process it. "Then they must have tracked us from the beginning. Why haven't they attacked already?"

Lil shrugged. "Maybe Cheyne was too out of it to focus. Maybe they wanted to see where we go. Who we meet. Whatever it was, they're on our trail now."

"Every tangle of snakes has a simple answer," Conroy said, starting

154

toward the trailer, "like just searching the damn case for a chip. I need more coffee."

We followed. Janelle and Kayla had given up on sleep so we gathered around the table to examine the transport case. The main body of the cylinder gleamed silvery. The keypad, ports, and readouts were set into plastic teardrop shapes of deep blue.

We poked, prodded, and turned it over. At last Conroy said, "Nothing there. Waste of time."

But Janelle picked up the case by the blue handle attached to one long side. "That handle's too big and clunky. It's too big in comparison to the case."

Kayla squinted at the case. "She's right."

I didn't see it myself, but they were the experts on Sape design. I reached for the case. The attachments for the handle looked typical – smooth metal rectangles passing through plastic openings like hinge knuckles. The plastic handle itself was roughly oval in cross-section, with decorative grooves running lengthwise. I used my knife to pry the rectangles far enough open to remove the handle. When I pried at the grooves, two split apart. And inside was a chip, mounted securely to prevent it rattling.

I was about to pry it out of its clip when Kayla said, "Stop! If the signal is interrupted or changed in any way, they might attack immediately."

She was right. I reassembled the handle and bent the attachments back together to attach it to the case. One mystery solved. It hadn't really made sense for a bigwig like Cheyne to come after us personally just for revenge. But sure, he'd come after us if we could expose whatever scam he was running with the prototypes.

We kicked possible solutions around and were talking about possibly jamming the signal when Uncle Wilbur emerged from his lair. The morning sun didn't do him any favors. He shuffled to the kitchen, grumbling about how no one had fixed him a second breakfast, even with three women in the house, scrounged a piece of toast, and shoved his chair in between Janelle and Lil.

A minute later he said, "Sounds like what you need, I got." He enjoyed our curiosity a few moments before adding, "Old GPS jammer around here somewhere. Cost you, though."

I believed him. The jammers have been illegal for years. Just the sort of thing Uncle Wilbur would love. "How much?"

Uncle Wilbur grinned so wide a crumb of toast fell from his teeth.

"We need another vehicle, too," Conroy added.

*

Two hours later, after searching through Uncle Wilbur's vehicle museum, we were ready to leave. Kayla carried the detached handle of the transport case and the jammer fitted with a new battery. She grinned with delight as she nudged Uncle Wilbur's old Harley panhead around the clearing. Uncle Wilbur sat behind the wheel of the Buick. The rest of us, along with the cats and our gear, crowded into a Ford Econovan with Conroy driving. At least my backpack was lighter since almost all the cash Andrei had left me now belonged to Uncle Wilbur.

I cased the clearing once more. Kayla sat astride the motorcycle ready to scream down the road at my signal. With the chip transmitting, she would ride almost to the highway, turn into the sparse trees, and head in a different direction before she jammed the signal. As she rode farther from us, jamming and unjamming, she'd lure away pursuers long enough for us to escape, while outrunning the bad guys herself. We hoped. She swore she could do it without getting caught. Using different routes, we would rendezvous on the other side of the Columbia River. The plan was insanely dangerous, most of all for Kayla, but it was the best we had.

When I raised my hand, she roared off. We waited two minutes before Uncle Wilbur put the Buick in gear and followed. Five minutes later Conroy started the Econovan. We planned to meet across the river at the Wenatchee Valley Mall, which, according to Wilbur, had become a giant U-squat and swap meet center. Then we'd head north for the border, skirting east of the lingering forest fires.

When we reached the highway it was empty in both directions. Conroy turned east toward Wenatchee. Still too tense to talk, we watched every vehicle we encountered as we followed the main street through downtown.

We made it safely across the bottleneck of the river bridge. At last Conroy turned into the mall parking lot and drove between rows of tents and tables loaded with stuff to sell. In the shadows cast by the almost deserted mall buildings, we found Wilbur, leaning against the fender of the Buick and smoking a huge, home-rolled cigar he'd bought from a peddler. We pulled in beside him, shielding as much of the Buick as possible from view. The girls got out to stretch and buy skewers of meat from a grill tent nearby. As my hunger waned, my worry grew. Thirty minutes later, Kayla had still not appeared.

# CHAPTER 24

From the unpublished Godunov manuscript
*Why We Came to Earth: The Yunko Voyages*

*The team adding human characteristics and organs to the ancestral Gliese-C body faced endless complexities on both the molecular and cellular levels. They also encountered a problem of the simplest kind. Our tripodal bodies, evolved on a heavy gravity planet, carry most of our mass in the legs, tail-leg and lower abdomen, tapering inward and upward to a small upper torso and arms. There simply wasn't room in our natural chest cavities to add a pair of human-size lungs.*

We paced the lanes of the huge market, worrying and watching the highway over the Wenatchee River bridge; one of its lanes fed directly into our derelict mall. We griped about how long Kayla was taking, but nobody dared say she might not make it back at all.

Conroy hovered over the Buick in a trance, caressing its glowing, deep blue finish. At last he shook himself and walked over to Uncle Wilbur and me. "Kayla ever gets her lazy ass back here, we can head up along the river, cut east on Highway 2, then head north and cross the Columbia again at Grand Coulee." He turned to me. "We're headed for the Kettle River area?"

No point in revealing details early. I nodded.

"Well," Conroy said, "just north of the dam there's a little place called Elmer City. We can take a back road from there across to Highway 21. It'll take us straight north."

Distracted by a faint rumbling, I nodded again. Conroy kept talking until the sound grew so loud people started looking around. A man down the row yelled, "Hit the deck! The 'Poons!" The market heaved like a kicked ant hill with people stowing away their goods and hiding their kids.

A glittering army of bikers topped the arch of the bridge and poured down the road into the mall. I nudged Uncle Wilbur. "Who's that?"

He spat. "Filthy, rotten, rat-roasting Harpoons, that's who." At our stares, he added. "Biker gang. Do jobs for whoever wants somebody intimidated. They carry harpoon guns along with knives, axes, and nunchaku."

"Will they attack us?" I asked.

Uncle Wilbur shrugged. "Probably just showing muscle. Unless they see something they want. Might oughta get the girls in the van."

The massed engines toned down enough for us to hear yelling and scrambling at the far end of the parking lot as the 'Poons checked out the merchandise. Conroy hustled Janelle and Lil into the van. I crammed the unhappy cats into their pack and added it to the huddle before we threw random clothing over them. The middle-aged woman in the stall next to us stuffed her trays of dried baby octopus into a large basket and sat down on it.

People melted back from the path between the stalls as the first hogs approached. The riders flaunted the usual motifs – skulls, demons, igloos, swastikas. The lead rider wore a sleeveless leather vest. Between the dark blue tats, his bare arms looked pale blue from cold. A gun with barbed harpoon stuck out of a holster made of brass pipe, an axe head gleamed over his shoulder, his chrome helmet and multiple chains glittered. The vanguard bristled at Conroy, Uncle Wilbur, and me as they passed.

Rank and status in the 'Poons were pretty obvious. The most grotesque-looking warriors led the pack, followed by average-looking guys on less impressive bikes. Then came the misfits and stragglers riding any sort of wreck they could find. The rag-tag tail-end of the force rolled by, dwindling to a final, puny figure in a vaguely familiar helmet and jacket, riding a bike that looked a half-century past its prime.

Uncle Wilbur tensed at the sight of the last bike. Its rider stuck out a foot and swerved in beside us, dismounted and bent over as if to catch his breath. No, catch *her* breath. Kayla pulled off the helmet, broke into a grin and wiped her eyes.

Two giant steps and I grabbed her in a bear hug. Swung her in a circle. Her laughter alternated with sobs. Must have been a pretty scary ride to make the indomitable Kayla cry. Conroy hurried over, and then Lil and Janelle jumped out of the van and joined the group hug. Uncle Wilbur inspected his Harley panhead.

We broke apart. "What took you so long? Conroy said.

"Had to lead the GenAge guys way up the other side of the river to lose them before I could double back," she said. "Those 'Poon goons went thundering past. Looked like good cover, so I turned on the jammer and tailed them."

A minute later, Uncle Wilbur said, "Everybody ready to head back to my place?"

We stared. "Why?" Lil said.

"Wuh . . . ? I can't drive the bike and the Buick both back."

Conroy took the bike keys from Kayla and handed them to him.

"Here. You ride the bike back home. We're going the other way."

Uncle Wilbur pushed into Conroy's space. "But you traded me the Buick."

"I did not. I gave you money for the van and to gas up the Buick. I'm not throwing the car in too. We just needed to get the GenAge guys off our tails."

I was as surprised as Uncle Wilbur, although probably not as red in the face. I'd thought we were leaving the Buick with Wilbur. "Buick's probably got all kinds of people looking for it by now."

"Then I'll drive the Buick by myself. I somebody attacks it, the risk is all mine. The rest of you can all be nice and anonymous in the van. We'll switch leads every once in a while. I'm not leaving my car here."

"You worthless sumbitch!" Uncle Wilbur roared. "My sister shoulda drowned you soon as she got enough strength back to stuff you in a sack."

His mouth was still flapping when our two-vehicle caravan drove away between the lines of stalls.

*

We followed the mighty Columbia north, then turned east onto a road between steep, bare slopes. Lil sat up front with me in the Econovan. Janelle and Kayla took the second seat, while the cats claimed the rear as their territory. Soon we climbed out of the canyon onto a high plateau patched with rolling wheat fields, studded with house-size glacial boulders, and cut by a straight road vanishing in the distance.

As I drove the monotonous stretch, my mind circled in on a thought I didn't know what to do with – how good my arms had felt when they were tight around Kayla. I didn't dare look at Lil sitting beside me half asleep, but the skin on my right cheek felt hot, as if she were X-raying my mind.

Dammit! I couldn't figure Kayla out, but she made life a lot more fun and a lot less scary. Lil, though, had sunk a hook in my heart. Between her ignoring me and hating me, life around Lil was usually painful.

Lil probably thought having sex with an alien would make tentacles grow out her nose. Why couldn't she see my genetic differences as improvements? We hadn't engineered ourselves to be stupider, slower, or weaker. I wondered if I could impress her by seeing long distances in bad light, courtesy of evolution on a twilight world. Or by filling a bathtub and holding my breath underwater for seven minutes, thanks to a dolphin gene for hyper-efficient red blood cells. I couldn't leap tall buildings in a single bound, but dense bones and heavy muscles evolved for high gravity offered other opportunities for showing off.

Maybe I should admit my true origins to Kayla. She was so in love with the weird that she'd probably want to get it on just for bragging rights to alien sex. I could explain any mistakes I made as Yunko mating rituals.

If only I could talk to Maks about it all, particularly about how he attracted girls like sugar draws ants, but I didn't even know if Maks was still alive. In frustration I shoved the accelerator pedal to the floor and the van lumbered into a gallop.

Lil jerked out of her slump. "What's wrong? Are they after us?" She twisted in the seat, trying to see out the small rear windows of the van.

"Nothing," I muttered. "Just checking max speed on this dinosaur."

Shadows stretched long by the time I spotted the Buick parked on the shoulder of the deserted road. Conroy leaned against the car, waving us to stop.

I pulled over, stopped, and got out.

"Everything okay?" he said.

"Yeah. See any sign of the bad guys?"

"Naw. Mile or two ahead, we turn north toward the dam. Maybe another half hour on to the town of Grand Coulee. We could stop and eat there. Not much else between here and the border and I'm hungry."

"Sure." I was starving too.

*

I'd started on my second loaded goatburger, feeling better by the minute, when Conroy yelled, "Hellfire! Get down!" I launched from our café booth and rolled across the floor, looked back and saw Conroy help Janelle under our window-side table. The other diners stared at us.

Feeling foolish, I followed Conroy's leopard crawl down the restaurant aisle to an empty booth. He slowly raised his head to look out.

"What?"

"Black SUV came past," he whispered. "Must have spotted the Buick parked across the street 'cause they slowed down. I think they turned right, maybe circling around the block."

"It's them?"

"Yeah. There they are, going by again."

"How'd they find us?" I blurted.

"Probably went back to check Uncle Wilbur's place. He knew we were headed for the dam. Stupid old eel-head either told them because he was pissed off, or they beat it out of him. I'll take the Buick, draw off the SUV and head for the bridge across the river. You get the girls away. Then call me." He rose to a crouch and launched himself out the door. I gestured the others forward and relayed the plan. The Buick screamed out of the parking lot and careened around the corner that the SUV had just turned.

We scrambled to our feet. I dropped money on the counter and led the race out the door. We piled into the Econovan and took off toward the back streets of Grand Coulee, climbing steadily as we looked for a place to lay low.

A couple of blocks later, Janelle said, "Turn off the jammer."

"What?" The jammer was in my zipper pocket.

"They're chasing the Buick. Turn off the jammer so they can hear the chip's signal. Then they'll start looking for us and leave Conroy alone." She sounded ready to cry. "Don't let them catch him!"

It wasn't a bad idea. "Sure, soon as I find a place where you can all hide. I'll let you out and then turn it off. If neither of us comes for you in, uh, thirty minutes, try to call." I turned right onto a street of houses. Lights were coming on as twilight deepened to full dark. We passed a school building on our right. Behind it, trees descended into a gully. I took two more quick rights, ending in a parking lot on the other side of the gully.

"You can hide down in there," I said. The heavily forested dip should keep them safe, at least for a while. Safer than they would be in the van with GenAge chasing me.

I couldn't risk GenAge discovering Yunko stuff. The girls each had a backpack but they needed to carry more. "Kayla, take Zax and Gwitchy. Keep them in their pack till we come find you." She dropped her own backpack long enough to sling the heavy cat carrier onto her shoulders.

"Lil, take the transport case. I'll take the handle and jammer so I can lead them away. Janelle, take my backpack." They rearranged their loads and started down the slope. I tried to watch in all directions until they disappeared.

Then I looked out over the small town. From the high ground, I could see the dam. It had to be a couple of miles away, but its gigantic size made it seem almost beneath my feet. It looked junky, though, as if it had acquired reefs of trash along each bank. I finally realized that the corp that bought it must have trucked in miles of rock and other debris, trying to fill in the reservoir enough to keep the water level higher than the intakes. Beyond the dam, lights picked out Conroy's escape route, the highway bridge across the river. Compared to the dam, it looked like a thread.

The street lights also outlined the layout of the town. Up in the hills across the highway, lights marked a web of roads for servicing the electric towers and transformers. Maybe I could lure the GenAge guys into that maze and lose them. I started the van and headed toward the highway. As soon as I crossed it, I turned off the jammer.

*

Fifteen minutes of cornering the clumsy old van through thickets of electrical equipment and forests of powerline towers, and the SUV still chased me. I skidded around a giant transmission station and saw light reflecting off the river below and to my left. I turned on the jammer and took the next turn in that direction. The route twisted downhill like a ski run and spat me out on the main road headed north toward the dam and bridge.

I floored the accelerator. Vertical cliffs rose on my left and the jagged fill threatened my right. The dam had grown to fill my windshield when, several hundred meters ahead, the cliff side exploded with debris. Boulders tumbled onto the road at the choke-point where the end of the dam rose on the other side of the road, blocking my escape route. Just ahead, an open gate on my right led into the dam's visitor parking lot. I slewed the Econovan off the road and into the lot, hoping I could get around the blockage on foot. The engineers were crazy not to have stabilized the slope in such a critical location.

The SUV swerved into the parking lot behind me. I jumped out and ran. A windowless building sat at the end of the lot nearest the dam. Its doors burst open and a dozen SWAT-type security guards poured out. They headed toward the landslide at a run, so intent they never noticed me or the GenAge guys chasing me. I veered the other way, toward the water and the dam. The GenAge guys started firing.

I tried to duck around the far corner of the building, but something tore into the back of my thigh, and suddenly my leg didn't work right. I slowed to a hobble. At a new noise behind me, I turned and looked. Four more dam security guards hurried out the open door. They yelled and fired at the GenAge guys in the darkness. I kept limping toward the dam. My thigh blazed with pain and my jeans were wet with blood but my leg didn't seem paralyzed. Maybe I'd been hit by a chunk of flying concrete or a ricochet instead of directly by a bullet.

The others needed to know what was happening. I hunkered behind a car parked at one end of the dam road, pulled out my pocket phone and hit Conroy's number.

"What?" he snapped.

"I'm at the dam. GenAge guys and guards chasing me. Gotta go." I clicked off, and pushed to my feet. Nowhere to go but across. Upriver to my right, the reservoir stretched away into the darkness. On my left, the dam's sloping face dropped over 200 feet to churning water. A gate blocked the road across the dam. I ran toward it, scrambled to the top of the waist-high guardrail and leaped for the top of the gate. If it was electrified, well, it wouldn't be any worse than getting caught by GenAge. It wasn't, and I hauled myself over the top and dropped to the road along the top of the mile-long dam.

As I ran, I mentally apologized to my people for my failure, and mentally begged Kayla to take care of Zax and Gwitchy. Then I set my mind to staying on my feet and set my eyes on the cluster of lights at the far end of the dam, imagining Lil, Kayla, and the others urging me on.

Below me, drifts of green and purple lights skittered across the dam's downriver face. Surreal. They'd turned on the laser light show. It usually runs in summer to entertain tourists; maybe they were trying to light up the place in hopes of spotting saboteurs. The laser beams were disorienting as the speeded up pictures danced across the dam.

The canned lecture and music bombarded me, along with the smell of water, and the humming tingle of electricity. I was nearly a third of the way across but my leg was getting weaker. The more I ran, the more my knee tried to bend the wrong way, giving me a flopping, hopping gait. I glanced back. Cheyne and his flunky were fifty yards behind. The flickering shadows of the dam guards trailed them. Still out of pistol range but closing up.

To any tourists in the viewing areas below, our life or death chase must have looked like random pixels, escaped from the main light show. Distracted by the thought, I stepped carelessly and my knee buckled. The momentum of the fall rolled me forward so hard I smashed my bad shoulder and the concrete scraped my skin through my clothing. Screaming with the pain, I scuttled on all fours, then scrambled awkwardly to my feet and hobbled on.

Above me, the sky went crazy with light and sound. Now they'd started the fireworks display too, lighting the bridge from above. As I hobbled past the mid-point of the dam, my eyes on the sky, the sparkling barrage of color and light suddenly changed directions. From shooting straight up toward the heavens, it veered to blow past me horizontally. The sudden, violent wind that blew the fireworks blew me down and rolled me across the concrete until the low guardrail stopped me.

I forced my head up against the wind's pressure enough to look back at Cheyne and the guards just as a gigantic gout of water rose forty feet above the surface of the reservoir like a monster from the deep. The mini-tsunami roared forward and washed my pursuers off the bridge. I saw them flopping like rag dolls in the chaotic deluge of rushing water and crazy light. Then the water's trailing edge picked me up too and carried me over the guardrail like a gum wrapper washed down a street drain.

# CHAPTER 25

From the unpublished Godunov manuscript
*Why We Came to Earth: The Yunko Voyages*

*The team adding Gliese-C genes to Earth's human genome had more luck. Whether because Earth's lifeforms evolved to resist more intense solar radiation, because of the endless redundancy typical of your creatures, or because of a a wildly varied and complex evolution, Earth's fauna seemed more capable of surviving drastic mutations.*

The wave slammed me down the face of the dam, smashing head, knees, and elbows on the concrete. Choking, coughing, retching in the tumble of water, I gulped air before the monstrous waterfall plunged me into the Columbia River.

Churning currents jerked me up, down, and sideways with a power that yanked in a memory from years ago. I was standing near the bow of a ship with five other eight-year-olds from my training group, bundled into so many layers we bulked as round as we were tall. Our teacher stopped lecturing about Bubble Drive physics and looked at her comm. Abruptly, she pointed forward and said "Now!" Pressed against the icy railing, peering across the frozen Beaufort Sea, we saw a geyser of ice and seawater erupt a mile ahead. Somewhere above, far higher than the vertical beam width of radar in the region, a Yunko shuttlecraft pilot was staging a science demonstration for us, using tiny jolts of the Bubble Drive to blast an open channel through the frozen sea ahead of our ship.

If I'd had control of my limbs, I would have smacked my forehead. First the sudden, rocky avalanche. Then the giant wave out of nowhere. Somewhere above the vertical beam width of local radar, a Yunko shuttlecraft pilot had used small, directed Bubble Drive bursts to take potshots at our chase below.

The tangle of currents flipped me over again. I glimpsed something large, dark and angular tumbling through the murky water toward my head.

*

My raw throat made suffocation feel even worse. I strained to blow away the choking, fuzzy filaments invading my nose and mouth, but a warm mass pressed them into my face. I couldn't move my arms.

"Get off, dammit," a voice murmured, and the mass disappeared from my face. I inhaled weakly before passing out, only to be roused again by the same suffocation.

The same voice said, "That's it, cat. I'm throwing you out!"

A sudden chill hit my side. I opened my eyes. Kayla, wearing only panties, tossed Gwitchy out a room's open door and then slammed it. I was too wrecked to fully appreciate the view. My head and my other side felt fairly warm, but the chilly side felt frozen all the way down to my gut. Kayla returned and wiggled under a heavy pile of blankets that covered me. I tilted my head enough to see Lil lying against my other side. The furry warmth capping my head suddenly squirmed. Must be Zax. The afterlife was not what I'd expected.

Sometime later, I floated to the surface again and considered the possibility that I was not dead after all. "Where am I?" I whispered.

A short silence before Lil's voice said, "An empty house near Elmer City. It had a For Rent sign. Conroy broke in a back window."

"They here?"

"Conroy's outside keeping watch," Kayla said. "Janelle's in the other bedroom, curled up in a ball. She's about as wasted as you are. Soaking in the river sent your core temperature way down. We're trying to get it back up."

Cozied up in half-consciousness, I checked as much of my body as I could reach with my hands hampered by the blankets. I wasn't wearing any clothes, although a scratchy feeling against my right thigh might be a bandage. The girls weren't wearing much either.

"Where're my clothes?"

Kayla's voice. "In the dryer."

If they'd noticed any physical oddities while they were stripping me, there was nothing I could do about it.

"Are you awake enough to pay attention?" Lil said.

When I nodded Zax dug his claws into my scalp, finishing the job of reviving me.

"About five minutes after you let us off, Conroy called. Said he'd lost his tail and he'd come back and pick us up. We linked up, then headed past the dam and toward the bridge. We were crossing the bridge when that landslide thing happened. Then Conroy got your call."

Gwitchy yowled outside the door. In a moment I said, "Where'd you find me?"

Kayla picked up the story. "Emergency vehicles were heading down the side of the river. We followed. They were parking near a place where the river bank curves around. One of the EMT people said that bank was where stuff that came off the dam usually washes up. They were searching for anyone who might have been in the tourist areas when the wave hit."

When she paused, Lil said, "I remembered how the cats found you in the forest, so I let them out of their pack. They took off and we followed. They found you down the beach a ways, tangled in debris." She stopped, then blurted, "We thought you were dead. Then Conroy pumped on you and you vomited a lot of water and gunk. Started breathing."

At last I said, "Are my clothes dry?" I felt like a slab of meat worked over by a tenderizing hammer. Being naked under the blankets made me feel even more vulnerable.

"We'll go see." They both went out, letting Gwitchy back in so she'd shut up. With only the cats for company, I faded out until they returned fully clad, Lil with my clothes, Kayla with a steaming bowl of broth. By now I felt close to my normal temperature, but I regretted they didn't get back in bed with me. Instead they left me to get dressed.

I was propped up on pillows finishing the broth when Lil returned with the medkit. "Anything in here that might help?"

It took everything I had to throw off the blankets and sit up. Zax and Gwitchy nosed me anxiously. Nothing seemed broken, but it all hurt so much I couldn't really tell. I pulled out the last two gel packs for my thigh and shoulder. Then I uncapped a pre-loaded syringe, twisted around and injected a full spectrum antibiotic through the bandage over the wound in my thigh. The last three bonbons rolled loose in the bottom of the kit. I munched them. Right now, I needed them more than Janelle.

I picked up the bowl of soup to finish but Lil lingered. When I glanced at her she said, "That explosion? And the wave? What actually happened? The ambulance guys at the scene thought it was probably a meteorite – one that broke up since there were two hits – but it was awfully convenient."

No big surprise. Sapes are fixated on meteorites. Even with evidence to the contrary, they still think our supply ship that crashed in central Siberia back in 1908 was a meteorite or a comet. When the ship entered orbit around Earth for the first time, the Yunko got a tragic lesson about using the Bubble Drive in any environment more crowded than a vacuum, particularly during a coronal mass ejection. Fortunately, the second ship, the personnel ship, stayed in orbit around Mars while the supply ship attempted the first close approach.

Our ancestors eventually re-engineered the second ship's two shuttlecraft so they could land on Earth. The first trip was to search out and collect even the smallest fragments of bone and metal left from the crash. Those fragments are preserved in the Hall of Heroes. Since then, Yunko pilots have learned how to maneuver in an atmosphere with pinpoint control. I wondered about the shuttlecraft pilot who blasted out the hillside and raised the wave. Was the pilot trying to save me or kill me? Or just a lousy shot?

It didn't make sense for the Yunko to risk exposing the Bubble Drive just to save me. So they must have been trying to save the culture. At last I said, "I think the Yunko caused the explosion and the wave. I'm not sure why, but it means they've been watching us all along. Don't tell the others."

She looked away. "They aren't fools, you know." Then once again she left me alone.

*

By mid-afternoon, I recovered enough to join the group, gathered around the kitchen counter. Kayla had made a meal out of every edible left in the house by real estate salespeople–a cup of yogurt, shriveled grapes, a baggie of jerky, a pile of cracker packets, and the four remaining bouillon cubes.

Conroy swept the last few cracker crumbs into his palm, licked them up and wiped his hand on his jeans. "Have I got this straight? The GenAge guys were about to kill you when a miraculous wave washed all of you off the dam? Way too convenient, Goran. Anything you're not telling us?"

I tried an intimidating stare. "You think I beat myself up falling down the dam and nearly drowning just for fun? Hunger making you lightheaded?"

"I'm not buying it either," Kayla chimed in. "There's had to be another player mixed up in that, a player with major resources. Some rival corp trying to take down GenAge? A foreign government?" And then, "Alien squid-bots?"

"You're hallucinating," I said. "I'm a high school kid, not some assassin or spy!" I backed away from the counter. If I had to escape them, I had no idea where to run.

"Yeah," Kayla said. "A high school kid none of us had anything to do with until a few weeks ago. Judging by your torso muscles, a high school kid who's been working out at a really strange gym. And those two weird scars high on your back. Where are you really from?"

Her manner was odd, almost joking, but with an edge of anger. I glanced at Lil. She shifted slightly back and forth between me and the rest of them. "Near Terrace, in northern British Columbia," I said. They had no way to check.

"Oh, sure," Kayla said. "Goran, you're lying. We're all running for our lives because we thought you were our friend. We saved your life. If you lie to your friends, you're not really their friend. The least you can do is come clean about what's actually going on. Or I'm outta here."

Conroy nodded agreement. Lil seemed turned to stone.

"Okay," I finally said, "You're right. I'd tell you the whole truth if I could, but I can't. I swear I'll tell you more once we cross the border." My brain wasn't functioning just then, but I could probably think up something by the time we reached Canada.

They stared at me. Kayla with an unreadable look. To break the silence I finally said, "Any idea what happened to Cheyne?"

"You were the one on the dam," Conroy said. "What do *you* think happened?" He added with an edge, "If you're allowed to tell us."

"Looked like the full force of the wave hit them. Just before the outer edge hit me. Probably threw them a lot farther and they hit a lot harder." I'd been incredibly lucky to survive myself, even with blood cells that carried more oxygen. "I don't think Cheyne could have survived." Lil's shoulders sank slowly out of the tension that gripped them.

"So what's next?" Kayla said.

"Get out of here fast and head north. Anybody know what happened to the van?"

"Dam Security's probably taking it apart right now," Conroy said.

"What was left of the cash, I put in the center console. So it's gone."

"I could peddle a couple of fake IDs," Kayla said.

"Too dangerous," Lil and I said almost in unison.

Conroy pulled out a wallet and threw cash on the table. "That's what I've got left."

I added a few folded bills, still damp from the river. The girls dug out whatever money they had and added it to the pile.

"Did Wilbur gas up the car?" I said.

"Yeah, he got one thing right at least," Conroy said.

Janelle peered sadly at the cash. "That's barely enough for a real meal."

"We need to load up," I said. "We have to cross the border at four o'clock tomorrow morning, and it's a slow drive and a hike to get there."

Once we made it out of town we took the back road to Highway 21. The steep, forested country slid past, interrupted by a farm every few miles. Occasionally a sign announced we were on the Colville Indian Reservation. A huge, beautiful, deserted country. All the Yunko on Earth could move here and just disappear into the background. We could claim we were a long-lost sub-tribe with several thousand members. Oh, yeah, sure. I could imagine how the Colville band would view another batch of strangers showing up and saying, "Hi. We've decided to live on your land."

We wouldn't have to worry about the dying world that humans called Gliese 667Cc. People there had probably forgotten about our mission. Or it had become just a legend. They might even all be dead by now – I was too far down the food chain to know if communication was going on. It was all so long ago, dozens of generations for us. Because of time dilation, much longer for those who stayed on Gliese-C. The bodies preserved in the Hall of Heroes memorialized our slow transition to creatures that breathed oxygen-rich air and looked more and more like local humans. So why couldn't we all just stay here?

Night fell. We drove on, Kayla took the wheel to relieve Conroy. The cats made burping, whimpering sounds to inform me they were disgusted with their situation. At last we spotted lights ahead, the village of Republic. Another little town that looked like a Western movie set. One café was still open. Conroy parked down a side street and we got out.

I let the cats loose. "We're going for a walk up that hill," I said. "Can you bring us two orders of something with meat?" Without waiting for an answer, I headed toward a finger of forest poking into town, hoping movement would ease my aches. Zax and Gwitchy streaked ahead. Yunko had tracked us to Grand Coulee, they must be tracking us now. They had to know I had Sapes with me, and by now they could guess we were headed for the Highline border crossing, a secret from outsiders.

But the cold, fresh air felt good. The cats darted from side to side and ran up and down trees while I mentally reviewed the logistics of our crossing. When the Buick's horn beeped, we headed back.

Conroy held out a paper bag. "Two elk jerky burritos. All they had left this late."

I smoothed out the bag and put it in my pocket. Leaning against the fender, I unwrapped the burritos, picked out most of the meat and the gravy-soaked potatoes for Zax and Gwitchy, and then wolfed down the remains.

After wrestling the cats back into their pack, I told Conroy, "Don't start the car yet. Far as we know, there's no widespread hunt for Janelle or Kayla, so here's what we need to do. We cut over to the Laurier road and a few miles later we turn onto a forest service road. We'll all drive up to where . . . where we have to start hiking, then Janelle and Kayla will drive back down and cross the border at Danville in the car. Pick us up on the other side."

Conroy erupted at the idea of Janelle and the Buick crossing the border with only Kayla for protection.

When he stopped for breath, I said, "I don't like it either, but you skipped bail. The same corporation that runs the jail facility in Seal Bay owns the timber company that operates the border stations here in Ferry County. Lots of times they informally pass around any info that might bring a profit, like the reward for a bail jumper. You'd keep Janelle safer by staying away from her."

He shut up and took out his frustrations in driving. It wasn't long before we followed a narrow road across the local mountains, and hit the highway to Laurier. Once we turned off on the forest road, I said, "Pull over."

Janelle exchanged her quilted coat lined with fake fur for Lil's light jacket, unsuitable for night hiking in snow. Conroy turned on the dome light so I could draw the girls' return route on the burrito sack. "If the Danville crossing is already open for the day, show 'em the fake IDs and tell them you're headed up to Kootenay Lake for the day." I drew another road they'd follow on the Canadian side that led to an abandoned quarry. "You should be able to reach it before it gets light. Drive down into the quarry far enough that no one can see the Buick from Gilpin Road. We'll come across the border near the quarry and find you." I turned the sack over and drew the roads and turns to where our hike started.

Lil had her phone out. "Show me where we are now so I can display the route."

"Won't work," I said. "After the second turn, this route doesn't show up on maps. Or on satellite views."

"Why not?" Conroy said.

"We didn't want it to."

"Other side of the border," he pointed at me, "you're telling us everything."

The gravel road wasn't bad at first, but snow increased as we climbed. It was late in the year to attempt the crossing. Higher and higher we snaked on switchbacks, dodging around trees like skiers, meandering across an occasional meadow. The road degenerated until it was marked only by gaps in the forest. Conroy kept up a steady stream of curses and worries, scared he'd puncture something under the car. The cats yowled when the Buick banged up and down. At last the track we were following took a sharp turn back to the south and I said, "Okay, this is it. It's a mile and a half hike from here." I didn't add that much of that distance was straight up and down.

# CHAPTER 26

From the unpublished Godunov manuscript
*Why We Came to Earth: The Yunko Voyages*

*It took seventy years to produce an analog of the Gliese-C gill trachea that would function in Earth mammals. But at last, researchers created a pig with gill trachea that didn't immediately dry out. The organ emerged from the back of the throat, ran between the lungs, branched to bypass the spine and exited just under each shoulder blade.*

*The last in a long line of pig specimens lived to breed. Although its piglets did not survive, necropsies showed that they possessed–that they had inherited–both lungs and gill tracheae. The creation of the pig solved many of the basic problems necessary to create a person who could survive on the surface of both planets. Having reached this milestone, the survivors of the second expedition packed up their results and left for home in 1402 C.E.*

Conroy, Lil, and I got out of the Buick. Around us, wind stirred tree tops, dimly visible in the moonlight. The humid air smelled of snow, pine, rotting duff, flinty rock, and stressed-out people, along with the faint trace of a nearby skunk tussle. I could barely make out the oily reek of the highway and railroad tracks at the Laurier crossing four miles away. Zax and Gwitchy whined to escape their pack and explore the delicious forest.

I slung the thirty-odd pounds of Pallas' cats onto my shoulders, handed Lil the transport case, and gave my backpack to Conroy. If Kayla and Janelle were stopped and the car searched, no way could they pass the stuff off as camping gear. But Conroy, Lil, and I might have a chance of ditching it. Conroy got in the Buick to turn it around in the snow. He backed it down the track until Lil yelled, "There! Back up toward the bank."

I wanted to clap a hand over her mouth. I wasn't sure how far the sensors could pick unexpected noises out of the forest's background sounds. Conroy turned the car on the frozen ground without getting stuck. He petted and fretted over Janelle and the car while I reviewed Kayla on the route to the abandoned quarry on the Canada side. Then Conroy watched his beloved Janelle disappear in his beloved Buick.

Two boulders the size of small cars marked the turn-off point for the crossing. We paused as if by mutual agreement before plunging into the forest.

"You ran us all over Washington State," Conroy said, "just to reach this butthole of nowhere? If we'd gone straight north and crossed at the Peace Arch like I wanted, we'd have been living high in Vancouver two days ago."

"Or been passed out in an interrogation room," I said. "C'mon."

I set out north, pushing through the trees and undergrowth down a slight decline between two rounded summits. The footing was tricky on the rocky, uneven ground littered with fallen limbs, all camouflaged by snow. None of us wore hiking boots. The creatures that thronged the forest emitted dim auras. Zax and Gwitchy mewled and struggled in their pack.

"Wish we had a flashlight," Conroy said.

"Couldn't use it," I panted, wanting nothing more than to lie down. Was I weakened by my wounds? Or had aging begun? "Once in a while a drone patrols the area. Or someone gets curious about a light up here."

At last we reached a saddle in the hills. An outcropping of rock created an open space in the trees. "Okay," I said, "sit down and take a break." They slumped on the boulders free of snow. The wound on the back of my thigh felt wet, the dampness warm for a few seconds before it turned icy from the cold. Probably fresh blood. I didn't want to leave a handy patch of DNA frozen to a boulder so I leaned awkwardly sideways against a tree, my injured shoulder aching from the weight of the cats. We all heaved for oxygen

"We're about to enter the security zone," I said. "We need to start the crossing procedures here."

"Yeah?" Conroy said. "What? Put on bear suits? Waddle on all fours?"

I stuck my hands under my armpits to warm them up and to keep from slugging Conroy. He and Lil were both too bright to bullshit about the situation, and Conroy probably knew as much as I did about illegal border crossings. "Just before the Big Crumble, the U.S. and Canada started setting up a new border surveillance system. It was based on something the Navy developed called Blue Rose technology."

"Blue rose?" Conroy flapped a hand. "How lovely."

"An acronym," I said. "Battlescape Land Undersea, uh, something. Rayleigh Optical Scattering something. It's a very sensitive fiber optic cable running along remote areas of the border. They installed it as far as Idaho before Congress cut off funding."

"So how do we get past this thing? Fly?"

"The cable's like a motion sensor. Picks up vibrations out to about

174

500 meters. The signal feed goes to a central command post in Kelowna, over a hundred miles away. It's cheaper than setting up receivers in individual border stations.

"From now on we'll approach one at a time, stepping randomly instead of in steady rhythm. I'll go first, then Lil, then Conroy. The sensors will pick up movement, but Kelowna doesn't alert a local border station unless they're sure it's people crossing. When the system first went up, they wasted way too much of the stockholders' profits chasing down bears and turkeys and woodland caribou.

"So we try to sound like foraging animals. A step, a pause, couple of steps, then a long pause – whatever, just so it's not a regular human stride. The cats'll be running around too, leaving a typical animal signature to increase the white noise."

They said nothing. I doubted they understood how hard the uneven walking would be. Harder for them than for a Yunko. Our ancestors used their tail-leg to give an extra push on every third step, like a Sape waltz rhythm, and Yunko still retain a tendency to switch uneven gaits with the usual Sape binary rhythm. "Okay, when we get to the point where the sensors get really dangerous, I'll wait, and we regroup. Then we run like hell."

"Uh, Goran," Conroy said, "you just contradicted your idiot scheme."

"No. Twice a day a freight train runs across the border at Laurier. The vibrations mask our steps when we get near the border."

"No way," Lil said. "Laurier's several miles away. Train vibrations don't travel more than a few blocks."

Yeah, too smart to bullshit. "Right before they started installing the Blue Rose system, our people concealed a chain of seismic generators from Laurier past the point where we cross the border. They transmit and amplify the train vibrations through here. They also minimize any regular vibration that's not the train."

"C'mon," Conroy said. "You want us to believe the Blue Rose people didn't notice a line of weird vibrations running off into the wilderness?"

"Of course they noticed. For a while they had people out here every time the train crossed into Canada. Border guards patrolling back and forth. Drones flying. But they never caught anyone – we use this crossing maybe once every few months. At last the crossing personnel announced it was just an odd geological fault and moved on. A full investigation would have cut into profits."

"Who's 'we'?" Conroy said. "Who are you linked up with?"

In the silence of my non-answer, I heard the far-off screech of an owl and an agonized scream from some small creature.

"Goran," he finally said, "you're telling us the whole thing later."

Time to stop talking. I flicked on my comm briefly. "Okay, it's 3:14 now. At 4:42 the train goes by. I'll hear it first and signal you to run. Once it's passed, we start the slow irregular walking again. It takes a lot of patience. It makes your muscles scream, it's hard to balance, and it's exhausting. So drink some water and we'll head out."

When we were all standing, I demonstrated how to walk. They could not believe how much time it took, how hard it was to walk against a natural rhythm. "Don't look at each other," I said, "or you'll automatically fall into the same rhythm." I released the cats from their backpack, glad to ditch the extra weight, and made a sharp tongue click to send them loping and circling ahead.

Meter by meter, we progressed up another steep hill. The moon cast our slow shadows on the snow, broken up by trees and grass. We spooked a couple of deer that bounded away, their hooves clattering on an occasional rock. I clicked the cats back, then forward again. If I survived it all, maybe I'd take up training sheep dogs.

We skirted another hill like crippled sloths, followed a short ravine, and then climbed up its side. From the higher ground I could see the long, straight band stripped bare of trees that marked the border. I halted the others.

Corny as it looked, I knelt, swept away the snow, and pressed a half frozen ear against the icy ground. I felt as much as heard a faint rumble coming from the southeast. I raised my head, rubbed my numb ear and listened again. This time I made out the drumming, track-clacking approach of the train. I counted off thirty seconds, sent the cats forward, counted off another fifteen, and whispered "Go!"

We spilled over the crest, racing, stumbling, flailing down the steep slope, knees screaming, balance out of control, falling off the edge of the country. Almost in unison, we galloped across the open line of the border, the cats racing back and forth in ecstasy. Then down through the trees again and across a lower shelf.

"Stop," I gasped. I could make out the pale scar of the abandoned quarry far below us, backed by the thin white line of Gilpin Road and the glinting Kettle River beyond. The train whistle dopplered off into the night. We doubled over, aching for breath.

When I could manage more than one word, I said, "Okay, back to the uneven walking, but we're across. Welcome to Canada."

"Oh, Caan-a-daaa," Conroy bellowed, "Our home and native land – "

"Shut up," I hissed. "We're still in sensor range, and people may be around." As if to back me up, lights came on in a distant farmhouse.

Across the valley, the moon sank below a line of mountains, making way for the sun. We inched down the slope, staying close to the trees. We were almost to the quarry when I heard the sound of an engine. Lights swept across the road.

"Down!" I said. Prone among the grass and scattered trees, we watched the headlights grow bigger until a farm truck rumbled by, headed toward Danville.

*

The Crowsnest Highway runs east-west across British Columbia, kissing the border, then retreating where the steep Cascades push it north. Flat farmland, foothills pocked with mining scars, and towering mountains passed in a blur. I wasn't asleep but I wasn't quite awake either.

From the back seat, Janelle murmured about outfits she would create once we reached Vancouver and she got a job designing clothes and everything was perfect. Vancouver didn't hold much promise for me, except a short delay before facing Yunko judgment. Making it across the border had left room for new flood of worries. I'd revealed secrets to Lil that no Sape should know. I'd raised the others' suspicions. I'd promised a cure for Davy with no idea how to deliver it. I wasn't even sure the culture was still viable, we were taking so long to deliver it.

Conroy broke into my miserable thoughts. "Once we get to Vancouver, I'll go see a guy down on East Hastings Street. He pays real good for certain errands."

"Speaking of pay," Kayla said, "anybody still have money? I'm starving."

I realized I hadn't eaten since . . . yesterday? I shifted to get the wallet out of my pocket and gasped at the pain in my thigh.

From the back seat Lil said, "You okay?" Her fingers felt icy on my neck. She reached around to feel my forehead. "Goran, you're burning up. Do you have fever?"

I shrugged. Maybe she was still cold. Everyone had been shivering by the time we found Janelle and Kayla huddled in the Buick parked at the quarry.

We had about enough money between us for an order of fries, but Conroy didn't look worried. "I've got something to trade."

"Surprised you have anything left," I said.

'It's not prime stuff, but these yokels won't know the difference."

He pulled in at a diner in Greenwood that seemed to meet his unspoken specifications and drove around until he was away from the windows. Then he had the girls get out so he could reach the hidden compartment behind the back seat. I didn't see what he took out, but it fit into his jacket pocket.

He soon returned with two greasy paper bags of sandwiches and a proud grin. "Make your pitch, then bait and switch."

Another half-mile down the highway we pulled onto a side road shielded with trees. I felt so bad I only ate a few bites of my sandwich. Maybe I did have fever. I wasn't hungry, and I couldn't put off contacting the Outpost any longer. I let the cats out, followed them into the trees, took out my burner comm, and tapped Andrei's old number. I hoped he'd ditched his comm and I wouldn't have to confront him.

But he answered, cautiously. "Who is this, please?"

My throat closed up at hearing his voice again. "Goran," I croaked. "I got the culture across the border."

A short silence, then, "You have done very well. A great victory."

I couldn't speak.

"The head Researchers are extremely excited. I've described the culture as exactly as I can, but we need the actual tissue. I . . .I'm very proud of you. Even though things are a bit unsettled. Tell me where you are and we'll fly an escort to the nearest airport immediately."

Andrei didn't seem to be in the Outpost's surveillance loop. "I'm pretty sure someone at the Outpost already knows where I am. Besides, I have to go to Vancouver first."

"Vancouver? Have you lost your mind? Nothing in Vancouver is more important than delivering the culture as soon as possible."

"I need to retrieve the comm helmet before it falls into the wrong hands."

"We'll send another team after it. We need you here immediately."

No way out. "I'm with four Sapes."

He made a tiny popping sound as he tried to form words. When he finally spoke, his voice had iced over. "Where is your honor? Where is your common sense?"

"I needed them to steal the culture and get out of Seal Bay." I clicked off. Then I whistled up the cats. "Come on," I said when I reached the Buick. "I'll drive so the rest of you can finish eating."

Worry turned me numb and dumb to the others' conversation. I drove through Osoyoos where we brought Vlad out of the tunnels – a light-hearted adventure in comparison. A mile or so past the town, my nose began to tingle from a faint smell. I was trying to identify it when Conroy said, "Okay, we're across the border. You said you'd tell us your story once we reached Canada, so start talking."

The smell was growing stronger, stinging my nostrils like caustic chemicals. I wondered if I had picked up a really serious illness from the polluted Columbia River. "Do you smell that?"

"Smell what?" Lil said. I didn't see how she could miss it. The cats grumbled with displeasure at the odor.

"What are we supposed to smell? Your lies?" Conroy sneered.

178

"That's the point," I heard myself saying. "You *can't* lie. The chemicals make you tell every single secret. Something about galvanic skin responses."

"Something's wrong with him," Lil said, reaching to feel my forehead again.

'No." Conroy blocked her hand. "Leave him alone. Maybe he'll finally spill what's really going on."

"It's like a natural lie detector," I rambled. "The chemicals eat at your skin if you start sweating. I'll never make it through."

"Pull over," Conroy ordered.

I speeded up instead. Even as the smell escalated my fear and guilt, I knew I had to reach it, like a soldier charging over a hill and straight at certain death. My thoughts fled into the foggy tunnel of ancestral memory. A line of figures picked their way toward me across puddles of toxic fluid, their upper limbs raised in supplication, their nostrils pinched tight against vapors rising from the pools.

I veered off the road, slammed on the brakes, got out, and stumbled across the highway. The smell overpowered me as I crawled the remaining yards to the fence around the lake, a vast distorted skull with 300 crumbling eye sockets, each set with colored jewels.

# CHAPTER 27

From the unpublished Godunov manuscript
*Why We Came to Earth: The Yunko Voyages*

*Back on Gliese-C, economies were so strained that it took over 130 years to mount the third expedition to Earth, which reached your solar system in 1609 C.E. However, a new technique for harvesting fuel in flight boosted our ships to approximately 80 percent of light speed.*

*These Third Expedition scientists developed a hybrid human anatomy that could survive, breed true, and function in the open air of both Earth and Gliese-C. Because these new creatures needed to move around on Earth's surface without provoking curiosity, scientists kept them looking as human as possible.*

The smell of the lake pulled me forward. It disordered my brain. Was I on Earth or Gliese-C? When voices mumbled behind me I tried to swivel my ears to hear better, but my entire head turned. Strange beings followed. No, they were just Sapes. I dug my fingers into the gravelly soil, clawing my way back to the here and now. I was on Earth.

The male Sape yelled, "What's the matter with you?"

I lifted a hand toward the strange, crusted pools of water.

"Yeah, it's Spotted Lake," he said. "So what?"

When I tried to answer, I stumbled over syllables from a time when our lips had a different shape. One of the Sapes ran toward me. Lil – that was her name. She dragged me to my knees.

I clung to reality enough to mumble "Car. Help me."

The male – Conroy – took my other side. They lugged me back across the highway and bundled me into the car.

"Smell," I said.

"Yeah, it's really odd." Janelle rolled up her window. "Let's get away from here."

"I can't smell anything," Conroy said. Lil and Kayla agreed.

"Well, I can. Maybe 'cause I'm pregnant," Janelle said.

Conroy started the car. Several miles down the highway, he pulled off at a shabby picnic table set up beside corrals built from old tires. "You okay?"

When I nodded he said, "I'm gonna help you over to that table. You're gonna take deep breaths of this nice, fresh air, maybe meditate on that goofy corral over there, and generally get your shit together. Then you're gonna tell us what the hell's going on with you. Or else we're taking that culture thing and leaving you here."

We made it to the picnic table. I followed Conroy's orders. The low, looping walls of tires dividing the meadow were oddly peaceful. The sun soothed my aching body, the mountains were overpowering but in a good way. Zax and Gwitchy twined around my legs. *Time has no duration.* I was briefly free from its endless whip.

A few minutes later Conroy said. "Okay, let's have it. Why did Spotted Lake wig you out like that?"

The truth was too strange to share. Ages ago, judges on Gliese-C tested an accused person's guilt by forcing that person to walk across the Lake of Ordeals, a depression dappled with pools of toxic chemicals dissolved from the surrounding rock strata. The Ordeal no more proved guilt than Earth customs like dunking witches, but we carry the Lake in our ancestral memories. The faint mineral smells rising from Spotted Lake, combined with stress and fever, triggered mine.

Nope. Couldn't go there. Conroy slapped the table with impatience. What would *he* do, facing a Yunko interrogation team? He was so proud of his scams, his bait-and-switch ability, I figured he'd decoy them in the wrong direction, mouth flapping in overdrive.

Might as well try. "I'm part of a group that's . . ." I groped, "had major genetic engineering. Sometimes chemical smells make us hallucinate. The smell from that lake started frying my brain. Thanks for getting me out of there."

Conroy stared at me, chin on his hands. "What group?"

"Scientists mostly."

"Scientists doing what?" he said. "Breeding super-soldiers? That how you took us out at that garden center? How you survived washing off Grand Coulee Dam?"

"Those are just side effects."

"Then tell us your main goal." Kayla leaned across the table toward me, launching a waft of pheromones that screamed curiosity.

I dredged up lessons from Earth's history. "Earth is on its third atmosphere. The first one was blown away by solar wind. Took a billion years for the second atmosphere to form, mostly nitrogen, with about thirty percent carbon dioxide. Early, simple life evolved in the second atmosphere."

Kayla got up as if bored, wandered away from the table and around behind me. Odd. I heard a tiny sound and turned to look. She threw another pebble at the scrubby earth. No one else noticed.

"I don't need a bleedin' biology lesson," Conroy said. "Get to the point."

"Okay. Those early life forms produced oxygen, which was deadly to them. After another billion years passed, they had changed Earth's second atmosphere to a third one, mostly nitrogen and oxygen. It triggered the Great Oxygenation Catastrophe. Almost every living thing died, poisoned by the free oxygen in the air.

"Life had to start all over again with creatures that could breathe oxygen. Took another billion years for the oxygen breathers to evolve to the level of multicellular organisms. All the extinction events since then have been minor in comparison."

Janelle gazed dreamily at the tires, off in her own world. Lil stared at me intently. Kayla returned to the table and listened.

"So what?" Conroy said. "Get to the point."

"So there's nothing to keep us from changing Earth to a fourth atmosphere if we raise the temperature a few more degrees." I rose unsteadily to my feet. "C'mon. We've wasted enough time. We need to get on the road."

"Waaaait a minute!" Kayla said. She moved to block my path. "You're leaving out a lot, Goran. Like, what does genetic engineering have to do with changing atmospheres?"

"We're trying to re-engineer ourselves so that, if we do trigger a runaway greenhouse effect, we might have a chance of surviving."

"What a crock." She paused. "Lil told me you gave her a different story two or three days ago. That's the one I believe."

They were all standing now. I glanced at Lil. She looked like the two halves of her brain were cracking apart.

"What did Lil tell you?" Conroy said.

Kayla stared at me while she answered him. "That Goran's either crazy or part alien. Like from another planet. It explains all the weird things about him."

"You're the one who's nuts, Kayla," Conroy said.

"Yeah?" Kayla said. "Then why can't you explain how Goran took out your whole gang? Or what happened at the dam. Or why we're running up to Canada to deliver some top secret culture thing?"

I struggled out of shock toward some sort of answer. "Hey, I was just messing with Lil's head. Uh, trying to take her mind off her brother." I didn't dare look at her.

"No." Kayla took a step forward. "You've got too many strange physical features."

"You're a doctor now, as well as a forger?" I blurted.

"No, I'm an artist. Been taking classes since I was nine. Anatomy classes, too. Drawing won't make you rich, but it'll make you see what's really there instead of what you expect to see. Your features are off. Your eyes are wider apart. One ear's slightly higher than another. I suspected your hearing was different. Just now when I tossed pebbles, you heard what no one else did, even when I was standing behind you."

"I – you think I'm alien because I have good hearing? Jeez. Lame." I started toward the car. I had to either get away from them or . . . somehow make sure they couldn't talk.

Kayla grabbed my arm. "I'm just working up to the really good stuff. After you went over the dam we stripped you. No offense, Goran, but your butt is really strange. Glutes anchored a little farther to the side. Then higher up, in the middle of your back, there's another muscle mass. Almost like you once had a tail. And those places under your shoulder blades. I couldn't figure them out. Until you started talking about breathing different atmospheres. Now, I'd guess they have something to do with breathing."

"That's too bloody freaking crazy to . . . to even answer. You're the freak, Kayla."

Conroy leaned forward on the balls of his feet, ready to attack if he could figure out his target. Lil had one arm around Janelle, who looked stunned. They all looked stunned. I couldn't read them well enough to know if they actually believed Kayla. And the weight of despair was crushing down too hard to find a good response.

At last I said, "Screw it. Dump me here or let's get a move on. We aren't getting any closer to Vancouver." I walked to the car and slumped in the passenger seat.

Oddly enough, the others didn't try to haul me out. But then for three decades, the country had been wandering lost in a swamp of lies. I suppose they just took conflicting evidence for granted. They piled in and we drove away. In the car's silence, I could feel the seething bubbles of their curiosity, feel Conroy struggling for a question to pin me down, feel Lil and Kayla's huddled apprehension, but none of them challenged me.

At last Janelle broke the tension. "So Goran . . . if you're a space alien, why did you and your people come to Earth?"

I didn't have the energy to concoct an answer.

Then, more timidly, "Are you gonna take over our planet? Herd us into corrals like cattle and . . . eat us?"

"C'mon, Janelle, give it a rest!" I scrubbed a hand over my face. "Even if we were aliens – which we aren't – coming to Earth just to eat people doesn't make sense. We'd use a million times more energy flying here than we'd get from gobbling up every mammal on the planet."

"Oh."

I suppose the answer satisfied her. When I looked back a few minutes later, she had dozed off. Next to vomiting, sleeping seemed her favorite occupation during pregnancy. I didn't have the     nerve to glance at Lil or Kayla.

By the time Janelle woke, the low sun pierced the windshield and we were driving through a patchwork of fields and suburbs east of Vancouver. "Goran!" she said, "The new clothing line I want to start? Your aliens and scientists? Did they wear any cool, weird outfits I could use for ideas? Like science fiction movies with plastic bodysuits and metal stuff?"

I was tempted to describe the unearthly gear worn by our ancestors in the Hall of Heroes, but I settled for "Just lab coats. Sorry."

*

The girls, the cats, and I sat on a low concrete platform under an eighteen-foot-tall sculpture of a sparrow, its enameled colors glowing in the sunset. Its mate stood on the far side of Vancouver's Olympic Village Square. We'd learned from a street kid that the Olympic Village apartments rented cheap – after a glamorous start housing the world's best athletes, their condition had deteriorated until they were as beat up as any squat in the city. But the sparrows were still cool. The cats mumbled uneasily, staring through the mesh window of their pack at the sparrows. I suppose the scale of the giant birds made them feel more like juicy worms than heroic hunters.

We'd been waiting – an hour of pure misery – for Conroy to set up a deal. The girls wouldn't talk to me so I rose and wandered down the central courtyard to the water. False Creek, the narrow inlet separating the former Olympic site from downtown Vancouver, was busy with rowboats, sail boats, and a few armored First Nation canoes. A ferry eased across the water to the terminal and docked. People streamed down the gangway and up the ramp to the street. Conroy's height and familiar gait caught my eye.

I angled over to intercept him before he reached the others. "What happened?"

He flicked his eyes at the small aluminum case he carried. "Picked up a job delivering product to Victoria. Got enough of an advance for food and a week's rent here."

"Bullshit! You just walked into some dive and said, 'Got any illegal deals you want done, payment up front?' You're lucky they didn't off you on the spot."

"Calm down, Alien. I've worked with them before. They know me."

"The police force still functions in Canada." I glanced back at the girls perched under the sparrow. "So how'd your gangsters know you weren't a narc? I don't trust it."

"You think I trust you? Just chill." Conroy jerked his head at the apartments. "We'll do it tomorrow morning soon as the ferries start running."

"We?"

"Yeah. Told them I had backup."

I ran one hand through my hair, yanking till it stood up straight, and tried to count the armed enforcers that wanted a piece of me by now: GenAge security, Seal Bay police, Grand Coulee Dam security, the Yunko. And by tomorrow, the Vancouver police and Conroy's sleazeball drug buddies.

We rejoined the others and gathered up our stuff. Lugging the cats, my backpack and the culture case, I followed Conroy to the building manager's office. Conroy peeled off bills and laid them on the desk.

The woman slammed a key in his hand. "Number 314."

"No!" Lil said. "It has to be on the first floor. Because of Davy."

"Only thing I've got. Take it or leave it."

"Is there an elevator in the building?" I said.

"Not one that works."

I thought about appealing to her better nature – poor sick kid in a wheelchair needs a place on the first floor – then snapped back to reality. "Lil, he's not that heavy. We can carry him up the stairs." Assuming we could get him to Canada, that is. I saw no way to deliver on my promise of a cure for Davy. And I couldn't convince myself that my current plan – dumping them all and taking off – was anything but dishonorable.

The apartment manager rounded her desk, led us up the stairs and into a hallway. Halfway down it, she unlocked a door and waved us in. Ruddy evening sunset light flooded through a glass wall patched with plywood. Must have been prime real estate once. Now, the interior walls were grimy and randomly studded with long nails that someone had used as a loom to weave a demented spider web of strings and strips of dirty cloth. A hole gaped in the floor in front of a blackened fireplace.

Conroy pointed at the hole. "You call this livable?" He stepped back into the hall with the manager, apparently intent on driving down the rental price. The hole didn't really bother me – it looked like an alternate escape route. I shoved a coffee table across the floor to cover the opening.

A glass door opened onto a balcony. I stepped out to check the lines of sight. Lil followed. They call Vancouver the "City of Glass." It still retained much of its glory. Reflections blazed off glass high rises against the dark wall of mountains inland. The huge silver ball of the children's science museum sat just across False Creek. Twinkling lights still marked the facets of the geodesic sphere, even though water now lapped over its seawall.

Lil gazed at the museum, a rare smile on her face. "We can take Davy. He'll love it."

When the building manager left, we explored the apartment. The place was trashed but it had lots of space – a main room and a kitchen, a big bedroom with a sagging king size bed and its own bathroom, a smaller bedroom, an extra bath, and a storage space the size of a ping pong table. I picked up the catpack to release them in the smaller bedroom, assuming Conroy and I would share it while the three girls took the large room.

I'd thought I'd grown to understand my new companions, how they acted, how they felt, how they manipulated other people. Wrong again. What happened next baffled me.

Kayla raised an inquiring eyebrow at Lil, who gave me a brief glance. Janelle placed one hand on her belly, Conroy draped a protective arm over her shoulders. And then, with no discussion, somehow Conroy and Janelle were in the big room, the other two were in the smaller room, and the cats and I were trying to fit into the windowless storage room.

I hadn't made much progress after all. I mean, I usually catch it now when Sapes talk in a way that doesn't fit what's happening, but their non-verbal stuff – a lifted shoulder, a sudden tension – still blows right past me. And I was still the odd one out. Even the cats deserted me sometime during the night to take up residence on the balcony.

# CHAPTER 28

From the unpublished Godunov manuscript
*Why We Came to Earth: The Yunko Voyages*

*Besides human characteristics, we also added certain genes and anatomical structures from Earth's animals to our hybrid genome to enhance our smell and hearing. To deal with Gliese-C's heavier gravity, we retained our denser, stronger bones. We modified the human pelvic girdle and lower torso musculature so that genes inserted to recreate our original tail-legs would find a sufficiently strong anatomical foundation. Above all, we worked to combine the human and Gliese-C brain and central nervous systems, trying to preserve the best of both species.*

The next morning, still groggy with fatigue, Conroy and I drove south to the ferry terminal at Tsawwassen, up a ramp, and into the belly of the boat. He stayed below decks with the Buick. I spent most of the two-hour voyage to Vancouver Island leaning on the railing, hypnotized by water flowing past the hull. The sea wind blew away the cloud of pheromones from the other passengers and the lingering fog of fever. Besides, standing wasn't as painful for the wound on the back of my thigh. I had nothing to do for the next few hours, unless my role as Conroy's hired muscle required beating up somebody when we reached Victoria.

Even that turned out to be unnecessary. The delivery, set at an elegant chocolate shop near Government Street, went off without a hitch. An armored porte-cochere stretched across the front, allowing the shop's elite customers to exit and return to their vehicles unseen by grubby commoners. We entered a small side door unchallenged. Conroy placed the metal satchel beside a display case, as if setting it out of the way, while he searched his pockets. A clerk behind the counter handed him a small, gold-foil shopping bag, and we left.

Back on the ferry, he dug cash out of the bag, peeled off high denomination bills, then handed me some, and returned the remainder to the bag. He made half-hearted threats to expose my secrets if I got out of line, but I didn't worry much about my companions leaking; claiming acquaintance with a space alien announced to the world that you were screaming bug-nuts. It was the Yunko reaction that froze my guts.

When we returned to the apartment that evening, it had transformed into something like home. Kayla and Lil sat at the dining table pecking away at the cumbersome laptops they'd hauled across Washington state like prosthetic brains.

Kayla looked up. "Since you keep claiming you're not an alien, I guess you can eat the whole range of human food?"

"Sure. Why?"

"Because we prepped a feast."

She wasn't exaggerating. Conroy had left money, and they had bought as much food as they could carry at what was left of the Granville Island farmers market. Soon, paper plates were heaped with crabs, oysters, and salmon steaks, almost hidden by the piles of vegetables and fruits, along with loaves of crusty bread and little iced cakes. The aromas threatened to burn out my circuits. The sight of so much food turned us all giddy. It temporarily overcame the haze of suspicion that blanketed the group. We ate, and we laughed.

When we could eat no more, Lil announced, "Mary Lee Griffin sneaked Davy out of her mother's house last night and took him to a hostel. She's bringing him across the border at Peace Arch Park day after tomorrow. Early in the morning."

"GenAge knows Davy's your brother," I said. "He's probably on a watch list at Customs." I was glad they had a plan, in spite of the fact I doubted it would succeed. I began making plans to get away from them the next day and head for the Outpost.

"We've been working on that all day, along with some other stuff," Lil said. "Mary Lee photographed the two of them and uploaded the pix so Kayla could make new IDs. We took them to the UPS store this afternoon and overnighted them to her."

"What if Customs asks the purpose of the trip?" Conroy said.

Kayla laughed. "To see a doctor, of course. Lil gave me all the details and I forged a letter from a Vancouver pediatric specialist verifying Davy's appointment."

We sat awhile longer talking about what they'd do the next day. Kayla had set up a job interview at an animation studio. Lil, who seemed happier than she'd been in days, wanted to shop for Davy. Conroy planned to take Janelle to visit a few high-ticket boutiques to spy out the fashion competition.

I mumbled something about taking the cats somewhere they could run free for a while. I didn't see any possible way to get treatment for Davy. My real plan was to take the cats, the culture, and disappear.

\*

Euphoria still wrapped us the next morning – we had plenty of leftovers and we didn't have to cram ourselves into the Buick. Kayla claimed first crack at the hot water so she could prep for her ten o'clock job interview. She finally emerged from the bathroom, emitting tendrils of steam, and disappeared into the bedroom. I joined the cats, who basked on the balcony, stuffed with salmon scraps.

At the sound of cheers, I went back inside. Kayla had emerged, ready to wow the animation jockeys. Her drab, unnoticeable camouflage was gone, replaced with a second skin of glowing deep red fabric from boots to collar. Somewhere in her gear, she'd brought along a wig like a shiny black mane. It crested her head, trailed down her back, and flopped a forelock over one eye. When she headed toward the kitchen for more coffee, the flowing tail attached low on her spine twitched from side to side as her buttocks tensed. It was very interesting to watch.

Lil, who sat at the table making one of her lists, noticed me noticing. "Hey, Goran. It's your turn in the shower."

Kayla grinned and whispered to Lil, "I'll be back by noon."

I grabbed a clean pair of dojo pants and headed for the bathroom. When I emerged, the others had left except for Lil. She stood in the living room wearing shorts and a t-shirt worn thin, one hand over her mouth, staring at the web of strings and fabric strung between long nails on the wall. She was so intent she didn't notice me.

I walked over. "What are you looking at?"

She jumped slightly. "This . . . this thing. The morning light? Its angle throws shadows on the wall. They look like, like people . . ."

She trailed off, but I could see what she hesitated to say. The knots and clumps and tendrils formed two naughty shadow puppets, busy with an activity I recognized from my old collection of manga porn.

I plucked at the web of strings and the figures vibrated. I felt an answering vibration of excitement myself. "Hey, if you're gonna tie yourself in a knot, that's the way to do it." I mimed threading my arms in a tangle around my torso.

"You goof," she laughed. She tried to wind her own slender arms into pretzels.

"No, no," I said. "You're doing it wrong." I looped my arms through hers, and then I brought her close enough for our bodies to touch. Her breathing turned shallow and her pheromone mix signaled we were heading down the same path.

I moved my arms to pin hers around me and kissed her. Then we were grasping at each other, mouths roving, pressing together so tightly we risked fusing our skin. I could hear her heart beating faster and faster. Her excitement fed my own. Unwilling to release each other, we stumbled toward the bedroom like sack racers. I kicked the door shut behind me. We freed hands long enough to jerk off clothing and fell across the bed.

"You're jumping on top of me again," she giggled.

Almost choked by pheromones, deafened by our racing hearts, I explored her silky skin, wanting to linger, wanting to plunge past any restraint. She moaned in anticipation.

Then abruptly, she changed. Like an airplane when the engine stalls – still gliding in the same direction but with no power behind it. She still caressed me, she still made noises deep in her throat, but the rhythm was wrong. Her heartbeat slowed. A confusing waft of anger and fear replaced the fragrance of desire. Then she gave up even faking it and lay there with her eyes squeezed shut.

I was baffled and angry. My own desire subsided in response. I raised myself on my elbows and tried to meet her eyes. "Lil?" I kept my voice low and non-threatening, hoping to restore the mood. Nothing. I rolled over, sat up and held her at arms' length.

Her eyes roamed the room, fixing on anything but me. "Sorry. Thought I could do it."

Okay, I'm hardly an expert lover, but I thought I was following the logical steps – not that I was thinking very much. And she had been eager too, until the moment she changed.

Had she panicked, afraid the pressure of desire might transform me into some slimy alien monster with tentacles? I forced my mind away from my own physical frustration and murmured, "Are you scared of me?"

She shook her head and curled into a fetal position.

But sex triggered some sort of fear. I heaved a sigh. She became unhinged whenever something reminded her of Erik Cheyne. Was the fear of sex connected? If that was the problem, it was probably so poisonous it required a professional. I swung my legs over the bed, eager to escape the room, escape the apartment, escape Lil, and resisted slamming my fist into the wall.

Something clinked faintly in the main room. I turned to ask her when the others were returning and saw a look of relief on her face that felt like a slap on mine. Then another faint, sneaky sound filtered through the bedroom wall. I held a finger to my lips, found my pants on the floor and pulled them on. She was sitting up too, pulling on her T-shirt.

An earsplitting squall erupted from the living room. Then another. Then a human shriek, followed by a woman screaming "Get away from me! Get away!"

My brain was still mired in confusion but my body went on emergency alert. I moved silently to the door. In one motion, I jerked it open, went through in a painful tuck and roll, and came up facing the building manager. She huddled in a corner, hugging the transport case to

192

her chest like a shield. Tails lashing, Zax and Gwitchy snarled and positioned themselves to lunge at her.

She gaped at me, then gabbled, "I'm supposed to check the apartments. Kids bring in illegal stuff." She jabbed the case toward the cats. "These . . . things. You're not supposed to have animals in here. That's illegal . . .."

I used my best command voice. "Put down the goods you stole." She probably snooped through the apartments regularly for anything to steal and sell for extra cash. Which prompted another thought: she must have started her search at my cubbyhole, next to the entrance door. If she grabbed something as odd looking as the transport case, she certainly would have stolen any cash. The cats, addicted to the balcony after too much time in a car, probably didn't sense her until she entered the living area. I veered around her to glance in my room. Sure enough, my empty wallet lay on the pile of blankets mounded on the floor.

When I turned back to the woman, I saw Lil standing in the bedroom door. I hoped she'd recovered enough to play along. "Lil, take photos. Then call 911. Tell them we caught a burglar on the premises and need an officer here immediately."

"I'm on it," she said in the voice of a bossy bureaucrat. Nothing slow about Lil, whatever her problems.

"No, wait!" The manager put down the case and stepped toward me. The cats screamed.

"Freeze," I ordered. I picked up the case and checked it for tampering. "Okay. Now hand over the cash you took from my wallet."

She glared and snorted at the same time, then dug a few bills out of her pants pocket.

"All of it. I know exactly how much there was." I handed the case to Lil, who was making a show of photographing the woman from different angles with her comm.

The manager glared at me and folded her arms. "Seize!" I ordered Zax. He launched himself at her leg and got a good four-paw grip. She screamed. "Hold!" I yelled. He froze in position, still gripping her leg.

"Hand it over," I said.

Trembling, eyes showing white all around, she pulled out more bills and threw them on the floor.

"Now get out of here," I said. "You come back, I'll let the cats work you over, then call the police to pick up what's left."

She nodded frantically. I ordered Zax to let go. Still eyeing the two cats, she backed out the door and slammed it.

I returned the transport case to my alcove and slumped on the sofa. Lil sat at the other end, hands limp by her sides. I reached over and took one. We sat that way a long time. I couldn't unscramble my thoughts. I had to get away from them all. I'd take the cats, go somewhere empty of humans long enough to calm down, then collect the transport case, contact the Outpost, and disappear forever from the lives of my "friends."

Bored with human relationships, Zax and Gwitchy whined. I rose, dressed, counted out half the money, and put it on the table. I stuffed the cats in their pack and said, "I'm taking these guys for a run. See you later." She kept staring at the floor.

# CHAPTER 29

From the unpublished Godunov manuscript
*Why We Came to Earth: The Yunko Voyages*

*Generations rolled past. Our Orbian ancestors gradually bred the evolving genome into their own offspring. We were no longer scientists working on specimens, but a single people transforming ourselves. Later generations wanted to live in the open air. Once on the surface, they often encountered the Evenki people who migrated through the area with their reindeer. They had been the original source of our human DNA.*

*Evenki reaction was unexpected. Perhaps the animism that permeates their culture encouraged more tolerance for "different" creatures. Perhaps the takeoffs and landings of our shuttles fit neatly into beliefs about Agdy, their god of fire and thunder. Perhaps our early, now abandoned, underground metal habitats resembled their legendary underground iron yurts peopled by the dead. For whatever reason, the Evenki went about their business throughout the vast taiga, or forest, and we went about ours.*

I waited on the dock with the seagulls, watching water taxis cruise False Creek. One headed my way and I waved it in.

The pilot glided to the dock. "Where you headed?"

"Stanley Park," I said. "How much?"

"Park's a thousand square acres. Narrow it down, mate."

I needed to be as far from people as possible. "Can you let me off along the north shore?"

"Let you off anywhere, you don't mind getting your feet wet." He gave the cat pack a brief, incurious glance and looped a rope around a bollard so I could board. We threaded through the small boats swarming False Creek and into the open waters of English Bay. Heading north, he rounded the rock seawall and dense forests of Stanley Park. At last, steep rocks gave way to a small slice of sand. The taxi pulled into the shallow water until its hull brushed the bottom. I went over the side, pack on my back and shoes in my hand, and waded ashore.

As I climbed into the trees, the cats jostled back and forth in their eagerness to escape the pack. I released them and they dashed around madly before falling in behind. I needed to get the transport case and get away. But even more I needed composure. I decided to hike across the Stanley Park peninsula the long way before returning to the apartment. We followed foot trails and plunged between towering stands of trees. Zax and Gwitchy nosed through undergrowth, chased squirrels, and startled river otters, who immediately dived out of danger.

Nearing the south shore, I dodged between the Aquarium and the stables and fantasized about the Yunko moving to Stanley Park, just another rare species observed by the park's ecologists. What I didn't think about was Lil. I couldn't solve her problems – no way was I an expert on human psychology. I didn't even know what *I* was. A Seal Bay High School senior? Cog in a research project? Tsimshian? Nisga'a? A son of central Siberia? My DNA was mostly Evenki, but I'd never met a native Evenk. It even seemed a tossup whether I was Sape or Yunko.

I headed for the park's famous totem poles. I vaguely remembered visiting the popular tourist attraction on a middle school outing. Our teacher had pointed out the pole carved by a Nisga'a artist and said, "Your people, Goran." My First Nation heritage was fake, but it was the nearest thing I had to a culture. I wanted, I needed, to put my hand on something solid.

At the edge of the wooded area, I put the cats back in their pack, then crossed the oval running track to the gathering of totem poles from different Nations. I stood among the people admiring the nine towering sculptures, ready to reconnect with my heritage. But for the life of me, I couldn't remember which pole was Nisga'a.

*

I got back to the apartment about five to find the others already there. Janelle gave us a summary of every fashion trend in the city. Lil acted as though nothing had happened. She'd gone out shopping and sat at the table sorting medicines, support cushions, nasal cannulas, and other stuff she'd bought for Davy. Kayla was using Lil's laptop for something. She logged off and set out boxes of Chinese carryout. We dug in.

Kayla took charge of the conversation, buzzing and bubbling about her new job. The animation studio had given her digital files of background characters to animate. Even more exciting, the studio wanted her to submit a portfolio of ideas for future characters and sets.

Even though she'd brought along her graphics screamer, she'd be working independently using equipment the company supplied. "Be cool if we could all stay together," she said. "Get a permanent place. Lil, once Davy's okay, you could come back and stay. Goran too."

Neither of us responded. Kayla gave me an odd look. I wondered if Lil had told her what happened, or if she picked up on our unease. I could hardly wait to finish eating. Hardly wait to gather up my stuff, leave, and contact the Outpost.

When we broke away from the table, I headed for my cubicle and the transport case. Gone. I followed Lil and Kayla into the small bedroom. "Where's the case? I want to check the gauges."

Lil tensed. "Somewhere safe."

"Where?" I looked around the space as if I could see through walls. She must have hidden it while I was moping around Stanley Park–I'd been gone most of the day.

"Goran, why don't you tell me exactly how your doctors plan to treat Davy. Tell me where we'll meet them, where we'll need to go, how long it will take, how hard it'll be on him."

"I don't know. I'm not a doctor, not even a scientist."

"You have to do better than that," she said.

I could have kicked myself for growing careless about the culture. But it obviously wasn't going anywhere while we were all cooped up in the Buick, and I'd been too distracted to tighten up security at the apartment. "You can't do anything with the culture. I can maybe use it to work out a deal with my people."

"No," she said. "The culture's my only bargaining chip. I won't hand it over until I'm convinced your people really will treat Davy."

Oddly, her voice sounded relaxed, as if she had gone beyond the tension of indecision. I stood motionless as a totem pole myself for long moments wondering how, short of torture, mind wiping, or murder, I could recover the culture and escape.

*

The next morning, the others rose early to drive to the Peace Arch border crossing to meet Mary Lee Griffin and Davy. I pleaded a flare-up of my earlier infection, moaned a bit, and stayed in bed.

As they left, Lil poked her head in the door of my storage room, sneered, and said, "Good luck."

I figured she had guessed exactly what I planned to do. Where else could she have hidden the transport case but the apartment? Far as I knew, she had no friends in Vancouver, no place she could stash the case unless she'd rented a locker somewhere. Vancouver was functioning better than anywhere in the U.S., but in 2037, it would be madness to leave something valuable lying around. In spite of her snark, odds were the case was hidden in the apartment.

So I jumped out of bed and started my search. I pawed through Lil and Kayla's backpacks and closet, searched under the bed, then under the mattress, pulled up a loose corner of the rug, tapped on walls, even looked in the toilet tank. Nothing. On to Conroy and Janelle's room to do the

197

same.

Then on to the kitchen and living area. Nothing in the cabinets, under the sink, taped to the bottom of the table. Nothing in the refrigerator but leftovers, or behind it, or in the oven. Nothing stuffed between the charred floor joists in front of the fireplace or up the chimney. I even loosened one end of the balcony railing so I could jackknife over the edge to look under its floor.

I was trying out passwords on Lil's laptop when a knock sounded on the door. I closed the machine and answered. They were back.

"Can you come downstairs and carry Davy up?" Lil said.

I followed although I did not want to confront Davy. It wasn't like I'd made his illness worse.

Or maybe I had by taking Lil away from him. His face looked thinner, purple smudges ringed his eyes, and his arms, beneath a sweater embroidered with raccoons, hardly bulked out the sleeves at all.

But he smiled and said, "Hi, Goran. I remember you."

I lifted him out of his wheelchair and started up the stairs, the others following with Davy's stuff. Inside, I deposited him on the couch and introduced him to Zax and Gwitchy, who immediately hissed. Davy shrank back.

"Don't worry," I said. "They haven't decided yet whether you're another cat. Just in case you are, they want to pull rank on you first." It drew a bigger smile from him than it deserved. In a few minutes the cats settled down and even favored Davy with a few leg rubs. They were still doing it when he fell asleep again.

Lil watched until he was gently snoring. Then she ordered me onto the balcony. I followed her into the bright morning rich with sea smells and leaned on the railing. She did the same. We didn't meet each other's eyes.

"You see his condition," she said. "I don't know how much more time he has. How soon can you set up things with your people?"

"I'll go pick up the comm helmet now and then contact the Outpost." The Yunko probably knew everything anyway, so I might as well pretend to set up a meeting. "So, uh, they'll either want me to go on to the Outpost or they'll send a pick-up team. Whichever it is, we'll all three meet them. With the cats. And . . . we'll tell them they have to heal Davy in exchange for the culture."

"Uh hunh," she said. "And what if they just pull out their ray guns, blow us away, and then take the culture?"

"They . . . we . . . don't operate like that." Of course they/we had never confronted such a massive security breach before.

"What about the others?" Lil jerked her head toward the apartment.

"Less they know, the better. We should get away from them for their own safety. I'll walk up to the UPS store and get the helmet right now."

"No," Lil said. "You'll wait till Davy's slept a little longer and then the three of us will go after the helmet."

"No! It might be dangerous for you two to show up with me before I've talked to them."

She turned her face toward me but wouldn't meet my eyes. "Might be more dangerous for you to go alone. Like, dangerous that we'd never see you again. Or dangerous that you can't deliver what you promised."

I walked to the other end of the balcony and stared unseeing at the science museum. The door clicked shut when she went inside. I considered jumping off the balcony, but I doubted a three-story fall would do a very good job of killing me. Eventually I heard Kayla laugh and Davy's high voice. I joined them with heavy steps.

"Goran," Lil said brightly, "Let's take Davy for a little outing as soon as I get him ready. Fresh air, see some new sights."

"Great." Kayla looked up from Lil's computer. "I'm ready for a break."

"Yeah," Conroy said. "We could drive to a decent beach."

"Oh, we're not going far," Lil said in a rush. "Just to pick up a couple of things. Goran can push the wheelchair. I don't think Davy should be out for too long."

"Yeah," I said, "I need to, uh, pick up cat food."

Conroy shrugged and resumed tinkering with the entertainment console. Kayla glanced from me to Lil to the computer screen and went back to work.

# CHAPTER 30

From the unpublished Godunov manuscript
*Why We Came to Earth: The Yunko Voyages*

*By the dawn of your nineteenth century, we were ready to return permanently to Gliese-C. At that point a dreadful problem arose. Our population had expanded to the point that we now lived primarily on the surface. But Earth's much stronger solar radiation proved almost as damaging as the supernova radiation that had fatally changed our atmosphere on Gliese-C. Skin cancers began to appear. But our scientists went to work and soon announced a breakthrough. They had altered the telomeres that protect against human cell death to make our own bodily defenses more effective at killing off cancerous cells. It was wonderful news, and the alterations were gene-spliced into every individual. Skin cancer cases fell dramatically.*

Thirty minutes later Lil and I had hiked uphill from the apartment on False Creek and cut through a leafy neighborhood to Cambie Street.

"Want a rest from pushing?" Lil said.

Maybe it was a peace offering. She took the handles of Davy's chair. His illness had warped her life as much as his, aging her into a cross between nurse and mother before she'd had time to be a child and teenager. Sort of like my job as Second, becoming bodyguard, mechanic, cook, and nurse at thirteen, without much to look forward to in "retirement." Maybe that was the bond between us. Odd, but deep. We made a bizarre family unit, but Canadians were still too polite to stare.

The city vibrated with sounds and smells. I constantly checked that no one was following us. Still, the skin on the back of my neck and ears felt supersensitive, as if I'd gotten a sunburn. As if we were being watched.

On busy Cambie Street people lunched at sidewalk tables, drifted into styling shops, or listened to street musicians. Davy fired off questions and demanded we halt in front of a pet shop. We finally reached the UPS Store sandwiched between a grocery and bistro.

Lil pointed to chairs in front of the bistro. "We'll wait out here."

I went in. The space for customers, lined with mail boxes, was the size of a large closet. The clerk finished with another customer. When she left I said, "Need to pick up a package for Charles Moody." I pulled the ID Kayla had made out of my wallet.

The clerk glanced at it. "Yessir. Just be a second." He turned and went through the accordion metal screen to the back room, returned and set the bulky package on the counter. I turned it over and around, looking for any sign of tampering. The door creaked open and I felt the air compress as someone else squeezed in.

The clerk glanced over my shoulder. "Just be a second, sir."

"No hurry," a familiar voice said.

Blood drained from my head. Delight filled my heart. I turned to see Maks, my first real friend. I wanted to bear-hug him. I wanted to tell him about our adventures. I wanted to run like hell.

Another guy squeezed in beside him, half a head taller with rock jaw and buzz cut, built like an action figure. He appeared to be in his forties, so he was probably about twenty-six, old enough for command in the security force. The Hawaiian shirt he wore looked as silly as a frilly pink bow tied around a granite boulder.

Maks leaned over to read the package address. "So, Charles," he said with a grin, "meet Anatol." Still holding the box, I nodded to the other man. Through the UPS Store's windows, I saw two more vaguely Asian-looking guys. One gripped Lil's elbow. The other grasped the handles of Davy's chair.

Maks followed my glance. "That the girl you were telling me about? Verrrry nice!" He punched my bicep, then snaked an arm over my shoulders. Anatol's fist clamped my other arm.

The clerk looked puzzled. "Is everything all right, gentlemen?"

"Just great," Maks said. "We're taking him to a surprise party." I swear, there was real affection in his voice.

I could have broken free, punched out one of them with the heavy helmet, reached the street, and disappeared. And abandoned Lil and Davy.

Maks and Anatol muscled me out the door. Lil looked at me as if I were the hangman. I guess she had finally absorbed what I really was. Her mouth opened a time or two like a goldfish's. "They said they were friends of yours."

Maks released me and approached her. He signaled the man holding Lil's arm to let go. It was amazing to hear his voice modulate. "We *are* Goran's friends. We knew he was in a tight spot and came along to help. You must be Lil."

The Yunko holding Davy's chair rolled it up the sidewalk out of the UPS clerk's view. Lil glanced back at Maks as she hurried to follow

He took the package from me. "Comm helmet?"

I nodded.

He stepped closer, lowered his voice. "Where's the culture?"

"I don't have it with me."

His head jerked back, his pupils flared. His chemical signature went mixed – confusion, wariness. "Then where is it?"

I couldn't speak.

"Get it together, Goran," he whispered. "You've been playing silly buggers all over the Northwest with these Sapes. The culture can't remain viable much longer. Where is it?"

Two of the others closed in around me. I felt like a rope, Maks pulling one end and Lil the other. My gaze must have flicked in her direction, because Maks gave me a hard stare and then stepped over to her. "Where's the culture?"

She didn't bother to protest her innocence, just braced herself and said, "I'll offer you a deal." Her shaky voice strengthened when she said, "My little brother has a genetic disease. The doctors haven't been able to figure it out. Goran said your people could fix it."

"Oh, he did?"

Lil seemed to grow three inches. She got right up in Maks' face. The air vibrated between them. "I was Goran's only chance to steal the culture. His brother failed and went on the run. Goran couldn't get inside the GenAge building. I worked there and knew how to sneak in, so I said I'd steal the culture for him if he could get treatment for Davy. He agreed."

"Yeah, Goran's very creative," Maks jibed. He looked at Davy, then said to the guy with slicked back hair, "Boris, check the chair for anything that could hide a transport case." Lil glared at Boris until he rose from his inspection and shook his head.

I admired her steel nerves even as I searched Cambie Street for an escape route.

Maks searched the street too. "We need somewhere private."

With a head jerk at the others, he led us around the corner and down a short block thick with trees and shrubbery onto a residential street. Davy's head twisted back and forth trying to watch us all. He didn't seem scared as much as excited at the drama playing out around him. Boris pushed the wheelchair, but Lil kept a hand on Davy's shoulder. Maks turned into an alley between residential back yards, empty of people, lined with cars, storage sheds and renegade greenery spilling over back fences. Anatol watched my every twitch. I figured he was the usual leader of the team but they'd brought Maks along because he knew me.

Maks drew me aside. "What have you been *doing*, man? You're driving the Researchers crazy. Where are the other three people traveling with you?"

The full awfulness of our situation hit me. "Look, leave them alone.

They don't know anything."

"They at that place you're staying? With the giant birds? Your guard animals there too?"

I didn't answer. He gestured for the other Yunko to join us, the one whose name I didn't know.

"Fetch the van for us," Maks ordered. "Then call the B team to pick you up. All of you go to their apartment and grab everyone, including two Pallas' cats. Sweep the place for anything incriminating, then head straight for the Outpost. Don't let them talk to each other."

No Name left to carry out his mission. I begged. "You don't have to grab them. Just memory-wipe them. We've only been together a few days. You can wipe back past that. Please." Maks stared at me, still giving off a chemical signature of confusion. Better, I guess, than hostility. "Do what you have to with me. I knew the risks, knew there was no clean way out. But they have no idea. They're innocent."

He cocked his head. "You actually care about these Sapes. Why?"

I couldn't answer. Why *had* finding a group of friends meant so much?

Minutes passed. Apparently we were waiting for the van. I conceived, then discarded, escape plans. Lil sneaked glances at Maks. At last, Officer No Name pulled a van into the alley, handed the key to Maks and left, presumably to join the backup team.

Maks suddenly forced my arms behind me in a bone-breaker grip. Anatol moved behind Lil and grasped her upper arms, while Boris took the handles of the wheelchair but watched us all intently. Looked like it was time to get serious.

"Lil, please tell us where the culture is," Maks said.

She shook her head and swallowed. "Not without a guarantee you'll cure Davy."

Maks tried quiet reason. "Lil, our people need the culture to survive. I don't know how much Goran revealed, but if you refuse to hand it over, you alone become responsible for killing off an entire intelligent species, including Goran and me. So I'll ask again, where's the culture?" His voice was as warm as fresh-baked bread.

Again she said, "Not without a guarantee you'll cure Davy."

Anatol said, also very calmly, "So your brother is the problem? Then if your brother is no longer here, there is no longer a problem. Correct?" He nodded to Boris, who moved his hands to Davy's shoulders, close to his neck.

Davy, long past exhaustion and running on sheer nerves, whined, "No. I don't want to go somewhere else. I want to stay with Lil."

# CHAPTER 31

From the unpublished Godunov manuscript
*Why We Came to Earth: The Yunko Voyages*

*The skin cancer problem apparently solved, we launched a communication pod to Gliese-C requesting that another ship come to Earth to take our expanded population home. Forty-five years later, we received an exciting reply – the experimental propulsion system commonly known as the Bubble Drive was operational. Two Bubble Drive ships, whose prolonged acceleration achieved near-light speeds, had left Gliese-C for Earth.*

*At the same time increasing emigration to Siberia by ethnic Russians from the west had begun to endanger us to the point that we sent personnel to begin constructing an emergency outpost in Western Canada*

Lil struggled in Anatol's grip, jerking toward Davy so hard I feared she'd dislocate her shoulders. She back-kicked the security officer between lunges, but he didn't seem to feel it.

Her tactics swung from physical to verbal. "There's a dead man switch, you idiots. You think I'd just hand over my only bargaining chip?"

Maks released me and approached her. She faced him, but I think she was too blind with fear to see him. "I put it all on the cloud," she yelled. "The ship that crashed, your short lifespans, the Outpost, the Researchers and the Seconds. Enough information to get everyone from National Security to GenAge after you."

Still in Anatol's grip, she leaned toward Maks. "Then I gave the password to someone. Told that person to change the password and send it to someone else – I don't know who, so you can't make me tell you. But if I don't make contact at regular intervals, that information go out to a dozen news sites on the Web."

"Okay," Maks said. "Okay, calm down." He turned to me. "Did you see her give a password to anyone?"

Time stuttered. Birds twittered. Breezes stirred the shrubbery spilling over backyard fences. Protect Lil, or side with my people?

Maks picked up on my paralyzing indecision. "Goran, what's the matter? Answer me. This is our future. It's all our people's work, our ancestors' heroic journeys. It's . . . it's Andrei making that last painful climb up the cliff to leave you what you needed – yeah, he told us about that."

I flinched at the thought.

"Goran, honor demands you do everything possible to save your people."

And then Maks seemed to run out of arguments. I'd been away from Lil most of yesterday and also this morning. Had she hidden the transport case away from the apartment? Had she given the password to her friend, Mary Lee Griffin? Or emailed or texted it to someone? I couldn't risk lying to another Yunko so I told the truth, technically. "I didn't actually see her pass anything on. But I was gone part of yesterday. She could have transferred something then."

Maks stepped next to Anatol and whispered, "Now what?"

Anatol answered in the same manner. "Don't ask me. I'm operations, not strategy."

Maks shuffled from one foot to the other as if eager to run from his own decision. "Okay," he said to Lil, "if you give us the tissue culture now, we'll take you and Davy to our base. I'll do everything I can to persuade the medics to treat him. Once you're there, they'll almost surely examine him, discuss his condition. Probably think it's an interesting bit of research, if nothing else. But if we don't have the culture, there's no point in any of us going back. If you think I've broken on my word, you can use your dead man switch."

I watched the struggle play across her exhausted face. At last she said, "Okay. I'll take you to it."

Maks jerked his head toward the van. Boris slid the side door open, got in the back, then gestured Lil and me to the two-person middle seat. Maks and Anatol lifted Davy in next to us, wheelchair and all.

As the door rumbled shut, I risked whispering to Lil. "Be careful. They can memory grab you, find out anything you know."

She leaned over Davy for a brief hug before murmuring, "There's another layer."

*

"Turn into the museum parking lot," Lil said.

Anatol pulled into a handicapped space at the World of Science children's museum. We lifted Davy's chair from the van and headed toward the building in a tense clot.

"Lil?" Maks stopped and waved at the entrance and its security scanners thirty feet ahead. "How'd you get the transport case through museum security?"

"I bought some cannulas and a carrying bag for a portable oxygen tank. Then I put the case in the bag, slung it over my shoulder, stuck a cannula in my nose, and walked in. No problem."

"So much for museum security," Maks said. "Come on. I'll buy tickets for us."

We entered the building amid streams of little people. The children's chatter, echoing inside the soaring sphere, made the building feel like an aviary. Lil pushed Davy slowly enough that he could look at the displays. I watched for possible hiding places, but the design was sleek and clean. Glass cases jutted from the walls, lacking any concealing cabinets below. Tables of puzzles and games were supported by single central columns. I kicked the base of a realistic mountain lion leaping to seize a grouse, but it sounded solid. Earth's life gathered into an architectural ark without one single hiding place.

"Speed it up," Anatol said. "We're in a hurry."

Lil responded by pushing Davy toward an upward ramp. "This may be Davy's only chance to see this place. He will, by God, visit as many exhibits as he wants."

Maks took Lil's arm. "We don't have time to wander around. Tell you what. Let Davy pick the thing he most wants to see. We'll visit that, then you'll get the culture."

She shrugged, knelt by Davy's chair and began to read the various attractions off a directory board. When she mentioned a sports science playroom, he said, "That one!"

"Okay." She ducked her head a moment then rose and resumed pushing, past a *Tyrannosaurus rex* skeleton and up the ramp to the next level.

Screams of excitement drew us toward the sports science exhibits. Davy stared in awe at kids racing each other until they slammed into pillowy safety stops, kids crowding around batters' cages and balance beams, kids jumping off a platform that measured how heavily they landed. A few minutes later, Anatol the Action Figure said, "Stop stalling. Get it now."

"Come this way." Lil led us up another turn of the ramp to an empty corridor. She faced Maks. "Run the Pocket Doc on Davy. Now. Before I turn over anything, I want to know if you can even diagnose him."

He whipped around to stare at me. "How does she know about that?"

I shrugged. I thought. "I passed out for a while after I went over Grand Coulee. They must have gone through my medkit and found it. It's pretty simple to use."

"Will it hurt?" Davy said.

"No, sweetie. You won't even feel it."

"I don't carry one around with me," Maks said.

"Well," Lil said, "get one from the van or get Goran's from that other team." Now, she seemed the impatient one.

"Get the one in the van," Maks ordered Boris. "And hurry." Boris took off.

I trailed after Lil and Davy, wondering if one teenage Sape would be able to back off our entire species. A few minutes later, Boris jogged up the ramp, found us, handed Maks the Pocket Doc, and ran a hand over his shiny black, slicked-back hair in case the trip had mussed it.

Maks took the device, about the size of a paperback book, knelt by Davy's chair and said, "Open wide, sunshine."

Davy looked nervously at Lil, who nodded. Maks pressed a button and the sampler probe extended. He stuck it in Davy's open mouth, angled it to the side and said. "Now close your lips like you're sucking on a straw." Davy's eyes went wide with surprise at a low, slurping sound. Maks pressed another button, said "All done" and withdrew the probe. He stepped away and waited, jiggling a foot, tugging at his collar.

"You and Kayla used that on me?" I said. "Pried my mouth open?"

"Didn't have to. You were drooling." She didn't take her eyes off Maks.

A soft chime signaled that a diagnosis was ready. Maks turned the device sideways and peered at it.

"What does it say?" Lil stepped closer to him.

He frowned. "Proximity consultation required."

"What's that mean?"

"The medics need to actually see him." He poked a couple more buttons. "Raw readout says, "Homo sapiens sapiens. Mutation in DMD gene, along with associated anomalies." He shrugged.

"DMD. Duchenne's muscular dystrophy," Lil said. "Plus a problem in another gene. Just what the doctors in Bellingham said, but it took them three months."

She twisted her mouth in thought, turned Davy's chair around to face the others and took her stance beside him. "I didn't tell you everything about the dead man switch. Switches, actually. There's two. Kayla's family owns a major corporation that does military stuff. Surveillance. She communicates secretly with one of the senior scientists – sounds like he was almost a second father to her. She and I managed to access the programs inside the Pocket Doc, and Kayla streamed everything to this scientist."

Maks was good. He wobbled on his axis a second, then recovered. "Nice try, but the Pocket Doc's encrypted."

"Not the IPs," Lil shot back. "So they have the locations of the Outpost and every computer in contact with it."

Three five-year-olds careened through our legs, screaming, and galloped off down the ramp. Maks said, "So what? A bunch of locations. What does that prove?"

"That's just for starters. I got as far as converting the actual program code for IPs into numbers. Kayla studied them for a while, said they look like strings of triple number combinations. Possibly X, Y, and Z coordinates. Maybe even . . . right ascension, declination and distance. Like they're vectors and distances from some point in space, used as the basis for a code."

"So this Kayla looks at some numbers and imagines something?" Maks grinned. "Sorry, but you're not scaring me yet."

"Too bad." She stared at him like an apex predator. "You see, Kayla's scientist has access to enough computing power to run the whole Northwest, along with the tightest security there is. And Kayla has this weird genius kink for visualizing stuff in three-dimensional space."

"Where's Kayla?" Davy grabbed for the one word he understood.

Lil laid a hand on his shoulder. "She's gone on ahead to the place we're headed. Where the doctors will fix you."

Maks pulled on his fingers, popping the knuckles, and studied Lil. We all jumped when an explosion rolled up from a science demonstration going on below, followed by excited cheers. "Give me a minute," Maks said. He walked out of earshot and put a comm to his ear.

I thought I'd learned to understand Sapes, but I'd been completely blindsided by what Lil and Kayla were really doing, why they'd lugged along their laptops that seemed so unnecessarily powerful. Neither side trusted me.

Maks walked back to us. Lil looked at him with an unreadable expression. "You've got your bargain," he said. "They'll allocate a full medical team to devise and perform whatever procedures and therapies it takes to heal your little brother. They'll begin as soon as we arrive at the Outpost."

She looked at him like he was clear dawn breaking after a hurricane. Tears leaked down her cheeks. Relief, I guess, and something else. I couldn't pull my gaze away from them, painful as it was to watch. I think that was the moment I finally understood. Lil's heart – along with the rest of her – would always belong to whoever had the power to help Davy.

Maks broke eye contact first. "So, take us to the culture."

Lil took the handles of the wheelchair and started back down the ramp, Maks beside her. Anatol, Boris, and I trailed behind. We spiraled to the ground floor and headed toward the entrance.

Maks put a hand on her arm. "Isn't the culture in the museum?"

"Through here," she said and veered left into an annex that held an exhibit about water. She continued through double glass doors to the outside, a patio turned into a natural science park crowded with planters and hanging green walls, busy with chickens roaming free. We moved through the crowd like a dark cloud passing over the bright, bouncing children.

Lil headed toward the far end of the park. We followed her through a forest of big red balls on poles. Ahead of us rose a gingerbread house built from trash. Every rickety molecule of higgledy-piggledy chaos banished from the museum's interior had piled up here.

Maks and I followed the ramp that wound around the house with its chimney of discarded tires, mosaics of bottle caps, cornices of plastic bottles, wall panels patched together from shoe soles, keyboards, dart boards, chopping boards, and one cracked toilet. Lil and Davy followed.

"Is this Hansel and Gretel's house?" Davy said doubtfully.

I stepped over to read the sign in front of it. "No, it's the non-organic trash a family throws away in a year, all 2,028 kilograms of it."

I took another couple of steps around to the back side of the cottage. My gaze traveled over a jangle of pots, pans, thermoses and toasters. One end of a cylindrical object in a canvas cover peeked out from the metal clutter.

"Maks," I said quietly, "here it is."

"How'd you get it up there?" Maks asked Lil.

She changed from steel-nerved warrior to guilty kid. "I, uh, kind of threw it."

He stared at the case a moment more, rose onto his toes and reached over the railing to hook a finger under the cannula. He jinked it up a couple of times to release the case from a drainboard hook. Then he carefully pulled our future from the house built of human trash.

# CHAPTER 32

From the unpublished Godunov manuscript
*Why We Came to Earth: The Yunko Voyages*

*Our two new Bubble Drive ships entered the solar system in spring of 1908. They planned to orbit Earth while the two shuttles on each vessel loaded our people and data. Then the fleet, including our 1609 ship still circling Mars, would leave for Gliese-C.*

*On June 30 the first ship approached Earth and prepared to enter orbit over Krasnoyarsk. Tragically, an unforeseen coronal mass ejection erupted simultaneously, compressing the upper atmosphere severely and disrupting the plasma flow of the Bubble Drive. Our supply ship was destroyed. Your histories record the detonation as the Tunguska Event. It lit up night skies as far away as London, registered on seismometers worldwide, and flattened about 800 square miles of forest. Several dozen of our personnel who were above ground in the area were killed.*

Huge, grotesquely muscled Anatol cradled the culture case like a newborn baby.

Maks touched Lil's cheek and said, "Thank you." She gazed back at him like a love-sick puma. He looked confused. Maybe he'd overshot his mark. I mean, Lil's instant obsession with Maks, or whatever it was, seemed strange even for a Sape. She always appeared so tough, so smart, so determined, but maybe her troubles had damaged her brain circuits more than I'd ever be able to understand.

After one last glance at Lil and another at the case, I pretended to watch the chickens. They pecked and fluffed and played keep away with a bottle cap, but I couldn't manage a smile. My great quest was done. Andrei would never go into the field again, so my job as his Second was also done. I'd given Lil a chance to grasp what she wanted, and then she'd moved on at light speed. Whatever I had hoped for with her was most definitely done. And it was my fault that four Sapes now knew about Yunko existence on Earth. About that, something drastic would no doubt be done.

The rest of my life looked like nothing but shame and misery for betraying the secrets of my people. I wished I could disappear – into the city around me or into oblivion. Didn't make much difference.

Maks broke away from staring into Lil's eyes and glanced at people nearby. Some watched us curiously. He hurried down the concrete ramp and headed toward the rear side of the elaborate chicken coop. I followed, hoping he might agree to a plan forming in my mind.

When I caught up, he was comming someone. "Yeah. Anatol Bobroff will be leaving in a cab for Abbotsford Airport east of Vancouver. Should arrive approximately forty minutes from now. Are you close enough to rendezvous with him that fast?" He turned and raised his hand as if forestalling interruptions. "Okay. We'll depart in a van. The other team will also head back with the other persons of interest. Right."

Anatol and Boris headed toward us. Last thing I needed was an audience. "I have to talk to you," I said. "Alone." I walked toward a wall covered with planting bags and veered behind it. Maks followed and then looked at me curiously as I failed to speak. Frayka knows what my body chemistry was transmitting.

At last I said. "I need a favor. It'll make everything simpler." When he nodded I continued, "You know the Big Dipper Mine? The open pit place on the way to the Outpost?"

He nodded.

"When we get there . . . I want the two of us to leave the others in the van and hike up to the mine." I finished in a rush. "Then hit me with a fatal dose of mind-wipe, weight me down and dump my body in that deep pond at the bottom of the mine. Okay?"

He stared at me with a mix of emotions too complicated to read.

"Oh, and promise me you'll find someone to take care of the cats."

His face twitched. He was trying not to laugh. I didn't expect Maks to break down sobbing over my imminent death, but mockery was unacceptable. "Well, say something!"

At that he actually laughed. "Oh! Noble One! I am speechless with awe at your heroic, self-sacrificing bullshit!" He sniggered.

It was too much. I shifted weight to attack.

Just then Anatol appeared around the wall and tapped him on the shoulder. Maks said, "Plane's headed for Abbotsford Airport, so you're good to go. See you at the Outpost." Anatol strode toward the museum's exit, past Lil, who was handing a chicken to Davy.

"Come over here, you idiot!" Maks walked toward the decorative fence around the park. He leaned on the railing and slapped it for me to do the same. He stared at the city, the mountains, and the sea. He jiggled the van keys over the fence, humming tunelessly.

Just as I was considering a jab to his kidney, he chuckled again and said, "Dude, the Change Lords and the senior scientists are working non-stop with Andrei. There's one last kink, but they suspect the culture contains the key. And they're really antsy for you to get to the Outpost. No way do I help you off yourself."

I grabbed his hand to stop the maddening key jangle. "They just want me there to punish me, or mind-wipe me into a vegetable or something."

"You're lousy at keeping secrets, that's for sure. But you're not in as bad a shape as you think you are. Everything – everything! – changed the moment they realized they might succeed. Right now there's this giant, smash-mouth, groin-kicking brawl going on. Even the Change Lords are acting like three people in a lifeboat – all cooperation until they reach an island, then fighting over who gets the boat for firewood."

The picture just would not form in my mind. "Arguing about what?"

"What to do next! Don't you get it? You and I might actually live long enough to go home! In the meantime, these three factions are pounding each other into mush over how to go about it."

His news didn't really penetrate the thick blanket of depression wrapping my brain.

Boris came over. "We need to get going."

"Head out. We'll follow." Maks didn't even look at him.

Boris strode away obediently and I said, "What factions?"

Maks started back toward the entrance, nodding at me to follow. "One faction wants to gene splice all of us with the cure and then sneak away. People on Earth would never know we had been here. Another faction says we're now more human than Orbian, so why not stay here on earth and quietly fade into the population."

The notion of quietly fading into the background seemed unbearably appealing. Earth was the only place I'd ever known. I'd spent my life bonding with every field mouse, every tree, every leaping salmon, and pooping gull. "So wouldn't either group punish me for blowing their secrets?"

He headed toward Lil and Davy. I followed. "Probably. Bad news for you if one of them wins."

"Okay, what does the third faction want?"

Maks grimaced. "Gene splice our whole population, then tell Earth we're here."

"Why?" I said, but he just aimed a sappy smile at Lil and laid a hand on Davy's shoulder. The boy dozed, with an exceptionally calm chicken half tucked under his jacket. "We need to go now," Maks said and took the chicken in his hands, triggering a flapping, clucking tornado.

Davy jerked in surprise and reached for the chicken. Maks, who now held it by the legs, lifted it away and released it to bustle back to its mates. Davy started crying. I walked away. Too much to think about. Beside,

Maks was the man of the hour; let him handle it.

I had exited the building when Maks came up behind me and flung an arm over my shoulder like he hadn't a care in the world.

"So why?" I muttered. "Why does the third faction want to reveal our presence?"

"As a warning." He said in a low voice, "Earth's wrecking its atmosphere, just like ours was wrecked. Except they're doing it in reverse. So we'd try to reach a deal. Some of the technology we've developed in exchange for territory to call our own."

I had never realized how little I cared about returning to Gliese-C. "Sounds reasonable."

"Not really." He was whispering now. "Sapes are terrified of other Sapes who're a slightly different color. Turn into howling, murdering mobs. What do you think they'd do to us? Particularly if they think we have some 'secret' for longer life? They'd skin us alive over slow fires to get it." He paused. "And there's something else. You ever feel like something's going on you don't know about? I've been feeling like the higher-ups at the Outpost are really jangled, like there's some other big crisis. I don't know what, but I'm pretty sure it's important."

Lil and Davy caught up with us. Lil wouldn't meet my eyes. Davy had stopped crying although he still looked grumpy.

"So, buddy," Maks said, "how'd you like the museum."

Davy wasn't buying the charm offensive. "Okay, I guess." Silently I cheered him on. "Wish I had a chicken," he added.

"We'll see if we can find one." Maks looked a little frazzled. He walked with them the rest of the way to the van. When they were loaded up, he gestured me around to the back as if checking something. "Okay. Back to your situation. Couple weeks ago, offing yourself might have made sense. But if the third faction wins the brawl, revealing our existence to outsiders may no longer be a termination offense."

Too complicated to think about. "So what happens to Lil and Davy? To the others?"

"Way above my clearance level." Maks laughed. "They only sent me along on this mission because I know you. We're dumping the whole bunch of you on the Change Lords. Give 'em something new to argue about."

Half an hour later, we were somewhere east of downtown Vancouver, but I had too much on my mind to notice landmarks. I sat beside Lil in the van's short middle row. Maks was driving. Boris, in the front passenger seat, twisted around to watch us.

Maks pulled out his phone and answered. "You sound funny," he said immediately. Then, "Where are you now?" Then "Still? How long will they be under?" At last he said. "Yeah, probably. Why?"

A minute later, he pulled into a parking lot, stopped, got out and gestured to Boris to take the wheel. "Head back to the apartment at False Creek."

Once we got back into traffic headed the other way, Maks turned to glare at me. "Where did you *find* these people?"

I shrugged.

"What's wrong?" Lil said. She reached for Davy's hand. "Are the others all right?"

"Oh, yeah. Your buddies are just fine," Maks said. "They're taking little naps right now. My buddies? Not so much. Karl has a broken nose – the big guy got in one punch before they subdued him. And Vassily's hands and arms are clawed up. Apparently your cats decided to protect that other girl – Kayla? – when Vassily tried to sedate her.

"Was she hurt?" I said.

"Hell, no. Vassily ended up spraying the whole screaming, yowling bunch of 'em. Those damn cats are just as confused about which side they're on as you are."

He turned to stare out the windshield, then blurted, "And Karl was ranting about some antique car we have to take along, so they need another driver. Karl's spooked. He wants us to all caravan to the Outpost. We're going back to the apartment to link up." He paused a moment. "Actually, I don't know what the staggering hell's going on."

I grinned. The future scared me stiff, but at least I'd face it with my homies.

Afterword, from *The Way of the Yunko*

*The first verified instance of Sacrifice for the People dates back to Gliese-C's semi-mythical War of Lies. King Lys'pithym IV, a.k.a. Lisp the Feckless, lusted for war. He and his ministers convinced the people to attack an enemy tribe, saying they had invented a great horn that, if blown, would shatter our bones. After many lives were lost and stores of treasure squandered, no great horn was ever found. We entombed our war dead in a towering memorial. Lisp the Feckless was escorted to the top, where he leaped (some say was pushed) to his death in atonement for the evil he had done his people. It established a precedent for those who fail at large responsibilities.*

Four hundred miles north of Vancouver, a deer sprang from deep forest and bounded across the highway. Boris stomped the van's brakes. A faint "Oof" sounded behind us. I looked back. Kayla lay on the middle seat, Zax spooned against her body. She wore her dark red catsuit, minus the mane and tail, plus restraints around wrists and ankles. Her eyes were closed, but her breathing changed and I caught a whiff of adrenaline.

I faced forward again, wearing a blank stare. I didn't know whether Boris and the others categorized me as Sape or Yunko. Whenever I looked at Boris, he seemed to be flicking glances my way – I figured him for Intelligence Division. On the other hand, he was the only member of the retrieval team assigned to our van for the 800-mile drive to the Outpost–for me, pretty good odds. Looked like they classified me as Yunko-on-probation.

Boris frowned and sniffed the air. "Is she awake?"

Impossible for me to choose sides. I hefted Gwitchy onto my lap with an exaggerated grunt of effort and said, "Still got her eyes closed. What'd they spray 'em with?"

"Sedative. Didn't use memory wipe since they'll probably interrogate you all as soon as we reach the Outpost."

A few miles later, Kayla herself settled the question. "Stop!" she said. "I have to pee."

"We'll stop in Prince George, about twenty miles farther," Boris said.

"I don't want to lag too far behind the others."

"Twenty miles! I have to go now!" For the remaining miles, she muttered unflattering speculations about our alien plumbing.

We had been the last vehicle to leave Vancouver for the Outpost. Lights from isolated farms sprinkled the darkness, little towns slept along the highway, and another vehicle swooshed by every fifteen miles or so.

Soon the glow of Prince George rose above the horizon. We crossed the Fraser River and Boris cut left onto the Yellowhead Highway, which meandered northwest across the Coast Range to the Pacific. Once past most of Prince George, he pulled off and drove behind an all-night gas and recharging station to its restroom doors.

When Boris fetched the restroom key, I marched Kayla to the Women's door and thrust her inside.

Two minutes later she yelled through the door, "Goran, can you hear me? Where are the others? Where are you taking us?"

Boris had pulled around to the charging stations so I yelled back, "Conroy and Janelle are about thirty minutes ahead of us. They're with Vassily and Karl in the Buick."

"The Buick? You aliens invade Earth for old cars?"

The "you aliens" stung. "Somebody said they had orders to keep Janelle – well, actually he said 'the pregnant one' – calm and happy. I guess keeping Janelle calm required keeping Conroy happy."

The door cracked open and Kayla peered out. "What about Lil and Davy?"

I was trying not to think about Lil. With a voice as toneless as possible, I said, "They left immediately. Fixed up a bed in the other van for Davy. Maks is driving."

"How's that feel, spaceman?" She smirked at me.

"It was the logical arrangement." I gripped her arm again as she emerged.

"So you're my jailer? What are you gonna do with us?"

I had no real answer to her questions, so I hauled her back to the van. Boris leaned against the side, dangling the restraints from one finger.

Kayla dug in her heels. "No way! My arms and legs are still numb from those things." She glanced toward cars parked at the gas pumps and opened her mouth to scream.

Okay," Boris said. With one movement he grabbed her head and clamped the sedative inhaler over her mouth and nose until her struggles faded.

At last the sky grew lighter in the rear view mirrors. We'd driven all night. High slopes splotched with clear cuts rose on both sides of the Bulkley River valley, topped by rugged mountains too steep for logging.

As we neared Hazelton, I began to see buildings, creeks and farms that looked familiar. No doubt the Outpost had recognized us too. The first perimeter – drones only – is fifty miles out. We stopped briefly in Hazelton and bought hockey-puck breakfast sandwiches. I was trying so desperately to soak up what might be my last sight of the outdoors that I hardly noticed the usual hassles with Kayla. Boris had let her stay awake for the last stretch. He probably wanted to make sure we were alert for interrogation. My gut clenched at the thought.

Twenty miles later the Skeena River flowed along the highway on our right and the jagged, snowy peaks of the Seven Sisters loomed above the tree line on our left. With no warning, the hum of the van's motor and the noise of the tires shimmered for an instant, like a brief mirage of sound instead of vision.

"What was that?" Kayla shook her head as if to knock water out of her ears. I shrugged, surprised she noticed, even though she had talked about a family surveillance business. Apparently she knew enough to notice the second defense perimeter taking a reading.

We turned off the highway onto a logging road. After several slow miles Boris stopped. Up ahead, two old guys leaned on two old pickups parked in the road, catching up on the morning's gossip.

One sauntered to Boris' window. "Where you folks headed?"

Boris checked his hair in the mirror and gave the correct response. "We plan to spend three days at a cabin past the village."

"What about this young lady?"

"Authorized."

Kayla yelled, "They're kidnapping me!" just before the old guy lifted a comm and pressed a button. He grinned. Obviously not a potential rescuer. She fell silent. He returned to his pickup and pulled forward so we could pass.

Three rings of security down, three more to go. The next one looked like an almost abandoned native settlement: half a dozen houses so gray and weathered that the walls had cracks and holes – with weaponry, both projectile and field generating, on the other side. The gas station's faded sign still read "No Gas Today." The elementary school I remembered well. It consisted of a metal "temporary classroom" beside an old double wide trailer, a two-bay carport, a swing set, and weedy baseball diamond. Half a dozen children played in the yard with a roll of chicken wire. The teacher watched us closely as we passed, one hand to her ear.

Farm buildings clustered at the end of the road, which narrowed into a driveway that ran past the house and curved behind the barn into the forest. We started down the ruts, which improved as soon as they were hidden by the trees.

Three miles later, a meadow glinted through the foliage. Beside a truck with a bumper-pull trailer, two guys with long guns stood in the road, holding the reins of saddled horses. Another armed guy stepped from the trees beside us.

"How's it going?" he asked.

"Can't complain." Boris reached out to swipe the pad he held. The guy nodded at his two buddies and they led the horses out of the way. We drove down across the sloping meadow and followed a track through the trees on the other side into a ravine. At one point the filtered light dimmed even more, and the tops of the trees went out of focus.

Kayla peered out and up at the now blurry sky. "Giant hologram? Making this crappy road invisible from above?"

I nodded. No point now in keeping secrets.

At last we approached the final barrier. The gravel road turned away from the stream and soon spread into a loose patch that lapped a cliff face. When the van stopped before the cliff, small cracks appeared in the rock strata, widened, and grew into weapons ports. A large rectangle, maybe twenty-five feet by twenty feet, sank back into the cliff space. Its vertical crack widened as huge doors rolled apart. We drove forward into the rock, into the Outpost.

Past the checkpoint, sunlight glowed through portals that pierced the rock on our left, framing views of sky and a steep-walled canyon. Thick arches, like flying buttresses carved from living granite, supported the roof that protected us. Against my will, I leaned forward, drinking in the sights of my childhood.

Kayla lapsed into open-mouthed concentration, either stunned or busily imprinting every detail in hopes of escape. I rolled down the van's window and inhaled. The Outpost's unique smell of biological and mechanical processes flavored with rock dust, the feel of the air, the look of the light, flooded me with memories. I wondered if I'd have time to look up childhood friends or visit the crèche – some of my crèche mothers might still be alive. I suppose it depended on whether my future stretched another couple of days or fifteen more years. I dreaded what awaited me, yet returning to my childhood home drained away a tension so familiar it had gone unnoticed.

The wall on our right, finished in mottled grays similar to the local rock, turned into a progression of bays, corridors, stairs, commissaries, and other necessities of life. A muted rumble signaled heavy construction underway somewhere. I couldn't tell if the noise came from the labs, warehouses, hydroponics, and mechanical services far below or from the living quarters that rose half a dozen floors above, their windows to the outside set back in crevices and under overhangs, covered with camouflage similar to the old bus wraps.

The van stopped in front of an entry labeled Security Services. Andrei and Maks waited beside the door to welcome us. I grabbed Andrei in a bear hug, for once forgetting his arthritis. He had tears in his eyes when we released. I didn't know if Maks was there as a guard or as a friend so I just stuck out a hand. He shook it. They herded us through the Security lobby, down a corridor, and into a large room for a sort of preliminary booking. The others were already there. Conroy, sitting with his arm around Janelle, focused his glazed eyes long enough to glare at me. Lil, fussing over Davy, simply nodded. Davy at least spoke. "Hi, Kayla. Hi, Goran."

# CHAPTER 34

From the unpublished Godunov manuscript
*Why We Came to Earth: The Yunko Voyages*

*Our second Bubble Drive vessel had remained in orbit around Mars. Those aboard spent the next few months re-engineering the ship's two shuttles so they could land safely on Earth. Their first task was cleaning up the Tunguska area until no trace of our connection with the explosion remained.*

*But before we could all leave for Gliese-C, the first of us began to die. To our horror, within three years, every Earth-dwelling individual older than thirty-two was gone. The solution we thought we had found to skin cancer was killing us.*

Few things are more uncomfortable than watching the interrogation of your friends, particularly when they're dosed with a truth drug. But I learned a lot of interesting background.

The room looked like every other bureaucratic processing room on Earth, maybe in the whole galaxy. They scanned our irises and took our hand prints. While they stuck med patches infused with truth drug between my comrades' shoulder blades, one woman in a lab coat said they'd interview me later. Then they started down the row with their questions, forms, and bio-monitors.

Dalton Conroy. Student. Mid-level drug dealer. Amateur mechanic. Mother died from unknown causes when he was three months old. Father unknown. Raised by uncle. Started working as a drug courier at eleven. Emotionally bonded to Janelle Higgins.

Janelle Maria Higgins. Student. Mother born to emigrants from Cuba. Father from a Puget Sound First Nation band, some Asian in the mix. Approximately thirteen weeks into pregnancy. Demanded that someone notify her parents that she was okay, assuming she was, in fact, okay, but not to let them know where she was or who she was with.

Ludmilla "Lil" Osborne. Student. Biotech company intern. Hacker. Caregiver for younger brother. Mother descended from early Russian settlers. Father arrived with a wave of refugees from California after the fire storms.

Kayla Midnight. Birth name Regina Sabine Theissen Martinez. Student. Artist. Forger. Parents of German-English and Spanish American descent. Ran away from home at the age of thirteen. No further contact with family.

And that information, combined with Kayla's enigmatic comments, finally told me who she really was. Four years ago when we first arrived in Seal Bay, newsfeeds had been full of the assumed kidnapping of Reggie Martinez, a thirteen-year-old girl from a wealthy East Coast family. Since I was then trying to imitate a thirteen-year-old Sapiens myself, I studied the stories. And I remembered "Monkey-Mart," the press's nickname for Montgomery-Martinez, the armaments and surveillance manufacturing empire controlled by her parents. Kayla had to be the missing heir, using her outrageous outfits to hide in plain sight.

I was still piecing it together as they led my companions past me for further questioning. "Thanks a lot, shithead," Conroy said.

Andrei and Maks corralled the cats and said they'd pick me up for lunch after my medical check-up and before my much longer personal interview, a.k.a. my trial. Lab Coat Lady then led me to a doctor's suite for a painfully thorough going-over.

When they finally released me, Andrei, Maks, and the cats were waiting in the lobby. We set out along the main concourse. Electric carts loaded with construction equipment or elderly passengers buzzed past us. A dozen youngsters followed a teacher on a school outing. A young woman strode past, the two biggest ravens I've ever seen perched on her leather-padded shoulders. Zax and Gwitchy sank into their butt-wiggling, I-see-a-bird crouch. Andrei and I grabbed them until the ravens were past.

It was mid-afternoon, but one cafe on the mezzanine was still open. Posters of Haida longhouses and the Seven Sisters peaks added color to its industrial décor. The cook, who came out to take our orders, looked vaguely familiar; maybe I'd known her as a child.

Maks smiled at her. "What's today's special?"

She smacked her head in exasperation. "Right now, the special's the only thing we've got. Chicken pudding with white potato pudding, sweet potato pudding, and green bean pudding. All reconstituted from powder. Sorry." When we hesitated she added, "The other two cafes are down to the same stuff, and the main dining hall's closed today until five. Maintenance has been changing out the hydroponics filtration system. And Big Ag enforcers raiding for illegal seeds hit a couple of our truck farms down near the border."

We ordered three specials. As soon as she headed to the kitchen I asked Maks, "Did Davy make the trip okay? And Lil?"

"More or less. The infirmary did a preliminary check on the kid soon

224

as we got here."

He looked uncomfortable, and he left out the information I really wanted – how he and Lil were getting along. "The Researchers agreed to treat Davy," he added. "Actually, they were drooling over him."

"Why?"

He shrugged.

"So what happens to the rest of us?"

"Don't know. But the lodging masters talked about prepping quarters for you. I guess they plan on keeping you all around for a while."

At least they wouldn't kill the others immediately. "Have they started working on the tissue sample?"

Andrei cleared his throat. "They reserved half of it for replication and are sectioning the rest for immediate testing."

His cadence implied he had more to say. "What else?"

He cupped his hands over his mouth for a moment as if to hold in the words. "They went as far as they could from my description and detailed notes. There is a strong theoretical probability that the sample may offer a way to reverse the damage." He didn't seem elated.

"Well, great!" I said. "Sounds like you've basically saved our people."

"I said 'theoretical probability,' not cure. And . . . the effect they hope for seems to be limited to people who carry a certain genetic combination." He paused. "My genome does not have that combination. Yours might, but your odds are not good."

I couldn't speak. The cook returned with our plates of colored mush. I was hungry, the mush was bland, but when I tried a bite of food, I struggled to swallow. I put my fork down and tried to feel happy that at least some of my people might be cured. My stomach clenched with spasms. I tried to find the bright side: if execution was my fate, it wouldn't matter that I lacked the life-saving gene.

Maks tried to restore normalcy, chattering on about how gorgeous Janelle was and how the researchers seemed extremely interested in her pregnancy. Our coffee arrived. I had managed one swallow when Boris and a security guy walked in and stopped behind my chair.

Boris tapped my shoulder. "They're ready for you."

*

At least they didn't drag me into the Council Room in chains. A handler took charge of the cats and I walked in with Boris and the guard flanking me. Andrei and Maks followed. I didn't know whether they were along for moral support or to give evidence.

The space was the size of a classroom. Its far end was concave. A dais filled the curve. On the dais sat a semicircular desk painted with Orbian

225

and First Nation symbols. Three shallow alcoves indented the curved wall behind the desk. By the time they take office, Change Lords are usually around thirty and afflicted with multiple physical problems. The alcoves were wired with medical devices from stimulus pumps to artificial breathing machines just to get our leaders through meetings without collapsing. I caught a medical smell above my own reek of two-day-old sweat.

The middle alcove was empty. The other two Change Lords sat in the side alcoves, legal assistants nearby. Boris took the seat at one end of the desk. At the other, Chief Recorder Yevgeny Godunov fussed with a voice-to-text recorder. I've read some of his stuff; sounds like he learned to write from a hundred-year-old etiquette book.

The Honorable Change Lord Nicolai, to my left, wore a pinkish-tan knitted cap snugged down to his eyebrows. It made him look like a wrinkly eraser. He had to be at least thirty-one, his face channeled with lines and dotted with splotches. "Would you rather sit?" he said.

I shook my head. The wound on the back of my thigh still hurt, and I was already a step below the dais. Seated, I'd feel even more intimidated.

Godunov rose and said, "The Honorable Change Lord Nickolai, The Honorable Change Lord Peter. Before you for judgment is Goran Helin, a Second previously posted to Washington State. Be it noted that the Honorable Change Lord Ekaterina is absent on other duties."

There went any hope for motherly leniency.

The Honorable Peter, his hair now sparse but still tinged with gray, adjusted his sunglasses. "Recount your experiences from the time Andrei Helin left Seal Bay until our team picked you up in Vancouver. Be thorough and don't try to lie."

I struggled to follow instructions, starting with Andrei's panicked phone call. By the time I described burning our house and barn, my voice had stopped shaking, but then came the long series of entanglements with ever more Sapes. Occasionally they interrupted for a clarification. At last I finished, "Lil and Davy and I went to the UPS Store to pick up the comm helmet, and Maks and Anatol walked in."

They called a brief break for nutrient drinks and other necessities. When we were back in place, they tapped keyboards briefly, glared at each other, and then started with the questions. The first ones I had expected – details about the extent of security breaches. What did Sapes think had happened at Grand Coulee Dam? Did the wider public have any idea of the truth? Was the tissue culture exposed to dangerous external conditions?

After an hour of that, the thrust of the questions shifted to Sape reactions. "You said," the Honorable Nicolai began, "that when Lil Osborne pulled the comm helmet off your head, she realized your claim to

Evenki ancestry was not the whole story. Did she believe what you said about your off-planet origins?"

I tried to think back through the mind-scrambling effect of jerking away the helmet. "At first she didn't. She thought I was crazy. Then, she sort of did and didn't believe me."

"Did the thought of an alien hybrid make her frightened or hostile?"

"I guess so. But mostly she was angry at me."

"Because you were alien?"

"No. Because I hadn't rescued her brother."

"Then why did she stay with you?" The Honorable Peter interjected, face blank behind his shades.

"She didn't have much choice. GenAge was after her too."

"Did she understand the significance of your interstellar origins?"

"I don't think she cared, except whether it meant we could cure her brother."

The two Change Lords stared at each other. Then Nicolai leaned forward as much as his tubes and needles would allow. "Just clarifying. This Sapiens girl believed you, yet didn't believe you. She was somewhat frightened at the thought you were alien, yet she saw no importance in an overt interstellar contact. She was angry with you for not carrying out an impossible task, yet believed you would do so in the future, yet she was still angry. Can this be correct?"

"As far as I could tell."

Next, they probed our conversation following the incident at Spotted Lake, which provoked more discussion of Sape ability to both believe and disbelieve something at the same time. I answered to the best of my understanding, but those questions were a picnic compared to the Honorable Peter's inquisition that followed. Did I risk breeding with any of the females? Were they receptive to mating only during the fertile part of their cycle? Did they seem more generally cooperative in that physiological state? I heard Maks snort when I described my experience with Lil.

I was regretting my choice not to use the chair when the Honorable Peter said, "We will withdraw for consultation. Do you have any questions?"

I had dozens, but I settled on two. "I heard there were factions arguing about our future. What's going on with that? And what will happen to my . . . friends? They're not at fault. They got dragged into this by accident."

Peter said, "The conditions that created the factions have recently become irrelevant." He nodded, handing off to Nicolai.

Nicolai glanced down at his tablet before speaking. "For the time being, your friends will remain here. Preliminary information indicates they might be helpful in the near future – understanding aspects of Sapiens pregnancy, testing how effective certain medical techniques are for Sapes, consulting on the defense industry. And we can always use good forgers. I am not able to explain further at this point. We will now begin private deliberation and announce our decision shortly."

A translucent shield descended from the ceiling, isolating the dais behind a wall of dead silence. I dropped into the chair. Nicolai seemed a bit less hostile than Peter but I couldn't guess the outcome. I twisted around and mouthed at Andrei and Maks, "What do you think?" Andrei shrugged. Maks gave me a thumbs up, then waggled it up and down. My life ticked away while we waited. At last the shield rose, and so did I.

The Honorable Nicolai cleared his throat and adjusted his cap. "By our laws, we could either reward you for what you have done, or punish you for the way you did it. You broke our most important law–never reveal our presence. One the other hand, we don't want to waste a potentially valuable asset. Without the Honorable Ekaterina here to break the tie, our vote was split. But we have agreed on a method to settle it." He took a deep breath and coughed. "A time of great crisis is upon us. Again, we disagreed on how to measure your usefulness in this emergency. So we each devised a test to measure your worth. If you succeed at both, you will continue forward. If not, you will be discarded."

My overloaded brain stuttered. What crisis? And how was *I* supposed to solve it?

# CHAPTER 35

From the unpublished Godunov manuscript
*Why We Came to Earth: The Yunko Voyages*

*The rapid aging that was killing us originated in the radiation suffered by our space-faring Orbian ancestors. Crews from our first two expeditions died soon after being revived from stasis, and from such a wide variety of radiation ills, that we did not realize the long-range dangers. Those on the third expedition, however, spent far less time in space, had better shielding, and survived considerably longer. Then, as we began incorporating Sapiens genes into our own population, those genes masked and counteracted the damage to our Orbian genes. But when we altered our human telomeres to destroy cancers caused by the Sun's radiation, we destroyed our immunity to the latent hyper-aging caused by interstellar radiation.*

The Honorable Nicolai spoke. "A ship from Gliese-C recently reached the solar system, decelerated, and advanced to the asteroid belt beyond the orbit of Mars. It is now positioned near our older interstellar transports – the single surviving Bubble Drive ship that arrived in 1908 and the ship that brought the expedition of 1609. One of our shuttles went to meet the Orbian ship, which holds most of the remaining population of our home world. That shuttle is bringing the Orbian ambassador back to the Outpost and should be landing very soon."

A trick? Some training game scenario? With Earth in such a mess, why in frozen hell would the remaining Orbians be coming here?

The Honorable Peter frowned behind his shades. "We expect that, one way or another, the arrival of the Orbian ship–along with your blundering–will reveal our presence to the people of Earth. Outpost security has been adequate to prevent our discovery, but once Sapes know we're here, we can expect an all-out military attack. We have to avoid getting bombed off the face of this planet until we can either negotiate or fully mobilize and install defense weaponry."

The Honorable Nicholai added, "Much depends on what kind of communication we can achieve between between Orbians, Yunko, and Sapes. You claim you've dealt with Sapes who know, or suspect, our true origin. You even brought several Sapes with you. Sometime during the next few days, we'll use those Sapes to test the limits of communications."

"I told you, none of this is my friends' fault. They shouldn't be punished."

"Be quiet. They'll suffer no harm. We only want to study their reactions."

"You're using us as lab rats."

"Precisely."

I saw no way to push forward on Nicolai's test, so I turned to the Honorable Peter, although he seemed a tougher case. "What test did you come up with?"

He leaned back in his alcove and stared at me through glasses so dark that I had no idea of his expression. He seemed to sneer a bit. "Goran, as the only living Yunko who's revealed his true nature to Sapes, we want you to give us one specific recommendation about how to avoid destruction in this approaching crisis."

My confused brain rebelled. Why did *I* have to fix their stupid, impossible problem when it wasn't my fault? I'd done what they wanted – brought them the cure – but it probably wouldn't help *me*. And I got no credit for bringing it. Screw it! "Even if I fixed this," I said, "you'd think up something else impossible." My voice rose to a yell. "Just execute me now and get it over with – "

Hands gripped me from both sides. Andrei and Maks.

"Chill," Maks murmured. "You can get through this. Looks to me like they're trying to find a way to *not* kill you."

"Goran, there's hope," Andrei said. "They haven't condemned you yet." He rubbed my shoulder in a way I remembered from childhood. "They're not looking for a detailed plan, just testing whether your viewpoint is useful."

I felt a bleeding chasm open between the human me and the Yunko me. On one side, rage because of all the things, all the time, I'd never have. On the other, a lifetime devoted to helping my people. And then, faintly, a curiosity about a new world of living openly. I tried to close the wound and center myself. *Time has no duration. The Past is over and done. The Future can't touch me till it turns into Now, and Now's the same length for everyone.*

Maybe I *could* come up with something in a few days. Maks and Andrei still grasped my arms. I took a deep breath and shrugged them off.

"Have you controlled yourself?" said the Honorable Peter. "You feel cheated by time? Then stop wasting it in babyish outbursts. You're past the midpoint of your life, but still lack wisdom. Answer as we requested."

The Honorable Nicolai was milder. "Think about what motivates your Sape companions. Perhaps that will help."

He might be friendlier than Peter, but he was just as determined. I tried to grab a thread, any thread, and follow it to an answer but I finally said, "I can't think with you staring at me."

"Then go sit in the back," Peter snapped. "Stare at the wall and *think* for five minutes. Then answer our question."

I walked to the back of the room, kicking a couple of chairs out of the way, then pulled one around to sit facing the corner. Like one of the cats, I stared intently at nothing. Through my fatigue and dread, I tried to understand what motivated my friends.

A tangle of love and fear, for sure. What else motivated Conroy besides love for Janelle and fear of a jail cell? Probably glee whenever he got the better of someone. In Kayla's case, maybe curiosity. And she and Janelle both seemed driven to create. Lil? Between her obsessive love for Davy and her fear of Erik Cheyne, she'd had no more chance to find out than I had.

I shook my head. It didn't matter. We wouldn't be dealing with my friends – none of them had power. And the people who did have power wanted . . . more power. To survive, we had to somehow perfectly balance love, fear, and power. We needed to display enough power to gain access to the leaders, but not enough to make them feel threatened by us. And we needed to dangle bait–the dream of more power–in front of them before they fully grasped what we were. Before they could mount their attack.

Sapes always wanted weapons more than anything else. No point denying our more advanced technology; after all, we succeeded in traveling here. But, as far as I knew, Sapes had no idea what Yunko tech could do or how it looked or how it could be weaponized.

We'd be fools to give them weapons, so we had to offer something else they valued. Maybe med tech. I thought about Janelle and the bonbons, but they seemed too similar to Earth supplements to impress anyone. The Pocket Doc could reveal too much about our locations and communications. Maybe Spitwad? I'd given it to Lil because she couldn't afford basic antibiotics; lots of other people were in the same boat. And bacteria were becoming resistant to Sape antibiotics so fast that their drugs were halfway useless anyway –

One of the security guards stopped beside me. "Your time is up."

I followed him back to my interrogation spot. We quickly agreed that all-out war was a lose-lose proposition: our technology was far more powerful, but there were billions of them up against a few thousand of us. Then I stumbled through my thoughts on Sape motivations. They seemed interested when I described an approach that combined sticks, carrots, and a juicy bribe, which we would need to offer before our presence was widely known.

"I'm sure there's other stuff I don't know about," I said, "but Spitwad might be a good trade for access to Sape leaders. I don't think they could use it against us."

"They might use it on their own forces and then try biological weapons," the Honorable Nicolai said. We discussed Earth's unsuccessful efforts at germ warfare and how distributing the cure to everyone might forestall bio-attacks.

"Lot of the damn fools reject science-based cures, and all of 'em should stop fighting and worry about their planet instead," the Honorable Peter contributed.

The Honorable Nicolai adjusted his cap again. "We have, of course, explored ways to initiate conversations with political and corporate leaders. But we hadn't thought of sending bribes out first as . . . as devices for clearing mine fields. If handled correctly, a Sape politician would become an immediate hero by offering a cure like Spitwad."

"Probably needs a different nickname," I said.

"Perhaps. But Sape demands for interstellar technology will be inevitable. If not for warfare, then as a source of energy."

We discussed the Bubble Drive, and whether we could keep Sapes from finding out it existed. But I hadn't really slept since they picked up Davy from the Peace Arch; my brain was dissolving into mush. Still, I realized that our meeting had turned into a cooperative planning session instead of a trial for execution. I wouldn't be immediately discarded. If I could somehow get a conversation started among the different species, I might live at least until the Sapes nuked us out of the mountain. Maybe even fifteen more years.

*

Maks walked us back to Andrei's apartment. Then Maks left to link up with Lil. I was too wasted to resent it. I was describing our hike over the border to Andrei when we heard angry voices. Familiar angry voices. My Sape friends with a Yunko escort. Through the peephole I saw Conroy and Kayla. Yevgeny Godunov and a security guard were trying to herd them into the apartment right across the hallway.

It made sense, I guess–I'd be the first in line to patch up anything they wrecked. I thought about going over and reassuring them, but I was too tired to put up with their abuse. They all went inside. A few minutes later, Yevgeny and the guard came back out.

Kayla stuck her head out the door and screamed, "And you hair looks like a gigolo, Ev Gimme."

At the sound of her voice, Zax and Gwitchy popped out of their pillow nest and trotted to the door, yowling at top decibel.

Silence. Then Kayla yelled, "Goran, are you in there?"

Impossibly, the yowling got louder.

"Goran, come on out. You gotta come over here. Conroy's losing it."

I wanted the unconsciousness of sleep, not another problem. But I heard fear in Kayla's voice. When I opened the door, the cats streaked out before I could grab them. I followed. Yevgeny had left but a guard remained in the corridor.

Conroy held a light-weight plastic chair with its legs pointed at the guard, who had drawn her weapon. He yelled at me without taking his eyes off the guard. "It's suppertime and she'll be getting hungry. I wanna see her! Now!"

"Janelle?" I guessed.

"Who do you think? They're keeping her prisoner in their med lab. I'm going after her." He started edging around the guard, who swiveled to maintain her aim.

I took a chance on grabbing his bicep. He couldn't attack me without dropping the chair. "No way you'll find her by stumbling around the Outpost. This place has at least eighteen levels and stretches for miles under the mountain. Come back inside and we'll figure out something that'll actually work."

He went still, then hurled the chair against the wall. "You better make this good, Goran."

Back inside the apartment I said, "Look, they're not gonna hurt her. They're treating her."

"Treating, hell! For what? They never saw a pregnant human before?"

"They've never seen a pregnant human who's been eating Yunko supplements." At Conroy's blank look, I said, "The bonbons. Remember? They've apparently affected her body chemistry in some way."

"Screw you, Goran, you gave them to her. Didn't you know what they'd do?"

"What I knew was, she was getting dehydrated, which is dangerous for sure."

"You take me to Janelle, or I'm gonna stuff you out that window." He jerked his head at a small window shaped like a skinny kite.

Actually, their lodging looked like choice quarters, with two windows to the outside. Even though they were small and oddly shaped to fit into the cliff's natural crevices for concealment, they helped prevent claustrophobia.

Meanwhile the cats kept shrieking, the fur on their tails standing straight out.

"Calm down," I ordered Conroy. "Stop yelling for just ten seconds."

He swung at me. I grabbed him and got him in a twisting wrist lock. He yelped before he could stop himself, then shook his head in disbelief.

He probably still thought I'd lucked out in the garden center fight. "I said calm down. My brother can probably find out when she'll be brought back up here." I kept up the pressure until he got control of himself.

Andrei crossed the hall at my summons and sidled in the door. He was visibly uneasy, but then he had spent a lifetime avoiding intimacy with Sapes. I explained the situation and he commed one of the medical bosses.

"They're still running some tests," he reported. "Might be another two hours."

Conroy grabbed my arm. "You're gonna take me to where she is. Right now."

Was this a pop quiz on whether I could facilitate Sape-Yunko communication? "Okay, okay. You can see for yourself she's okay." I pulled his hand away. "But don't start attacking people at the medical center. Just politely ask what's going on, and they'll probably tell you."

At the medical facility I told Conroy to keep his mouth shut and hauled him up to the front desk. "Uh, you've had a Janelle Higgins here for hours. She's pregnant. This is the baby's father. He really, really needs to talk to her. Can he possibly see her between tests?"

The pallid guy manning the entrance gave me a long stare and punched a button on his console. Conroy jittered. Several minutes later a senior med tech came out. She spouted a stream of med-speak. Conroy looked blank and so did I.

"I want to see her now!" Conroy said.

"You may enter her room, but you'll have to stay on the opposite side of a contamination screen until the tests are finished." The med tech turned back to the treatment areas and Conroy followed, practically stepping on her heels.

I collapsed on a couch.

# CHAPTER 36

From the unpublished Godunov manuscript
*Why We Came to Earth: The Yunko Voyages*

*While we struggled to repair the aging problem, more troubles descended on us from the outside. The new political order that arose during the first Russian Revolution and World War I became much more intrusive on the lives of Siberia's indigenous peoples. And it showed far too much curiosity about rumors and legends of those who were different. We speeded up the move from central Siberia to Western Canada.*

A commotion at the inner door woke me about an hour later. The med tech escorted Janelle into the lobby, Conroy hovering over her like a dog with new puppies.

"Are you okay?" I said.

"Sure." Janelle smiled. "They treated me like a rock star. Except I'm starving–they wouldn't let me eat anything."

"Well, what's happening?"

She shrugged. "They think something may show up in my cord blood when the baby's born. A catalyst. It might help you all live longer. Can we get something to eat?"

I took a step back and stared at her. Then I looked at Conroy with a question.

"Oh, yeah," he said. "You Yunko better treat her right. All your freaking lives may depend on it."

Like I was gonna believe that. "What did they say?"

He beamed at Janelle's uniqueness. "There's something in her urine. They were talking about . . . uh . . . an epicene and mentholatum. Her Yamaka cells–she's not Japanese; that's some guy that discovered something about aging. Her epigenome. That's it! The doctor said, if her DNA is the machine, then the epigenome is like its operating manual." He looked as proud as if he'd figured out the cure himself. "You were right, Goran. They think it's because she ate all those bonbons at just the right time in her pregnancy."

Probably another dead end. I would not allow myself to hope. Besides, Conroy was spouting garble without understanding any of it; no telling what the real situation was. Maybe I'd ask Andrei about it, not like I thought it was true, but to show him how Conroy was always running off the tracks.

Then I laughed at the irony. Suppose it *was* true. Here we all were, struggling, fighting, trying to survive, trying to save Davy, run from Kayla's father, keep Conroy out of prison. And Janelle wasn't struggling at all, just sailing serenely along, wanting nothing but to be with Conroy and to design her dresses. And she might be the one who saved my people.

After the long wrangle at the med facility, we detoured by the apartment for Kayla and headed for the dining hall. Picture a pile of soap bubbles swelling to giant size inside the mountain, pushing away the solid rock before they burst, leaving a high-domed, open space half the size of a football field.

The place was now crowded after being closed all day. We joined the shortest serving line in the central space but a dozen people were ahead of us. Janelle stood in front of Conroy, who massaged her shoulders. I suppose the food production systems were back in order because the PA system repeated the day's menu choices: venison meatballs in mushroom sauce; lentil-vegetable stew; spinach and cheese omelet.

We shuffled forward. Janelle stepped on the weight mat. She pointed to the lentil stew and received a medium serving. Then Conroy stepped on the mat and pointed to the venison meat balls. The server reached for a platter, filled it, and handed it over. Servings varied according to weight categories, and Conroy the Six-Foot-Three Monster got a double portion. I chose the stew and nudged Conroy to stop popping meatballs into his mouth and move on down the line.

"These things are good," he mumbled through chomps. Then he lurched away from the serving line and fell to all fours. His platter skidded across the floor. He crawled a step, reared up to grab his chest, and emitted a coughing shriek. Choking sounds burbled from his mouth. He screamed again, convulsed, and collapsed on the floor.

Janelle, who had turned at the first sound, broke her paralysis and rushed to his side. She dropped her bowl, shook him, shouted his name, and tugged on his blond scalp lock trying to get a response.

I knelt beside her. "It's okay. He'll come around in a few seconds. He's not hurt."

She looked at me with horror.

"He ate the chip," I added. She inched away from me. "Just a little nanochip. Makes him, uh, hallucinate, but there's no physical damage. Except maybe bruises from falling."

Conroy's eyes focused and he lifted his head. Polite applause broke out among the people in line.

"Let's get him over to a table." I grasped one arm. Janelle hesitated between aiding Conroy and cleaning up the mess on the floor.

"The suckervac'll get it," I said.

Sure enough, one of the wastebasket-size robots trundled out a service door and headed across the smooth stone floor, its protein recovery nozzle already slurping at the far-flung drops of Conroy's meal. We helped Conroy to a table. He walked almost normally but still looked confused. He slid around the booth's seat, rubbed his throat and one knee, and took a deep breath. "What the hell happened to me?"

Janelle and Kayla sat on either side as if to guard him. I sat across the table. "Whenever the cafeteria serves something made with meat, they put one nanochip in it. Whoever killed the animal remote-records the brain patterns triggered by its sensory inputs from just before the animal is hit until after its death. The patterns are imprinted on the nanochip, and when someone eats it, saliva activates the chip. It imposes the animal's final sensory patterns onto that person's brain. You're lucky the deer died quickly."

"I don't understand." Janelle grasped Conroy's arm.

I sighed. "Basically, Conroy relived the animal's experience when it died. The chips acknowledge the animal's sacrifice and remind us that nothing is free. And that we only have a short time to live. Also, they discourage us from eating lots of meat from actual animals, which cuts our energy use way down."

Conroy still looked fuddled with shock. "Yeah, it was like I was suddenly outside. Couldn't balance on two legs. Then this incredible pain, then another one, and everything turned black. I sure felt like I was dying."

Janelle sniffled. "I thought you *were* dead! Janelle scanned the busy room. "And those horrible people clapped like it was entertainment!"

"They were thanking him for eating the chip," I said. "They know it's now safe to eat today's meatballs." I turned to Conroy. "Want another serving?"

He shuddered. When Janelle whimpered, he put his arm around her. "Shhh. I'm okay. You need to eat something, though. Think about our baby." He turned to me. "Stop scaring Janelle, okay?" His face was pinched and white.

"I'll get you bowls of lentil stew." I rose and walked to the end of another serving line. I was beginning to realize I didn't understand my Sape friends nearly as well as I had thought. Conroy just now, demanding that I stop scaring Janelle? Conroy's scent, the undertones of his voice, and the look on his face insisted that big, bad Conroy was terrified, while Janelle seemed to be relaxing back into her placid pregnant glow.

Conroy picked at his stew while Janelle shoveled hers down. Kayla watched it all intently but said nothing. Full at last, Janelle started to yawn. The whole ragged bunch of us headed back to our quarters.

*

I actually sacked out for nine hours before Boris woke me. "The shuttle will be landing in forty-five minutes. The Change Lords have decided an encounter with the alien ambassador might be helpful before your communication test."

I was too groggy to respond, but a shower cleared my head. Guards led us down a corridor deeper into the mountain. New living spaces were under construction along the route. Boris said they were quarters for more people. Yunko teams were being called in from all over the world.

A lift tube shot our capsule up past the winding ramps and displays of the Hall of Heroes where we displayed the honored, misshapen bodies of those who had not survived genetic engineering. The capsule slowed and stopped. Its doors slid open on another short corridor. I knew what was coming, but still, entering the Great Chamber was disorienting.

The Outpost's architecture is mostly cramped and utilitarian, but in the stadium-sized Great Chamber, the builders went all out to remind us of home. Gliese-C's dark side, always turned away from our sun, is covered with glaciers several kilometers thick. Where the glaciers give way to the fertile, habitable ring around the planet, waterfalls gush from holes and crevices in the edge of the ice sheets. The architects of the Great Chamber replicated the effect with holograms of water pouring from openings between the piers of living rock that helped support the vaulted ceiling. We use the Chamber for anything that takes lots of space – shuttle landings, team sports, Remembrance Day ceremonies.

I jumped when overhead panels the size of racquetball courts slid open. They revealed skylights that admitted an icy, snow-filtered glare. Then, on the far wall, enormous doors folded back until we gazed out at empty space through a 120-foot by 40-foot slot in the side of the mountain, flanked by two shuttle spaces.

The forty people in the Chamber drifted toward the opening. We passed a side cavern where one shuttle was berthed. The other hangar was empty. In the freezing air, I pulled my jacket tighter around me.

Andrei stood beside Yevgeny Godunov. I started toward them. "Who's on the shuttle coming in?" I whispered.

Literal as always, Andrei rattled off the roster. "Two pilots, a navigator and engineer, diplomatic staff, medical and translation staff, security personnel, The Honorable Change Lord Ekaterina, and the Orbian Ambassador."

Outside, the view went out of focus like the beginning of a migraine. Our stealth tech could not only hide a shuttle from radar but also from actual human vision. The shuttle materialized in the mid-air void between us and the peaks of the Seven Sisters. It aligned itself with the entrance, slowly slid into the Chamber, and landed with the delicacy of a butterfly. Obviously these were the *good* pilots. They must have been traveling to collect the Orbian ambassador while the not-so-good backup pilots took potshots at Grand Coulee Dam.

An opening appeared on the shuttle's side and a lift tube angled down to the floor. Flight-suited personnel descended and formed into two lines as the Honorable Ekaterina exited in a support chair that was basically a mobile ICU. As soon as she was safely delivered to her attendants, the crew members hurried to a large door into the cargo bay, un-secured it and stood at attention. The door swung down to the floor, forming a ramp. Something in the dark hold moved.

The thing emerged. It looked like a translucent eight-foot tall, wedding cake made of melting metal-flake paraffin. It descended, riding a foot above the ramp on hoverpacks. Then it glided between the honor guard and turned sharply toward the cavern's opening that framed the Seven Sisters peaks, giant ice fangs against the clear blue sky.

Three security guards ran to catch it, presumably before it could glide over the lip of the cavern and plunge several hundred feet when its hoverpack resistance disappeared. Everyone in the cavern trailed after.

A proximity alert on the capsule's – the suit's? the pod's? – surface flashed the pushing-away symbol that meant "Do not approach." The guards stopped. The figure inside apparently settled in to contemplate the alien world it had reached.

Against the bright snowy landscape, I could make out the dark silhouette of the Orbian's body through the clouded material of the pod. Bulky lower limbs blended with the mass of its seat. A slender upper torso, a long head topped with erect ears, one slightly cocked, perhaps from an accident.

The Honorable Ekaterina glided over to speak with Yevgeny, the Chief Recorder. Her deep wrinkles hinted that she must have been almost thirty-two. She turned the gaze of a tired old eagle toward the Orbian. "She demanded to come back with us. They're eager to begin negotiations for settling on Earth." She grimaced. "Somewhere away from Sapes and preferably even Yunko – they seem to find our presence repulsive."

Godunov flinched as if the Honorable had slapped him. "How gracious. Have they any idea of the complications?'

The Honorable shook her head. "They have more immediate problems. Gliese-C has suffered a tipping point. As the dark side glaciers melt, the weight shift has become so enormous that the planet's crust has destabilized. Earthquakes threaten the underground habitats and even those living in the High Peaks. When their ship left, the population that remained on the home world wasn't expected to survive more than sixty or seventy years." She glanced at the shuttle. "Right now I'm too exhausted to calculate back-to-back time dilation, but there's no way we could reach them quickly enough to evacuate." She nodded toward the Orbian. "The ship's passengers are the surviving remnant of our race, and the ones not in stasis are in bad shape. They need treatment. Even more, they need a planet."

The two drew nearer the alien. The last thing I heard was Godunov asking Ekaterina about moving some of the Orbians to our own interstellar ships until we could figure out what to do with them.

I tried to imagine my Sape friends' reaction to the Ambassador. Would she satisfy their notion that aliens *had* to look like monsters and that I must be wearing some sort of human camouflage suit? I was trying to make out details of the Orbian's form inside the pod when it swiveled around and headed toward our assembled welcoming committee. At last it – she, I guess – cut the hoverpacks, stopped, and increased the transparency of the pod.

In spite of my effort to remain calm, I flinched. Since childhood, I'd seen images and holos of our ancestors, but they must have been as idealized as video models.

The Orbian ambassador looked ancient, well past the 350 years considered the normal Orbian lifespan, not just the geriatric thirties we Yunko struggle to achieve. Her skin was grayed and dull, no longer the gleaming, fine-grained texture of a leaping orca but the channeled, splotched, and barnacled hide of a beached sperm whale. Between the bronze scales of the torso harness that protected the spiracles of her tracheae, those breathing openings looked stiff and pale. Her eyes were still huge, dark and lustrous. Below them the black caverns of her nostrils flared so large they looked like another set of eyes. Her ears, long as a mule's, furled and curled like calla lilies.

She activated the audio feed. I heard the clicking, humming language of my ancestors, punctuated with occasional sounds like farts or breaking glass. All three segments of her mouth moved as she talked. At last the translation panel lit up. She had spoken at length but the translation text, apparently eliminating all allusions and emotional shadings, appeared as one short sentence: "[NOW-FUTURE] LAST REFUGE FOR ORBIANS IS YOU."

I looked with awe at my distant relative. All my life I've seen images of our ancestors, but I never felt any real, bone-deep connection before confronting this living, breathing Orbian. At the same time, I'd never felt so human.

# CHAPTER 37

From the unpublished Godunov manuscript
*Why We Came to Earth: The Yunko Voyages*

*Then, by the 1960s and 1970s, medical research by Earth's scientists had progressed so rapidly that we began sending out Yunko researchers to work undercover in your laboratories with their vast human tissue banks, even as our own scientists at the Outpost labored non-stop to restore our normal lifespans.*

Every step I took heading back to our apartment brought my thoughts circling back to the Ambassador. How did it feel to float, sealed off from everything? I assumed–I hoped–they had prepared some sort of chamber for her so she could escape from her pod. And how did she feel, traveling to a planet where any breath of open air was lethal? Did she even *have* feelings after so long? We shared DNA with Orbians, but we had transformed ourselves to the point we seemed completely human in comparison.

I was soon reminded of my alien status. Kayla sat on the floor in our apartment corridor, her back against the wall.

She slid up the surface until she was standing. "Where'd you go so early?"

They weren't supposed to know about the Orbian. "Talking to Yevgeny about some work I'm doing for him."

"Oh, great. So what's *our* job future gonna be? Chain gang? Item on the menu? Having our brains sucked out in some horrid alien experiment?"

I was still unpacking her words when she blurted, "Why won't somebody tell us? Will we be released? Imprisoned? Killed? What!?"

"Where's everyone else?"

"Inside."

"C'mon." I took her arm and opened their door.

Conroy and Janelle huddled on the couch, staring at the opposite wall as if they had a TV. Lil coaxed Davy to eat more Outpost Porridge. They deserved to hear something. I just couldn't figure out exactly what. "Uh, Kayla's been telling me how you all want to know what's happening."

"No shit," Conroy muttered.

I plowed on. "You've pretty much figured out the situation. Our people have been on Earth for centuries. We've survived because no group ever found out we were here."

"Group?" Kayla said. "What about individuals finding out, like us? Do you kill individuals who find out?"

"We simply wipe their memories of the encounter if possible."

"What if not possible?"

"Look, give me a chance to explain, will you? Recently, several things have happened that make it likely Earth will find out about us in a very short time."

Lil looked up. "Was our trip to blame?"

"Partly. And other things. But that's on me, not on you, so don't worry about it. The main thing is, the Outpost is on emergency footing right now. We're trying to prevent, or prepare for, possibly being attacked."

Silence.

"Kayla, your dad's from New Mexico—you ever hear about the Manhattan Project? Well, that's like what's going on right now."

"You're building a nuclear bomb?"

"No! But it's like all those people marooned in the middle of nowhere working themselves to death on a project. No one's had time to figure out what to do with you. My guess is they'll keep you here—both for our protection and yours—until we know what happens next."

"You're kidding," Conroy shouted. "We can't stay here—the baby! Our baby's gonna be born free!"

"Free? Where?" Why couldn't they see the obvious? "Back in Seal Bay with its father in prison and its mother catching hell from her family? Born free in Vancouver with daddy dead in a drug war? You baby's safer here than anywhere else, long as we can keep you Sapes from trying to wipe us out."

"Yeah, safey safe safe as a prison can be," Kayla chanted.

"You too! You've been hiding and running away from your father since . . . whenever. Well, your father can't get to you here, so stop complaining!"

Her face turned blank. Then she said, "Where are the cats?"

God, Sapes drive me crazy, the way they bounce all over the place. Or maybe not. Kayla was more bonded to Zax and Gwitchy than to anyone else in the place except possibly Lil. "Andrei took them down to the Animal Facility yesterday for a check up and to get some outdoor time."

"Outdoor time?"

"There's a sort of play area outside the mountain. I need to pick them up this morning."

"I'm going along."

"Why?"

"Because we're all going stir crazy sitting around and worrying. I don't even have paper to draw on, much less a graphics program."

It couldn't hurt and might calm her down. "Okay."

Conroy rose. "I want to check on my car. God knows what you aliens have done to it."

"We need to go to the medical facility," Lil said.

"Okay, okay. We'll all go. Have a tour of the Outpost. Take Your Kids to Work Day–as much as is allowed."

*

We set out for the nearest lift tube, which descended past training facilities, past the dining hall and food processing, past warehousing and several manufacturing levels for the bio-engineered products like simulated yew bark or horseshoe crab blood that we sell to the outside world. The med facilities were deeper–and safer from attack–than anything else in the Outpost except data storage. Lil was actually more familiar with the route than I was, since she and Davy spent most of their time here.

Davy was still in his wheelchair, but he seemed livelier. His color was better, and his flesh didn't seem as sunken. He asked about everything we passed, until we reached the med facility lobby and found Maks waiting. Davy immediately wheeled over for a hug. Like sister, like brother. I felt ridiculously deserted. We hung around a few minutes until a tech took them back to the labs. Then Janelle wanted to ask her obstetrician something. I went out to a waiting area in the hallway and Kayla trailed after me. We both flopped on an old couch.

In a moment, she took a deep breath and said, "How much do you mind it?"

"Mind what?"

"Lil linking up with Maks."

I shrugged. "Hope they're happy."

"Oh, c'mon. I saw the way you looked at her. Trailed after her like a sick puppy."

"I did not!"

"Doesn't matter. It wouldn't have worked with you and it's not gonna work with Maks. Even if he's a good enough lover to get her past Erik Cheyne . . . working her over–"

"What!?"

"Yeah. That's why Cheyne freaks her out so much. I'm pretty sure rape was involved, but don't ask for details because she's never revealed them. Besides, there's still her obsession with Davy. Lil's purpose in life is

243

taking care of Davy, and god knows what she'll do if the Outpost actually heals him. I'll bet . . . I'll bet you an afternoon in that outdoor cat playground that Lil'll move on from Maks to whichever doctor–male or female–is in charge of Davy's treatment. Within, um, a month, if we're still here."

I stared at her, groping for words. "She . . . you're supposed to be her friend, but you're saying all this awful stuff–"

"I am her friend. My heart breaks for her. And she can't help what she does. The stuff that's happened to her . . . she grabbed onto whatever kept her afloat."

She glanced back as Conroy and Janelle exited the med facility. "But I don't enjoy seeing you suffer, either. For several reasons."

With the others joining us, I didn't have a chance to ask what she meant. The four of us cut across laterally to the other main lift tube. I hardly spoke, my mind churning through this new view of Lil Osborne. Kayla kept glancing at me with what seemed like concern.

We rose past waste recycling, the geo-thermal plant and several hydroponics levels. The Transport Depot and the Animal Facility, both at ground level, had "back doors" leading from the Outpost into the small, stream-carved valley behind it.

The Transport Depot consisted of a vast, shadowy garage with its office near the inside entrance. I paced the waiting area, tormented by horrible mental images of Lil at the mercy of Cheyne. Janelle and Conroy stood nearby, oblivious.

After a few minutes, Anna Itskova, Boss of the Transport Depot, emerged from her inner office. She always smiled, but she had the saddest eyes I've ever seen – the outside corners drooped like a Weeping Nootka Cypress. Short and round with braids crowning her head, she looked like a Russian grandmother.

She bustled over. "So you're the infamous Goran Helin. Someday you must tell me about your adventures. And who is this?" She patted Janelle's hand and craned to look up at Conroy.

"Conroy," he said. "That antique Buick you have down here is my car."

"It's in excellent condition. Mmm, including the hidden compartment." She twinkled. "Did you restore it?"

"Sure. Mostly. Mainly I need to check it. It probably needs to be started and driven. The battery, you know."

She cocked her head. "And you, of course, want to be the driver?"

"Of course."

"My assistant will be back shortly. He'll go with you for a drive. Meanwhile, let's check it out." She trotted toward the door and started across the garage. We followed. The echo of our footsteps sounded gave no hint there was a mountain over us.

We passed electric vehicles of all types before the Buick came in sight. "We keep a few gasoline vehicles to use outside," Anna said. "Next to the outside doors to reduce pollution."

And there it was, Conroy's humongous four-hole baby. Someone had washed away the mud accumulated on our 800-mile dash from Vancouver over snowy, muddy roads. Conroy caressed the hood, peered through the windshield at the keys hanging from the ignition, and looked at Anna, who nodded. He escorted Janelle around to the passenger door, then jumped in himself. The engine roared to life. Conroy looked at the heavy, reinforced doors to the outside, sighed and turned her off. I caught a tiny whiff of disappointment from the well-rested car.

Anna Itskova held the comm to her ear, made a 'role down the window' motion, then announced, "My tech won't be back for nearly thirty minutes. Do you want to wait?"

"Yeah, sure. We'll just sit in the car." Conroy actually looked happy at the prospect.

"We need to leave," I told Anna. "Can someone escort them back afterward?"

"Yes." She gave Conroy a calculating look and said in a low voice, "I could use a good gasoline/diesel mechanic."

"Why don't you hire him?" I said. "It would solve more than one problem."

When I walked away, Kayla followed. "What a happy little family," she said. "Conroy, Janelle, the Buick and the baby." I couldn't understand her tone.

At the Animal Facility, I gave my name and the cats' to Natasha, the manager. She disappeared, then returned with Zax and Gwitchy following. When they spotted me, they pulled up into their snooty "Well, if you don't need us, we don't need you" poses and stalked ahead. Then they saw Kayla and hurried toward her, bumping each other in their haste.

She sank to the floor for maximum contact. After a first flurry of petting, she laughed. "Whaddaya know? Our own little family of four."

It sounded snarky, but something else was also in her voice.

# CHAPTER 38

From the unpublished Godunov manuscript
*Why We Came to Earth: The Yunko Voyages*

*We come now to speculations about the future. Allow us to share one theory with you.*

*For more than nine centuries, we have visited Earth, constantly accumulating data about our biological transformation and the effects of interstellar travel: thousands of genetic alterations, ship speeds and accelerations, radiation levels and shielding, percentage of voyage spent in stasis, and planetary atmospheres. Our Researchers recently subjected those centuries of data to what you might consider a meta-analysis of meta-analyses. A pattern became apparent.*

The next morning Yevgeny came to fetch me. He said, "You're required at a meeting," and then clammed up in spite of my questions. His silence and his solemn manner made me suspect we were headed for my second big test. That thought set me to shaking, so I grabbed a jacket before following him and tried to keep my teeth from chattering.

Two levels down from our quarters, we reached the administration area, then followed a corridor to a large, empty room I'd never seen. Inside it, a second door opened to my right, and on the left, a double door loomed, big enough to admit a twelve-person electric cart. The vehicle doors, plus the scratched and scruffed walls, hinted at industrial use. A work table ran along the back wall with a few folded chairs stacked against it. The floor sloped slightly to a drain.

Yevgeny opened the door on my right and waved Conroy, Kayla, and Lil into the room.

Conroy stopped. "What's going on?"

I shrugged. My survival test maybe, but I didn't think my Sape friends were in danger.

The door behind me opened again to admit an elderly woman with a voice synthesizer hanging loosely around her neck—an interpreter, one of a handful in each generation who spent their lives mastering Orbian speech. She pulled the voice synthesizer up and adjusted it to fit over her mouth and nose.

"Who's that," Conroy demanded. "What's that on her face? Is the air bad in here?"

"Air's okay," I said. "It's a translation device." Yep. This had to be the critical test.

"What does–" he was saying when Yevgeny pressed a button to open the large doors. The Orbian Ambassador floated in from the dark corridor, her eight-foot pod fully transparent. As we watched, her skin lightened to a misty gray, adjusting to the brighter illumination. Maybe her few days on Earth had helped her. She still looked like the biological version of an ancient ruin. Her long ears drooped a little, and her skin out-wrinkled an elephant. But she sat a little straighter and seemed ready to take on an alien planet.

Conroy's question turned into a high squeak. The three Sapes shrank back against the wall. Conroy spread his arms as if to protect Kayla and Lil, but Kayla was having none of it. She pushed around him and took a step toward me, primed for a fight.

Lil stared at the Ambassador. "So that's what you really look like."

Not again! "No. I really look exactly the way I look right now." Sapes spent way too much time watching videos of monstrous transformations that violate the laws of physics.

Conroy voice wavered. "That's like, uh, your great-great-granny? Grandpa? Smells like a machine shop."

"That's the mechanics of her pod. And the gurgle's from her breathing tanks."

Looking slightly offended by the unruliness before her, the Orbian spoke.

Kayla giggled nervously at the clicking, humming sounds.

The pod's translation panel activated: UNDERSTAND SUPERIOR WORDS MAKE HURT SAPE. AGAINST THREAT/FEAR ROCK GENTLE. [FUTURE MEDIUM LONG>] SPACE FOR TECH. It didn't make sense but words like hurt, threat, and fear felt ominous.

Conroy's lips moved as he read. He trembled a little but stepped forward. "Well, Mr. or Ms. Superior Kangaroo, maybe we'll just rock gentle your ass right off the nearest cliff."

"Shut up, Conroy." Of course. Instant aggression from the most likely source. Communication emergency here. I managed, "Something's wrong with the translator panel," and asked the interpreter beside me for a full rendering of the Ambassador's speech.

She responded in a voice that sounded both raspy and hollow through the synthesizer: *"It's difficult to make sure what our two species are saying, so we should try to use the simplest words possible. If something sounds like a threat, we should first respond with comforting gentleness rather than hostility."*

The interpreter was good. I suspected the Orbian's speech had been a bit more insulting. "Comforting gentleness. Got that, Conroy?"

Kayla hugged herself and edged around for a side view of the pod. "What about 'Space for tech'?"

The interpreter hesitated, perhaps unsure about security clearances. When I nodded, she continued: *"They want to make some sort of long term agreement to trade living space for Orbian technology."*

"Trade? Bullshit!" Conroy was still shaking slightly, but back on the attack. "Some clown's always spouting virtuous reasons for invading another country, but it always ends up with bombing them and taking over. So tell us why you're *really* here."

"Soften it," I told the interpreter. She must have; the Ambassador listened, then hummed and clicked at length and made a few sounds like breaking glass. The panel activated: TO KILL ORBIANS SOME SAPES DESIRE. NEED AGREE BEFORE ALL DIE.

"What's this 'all die' shit?" Conroy spat. "If you're threatening us you're heading for a world of hurt!"

I didn't like the sound of it myself but said, "I told you–ignore the translator panel."

Conroy quivered for a moment, then stepped back to the door, yanked it open, and left.

"Hold the fort," I told the interpreter and went after him.

He'd made it through the adjacent room and reached the corridor. A few meters away, he was jerking at doors looking for a way out, cursing in a high, shaky voice. The other exits were locked. Any minute now, Security would send someone to immobilize him. And I would fail my test.

He hadn't yet noticed my presence. I started to yell, then stopped, almost too frightened to act lest I flunked. Too many shocks too fast had pushed Conroy completely away from rationality: kidnapped by aliens, interrogated, informed that his darling Janelle might be the savior of another race, taken down by my own battle training, experiencing the deer's death. And now, seeing the Orbian.

He was operating on pure fight-or-flight. I needed to approach him like a wild animal. I sat down with my back against a wall. To look even less threatening, I dropped my face to my knees. "Sorry." I tried to keep my voice normal. "I was under orders not to tell you anything about the Orbian." His racket stopped. I continued. "Must have been a real shock when she suddenly rolled into the room. I mean, they do look like something out of a horror video, but they're actually okay." His steps approached, stopped just out of grabbing range. "She's probably more scared of us than we are of her. I mean, I think she's really old, and she's the only one of her kind on Earth."

I risked a quick glance up, then dropped my eyes again. "I saw her for the first time yesterday, and it rattled *me*, and I've seen pix of Orbians since childhood. You think other people would maybe not freak if they saw pictures of her before they actually met her?"

He was silent, but he slid down the wall to sit beside me. "You shouldn't have pulled that on us, Goran."

"Wasn't my choice." We sat a few more minutes in silence. When I heard his breathing and heartbeat slow, I said, "Jeez! Lil and Kayla. We left them in there alone. We better get back before they panic."

Conroy just grunted, but he rose to follow me back to the meeting room.

When we returned, Kayla had stepped closer to the Ambassador's pod. She leaned forward with the intense stare she used when drawing something. "So you have to stay in that pod-thing to breathe. Is it bulletproof?"

I wanted to slap my hand over her mouth. The interpreter repeated the question in Orbian. The Ambassador spoke at length. The translator panel was garbled.

The interpreter raised her eyebrows. I nodded.

*"I am not an expert on Earth's personal weaponry. However, the pod's shell is similar to the material of our ship's hull, except much thinner. The hull will accept and deform to enclose small particles of the interstellar medium that hit us at speeds up to 37,500 miles per hour. Your bullets seem larger, but much, much slower."*

Kayla nodded like she understood. Odd, until I remembered her background. No telling what the watchers would think of the exchange, but it was a sure bet that someone, maybe even the Change Lords, was watching us.

Time for a subject change. I turned to the interpreter. "So what was the Ambassador actually saying just before I left the room?

The interpreter looked from me to the Ambassador to Conroy. "She wants to reach an agreement before all the Sapes are dead, but she didn't inflect the words to imply that Orbians intend to kill Sapes."

Any port in a storm. "So she probably means they hope for an agreement before we–I mean we Yunko–die of old age. And that they understand that other Sapes oppose us."

Kayla said, "So why doesn't she go back to her ship and get everyone together, then come back to Earth and have a meeting?"

The interpreter hummed and clicked at the Ambassador.

The translator panel activated: MANY 8-MONTHS TO MEET.

[FUTURE SOON>] SAPES KILL OUTPOST.

"No!" I pointed at Conroy. "Whatever it is, don't say it." I shucked my jacket and, with a nod of apology at the Ambassador, draped it over the translator panel. Drawing on shaky school memories, I said, "It would take many 8-month periods to hold a meeting, and she has apparently learned from the Change Lords that a group of Sapes might attack us soon."

Lil said, "I don't know how long it takes to fly out to their ship but surely you have comm gear to hold a video meeting, even if there's a time lag. It shouldn't take that long."

The Ambassador spoke. The interpreter said, "She's just verifying that 'meeting' means many individuals coming together at the same time to discuss something."

The Ambassador looked at her hands, each of which had four digits–one offset–and spoke. The interpreter said, *"There are at least eight times eight officials and craft leaders who must be consulted for their agreement."*

Conroy said, "Sounds like a mob, but get 'em all in a room and lay it out."

The interpreter translated Conroy's message, then the Ambassador's response. *"They will not all come into the correct phase for discussing something of this nature at the same time, but over a long period."*

"I don't get it," Conroy said. "Tomorrow morning when they've all finished their second cup of coffee, just round 'em up and call a meeting."

Before the Ambassador could respond, I said, "That's a problem. Gliese-C is tidally locked, which means there are no mornings. No day and night at all."

Kayla, in exasperation, spoke. "Then how do you ever schedule working together on anything?"

Eventually the interpreter relayed: *"We consult each one of us as we come into a state in which we are ready to consider a problem. Then we calculate the consequences of each solution out to at least one-eighth of a Great Orbit. Each of us records our thoughts and conclusions, and at the appropriate time, studies the recordings of everyone involved. I don't understand why you Sapes don't do the same, since it prevents so much trouble."*

Lil frowned. "Hey, wait a minute, how long do your people live? I mean, on Gliese-C before you screwed up your biology turning yourselves into us?"

*"I myself have just passed one-third of a Great Orbit."*

My friends looked blank. I dredged up the calculations. "The Great Orbit is how long it takes Gliese 667C to complete an orbit around the other two suns, Gliese 667A and B. Uh. . .she's about 490 years old."

"Well, no wonder you do things so inefficiently." As always, inefficiency offended Lil. "We humans don't have time to mess around like that."

I whispered to the interpreter to soften the comment.

The Orbian pondered. *"That belief provides a partial answer to why you Sapes make such bad decisions–you jump into the first solution your brains are able to process."*

Kayla spoke up. "It's not that we can't think of other things. It's that our lives are too short to do much except choose the fastest solution–"

Conroy interrupted her. "Yeah, we evolved to, uh, catch the next antelope or starve. And we still think like that because of our lizard brains."

The interpreter relayed the exchange, then shushed my friends with a hand gesture as the Ambassador launched a long speech. She began the translation: *"The lizard you speak of looks nothing like you. However, the regrettably unappealing form our Yunko colleagues on Earth have taken looks nothing like those of us who stayed on our home planet. So I suppose your lizard brain is a true entity. We have a slightly similar early organ, although our own evolutionary period was so long ago our lower brain does little now but regulate metabolic functions.*

*"It does not affect our actions except in an occasional individual who has been injured in such a way as to revert to our Orbian version of a lizard brain. We understand how such an individual would be miserable in a slow-paced, peaceful world. But it is also a world of correct and incorrect action. Such a one who is hostile to good outcomes for all must be . . . "* the interpreter paused, *"put down because of the damage it is capable of causing."*

My three friends took an involuntary step back.

*"Just in the short years since our tragic expedition of 1908, we have seen your species destroying your planet at an ever accelerating rate. We concluded that you wished to die. Is this because you can only think a few years, at most your short lifespan, ahead?"*

A silence, then Kayla slowly picked her words, "Not exactly. When we see some action that would benefit ourselves, we think, 'Well, that would help me more than it would hurt any other one person.' That's how we convince ourselves it's okay. We don't think about how the little bit of damage we do to many, many other people adds up to far more than the benefit we personally receive."

Another discussion back and forth, then *"Do most Sapes not understand science, or do you think it is a made-up story?"*

The question seemed clear enough, so I held back. Still, I was surprised when Lil answered. "We can sort of believe two things at once.

All of us do it, because sometimes it's the only way we can get through."

I remembered my own interrogation and my theory that Lil could somehow believe two contradictory things at once. She was aware of her own illogic.

The Ambassador's brow wrinkled. *"What a terrible condition. Our laws and customs are so clear, so refined, that we never have to question whether something is the right thing to do. It's as black and white as our planet."*

Trust Conroy. "Yeah, I bet you people really love having a law for every little thing."

The interpreter must have successfully indicated the sarcasm: *"Sometimes it is a very hard thing to do."*

No one argued with the Ambassador's conclusion. Kayla finally said, "Well, yeah, if you're still split, still have the last remnants of your lizard brain, you're not so different from us after all."

Long pause. *"We have observed two other intelligent species quite closely, and their actions also fit the pattern of brains at war within themselves. Perhaps the cradle of intelligence is the long evolutionary battle between different stages of our brains."*

# CHAPTER 39

From the unpublished Godunov manuscript
*Why We Came to Earth: The Yunko Voyages*

*After concluding all their studies, our Researchers formed the following hypothesis: even with advanced shielding and near-light speeds, the radiation of interstellar voyages has numerous deadly effects. A high percentage of those with Gliese-C genes can only survive it if we obtain an infusion of healthy, unexposed genes from the only source available–our destination planet's native species. In our case, that meant Earth's humans. Many questions are still unanswered, such as whether Earth's humans themselves can survive interstellar travel without hybridization.*

My Sape friends looked ready for the interstellar version of a bull session, but the interpreter slumped with fatigue. Still, I hauled over chairs for the group and sat down myself. While the others poked at evolution and planetary survival, my own thoughts wandered–to Conroy's basic aggression versus his adoration of Janelle. To Kayla's bravado versus a vulnerability so intense she didn't even trust her family. To Lil's infinite tenderness and patience with Davy versus her robot-like efficiency elsewhere. All of them torn and conflicted, split nearly in two, and they didn't even have an inter-species issue to blame it on. Maybe I was just being a typical human.

I half-listened as Kayla tried to get a handle on Orbian art. Then I went back to full alert when Conroy started asking about Yunko reproduction. I think he was looking for anything that might harm Janelle's pregnancy, but the conversation went downhill from there.

Soon after, the interpreter said she needed to leave and we broke up. We drifted out the door I'd entered and headed for the main concourse.

"Janelle's not gonna believe this," Conroy said, pulling another of his maddening shifts between lover and fighter. I watched him lope toward the lift tube.

Lil rotated her shoulders as if to relax them. "I'm heading back to Medical. I'll see you this evening," she said to Kayla and walked away.

"Well," Kayla said, "Conroy's racing back to Janelle. Lil can't wait to start hovering over Davy again. So I guess I'll tag along after you. If that's all right, I mean if you're not busy?"

She seemed so forlorn I said, "Sure. I need to pick up the cats again. Let's go."

The cats greeted us with their usual attitudes–boredom re me, ecstasy at the sight of Kayla. Natasha said it was okay to take them outside again for a few minutes.

The Animal Facility's glass outside door was set in a two-foot-deep niche in the Outpost's rock wall. It gave onto a small, snow-covered valley that looked as innocent as a hundred other stream-carved valleys in British Columbia. A casual hiker would never suspect it was the playground for the guard animals of several thousand human-alien hybrids.

Kayla stopped and breathed deeply. I did the same, happy at any distraction from my fear and tension over whether I'd passed the tests. We ambled downhill while Zax and Gwitchy romped in drifts and windfalls.

Beside the stream, we watched dark water undercut banks puffy with snow. Kayla said, "If I just kept walking, would you let me go? Or would you be a loyal Yunko and stop me?"

I couldn't begin to unpack where she was going with that. "Stop you. Mostly because you'd die trying to hike out of here." I pointed roughly south. "Vancouver's hundreds of miles that way as the crow flies, with nothing much in between but wilderness."

She pinched needles off a small spruce and flicked them one by one into the stream. They were too light to make a satisfying plop.

"Besides, aren't you afraid of your father? And I thought you were sick of Seal Bay?"

"I wouldn't go back to Seal Bay," she said.

"Well, where would you go?"

She shrugged. "Maybe I'd link up with Forrest."

"Who's that? Your boyfriend?" Whoever he was, he surely wasn't good enough for her.

Her smile brightened at my irritation. "No, He's old. Same age as my parents. And more my parent than either of my real ones."

I needed to make her see reality. "Maybe this guy *would* be like a foster parent, but then what? I thought Lil and Janelle were your best friends. They're both here. And Conroy." I couldn't help adding, "And me."

She huffed in exasperation. "But what do I *do* all day? Yoga? Sit around wondering if your Yunko are going to kill me? Paint murals on the walls with leftover food?"

I was about to propose getting art supplies for her when I heard a voice in the distance. "Hush."

"What?"

"Someone's calling me. Sounds like Yevgeny." I heard another faint yell. "We better go back. Might be important."

"Why?"

"Well, finding out whether I'll live or die, for one thing."

"What!?"

"I'm pretty sure today was a test to see whether I could get Sapes and Orbians to communicate. Yevgeny's probably coming to tell me whether I passed."

She hesitated, then pulled her hand out of her padded jacket and took mine, a touch of warmth in the frigid air. We headed back to the Animal Facility.

Trees iced in white, sharp-smelling air, brilliant sky, snow crunching underfoot. Kayla's hand in mine. The world was too beautiful to leave. I tried to suspend myself like Schrodinger's poor kitty, existing and not existing at the same time.

Yevgeny waited outside the door, hands tucked in armpits. His smile seemed to crack his frozen face. "Congratulations," he called.

Something in my chest loosened.

"The Change Lords think your familiarity with Sape psychology might help us in the coming weeks and months."

I almost laughed, considering how blind-sided I'd been by Kayla's "Sape psychology."

"They were impressed by your handling of Conroy's hostility, which will not be uncommon in future negotiations with Sapes. In short, you did well enough at your two tests that they want to keep you around."

I'd braced myself against the tension for so long, it's ending seemed to melt me. My limbs turned into spaghetti. I thought I was standing normally but Kayla sensed the change and propped me up with all her strength. In an hour or two, I'd probably be wild with deep joy, with carefree happiness, but right now all I felt was the hollowness where fear had departed. I fought back the urge to sob.

"Your experiment today warned us off using Orbian translation algorithms with Sapes until we've done major upgrading. And we have more information on what types of questions Earth's ordinary citizens will probably ask, questions for which we can prepare more reassuring answers. In short, communication seems very . . . tricky but not impossible." He paused and stood more erect. "Not only will you survive, the Honorable Ekaterina has suggested that I train you as my successor."

I blurted my first reaction. "I'd be an awful Chief Recorder."

Yevgeny's smile tightened. "Next month I turn twenty-eight. I'll probably have a couple more viable years in which to train you. So you should be fully ready by the time I become too feeble to continue."

I clutched Kayla's hand for dear life. In spite of the hope offered by the tissue culture and Janelle's unique physiology, there was no guarantee any of us had much time left. But we had today. And probably tomorrow. And good odds for at least another month or two. And yes, I could feel the joy start to trickle in.

*Time has no duration.*
*The Past is over and done.*
*The Future can't touch us till it turns into Now,*
*and Now's the same length for everyone.*

## ACKNOWLEDGMENTS:

There's been lots of help on this long and winding road. Thanks first to Alex Sanchez for an infinite number of things, including being my first reader, constant support, and verification expert for the critical question, "Would a seventeen-year-old guy use that word?"

Thanks to John Finger for lots of good technical tips.

Thanks to my writers group who shared the entire *Alien Crossings* ride for their many excellent suggestions: Lisa Cherpelis, Karen Glinski, Helen Pilz, and Sandy Schauer.

Thanks to the folks at critters.org, particularly writers Noeleen Kavanagh and Dr. Scott M. Reed for their suggestions.

Thanks to University of New Mexico-Valencia science faculty, Dr. Claudia Barreto, Dr. Miriam R. Chavez, and Dr. Clifton Murray, who read an early draft. Thanks to Ted Christman for a medical read-through. Any science bloopers are entirely my fault.

Thanks to friends from 2016 Taos Toolbox, most particularly Stephen Loftus-Mercer and Shannon Rampe for their suggestions that improved the book significantly, along with instructors extraordinaire, Nancy Kress and Walter Jon Williams.

Thanks to the team at Aakenbaaken & Kent for bringing the book into existence.

CPSIA information can be obtained
at www.ICGtesting.com
Printed in the USA
JSHW052232140123
36127JS00002B/67

9 781958 022047